THE SHADOW MAN

A novel by

Karin Coddon

ISBN 978-0-615-16399-4

ACKNOWLEDGMENTS

Special thanks to David and Eve Coddon, Renie Henchy, and Sandy Wehe for their suggestions and encouragement, and to Warlock, "the slobbering Dutchman," for the pleasure of his company. I would also like to acknowledge the late Dorothy Macardle, author of *The Uninvited*, which remains the gold standard for the intelligent, gorgeously imagined, and genuinely scary haunted house novel.

Part One: <u>Maggie</u>

"I am stretched on your grave and will lie there forever"

Traditional Irish song

PROLOGUE

At ten past midnight Tim showed up at her door.

"I was wondering if maybe I could see Kat."

Maggie was incredulous – and then not. "She's been asleep for hours."

"What time is it?"

She didn't widen the door. Not this time. "Late."

He looked bad, even for him. The gray skin stretched across his face was dotted with tiny scabs. His eyes were as black and dull as charcoal. And in a ratty knit cap, old sweatshirt, torn jeans, and workboots, he was dressed too warmly for a humid July night. "Can I come in for a little?" he asked, inevitably.

Now Thumper, the anti-watchdog toy spaniel, was nosing excitedly at Tim's feet, remembering him. Tim stooped down to pet the quivering dog. "Hey, boy."

Maggie sighed. Her therapist would kill her, after all the hours devoted to "enabling." But resistance seemed less daunting when he wasn't standing right before her, petting the dog and looking like a wraith. "OK, but only for half an hour. And keep your voice down so we don't wake Kat."

He drifted inside. She closed the Window she'd been working on, shut her laptop, and took a sip from the small bottle of Pellegrino water next to the computer on the small pine dining table that did double-duty as her desk. She didn't offer him anything to drink.

Tim sank down into the overstuffed shabby-chic sofa. "Ed kicked my fucking ass out," he said, then burst into a horrible rale of sobs.

"Jesus Christ!" she hissed. "Tim, don't – you'll wake Kat!" But she was unnerved. Sober or tweaking, he'd never wept like this before. "Please, Tim!" She fell to her knees in front of him, clutching at the lightly scabbed hands that covered his face as if to try, in vain, to stem the flood of what remained of his very self, both the Tim he had been and the Tim he had become.

"It's so … humiliating. All of it." His sobs were now hoarse, heavy breaths.

"Tell me about it," she couldn't resist carping, straightening up and striding back over to the table to retrieve her water. Her own humiliation that day four months before at the prison in Lancaster, when he had told her of his involvement with another inmate with whom he planned to move in upon their release, was still too raw. Though really, why had she dreamed Tim would be any different, if not even more contagiously screwed up and self-destructive, after three-quarters of a year behind bars? Perhaps she'd been wishing for him only to remain at the same general level of Fucked-Uppedness, as he called it, and even that had proven too much to hope for.

"I don't blame you for hating me, Mags." Now his voice was still, barely audible.

"I've heard that before too." That familiar sick feeling was seeping into her blood as surely as the meth (or was it heroin this time?) coursed through his.

"I knew I was in no shape to see Kat. People like me shouldn't be around kids, not even my own."

"Then why are you here, Tim?"

"I've been living in my car the last two or three days. I lost count... I got weak and I came over here." His voice remained quiet, almost a low hum. Red-rimmed black coals fixed on her, no embers flickering in them.

She was growing impatient. "So how come Ed kicked you out? Or do I want to know?"

"I forgot to lock the door. Some people ripped off a lot of shit."

"Drugs?"

He nodded. "And some guns. A computer."

"And here he was going to help you keep off drugs."

He seemed oblivious of her mockery. "He tried, but ... you know how it is."

Indeed she did; she'd wasted over a decade on the Sisyphusian endeavor. Nonetheless, she bristled at his passing comparison of her ordeal to that endured by his now-ex-lover, some human pit bull who'd latched on to him at Lancaster with God only knew what sordid ulterior motives. "You know, maybe you should go, Tim. I'm just not up for this. I've got a ton of work and a Monday deadline."

"What're you working on?" He took out a cigarette, lit it with a shaking hand.

"Copy for a photography studio's website." A studio that specialized in wedding photos and video albums.

"I love you, Mags, and Kat too. I wish so much I could quit fucking up." He tapped his cigarette ash into a cupped hand.

Irritated, she located an ashtray. "Tim, I'm *through*. I can't do this anymore. I know I've said it a thousand times. But – " She broke off.

"But I never cheated on you before," he finished for her. "I never would have, Maggie, but it seemed like my only chance to get clean –"

"Oh, cut the crap. I know damn well why you did it. He'd supply you with crystal on the outside, just as I'm sure he did on the inside. I wish you'd had the *cahones* to tell me the truth instead of that bullshit about how he was helping you kick drugs."

The gray skinned tautened further over his cheekbones, but otherwise his expression remained dull. "You wish I'd told you I was pimping my ass for crystal? You'd have rather heard that?"

"You broke into your neighbor's house for it. Why would I be shocked you'd come to prostituting yourself for it too?"

For a moment he looked to be on the verge of simply disintegrating, dissolving into the smoke from his cigarette. But then he seemed to literally hold himself together by a stubborn force of will. She could see it in his slight grimace.

She wished he hadn't betrayed that glimmer of the old Tim, the one she used to love. The one back in college, the one who used meth occasionally but could always will himself to stop, at least for a little while. The ace lefty pitcher on the varsity team, the Academic All-American with the unlikely philosophy major, the bigtime college jock with an edge. All his contradictions had enchanted her from the very night they met, at the apartment of a mutual friend, Dan Ullman, who was a part-time student, part-time

runner for a local meth dealer.

But now, as for the last several years, the edge had severed whatever fragile knot

that had held together his contradictions, and there was almost nothing of the old Tim

left. Only edge remained, and tonight he seemed hardly a creature of substance at all.

"I want to get clean, Maggie," he said at length. "I just don't think it's possible

anymore."

"I don't either," she replied, honestly. Tim's dad, a doctor of sports medicine and

a Ph.D. in the School of Tough Love, had felt so sure that a stint in state prison would

finally be his son's wakeup call that Jack Emerson almost convinced Maggie as well. As

it turned out, tough love had been just as ineffectual as her own twelve years of

"enabling" and forgiving and faith that he would one day be able to free himself of his

addiction.

"Could I have some water?"

"Sure." She watched as he floated off the sofa, into the kitchen to get a bottle of

Aquafina. He struck her as less wired than usual, but all that likely denoted was that

tonight's intoxicant of choice included some opiate along with the methamphetamine.

As he twisted off the bottle cap, she suddenly found herself feeling sad and sorry for him.

"Oh Tim, maybe if you gave rehab just one more shot."

Standing there beside her, towering over her like an elongated shadow, he shook

his head. "Three times I've been through it, Mags, plus counseling in the pen. It's no

use."

"Maybe a different kind of program, Tim. Maybe it's just the Twelve-Step thing you don't respond to." In fact, she had researched such alternate rehabilitation centers and hospitals when he'd first gone into prison and she'd been foolish enough to try to plan for their future after he was released.

"Like what kind of programs?"

"They're called things like Rational Recovery and Smart Recovery ... they use cognitive approaches, you know, behavior modification instead of Twelve Steps."

"Like *A Clockwork Orange*?" he joked.

She bit back a smile. "I'm sure nothing quite that extreme."

"And these places – they don't try and force you to do all this psychobabble navel-gazing and Higher Power shit?"

Maggie was a little unprepared for his interest. "No, they don't, that's the whole point of them. They focus on changing behavior, not so much on ... the spiritual, I guess you'd say."

"Do they have these places here, in LA?"

"Yes – I looked into a few of them when you were at Lancaster." But then he had told her how well he was doing in group therapy, and what a relief it was to be in a drug-free environment, however oppressive. Shit. What an idiot she had been. Everyone knew drugs were rampant in prisons. She'd believed Tim only because she so desperately wanted to.

Just as she was probably still doing, right now. She decided to put his apparent sincerity to the test. "I'll take you to one of these places, Tim, first thing in the morning after I drop Kat off at day-camp. No promises from me. No carrots. You have to do this for you."

"OK."

"You mean it?"

He nodded. "Can I crash on the couch?"

"No, I won't risk Kat getting up in the middle of the night and finding you there. You can sleep in my bedroom, and I'll take the sofa." She was wholly certain that he would be gone long before either she or Kat were up. But that "what if?" that had haunted her over the years would not be satisfied unless she took this one final chance.

"One favor, Mags, and if you say no I'll understand. Could I just peek in at Kat? I mean, assuming she still sleeps with the light on."

She hesitated. Then she shrugged. "Only if you promise to be really, really quiet." A silly request, given the almost eerie quiet that had befallen him in the wake of his fit of raspy sobbing.

They padded down the apartment's short hallway, past the open door of the unlit master bedroom, to a shut door, under which faint light gleamed. Kat wasn't afraid of the dark, she said; she just preferred to sleep with the bedside lamp on. For a child who had spent her first eight years largely in the shadow of upset and upheaval that had continued even after her parents' divorce three years before, Kat was an unusually serene little girl, placid and sunny despite the emotional free-for-alls that characterized Maggie and Tim's relationship.

They stole into the room, moving noiselessly to her bedside. Kat slept with one small arm flung above her head. She had Tim's coloring – fair skin and taffy-colored hair that would likely darken to a sun-flecked brown like her father's someday. The shape of her face and features, and her slight frame, were her mother's. But her name was her own. Tim Emerson was of Scots-Irish descent and Maggie Flores was Mexican American. They chose the name "Katya" because in college they'd shared a fondness for dark, complicated Russian novels. In fact, the sole class they'd taken together at UCLA – Tim, the baseball hero philosopher and Maggie the Comp Lit major and campus newspaper editor – was Dostoevsky, in translation.

She watched him watch Kat. He looked so sad and tender. What a shame, she thought. What a goddamn shame.

They slipped back out into the living room. "I just need to grab some stuff from the car," Tim said. "Toothpaste, razor, and shit."

"No drugs in here, Tim. I'm serious."

"I promise."

He left, and she went into her bedroom to change into her pajamas – cotton shorts and a tank from the Victoria's Secret comfy rather than sexy line. The overhead fan whirred, but the room was nonetheless stuffy. Nor did the rented condo have air conditioning, probably because it was only a mile from the Manhattan Beach Strand. But on humid nights such as this, she might as well be living in the San Fernando Valley.

She brushed her teeth, pulled back her hair in a ponytail. She was removing an extra pillow and lightweight thermal blanket from the bedroom armoire when Tim returned with his rectangular shaving bag. "See, no contraband." He extended the open kit for her inspection.

True enough, its contents were mundane. A toothbrush, small tube of paste. Gillette deodorant, the brand he'd used for as long as she'd known him. A couple of disposable razors. It was one of his peculiarities that even as he sunk deeper into drug addiction he remained scrupulously clean in his personal hygiene. Even tonight in his ratty clothes and meth scabs, he didn't smell bad, his shaggy hair protruding under the knit cap wasn't greasy, no dark crescents tipped his fingernails. He'd obviously been using public facilities.

"Good boy," she said, waving away the shaving kit. Of course, for all she knew he had his stash in a jean pocket or had topped off his buzz outside in his car. But at least he was making an effort to appear to be honoring her request.

He started removing his clothes, throwing off the knit cap, yanking the sweatshirt over his head, then the tattered blue T-shirt he wore beneath it. "Will you stay and talk to me for a few minutes, just until the OxyContin kicks in?" He sat on the foot of the bed, bent to unlace his boots.

Maggie moved closer to eye the new tattoos that had joined the single one he'd sported last time she had seen him shirtless, a cat, for Kat, on his right bicep. Now an elaborate crimson heart, bleeding tears, had been etched below the cat, her own name snaked around it in black quasi-Gothic lettering. On his left bicep was a stranger image still, an elongated old man, gray-bearded, in some kind of Christ-like loincloth. The head sat backwards on the body, black eye sockets staring out above the figure's shoulder blades and bony spine. "Tiresius, the blind seer, " she said, tracing the tattoo with her index fingertip. "Why?"

He jerked his arm back to rub his left elbow with his right hand. The elbow whose shattering had ended what little was left of his minor-league career and major-league prospects. "It's been bothering me lately." He nodded toward the lamp on the nightstand. "Can you dim that, Mags? The pain's somehow easier to deal with in the dark."

She stepped away to switch the three-way bulb to its lowest wattage. "I think I'm going to bed, Tim. I'm tired."

"Why Tiresius?" He was pulling off his boots, socks, then his jeans as if he hadn't heard her last utterance. Tim had always slept naked. Once she had given him a pair of garish red silk pajamas as a joke. How he'd laughed, and laughed harder still when he tried them on; they looked as incongruous on him as a clown suit. "I just thought of it one day. From *The Inferno*." Nude, he pulled himself back onto the bed, wretchedly thin and tattooed, and yanked the comforter over him as if chilled.

"Tim, can I ask you something?" She stood in the doorway clutching the extra pillow and blanket close to her for protection.

"Only if you'll stay. Just five more minutes." He reached over to grab his hard-pack Marlboros from the pocket of his crumpled jeans.

She placed an empty tumbler on the night-table for him to use as an ashtray. "Were you lying to me when you told me about Ed, at Lancaster? Was that just to make me think you weren't using again?"

A long silence, followed by a quick inhale, then slow exhale, of smoke. "No, and yes."

"Are you gay? Is that what this has been about all along?" Now she was upset, and she expected to see her anguish mirrored in his face as well.

Instead, he regarded her with a mix of confusion and exasperation. "Now why would I be gay all of a sudden?"

She didn't respond, so he continued. "Ed was the only one, and I sure as hell didn't plan that. Foucault was right, you know?"

Now she was confused. "What, about prisons?"

"About fucking. It doesn't determine who you are. Only what you do, or've done." He exhaled more smoke. "Bodies and pleasures." Only in this last remark he sounded patently, and painfully, ironic.

His inappropriate philosophizing angered her. "You hurt me so bad, Tim – you made me fucking doubt the one thing that kept me sane all these years! How *dare* you make me doubt that you loved me?" She threw aside the pillow and blanket and strode over to him, needing to be in his face, needing to make physically aware of the betrayal.

"I didn't mean to," he said meekly. "Prison was just so goddamn – " Abruptly he snuffed out his cigarette in the plastic tumbler, yanked her to him, and kissed her, hard.

She struggled against his arms, his mouth. "Don't – "

"Don't doubt, Maggie. Never doubt." He pressed her hand to his penis, made her feel him stiffen.

She tried to pull her hand away. "Very impressive. But – "

He kissed her again, still squeezing her hand over his erection. "Don't make me stop," he breathed against her throat.

For a moment she ceased to fight, to allow herself to be aroused. And then she stopped fighting altogether. "Oh God," she moaned, her desire and despair hopelessly entangled. He slipped off her tank top and shorts, and only then did she remember to fumble in the nightstand drawer for a condom, which she helped him put on. Her thighs clasped his hips as he entered her, his thumb rubbing her clitoris as they rocked together, sitting up on the bed, the other thumb circling her nipple.

Still inside her, he eased her back on the bed. Losing herself in their inevitable coupling, she was incapable of second thoughts until at last he fell away from her and rested against the pillow. He seemed to sleep.

She studied him in the near-darkness. Despite his haggardness and the sprinkle of scabs from "meth bugs," his face was still beautiful. Yes, he'd always been more beautiful than handsome, even when his body was healthy and athletic and his suntanned skin was smooth. His brown eyes were large, long-lashed, his nose strong and straight over symmetrically sculpted lips. When she'd first met him she thought he looked like Rimbaud as Fantin-Latour portrayed him, or like Caravaggio's Narciso. Now he was little more than an amateur's preliminary sketch, absent sparkle in his eyes, color in his cracked lips and complexion. But impossibly, he was still beautiful, and he was part of her, and right now the recognition of each made her almost physically ill.

He was wrong about pain being more easily endured in the dark. A part of her longed to throw on every light in the room, as if like Kat she could find repose only under a 75-watt glow. God oh God, she had come damn close to forgetting about the condom. He was a drug addict who slammed, or shot up, meth as often as he smoked and snorted it. And Foucault or not, he was fresh out of a homosexual liaison with a fellow ex-con of highly dubious character. What if she had forgotten the condom, and he'd come inside of her, or one of them had a cut or sore? How could she have slept with him again in the first place, regardless of the condom?

She'd vowed his prison betrayal was the final, decisive blow to their relationship. Never again would she allow him to manipulate and deceive her, breaking her heart along with all of his ephemeral promises. She had even begun to see someone else, however casually, another freelance writer named Brian whom she'd met in the lobby of a textbook publisher for whom they both did projects. She'd even bought the damn condoms on the chance that something more might develop out of their handful of pleasant, superficial dates. And here she had relapsed yet again.

But unlike Tim's relapses, hers, she swore, was not going to launch an extended binge. She climbed out of bed and went into the bathroom. Even though she felt somewhat hypocritical, she took a bottle of Sonata from the medicine chest and washed down a capsule with a gulp from the faucet. She had to smother her frantic thoughts, her self-hatred, if only for a few hours. If Tim proved true to form, he'd be gone by the time she woke up, his promise to check into an alternative rehab clinic as forgotten as the sensation of really, truly starting over.

She must have been dreaming; how could that actually be the distinctive fatty aroma of bacon she was whiffing?

Maggie opened her eyes but the bacon smell didn't dissipate. "What the hell?" Throwing on her robe, she glanced at the clock. 8:46 a.m.

In the kitchen she discovered Tim removing a plate of crisp bacon from the microwave, Kat seated at the breakfast table, in her jammies, before a plate of Eggo toaster waffles. "Daddy's making breakfast!" she announced to Maggie. Kat adored Tim, despite his sporadic visits and the constant gentle warning that "Daddy's not feeling well" that generally accompanied them.

"Breakfast, such as it is," Tim said, lifting off the top, grease-lined paper towel from the bacon and extending the plate to Kat. She picked up a strip and took a bite.

Groggy, Maggie was still attempting to process the bizarrely domestic tableau. "Coffee," she mumbled, moving toward the Krups espresso machine on the counter, then stopping cold as she spotted, near the coffee maker, a syringe, a scorched spoon, and a short length of plastic cord.

"Kat, go get dressed for camp!" she barked. "Right now!"

"But I'm not done with my waffles – "

"*Now!*"

Startled by her mother's urgency, Kat scampered obediently out of the kitchen.

Tim stood there frozen, his eyes fixed on Maggie. "What?"

"You take that shit on the counter and get the hell out of here!" It was all she could do not to scream, not to attack him physically. "And never, ever come back! I swear, Tim, if I have to get a restraining order – "

"She didn't see it, Mags. I was gonna do it outside but I thought I saw a cop car."

"Get the *fuck* out of here! You show up again and you're damn right you'll see a cop car, and I'll have them drag your sorry ass back to prison! Get *out!*"

He swept up the paraphernalia. "She didn't see anything – "

Maggie reached for the telephone, and he was gone.

Still holding the phone, Maggie fought to catch her breath. Her heart was pounding. Twelve years of heartache, disappointment, anger, but this savage rage was new. And to think she had opened her door, her legs, to him, had only hours before panted under their orgasms. Why? To salvage her shredded ego after he rejected her for a man and a steady supply of crystal meth?

"Mommy?"

"It's OK, Kat. Run and get dressed for camp."

Wrenching, too, that it had been years since Kat had asked her why she and Daddy were fighting.

Unsatisfied with resolution alone, this time Maggie decided to take action.

"Hi Dad? This is Maggie."

"Maggie. I hope nothing's the matter with Katya." Jack Emerson's steady, dispassionate voice belied any real worry he might have had about the nature of her call.

"Kat's fine. Look, I just thought you should know, in case Tim drops dead, I've changed my number and I'm staying with my folks in Orange County until I can find a new apartment. Tim *cannot* know any of this."

"I applaud your good sense, Maggie. Tim knows he's not to have any contact with his mother or me so long as he's using drugs."

Maggie knew she could count on Dr. Emerson's strict adherence to the tough-love credo, a posture that for a long time had struck her as needlessly cold-hearted and counterproductive. Now she understood.

She gave him her new cellphone number, promised to provide periodic updates about his and Beth's only grandchild. Her own parents had changed their number years before to discourage Tim's raving, paranoid calls after the divorce; and they lived in a gated Newport Beach community with security codes and an on-site guard.

She kept up with work on her laptop, enrolled Kat in another day-camp. But three weeks into her flight from Manhattan Beach and accessibility, she had yet to formulate a concrete plan. Her parents, of course, wanted her and Kat to move in permanently, and they never missed an opportunity to remind Maggie how loved and cherished she and her daughter were, and how safe from Tim the environment was. But while she appreciated her parents' support and generosity, she was soon missing her privacy.

Tomorrow's August first, she mused one night as she prepared to retire in her old bedroom with its girlish tester bed and colorful folk art dolls and marionettes. Tomorrow I make a plan.

She half-hoped for inspiration from her dreams, but instead she had one of the most vivid nightmares of her life, more terrifying than the childhood one that had the snarling Werewolf pounding on her bedroom window, more unnervingly real than the one she'd had just after Tim's first arrest, in New Mexico, in which her subconscious sent federal agents bursting into their apartment, guns drawn. In the dream one of the agents had fired directly into her face. *Oh my God, I'm going to die!* she seemed to realize. She'd been genuinely relieved to awaken and find herself still whole.

No, in this new, terrible dream the skies rained down on LA and Tim Emerson was being buried. Rained so mercilessly that she wondered, standing there with a dozen faceless mourners at his gravesite, if Nature was expressing Tim's outrage that his wish to be cremated was being dishonored. "Better to burn out than to fade away," he often remarked. Strange how he'd somehow managed to do both. Her hands clutched the folded newspaper with his brief obituary: *"Tim Emerson, 32, Former UCLA Pitcher, Dodgers Prospect."* But the rain was disintegrating the paper even as she tried to reread the modest death notice, making it impossible to tell if she and Kat had been named as survivors.

The priest in his ornate green and white vestments ceased his sonorous mumbo-jumbo, and handed her a red rose. She understood; she was to drop it on top of the casket as it was lowered into the earth. But when the pallbearers appeared through curtains of rain, the coffin they were hoisting was far too small to have contained Tim's 6"2 corpse. It was unmistakably a child's coffin, and even though Kat stood beside her with a somber little expression on her face, Maggie's hands flew to her lips too late to smother a scream.

She shot up in bed but it was minutes before she could shake the dream and the terror. To reassure herself, she first checked Kat, sound asleep with the light on in the next room, then her cellphone voice-mail for any dire messages.

Nothing. The nightmare was nothing.

Yet the next morning, when she was driving back from dropping Kat off at camp and her phone rang, the caller ID indicating Jack Emerson's office, she *knew*. She was so sure that she pulled over to a curb before answering. "What is it, Dad? Is he ... gone?"

"Not that I've heard," Emerson replied in his typical composed manner. "But something's come up that interests you, more specifically, Katya." With no further preamble he informed her that Tim's grandmother had recently died, bequeathing her home in Del Mar to Kat to be either lived in or held in trust until she reached eighteen.

"Mother hasn't lived there for ten years – she's been in assisted living. Beth and I have always wondered why she held on to that house."

"Dad, I don't know what to say. I'm sorry about your mom. Will there be a funeral Mass?"

"Just a small service. Mother's never been one for fuss."

"Tim never said much about his grandparents. But she must have loved him to have left the house to Kat when she'd never even met her."

"Mother was aware of Tim's problems. She knew better than to leave the house directly to him."

She was oddly relieved that Emerson was at last referring to his late mother in the past tense.

"The estate lawyer will be contacting you," he went on. "I've no doubt he'll tell you that you can either continue to rent out the house, with the income going into a trust for Katya, or live there yourself. The only thing you can't do is sell it. That's for Katya to decide when she's eighteen."

"It'll pay for her college," Maggie murmured. "Bless your mother's heart."

"You really should consider moving there, Maggie," he said, all business as usual. "It's in a prime area and completely paid for. Property taxes are paid by the trust."

"Gee, Dad, I don't know. What if Tim figured out we were there?"

"I can't imagine how he would. I'm sure he assumes the house was sold years ago after my father passed and Mother went into assisted living. That is, if he even remembers his grandparents."

She winced at the undisguised contempt. "I'll have to think it over."

He gave her the lawyer's name and reminded her to expect a call, then efficiently

ended the conversation.

CHAPTER 1

The house itself was architecturally undistinguished, a two-story light brown

stucco with apparently random stylistic touches of Craftsman and California-Ranch. But

its location was exceptional, just up the hill from the Pacific Coast Highway on a woodsy

street with the sparkling ocean just beyond the doorstep.

"Oh my God, don't tell me there's no central air," Maggie groaned, struggling to

peer between floor-to-ceiling Bekins cartons and the wall of the front hallway.

"I have no sympathy." Ryan gestured toward the redwood deck just off the living

room and the horizontal blues of sky and sea visible down the hill through the trees. "It's

three times this humid in Hillcrest, and the fans don't do anything except blow around hot

air. Kind of like my boss."

Maggie had arrived around the same time as the Bekins van, at ten that morning;

Ryan, who had taken this Friday off from his job as head of electronic cataloguing at

UCSD library, showed up at noon with some beers and his toolbox, the latter in the all too likely event that the movers had neglected to fully reassemble a bed frame or had loosened a table-leg or armoire door.

"OK, here's the thermostat – Jeez, it's 85 degrees in here." Maggie tooled with the panel just outside the circa-1980 kitchen. No SubZero, no granite counters, no built-in microwaves or custom cabinets, but definitely workable, and vastly larger than the one in her Manhattan Beach condo.

Soon the purr of the AC was followed by the first wafts of cool air. "Ahhhh," Ryan said, stooping to sit on the bottom step of the carpeted staircase that led to the three upstairs bedrooms and two baths. "I'm moving in."

Maggie grabbed two Coronas from the six-pack he'd deposited in the fridge ten minutes earlier. She handed one bottle to him, twisted off the cap of her own. "No lime. My dad would have a conniption." She took a gulp of the icy, pleasantly bitter beer.

"Hey, did I tell you there's an Armando's in La Jolla now? I was just there last week with some people from work. Great happy hour."

"Are you kidding? My dad has this giant magnetic map of California in the family room, and he adds a new little sombrero marker every time another restaurant opens. It's like a new branch on the family tree." Not even 35 years as a successful restaurateur had dimmed Armando Flores's pride in his popular chain of upscale Tex-Mex cantinas, though nowadays he seldom mentioned his humble inaugural eatery, a ten-table tacqueria in downtown Santa Ana long since transformed and relocated to swanky Newport Beach. No, he'd pretty much ceased mentioning the original Armando's right around the time he re-registered Republican and forbade his wife and children to speak

Spanish in the home. *"Estamos asimilados!"* he would roar if he'd had too much to drink to appreciate the irony of his imperative.

Ryan set down his half-empty beer. "Well, we might as well begin before we break out the seconds. Where do you want to start?"

"Don't hate me – lining the kitchen cupboards."

Maggie hadn't seen Ryan, her best friend since freshman orientation at UCLA, in nearly three years, since right after her divorce. She'd driven down to San Diego, dropping Kat off in Newport along the way, and she and Ryan had proceeded to cut a drunken swathe through the Hillcrest area for an entire weekend, hitting every gay bar that welcomed straight women disgusted with straight men. Ryan himself had been between relationships and equally, if temporarily, disenchanted, which mitigated any guilt she might have had for monopolizing his company at Flick's, Numbers, Bourbon Street, or over a drunken, expensive meal at California Cuisine, a fine restaurant infamous for having been the site of future Versace-killer Andrew Cunanan's lavish going-away dinner.

Though they spoke on the phone only occasionally and e-mailed slightly more often, their longstanding easy rapport had weathered the infrequent contact, resurging from the moment she'd rung him two weeks before to inform him that she and Kat were moving to Del Mar just fifteen miles north of San Diego. He'd even volunteered to help her unpack, assistance she accepted without hesitation. On Sunday her mother would bring Kat and Thumper down from Orange County, and Maggie hoped that two days were sufficient time to whip the unfamiliar into some semblance of order, some *trompe l'oeil* of homey familiarity.

She rifled through a Ralph's grocery bag on the dining room table, locating the shelfpaper and scissors. "Let me just go pee and we'll get to work."

She wisely remembered to grab a roll of toilet paper from another bag on the table before heading down the short hallway to the half-bathroom just off the kitchen.

What a godsend this whirlwind move had turned out to be, she mused as she unknotted the drawstring of her shorts. The packing and the planning and the tightwire of coordinating the shutoff of utilities at her former place with the startup down here had absorbed her waking hours and left her too mentally spent to dream when she slept. Her freelance assignments were just as easily transferred to San Diego, consisting as they did mostly of Website copyediting and assembling classic literary anthologies for a publisher specializing in high school textbooks. Whenever people learned she was a freelance writer they always assumed her work was somehow glamorous – short stories, travel pieces, articles in national women's magazines. They often acted vaguely insulted, as if misled, upon her explanation of the rather more mundane nature of her publications.

She flushed the toilet and washed her hands. From the other room she heard Ryan call out something. "Hold your horses!" she called back, stepping out of the bathroom. "Can't a girl pee in peace?"

He stood in the kitchen, looking perplexed. "That was really strange."

"What?"

"I was in the dining room and I could have sworn I heard you putting silverware into the drawers."

"How bizarre. Must have been wind-chimes from next door or something."

She put Ryan, who was 5'10, in charge of lining the tallest shelves, while she unwrapped the bone china and other fragile items that she'd rather have out of Kat's – or Thumper's – way. They chatted idly as they labored, about impersonal things like movies and politics (they both loathed Bush, or as Ryan called him, "the Chimp"). He gave her tips on nearby restaurants, bookstores, the location of the nearest Kinko's. "Traffic's still pretty brutal in and out of here because of racing season," he said. "But a month from now it'll feel like a smallish beach town again."

"Speaking of racing, I promised Kat she could start horseback riding lessons once we're settled in. She's been begging me for months. But frankly, until now all my expendable income has gone into paying rent and groceries."

He measured and cut another rectangle of shelfpaper. "Yeah, there are a few stables just on the other side of the freeway. I'm sure Kat will be thrilled."

"Of course, I'm terrified she'll break her neck. But then I remind myself that the only bone I ever broke as a kid was from thinking if I flapped my arms fast enough I could fly, and leaping off the garage roof. I was lucky only to break my ankle."

"You just weren't flapping fast enough."

She smiled. "You're telling me!"

From the kitchen they moved on to unboxing crates of books and shelving them in cases first in the living room, then in the smallest of the three upstairs bedrooms she'd designated her office. "Don't worry about Kat's books. I'll put them away in her room."

Ryan held up a copy of Octavio Paz's poetry. "Remember when you told Dan you were doing your honors thesis on Octavio Paz, and he thought you were writing on the Roman Empire?"

She chuckled. "Yeah – he thought Octavio Paz was the same person as Octavius Caesar. How is Dan anyway? He still up in Portland?"

Ryan nodded. "I had an e-mail from him last week. He's still really involved in gay AA groups. Can you believe he's been sober for five years now?"

They both fell silent. The obvious sore subject hung suspended over the little study like motes in a sunbeam. Maggie brushed dust off the beautiful old oak desk her mother had given her from her former Newport Beach bedroom. "Isn't this nice?" she said at length. "Mama donated this, and the little kitchen table set, to our cause."

Ryan brushed his hands on the front of his baggy shorts. "What next?"

She checked her watch. "Wow, it's four thirty. I say we take another break. Want to go have a drink somewhere?"

"Twist my arm."

"I'm pretty grungey, so it'll have to be some place casual," she said, glimpsing herself in the mirrored closet door. "Or maybe I should change."

"I know a place on the beach where anything other than the proverbial tangerine Speedos is fine."

She didn't hear him. She was staring into the mirror at what had to be an optical illusion. In a dim corner a man's gray fedora hat appeared to be hanging from a peg.

She slowly turned around, looking past Ryan to the corner. She exhaled, almost amused by herself. The "hat" was simply a shadow from an overhanging tree branch outside the window.

"What?" Ryan said.

"Nothing – I was just wondering if I'd forgotten anything." The white lie seemed easier than trying to explain the silly, now dissipated, mirage.

Fifteen minutes later they perched at a table at the open beachfront bar of the Poseidon Restaurant, before them the ocean and countless sunbathers as golden and blandly beautiful as extras in an old *Beach Party* movie. This panorama, too, seemed faintly chimerical to her, and she surmised she was more exhausted than she'd realized.

Nonetheless, the ocean wind was reinvigorating. They ordered margaritas and shrimp cocktails. When the drinks arrived Ryan raised his glass to her. "To your new house, Maggie. May you and Kat be happy in it."

They clicked salt-frosted rims. "I'm just so glad you're here. I don't know a single soul in San Diego County other than you."

"Christy Tobias is in the Ph.D. program in history at UCSD."

"Really? God, I haven't thought of her in eons." Christy had been one of the "night people," the group of black-clad, drug-ingesting undergrads who used to hang out almost every night of the week at Dan Ullman's apartment.

"Every once in a while we have a drink and reminisce about the crazy days. But she's pretty busy studying for her qualifying exams."

Maggie studied the glass circled by her hands. "I saw Tim several weeks ago. First time since he got out."

"He's out? Good. Did he survive OK?"

She still couldn't meet his eyes. "I didn't tell you, but before Tim went into prison, we'd pretty much gotten back together. He'd gone through rehab again and this time it really seemed to have taken. All we had to do was somehow get through his nine

months at LA State." Finally she lifted her eyes. "I could not have been stupider, or

more naïve, Ryan."

"I'm sure you were neither. I'm sorry it didn't work out. I've always liked Tim

and hoped one day he'd get his act together."

"He started fucking one of his fellow inmates. Or was it the other way around?

He told me this two weeks before he was scheduled to be released." Her voice was

brittle.

Ryan looked momentarily taken aback. "Shit. Shit. But … I guess that happens

all the time in prisons."

"When he got out he went to live with this person, who I suppose had been

released around the same time. Then one night last month he just shows up at my

apartment with some crap about getting kicked out by his boyfriend."

"Was he tweaking?" Ryan asked quietly.

"You even need to ask?" She sipped her margarita. It was weaker than those

served at Armando's; she'd have to tell Pa. It would please him.

Ryan signaled for two more cocktails, then turned back to her. "Maggie, if I

believed he'd really switched teams I'd hit on him myself. But – I don't know how to put

this in a nice way."

"Don't worry about being nice. It's an incredibly not-nice situation."

"OK. I haven't seen Tim in probably five years, and even back then … it was like

he wasn't there anymore. Just crystal with a human shell. And everything you've said to

me about him since tells me that nothing's changed in that regard."

Even though the waning afternoon remained warm, she shuddered. "It's true. Every once in a while I try to convince myself I see a flicker of him, and not just the drugs talking and acting through him. And I'm always just plain wrong. You know, Ryan, I'm done with seeing mirages. This time I've broken off with him for good."

The waitress reappeared with their second round, efficiently shifting the empty glasses onto her tray. "I think that's probably for the best," Ryan said. "It doesn't look like Tim's going to outgrow it like the rest of us did."

"I know. Damn it, Ryan! If even Dan could get clean … " Her voice trailed off. "But it's useless to think in those terms." She actually felt better for having unburdened herself. Now that Tim had been evoked and acknowledged, he could be exorcised. "Thanks for letting me cry on your shoulder."

"*De nada.* What do you say – shall we go whole-hog and order dinner?"

Drinks and dinner staved off her fatigue a while longer, but by the time they got back to the house she could scarcely keep from falling asleep on her feet. She invited Ryan to stay and sleep in Kat's bedroom, but he opted to return to San Diego. "Rufus will kill me as it is for being late with the Fancy Feast." Maggie hugged him goodbye and started heavily up the rather narrow, dark staircase. In fact, the staircase was one of the few features of the house she thought downright ugly. It seemed a failure of architectural imagination; absent sweep or interest, it was merely a graceless ascending hallway, walled in on each side, connecting first to second floor. Perhaps the house's second story had been an addition.

She had not made up her bed, and now lacking the energy to do so, she crawled onto the bare mattress and pulled the comforter over her. She should have turned off the AC, but the cool that washed over her skin felt so lovely. In moments she was asleep.

In her dream, Kat and a group of her little friends were giggling and shrieking as they explored the new house, opening and shutting cupboards, jumping on the furniture, with Thumper yapping at their heels. In vain Maggie tried to settle the girls down, but ignoring her, they began to race each other up and down the ugly staircase. "Come on, you guys, chill," she pleaded to no avail. Then Kat, at the top of the stairs, started to flap her arms wildly. "Mommy, I can fly!" Just as she leaped from the landing, Maggie woke up.

And distinctly heard *stomp stomp stomp* on the stairs.

By morning she had persuaded herself that the thumping on the stairs had been no more than old pipes and that the panicky few minutes she'd lain in the dark, terrified by the burglar she was certain was about to burst into her room, were only the residue of new-house anxiety. No one had been in the house. The property managers had assured her that all the locks were changed after the previous tenants left. And daylight embarrassed her with the sunny benignity of her home and sparkling blue of the horizon. She put on some coffee and called her folks, reassuring each of them that the house was fantastic and that she and Ryan had gotten a lot of work accomplished. Then Mama put Kat on the phone. "Mommy, when do I get to start my riding lessons?"

"Soon, sweetie," Maggie promised. "Now, kiss Thumper for me and I'll see you and Abuelita tomorrow afternoon."

She knew how single-minded Kat could be, so after her second cup of coffee she dragged out the Yellow Pages to look up "Riding Academies." Despite having spent most of her adult life with a natural athlete who, once upon a time, had been not only a Major-League-caliber pitcher but also an outstanding tennis player, golfer, sprinter, and surfer, Maggie didn't have an athletic bone in her body. She liked to swim but even ping-pong taxed her limited hand-eye coordination. As for equestrian sports, she'd been on a couple of trail rides astride geriatric horses, once as a kid vacationing in Maui with her parents and older brother Juan-Gil, the other time in Puerto Vallarta with Tim.

She located three stables in Del Mar whose ads offered lessons. She called the first one, Camino Equestrian, and spoke with a cheery-sounding woman who told her that children as young as five and six took lessons there. "All our school-horses are gentle and totally bomb-proof," she boasted, adding that her teachers were experienced and patient with kids. Group lessons ran $40 an hour, with a discount if Kat signed up for an entire month.

"Let's play it safe and sign up for weekly lessons," Maggie said, less because she questioned Kat's stick-to-it-iveness than because she wanted to make sure the facilities and instruction were as top-notch as the woman on the phone promised.

"Okie-dokie. How's Tuesday at noon?"

"Fine. She doesn't start school until September 19th." Maggie circled Tuesday in her appointment book, adding, "noon."

"And your daughter's name is Kathy, you said?"

"Katya. K-A-T-Y-A. Katya Emerson."

"Katya, what a cute name!" the woman bubbled. "See you Tuesday!"

Maggie spent the rest of the day hanging pictures, making up the beds, putting

clothes in closets and drawers. She played Miles Davis and Etta James and Rage Against

the Machine on the stereo to drown out her loneliness for Kat, even for Ryan. She went

grocery shopping at a nearby Vons and had a solitary dinner of supermarket sushi and

Pinot Grigio on the redwood deck, where she lingered until the sun at last disappeared

into the ocean.

With her bed now fully made up with crisp clean sheets and the pale pink cotton

thermal blanket from Pottery Barn, she slept deeply, disturbed neither by her dreams nor

their waking echoes on the staircase.

Mama called her ten minutes from Del Mar to confirm directions. Maggie waited

in the driveway as her mother's silver Mercedes sedan cruised to a stop. Kat, clutching a

barking Thumper, jumped out of the passenger side even as Mama was unfastening her

own shoulder-belt.

Maggie embraced her daughter and, by necessity, dog. *Now* she felt at home.

"Sweetie, I missed you so much!"

"Me too, and Thumper too." Kat squirmed free and set the toy spaniel on the

ground where he promptly found some ivy to urinate on.

Mama, wearing a colorful print shift and her signature Bruno Magli pumps and

Prada purse, was reaching into the open trunk for Kat's overnight bags. Maggie gave her

a hand. "Your car looks a lot more at home here than my old Accord does, Mama. Come

on in and get the tour."

Kat and Thumper had already charged ahead into the house. "This location is out-standing," Mama pronounced, invoking her favorite adjective as she appraised the view. Her lightly accented voice, like her faint scent of L'Air du Temps, never failed to strike Maggie as comforting.

Like her daughter, Eva Flores was a petite woman, but she always wore three-inch heels and had an aristocratic bearing that belied her stature regardless of the stilettos. As much as Maggie loved her mother, Eva always made her feel underdressed.

Inside, Kat and Thumper dashed onto the redwood deck, while the two women lingered just behind them in the living room. "Oh, Magdalena, the view is even lovelier from here."

"Come on, it's nothing compared to the one you and Pa have, but it's pretty nice. Want some coffee, Mama, or an iced tea?"

Kat and the dog came back inside. "Can I see my room? Is it upstairs?"

For some reason Maggie had to suppress a shiver when Kat flew up the stairs, followed by the dog. Eva noticed her expression. "What, it's still a mess up there?"

"Sort of. Not that Kat will mind. Let me show you the rest of the downstairs."

Eva was thrilled to see the brightly painted wooden table and chairs that she'd given Maggie in the kitchen to replace the ugly pressboard set from Sears. "You finally have a pretty breakfast nook. Now you can use your dining room for guests."

"Yes, I do so much formal entertaining," Maggie joked, locking her arm in her mother's.

"Well, you never know, Maggie. And with this big house, you have to let me take you shopping for some other nice things."

"No, Mama – you've already given us plenty."

They headed for the stairs. "Have you enrolled Katya in school?" Included in her parents' bounty, at their insistence, was the tuition for Kat's Catholic schooling from kindergarten onward. Maggie wasn't thrilled about subjecting her daughter to the same kind of guilt-infused curriculum she'd endured for thirteen years, but she could hardly quarrel with the quality of the education.

Both women were momentarily startled to round the corner to the stairs and find Kat and the spaniel perched about three steps from the landing. "Mommy, 'Lita, I love these stairs! They're cool."

I'm glad somebody does, Maggie thought.

"This is your first home with stairs, isn't it, *me hija*," Eva replied indulgently.

Again Maggie had to smother a vague sense of unease. Damn that stupid dream. "I'm afraid you have to move, honey, so Abuelita and I can come up and see the bedrooms."

Kat obligingly scampered all the way up. "Here's my room, 'Lita."

Maggie had taken care in preparing the room for her daughter. The frilly lavender comforter and shams were on the white wicker bed, favorite dolls and stuffed toys displayed on the étagère, framed posters of *Spirit, Stallion of the Cimarron* and fairies with unicorns hung on the walls.

Thumper mischievously scooted under the bed. "Hey, don't be shy, Thumper," Kat admonished, getting down on all fours and poking her head under the bedskirt.

"Oh, Maggie, don't let her crawl around on the floor until you've vacuumed," Eva started to advise.

Kat popped up, holding what appeared to be a dust-caked red toy kaleidoscope. "Look what I found!"

"Honey, that's dirty. The movers must have kicked it under the bed." But did Kat even own such a toy?

Kat wiped the kaleidoscope on her jeans, then peered into it. "Wow."

It was clearly *not* her toy. The previous tenants must have had a child who had left it.

"*Me hija*, put that down and wash your hands," Eva was urging Kat.

"Let me see that," Maggie said, easing the scope out of Kat's grasp. It looked old, sort of retro. Irresistibly she raised it to her eye, twisting the ring around the lens piece.

Cloudy blue and green crystals coalesced, broke apart, reconfigured with each rotation. The toy was so low-tech that she was surprised Kat even found it intriguing. Maybe it was true that kids today were so jaded by their electronic PlayStations and bells-and-whistles videogames that they found "vintage" toys as quaintly fascinating as fossils.

She set the kaleidoscope on the dresser, and ushered her mother and daughter out of the room toward the master suite. It was only when Maggie was showing them onto the small balcony that she noticed Kat was again holding the kaleidoscope.

She was half-relieved Kat didn't sneak the toy along to dinner later. Her mother's treat, at the oceanfront Chart House in nearby Cardiff by the Sea. Eva knew San Diego's coastal North County far better than did Maggie, from years of day-trips during racing season. "Now Papa and I have two reasons to make the drive," she exclaimed. After seeing Maggie and Kat safely inside the house and exchanging multiple hugs and kisses, Eva departed for the hour-long drive back to Newport Beach.

It was only nine, but Maggie was tired and could tell that Kat was too. All the excitement and disorientation, for both of them. She ran a bath for Kat, resolving to take a long one herself as soon as her daughter was tucked in.

She went downstairs to switch off all but the hall light, double-checking the locks, the sliding glass door on the deck. When she returned upstairs with Kat's customary plastic tumbler of water, she found her already in her pajamas and under the covers – again clutching that goddamn red kaleidoscope. Thumper was snoring lightly at the foot of the bed.

Maggie sat down beside her, wondering whether to mention the toy. "You gonna sleep well, nina?"

Kat nodded. "I like our house. And day after tomorrow I get to go riding."

"That's right, so you need to rest up between now and then so you'll have lots of energy for the horses." She brushed back a stray curl from her daughter's brow.

"Mommy?"

"Uh-huh, sweetie?"

"Will Daddy ever come to see us here?"

Maggie was silent, torn between a comforting lie and a watered-down truth.

"It's OK," Kat said serenely. "I know he loves me."

"He does, Kat. More than anything in the world."

"I know, 'cause he gave me this," she replied, cradling the kaleidoscope.

"He did? When?"

"You saw. He left it under my bed, and Thumper found it."

Maggie kissed her. "I'm sure you're right, sweetie." Her heart ached. Kat's way of coping with Tim's likely permanent absence, along with the changes and dislocations of the last month and a half, was to imagine her father had left a surprise gift for her. Even if it was only a crummy old plastic kaleidoscope.

All the same, Maggie was especially glad she had set up the riding lessons. She only regretted they didn't start tomorrow.

CHAPTER 2

It was hard to believe that a small patch of horse country was only ten minutes away, just on the other side of the freeway, nestled between encroaching "planned communities" and a few patches of tomato fields. Eucalyptus, pepper, willow, and pine trees fringed the dirt road leading into Camino Equestrian. Kat squealed with delight at the rows and rows of pipe corrals housing horses and ponies. "Mommy, look at the white one!"

"Very pretty, sweetie." Maggie reached a clearing between a barn, an arena, a row of crossties, and a hut that looked to be a combination tack room and office, outside of which a wooden sign read "CAMINO EQUESTRIAN." She eased her Honda between two SUVs, shifted into park.

The pleasant smell of dust, hay, and horses perfumed the air. Kat dashed right over to the riding arena to watch a denim-clad young woman with a lunge-whip exercising a gray appaloosa mare. Two other mothers with children – daughters, inevitably – perched at a redwood picnic table nearby.

Maggie waved a reluctant Kat back over to her side as she leaned into the tack room/office. A woman of about sixty, in jeans and a graying red ponytail, her tanned face as weathered as one of Tim's old baseball mitts, greeted them. "Is this Katya? I'm Rhonda – we spoke the other day."

Rhonda dispatched Kat to choose a pair of riding boots from a ragtag selection on a shelf between the bridles and saddles. Maggie was given a three-page release form to scan and sign.

Horseback riding accidents were only the seventy-third leading cause of sports-related hospitalizations, she mused, impressed. "Here you go," she said, handing the form back to Rhonda along with a check.

"Thank you," Rhonda said in her bright, speaking-to-kindergartners tone. "Sandy will be your teacher, Katya. As soon as she's done turning out Lancer she'll get the horses. Do you want to ride English or Western?"

"English, please," Kat said, as though she had already given the matter serious thought.

"Are you sure, Kat?" Maggie eyed the slender English saddles that appeared so much less substantial than their heavy-tooled Western counterparts.

"Yes, Mom." Kat called her "Mom" only when she was especially trying to act grown up.

"She'll be fine," Rhonda said. "You're welcome to have a seat at the picnic table and watch with the other parents. There's a Coke machine out back just behind the big barn, next to the tack store."

"It's so nice and peaceful here, I think I will hang out." Maggie hoped that Kat accepted the premise rather than suspecting maternal overprotectiveness.

"Great!" Rhonda enthused. "I'm going to help Sandy get out the horses. Kat is going to ride Sugar today. She's one of our gentlest." She lifted a small English saddle and blanket from a saddle-tree and handed them to Kat, who was beside herself.

Maggie didn't want to hover, so she wandered over to the picnic table. The two other women, one around her own age and the other closer to 40, sat chattering about their children who were now swarming around the tack room to gather up their own saddles, pads, and bridles. Kat was waiting impatiently by the crossties, wearing a riding helmet and clasping her saddle as tenderly as she cuddled Thumper. Maggie had to smile at her daughter's palpable excitement.

"Is this her first time riding?" asked the fortyish woman, an ash blonde in a tanktop and sweatpants.

Maggie couldn't see her eyes behind the sunglasses, but the voice was kind. She nodded. "She's on cloud nine."

"My Brittany is still that way, and she's been riding eight whole weeks," the woman replied.

The other, younger woman, a white-blonde in low-rise jeans, cropped top over conspicuously round and perky breasts, and giant Jackie-O eyewear spoke up. "Lauren, did I tell you I'm buying Bianca her own pony? She's already outgrown these poky school horses."

"Great," Lauren said noncommittally.

The white-blonde turned to Maggie. "Are the little girl's parents riders? I know Bianca got her talent from me and her dad."

Maggie was baffled. "Excuse me?"

"The little girl," the woman repeated, pointing at Kat. "Do you know if her parents ride?"

At once Maggie gleaned the nature of the woman's misapprehension. *Jesus Christ, she thinks I'm the au pair because Kat's fair and I'm Latina!* At a loss for a lacerating rejoinder, all she could muster was an icy, "I'm her mother, and no, I don't ride."

If Lauren looked mortified, the transgressor herself seemed unembarrassed. "Oh, that's cool. I'm Tatiana, by the way."

"And I'm Lauren – so nice to meet you … "

"Maggie." She was still reeling over having been mistaken for the nanny.

"Mom, look at my horse!" Kat called as Rhonda led a pretty palomino mare into the crossties. The other little girls, plus a newly arrived third, were leading in their own horses, presumably a privilege of relative seniority.

Tatiana's cellphone rang, and she stepped away to answer. Lauren touched Maggie's arm. "I'm so sorry about what she said to you. She's a total ditz."

"Damn, I wish I'd had a good comeback, but I was so taken aback," Maggie admitted.

"Half the time she has her own au pair bring Bianca," Lauren said, then blushed. "Ugh – I'm making it worse, aren't I."

Several feet away Tatiana was chattering into her phone, swinging her car keys obliviously.

"Don't worry about it," Maggie said to Lauren. "Just tell me her name isn't really Tatiana."

"It gets worse. She says she's from Paris, and that her ex is a Formula One driver. I think she's some rich sugar daddy's trophy mistress."

"If her accent's any indication, I'd guess she means Paris, Texas," Maggie chuckled. "You know, my mother used to tell people she was Cuban because she thought that sounded somehow classier than Mexican. Maybe I should say I'm Desi Arnaz's granddaughter and Tatiana will quit confusing me with the hired help."

"As long as she thinks you're rich, she'll be your best friend. The first time I met her she thought another mom's Jaguar was mine. She was really chummy until she saw Brit and me drive off in our Toyota 4-Runner."

"Did she make it her business to meet the Jag's real owner?" Maggie had forgotten the small diversion of idle gossip with another woman. The nature of her work kept her isolated, and she had lost contact with most of her college girlfriends over the years, not the least because of her private shame over remaining involved with Tim. *Co-dependent. Enabler.*

"Oh, you can bet she did."

"Which one is Brittany?" Maggie asked, watching Rhonda demonstrate to Kat the mechanics of grooming with brush and curry on the placid palomino.

"The one in pigtails and the blue top, with the brownish-red horse. I mean, chestnut."

Tatiana was still on the phone when another parent, this one a tall, tanned man in his 50s with a thick head of silver hair, ambled up to them. The masculine presence was almost jarring amid all the women and little girls. "Beautiful day!" he boomed, then, without further preamble, launched into a monologue about his family's recent vacation on the Italian Riviera.

While Lauren made polite noises, Maggie returned her focus to Kat, who was taking her turn at the mounting block. She looked absolutely beatific as she swung a leg over the saddle and took hold of the leather reins.

Maggie followed the lesson as closely as if she too were among the student riders. The four little girls rode slowly around the ring as Sandy, the teacher, reminded them to sit up straight and keep their heels down. Occasionally she warned a child that her horse was getting too close to the animal in front of it. Maggie held her breath as all the riders, per Sandy's instructions, cued for a jog and the horses broke into slow trots. But Kat seemed to catch on immediately, her eyes still sparkling but her face otherwise a study in concentration. "Good, Katya, good," Sandy encouraged. Maggie could barely suppress her relief and happiness for Kat. How rare was it that sky-high hopes were rewarded by the reality of the thing so dearly anticipated. She treasured the moment for Kat, and for herself.

The lesson ended just after one. Far from running to her mother triumphantly, Kat busily untacked Sugar and took up the grooming brush again, chatting merrily with the other children likewise occupied with their horses. Lauren broke free of the still-pontificating continental traveler, and said to Maggie, "She did great! You must be proud."

"I am. This was her dream, and I was terrified that the experience couldn't possibly live up to it."

Kat and Brittany raced over. "Mom, Brittany takes lessons Thursday, too! Can I?"

"We'll see," Maggie hedged. Even living rent-free, twice-a-week lessons would be a stretch.

"But Mom!"

"Brit's going back to once a week when school starts," Lauren said diplomatically. "We just can't afford them that often year-round."

Kat turned to a crestfallen Brittany. "I bet my abuella will pay for more," she said confidently, and before Maggie could admonish her, the two girls ran back to finish grooming their horses.

"And so my wife said, 'Paul, if we don't stop off at Armani, the terrorists will win,'" the tedious tourist still rambled on, now to Tatiana, who actually looked impressed.

"My parents would spoil her rotten if I let them," Maggie said to Lauren.

"Mine are the same way, and so are my husband's parents. Sometimes it's hard to keep Brit grounded when she lives around kids with their own horses and catered slumber parties. My ex, Brit's dad, is always trying to buy her love, and they're at that age where they can be bought."

"Katya's father is … out of the picture." She said it only because she felt she had to say something. "I have to fight myself, too, not to spoil her."

Lauren nodded sympathetically.

Rhonda strode up to them. "Well, ladies? Am I going to see you two at Coffee Club on Friday?"

"What's that?" Maggie asked.

"I keep meaning to go, " Lauren laughed. "It's a group lesson for the moms."

"It's lots of fun," Rhonda pitched. "We all just dish and learn a little basic equitation in the process. And then we have coffee and doughnuts. Only $25 a session."

"I don't want to disillusion my daughter by promptly getting myself bucked off a horse," Maggie demurred.

"Oh, you won't," Rhonda chirped before turning to address the man. "Paul, is Skylar going to take her make-up lesson this week or next?"

Lauren fiddled in her purse for her keys. "Look, Brittany and I need to go. But we should have coffee – minus the horses – some time."

"I'd like that. I'm new to Del Mar and I don't know many people."

"You might not want to," Lauren grinned. "Here's my business card. Call me, OK?"

The Coldwell-Banker card read "LAUREN BYERS, SALES REPRESENTATIVE," and included both work and cell numbers. Maggie slipped it into her bag. "I will. And I'm sure I'll see you around here." Maybe she actually would call Lauren for coffee.

With Rhonda as an escort, Kat led Sugar back to her corral. When she returned, her cheeks were bright. "Mommy, Rhonda showed me the cutest little foal and its mama. Will you come see them too?" She seized Maggie's hand.

"Lead the way."

Kat pulled her along, over a shallow dry riverbed and up to another maze of horses behind pipe corrals. Kat acted as if she had been coming to these stables all her life. The bay mare and her fuzzy little rocking-horse of a foal were indeed charming, and Kat was entranced. But Maggie was distracted by a very tall, muscular black horse across the way with a black mane like a long silk curtain and a curious yet kind eye riveted on them. She left Kat cooing over the mare and foal to approach the black horse. "Hi there," she said, tentatively reaching out to stroke his nose. For it was a he; she didn't know how to tell a stallion from a gelding, but there was no doubt this great horse was male.

He nickered, pushing his immense head farther over the top rail to slobber, dog-like, on her shoulder. She noticed the bell-bottom-like fur over his huge hooves. Did Clydesdales come in black? Regardless, this magnificent animal was obviously no school horse but rather some seasoned equestrian's crown jewel.

Then the horse neighed and flared as he spied the dark-skinned man in the golf cart rolling up with bales of alfalfa and timothy. "Hola," he greeted Maggie, stopping the cart and stepping around to grab a bale from the back.

"Como esta?"

"Bien, gracias!" He tossed the hay into the large bin inside the black horse's stall. The black giant neighed again as he attacked it.

"Este caballo es mu grande, si?" the fellow said to Maggie.

"Si. Muy guapo, verdad."

Kat jogged up. "I'm telling abuelito on you, Mommy," she teased.

"He just doesn't want us speaking Spanish around *him*," Maggie rejoined.

Strangely, Kat barely gave the big horse a glance. "Can I come back on Thursday?"

"Buenos tardes," she said to the feed man.

"Buenos tardes, senorita."

The black horse raised his head briefly toward her, then returned to his hay.

She expected Kat to pester her all the way home about the additional lesson, but instead the little girl seemed content to verbally relive every moment of today's riding experience. She adored Sugar, loved trotting, couldn't wait to canter. Had her mommy seen her make the circles? Hadn't she done well? Did Mommy see her post? She had to remind Maggie what posting was – "Up and down in the saddle."

"You were wonderful, sweetie."

Thumper greeted them at the door, yapping. Kat swept him up for a kiss. "Put him out in case he has to go," Maggie said. There was no doggie door, but the small side yard was fenced in, a perfect run for a toy breed. "I'll fix us some lunch."

Kat wanted BLTs, but Maggie couldn't yet bear the aroma of bacon. Tim had so plainly chosen it to mask the smell of the meth he'd "burned" earlier in her kitchen. Instead she made grilled cheese and tomato sandwiches and a quick fruit salad of bananas, cantaloupe, and apples.

"Next time I want to bring some apples for Sugar," Kat said, inspired. Then, "I told Brittany I'd be there Thursday."

"I'm still thinking about it, Kat. I'll let you know when I've made up my mind."

Kat recognized that her mother meant business, and returned to her sandwich.

After lunch Maggie took her laptop up to her office. She switched on the overhead light – this week she *had* to buy a desk lamp – and sat down to resume work on her current project, revising copy for an HMO human resources brochure. From downstairs she could hear the hum of the TV, Kat's occasional giggle at something on Nickelodeon.

Perking up the dry, flat-footed HR prose was absorbing if not exciting; thus she had no idea how much time had elapsed when she heard not the hum of the TV but rather Kat's voice, closer, talking softly.

Maggie cocked her head, listening. Was Kat on the cellphone, perhaps calling her grandparents to ask for the extra riding lesson? She couldn't make out what the child was saying. It was as though Kat was deliberately trying to be quiet.

Maggie got up from her desk and stepped into the hallway.

Kat sat two steps from the landing, on the stairs, squinting into the kaleidoscope. She spoke very softly. "It was so much fun. You should have seen me."

"Kat!"

The little girl twisted around, more quizzical than startled. "I was just telling Thumper about my lesson, Mommy."

But the dog was nowhere in sight. "Are you sure you were talking to Thumper?" Maggie pressed.

"Uh-huh. He ran downstairs."

And then Thumper appeared at the bottom of the stairs, panting and wagging his tail. Kat scampered down to him. "Let's go find your ball, Thumper!"

Maggie remained at the top of the stairs, frowning. Maybe the dog had been there all along, she tried to convince herself. And maybe the scenario would strike her as more plausible if only Kat had not been peering into that damnable kaleidoscope. The ostensible "present from Daddy." And why was Kat so obsessed with this staircase?

Because Kat had always been so serene despite the instability of her home life and the countless upsetting arguments, Maggie had never felt it necessary to put her in therapy. Her own shrink had suggested it might not be a bad idea, but Maggie resisted for fear that therapy would serve to reinforce the notion that there was something seriously wrong with Kat's family. But now Maggie was second-guessing that decision. Barring any further strange incident, she resolved to give Kat a few more days to settle in. But if by week's end Kat was still behaving oddly, then it was time to make an appointment with a child psychologist.

Her concentration shattered, Maggie went to the phone and called Camino Equestrian. She signed Kat up for Thursday lessons as well.

To her mild disappointment, Lauren Byers was just leaving as Maggie and Kat trudged toward the crossties. "I've got to show a house in Carmel Mountain," Lauren apologized. "I'll be back in an hour and a half. Do you want to do coffee then?"

"What about the girls?"

Kat had already run over to join Brittany, who was grooming the old chestnut gelding, Rev.

"We can get our coffees at Starbucks and then let the girls play at McDonalds. They're both at the Highlands shopping center on Del Mar Heights."

"That big center with the Ralphs? That sounds fine." At least the outing would

serve to forestall returning home again to find Kat on the stairs with the kaleidoscope

telling "Thumper" about her ride. Yesterday she had taken Kat to the beach, where they

had played in the surf and built sandcastles. On the way home they'd stopped at Barnes

and Noble, and she'd bought Kat a book about horses and riding. Kat still kept the

kaleidoscope on her nightstand, but her attention was now solely directed on the book.

Maggie hoped that her fascination with the old toy was ebbing.

Today's group lesson was larger than Tuesday's, with seven little girls who

looked to be between seven and twelve years old. No sign of Tatiana or her daughter, but

the silver bore Paul was again holding court at the picnic table, monologizing to one

woman in a "Supermom" T-shirt and another bombshell type in hip-huggers and a

collagen pout.

Minus Lauren's presence Maggie was disinclined to join the picnic table klatsch.

Instead, she watched Kat grooming Sugar. "Want to give her a carrot?" Maggie asked,

petting the sweet palomino's neck. She had a one-pound bag of carrots in her hobo-style

leather satchel. A Prada – from Mama, of course. Out here she half-wished it had come

from Target.

"My book says it's better to give treats after the lesson," Kat replied in learned

manner, bending down to lift up Sugar's left front hoof and clean it expertly with the

little brushed pick.

Maggie was impressed by how quickly Kat had become comfortable with the

rudiments of grooming. She probably already had her horse book memorized.

Once the lesson started, Kat was oblivious of everything but the horse and instruction. Was this what Tim had meant, so many years ago, when describing his mental state while pitching, especially in a close game? He'd called it "being in the zone," a state of sublime concentration, pure fusion between mind and activity.

"Aren't these kids just amazing. There's nothing sweeter than little girls and their horses."

Maggie was startled. Paul's platitude was directed at her. And there was something faintly unctuous about the way he said "little girls." "True. Will you excuse me? I'm going to get a Coke."

She headed off in the direction of the tack store. Passing the dry riverbed, she remembered the gorgeous black horse. Maybe he would like a carrot.

He came right over to the rail at her approach. Bright black eyes regarded her from beneath his long forelock. "You are such a big boy," Maggie praised, petting his nose. She reached into her satchel for a carrot.

"Excuse me," scolded a high-pitched female voice from behind her. "Are you supposed to be hanging around that horse?" A tow-headed woman with a vaguely bovine face was trudging over.

Not another out-of-control blonde. But perhaps this officious cow-woman was the horse's owner. "I'm sorry – am I not supposed to be?" Maggie replied coolly, although she did step back from the railing.

Behind the woman a young man in jeans, T-shirt, and riding boots appeared. "Warlock loves people," he snapped to the tow-head. "Christ, Stacey, mind your own damn horse's business."

"I was only wondering, Billy," Stacey muttered, red-faced, as she backed away.

Maggie regarded Billy with gratitude. "Your horse is beautiful. And maybe I shouldn't have been giving him treats without permission."

"He's not my horse. I'm just training him. The owner bought him to ride but he's used to pulling a cart." He began unknotting the lead rope that was looped around the gate of the stall.

"He has such intelligent eyes. I bet he's a quick learner." She felt free to again caress Warlock's muzzle. He nosed her hand in hopes of another carrot.

"He's too smart for his own damn good. And riding him's like riding a jackhammer."

"Really?"

"Friesians are built for style, not comfort," he said with a sly wink. He extended a calloused hand. "Billy O'Donnell. You board here?"

She shook his hand, liking him despite his slightly brusque, no-nonsense manner. Liking him instinctively, as she had Lauren. "Maggie Flores. And no, I know next to nothing about horses. My daughter's just started lessons."

He was a good-looking guy, she found herself noticing, with sandy-brown hair, keen blue eyes, and a ruddy complexion as Irish as his name. Mid-thirties, she guessed. "You should ride too, Maggie," he said, stepping inside Warlock's stall and slipping the halter over his nose. Warlock looked at her plaintively.

"Maybe," she said, amused by the horse's pleading expression. "Can I give him one last carrot?"

"Go ahead, but don't let him take your hand with it. He doesn't have a mean bone in his body, but his ground manners need work."

Warlock chonked the carrot, spraying organge-flecked slobber. Maggie laughed. "He's certainly an enthusiastic eater."

"You gotta be tough with 'em or else they'll walk all over you." He led the drooling Friesian through the gate. "Nice meeting you, Maggie. See you around."

"You too." She smiled after him as he walked the big horse away toward an empty wood-railed arena.

She was a little surprised to find Lauren already returned from her appointment nursing a Diet-Pepsi and watching the little girls posting and trotting. "My client crapped out on me," she explained. "It happens. How are you liking Del Mar so far?"

"It's beautiful, but … I still feel like a guest in our new house, you know? It still feels strange."

"When did you move in?"

"A week ago tomorrow," Maggie conceded, a bit sheepish.

"Well, no wonder! When we moved into the new house last year, I was so overwhelmed I made us all go on vacation to Hawaii before we'd even finished unpacking."

Maggie felt a little better. "I never even saw the house until moving day. A relative on my ex-husband's side left it to my daughter in her will, and it was kind of a whirlwind move."

"Just give yourself some time. Where is the house?"

"La Amatista Road – it's just off – "

"That is a fantastic location! Once you're all settled in you're going to adore living there."

Kat remained a study in concentration as she struck the two-point seat, her small body leaning forward in the saddle ramrod-straight from heels to shoulders. *In the zone.* Maggie fought back a wave of sadness.

"Excellent, Katya!" exclaimed Sandy.

Not even the praise registered on Kat's face as she trotted along astride the palomino. Maggie pushed the sadness away and was simply happy for her.

It wasn't until after the adults had purchased Frappaccinos for themselves and Happy Meals for the girls that Maggie told Lauren about the latest officious blonde to diss her for presuming to visit with the huge Friesian. "Thank God the trainer came to my rescue and told the woman to mind her own damn business."

"I can't believe that wasn't even her horse. I don't think I know that particular bitch, but I've seen the horse. It's magnificent – belongs to this German woman who looks like a model but is actually a big-shot biotech executive."

They sat in the McDonalds patio area; Kat and Brittany had already bolted their meals and were jittering around the Crayola-colored inflatable playground. "I feel like I've fallen into a *Desperate Housewives* for the horsy set," Maggie said, enjoying Lauren's cheery dishing.

"It's true. Throw in Paul the Bore and we've got a spinoff."

Maggie swirled her straw through whipped cream. "This trainer, Billy, was pretty cute. He'd have to be the sexy plumber across the street."

"Cute? I don't think I've seen him," Lauren said ruefully. "What does he look like?"

"Irish-looking. Light brown hair, blue eyes. Maybe 5'9 or '10. Slim but nice bod."

"I guess you didn't get a very good look at him," Lauren teased. "Actually, I do know who that is, but I thought he was an owner. He and Rhonda got into it a few weeks ago – he read her the riot act for putting a kid on a really spooky horse. The horse started bucking and rearing. God only knows how the little girl stayed on. She was in hysterics."

"That's awful. I bet she hasn't been back for lessons."

Lauren shook her head. "It was kind of scary. According to that guy, the trainer, the same horse had acted up before."

Maggie frowned. "I hope Rhonda doesn't put Kat on that horse. Kat knows no fear, but I'm her mother and entitled to be neurotic."

"I hear that. I live in terror Brit's going to fall." Lauren tossed her empty Starbucks cup into the trash. "So tell me about your new house. Maybe I can help you brainstorm about how to feel more at home there."

"It's nicer than any place I've lived since moving out of my parents' house to go to college. I mean, it has an ocean view from both the living room and my bedroom. But … " She felt guilty, as if in the confessional booth.

But Lauren was no stern silhouetted priest. "The house probably feels all the stranger because you didn't pick it out yourself and go through that whole decision-making process. Regardless of how nice it is."

Maggie found the explanation both plausible and reassuring. "True. And it's in a new city, and since I work at home, it feels especially isolated."

"What do you do?"

"Freelance writer and editor, mostly textbooks and website copy."

Happily, Lauren didn't respond with that familiar look of vague disappointment. "How cool. You can work in your PJs and be home for your daughter too."

"I've been doing it practically since Kat was born. I'm surprised she's not downright sick of me by now."

"How does she like the new digs?"

"She loves it. Kids are so adaptable, aren't they? I'm the one who's being the stick in the mud."

"No you're not – you just need to enhance your feng shui. How about throwing a housewarming?"

Maggie had to laugh. "Lauren, I know only you and my friend Ryan. It'd be one lonely party, and he's gay so we couldn't even have a ménage a trois."

"You could invite that cute trainer."

"Right. I talked to him for all of thirty seconds."

Lauren seemed to consider it. "OK, let's table the housewarming for the time being. Why don't you buy a bunch of small frames and put up some family pictures here and there around the house? That would make it feel more like yours."

"I could do that, I suppose."

"Family photos and fresh flowers always do it for me."

"Those are both good ideas. Thanks, Lauren. I feel like such a baby."

"Not at all. Haven't you heard that moving is the third most stressful life event after a death and divorce?"

"Trust me, I'd move a dozen more times before going through a divorce again."

Lauren chuckled. "Same here. We'll trade war stories next time we do coffee, when the girls aren't within earshot."

Maggie was relieved to be let off the hook.

Encouraged by Lauren's suggestions, she stopped at Ralphs for a half dozen 5 x 7 frames and a bunch of bright if overpriced blue daisies. Once home, however, she found herself compelled to preempt any replay of Kat's staircase report "to Thumper." After trimming the daisies and arranging them in a water-filled cut glass vase, she proposed to Kat they call Abuelo and Abuelita to tell them about the riding lessons.

First Kat, then Maggie, spoke with Eva; Armando was at one of the LA restaurants but Eva promised to have him call when he got home. Maggie made no mention of her adjustment difficulties, painting for her mother only the positive – the view, the stables, the budding friendship with Lauren, the lovely afternoon at the beach. She had given her parents so much to worry about for so long. Why trouble Mama with her childish, nebulous sense that she didn't really want to be in this house?

By the time she got off the phone, Kat was outside in the little yard playing with Thumper. Good. Maggie was repositioning the flowers on the living room's brick mantle when Ryan called. "I can't talk long – I'm on a break," he said. "I just wanted to hear how things are going."

"OK – I mean, really well." She sat down on the sofa, focusing on the ocean view in front of her rather than the dreary staircase to her right. "Kat's started riding lessons, and she's ecstatic."

"Cool. Can I take you two to dinner tonight, or is this too short notice?"

"It so happens that my dance-card's completely open. But why don't you come over here and we'll order pizza? You can be my first official dinner guest."

"Sounds great. Is seven good?"

"For sure, because then we can watch the sunset – " Out of the corner of her right eye she glimpsed something, something between a long shape and a long shadow by the foot of the stairs.

"Maggie?"

Nothing was there, not even a shadow. Then Kat and the dog scurried in, and Maggie concluded that the glimmer was somehow caused by her daughter's reentry from the side door. "Sorry," she said to Ryan. "I had an eyelash in my eye. I'll see you around seven."

Ryan brought a bottle of Fetzer cabernet and a bakery box with six white frosted cupcakes. "The wine's for your daughter, of course," he joked.

Not surprisingly, Kat didn't remember having met him twice before, when she'd been three and five, respectively. But she was impressed by the cupcakes. "They're my favorites," she declared, peering into the box as Maggie uncorked the wine.

"I hear Del Mar Pizza in the village is pretty good," Ryan said, accepting a goblet.

"I like Pizza Hut!" Kat said.

"Pizza Hut's good too," Ryan said diplomatically.

"No, let's try the new place, sweetie," Maggie said to Kat with a smile. "I don't think they have Pizza Hut here in Del Mar."

Kat accepted the white lie philosophically. "Maybe the new place is good too."

Maggie ordered the pizza and an antipasto salad, then the three of them, plus Thumper, slipped outside onto the redwood deck. While Kat chattered to Ryan about her riding lessons and Sugar, Maggie lost herself in the sunset: crayon smudges of violet, pink, and burnt orange against the white-blue sky and glittery ocean. How she had missed these Pacific sunsets those years she'd spent away from the coast with Tim when he was pitching in the Dodger farm system. So far from the ocean she had felt landlocked and claustrophobic. The combination of sunset and wine was sufficient to coax her into thinking, however briefly, *I'm glad we're here.*

The pizza didn't arrive until well after eight. By the time they were done eating Kat was noticeably heavy-lidded. Maggie saw her to bed and kissed her goodnight. Rejoining Ryan at the dining room table, she asked, "Will you think me a hopeless lush if I open us another bottle of wine?"

"No, I'd think you a rude hostess if you didn't."

She refilled their glasses with a Meridian pinot noir. "I hope Kat didn't drive you too crazy with her horse talk."

"Not at all. She's a neat kid, Maggie. You and Tim sure got that part right."

"If little else," she quipped wryly. "But she's been my rock."

"Hey, speaking of rocks, I saw a great bumpersticker at UCSD the other day. A picture of the Chimp-in-Chief, with the caption 'Like a rock – only dumber.'"

She whooped. "I want one! It'd be another great way to thumb my nose at some of the snobs at the stables. Did I tell you that this one ditz thought I was Kat's au pair?"

"No fucking way!"

"Yes fucking way. I was literally shocked speechless."

"People are so vile."

"Yes, as Seinfeld said, 'they're the worst.' But I've met one nice woman out there. Her daughter and Kat have hit it off."

"Just don't ask the nice woman her political affiliation."

"I won't." She remembered the picture frames. "In fact, Lauren told me I should display some of my pictures to give this place the right feng shui."

"She actually said 'feng shui'? That's so nineties."

"Be that as it may – will you help me choose a few?"

"As long as they don't feature me in some flagrant state of intoxication."

Maggie knelt down next to the distressed-blue pine buffet. "Damn, I wish I could find those pictures from the graduation party your grandmother had for us all." She removed three stacked shoeboxes and set them on the table.

"*That* party? Even my grandma was shit-faced."

Maggie lifted the lids from the boxes, revealing dozens and dozens of stuffed Kodak envelopes. "Yes, that party. Remember what your grandmother said about Tim in front of the whole room?"

"'That boy is so handsome he just fascinates me'!"

They both howled. "Tim turned the color of a strawberry!" Maggie squealed.

Ryan picked up one envelope. "I take it you don't believe in photo albums."

She groaned. "My mom gave me three or four extra-large albums years ago, but I still haven't gotten around to putting any pictures in them." She sipped her wine and started paging through envelopes herself. At least they were dated; chances were that any marked 1997 or later would contain some cute pictures of Kat. "Ah-ha. Christmas 2002."

Sure enough, the pictures inside were strong candidates for framing: Kat opening gifts at her maternal grandparents' house; Armando and Eva beaming in front of the sparkling Christmas tree; Maggie with her older brother Juan-Gil and his wife Tina, all wearing Santa caps. "What do you think of these?"

Ryan was focused on his own discovery. "This one's from June '95, and so's this other one." He held up two envelopes. "The graduation party pictures have got to be in one of these."

She danced around to his side of the table and leaned over his shoulder as he opened the first. The date was right, but these were shots taken a week before graduation – at the reception thrown by her family at her father's Marina del Rey restaurant in honor of the surprise newlyweds Tim and Maggie Emerson. They'd eloped to Las Vegas the previous weekend, on an impulse, to jolt themselves out of honors-thesis obsession and an equally shared, lingering heartache over his accidental drug overdose in January that had landed him in the hospital for three days and earned him a suspension from the baseball program for his entire, crucial senior season. She had felt as responsible for the incident as if she'd forced the near-lethal combination of meth and about 50 Valium tablets into him herself. Though agreeing abortion was the lone sensible option, they'd both struggled mightily against Catholic guilt. She believed to this day that her parents would disown her if they ever learned about the abortion.

The whirlwind wedding hadn't exactly thrilled either set of parents, but the families were somewhat appeased when Tim and Maggie agreed to secure a priest's blessing for their union. Hence the margarita-drenched and mariachi-scored reception. It hurt to look at Tim and herself, he in a suit and she in the flowery dress they'd worn to church, young and beautiful and glowing with tequila and reborn hope. "There should be some of you and Dan and Julie in here," she said, flipping past the shots of herself and Tim. "I feel like I should put on 'Pictures of You' by the Cure."

"That was a killer reception. Even if Dan did puke up about two gallons of margaritas and a carne asada burrito on the drive home."

"Ha – what a perfect omen."

She finally came across a shot of Dan, Julie, and Ryan grinning over nachos and a pitcher of margaritas, the mariachi band in the background. Ryan scrutinized the picture. "We all look so young. How depressing."

She picked up the other June '95 envelope. "OK, these ones are from graduation. Your grandmother's party has to be in here." In rapid succession she passed him pictures of herself, Tim, herself and Tim, herself and Ryan, Dan and Julie, and her friend Ellen, all donning mortarboards and gowns and flanked by assorted proud family members.

Ryan gave each a cursory glance, then returned to a particular photo, raising it closer to his eyes. "This one has the most bizarre optical illusion. What do you see in the trees?" He handed it to her.

It was Tim and his parents, all smiling with their lips but not their eyes. "Yeah, he always had a tense relationship with them."

"No, look at the trees, just behind Tim and his folks," he urged.

And then she saw it. In the peculiar configuration of the branches, leaves, and patches of sky seemed to be the visage of a scowling old man. She shuddered. "Ugh, that's downright creepy. It looks just like a mean old man, doesn't it?"

"No shit. You never noticed before?"

She shook her head, still staring at the unnerving image – or apparent image – in the trees.

"It's not in any of the other graduation shots, not even ones taken from the same angle."

"A cloud must have passed over the sun." She lay the weird photograph back on the table.

Ryan had moved on to the remainder of the set. "OK, here we go – the party pictures!"

Soon they were laughing hysterically over various shots of themselves, Tim, Dan, all their stoner friends, and of course, Ryan's ordinarily dignified grandmother grinning tipsily and toasting the camera with her champagne flute. "She was so adorable," Maggie said, her nostalgia here warm rather than bittersweet. "Is she still doing well?"

"Eight-five and hasn't missed a beat. Look at her in this one – she's chug-a-lugging her champagne like a parched man in the desert."

They ended up killing the second bottle of wine, and this time Ryan agreed to spend the night on the couch. "I'm gonna leave early so don't get up," he said as they spread a sheet and light thermal blanket over the chintz upholstery.

"Kat's an early riser, so she may be up before either of us."

"Good, then I won't need an alarm clock."

She hugged him goodnight. Upstairs, she looked in on Kat, who slept placidly with the light on, before retiring to her own bedroom for the night.

Ryan was already gone when she padded downstairs the next morning just before eight. Kat, in her Little Mermaid pajamas, informed her that Thumper had given Ryan a wakeup kiss. "Isn't that cute, Mommy?"

"It sure is, sweetie." Good thing that Ryan was an animal lover.

Kat trailed her into the kitchen. "Can I have one of your new frames?"

Maggie groggily scooped coffee into the filter basket. "Sure. You want me to take a picture of you with Sugar to put in it?"

"Then I'll need two frames!" Kat said excitedly.

Maggie was confused. "Two?"

Kat nodded. "I want to put this picture of Daddy with Nana and Grampa in my room." She held up a photograph.

It was all Maggie could do not to gasp. Somehow Kat had gravitated to the picture with the unnerving optical illusion from the set left on the dining room table. "Oh sweetie, I'm sure we can find a better picture of Daddy for you," she said hurriedly, gently reaching for the photo.

"I like this one," Kat insisted, gazing at it with a smile.

Maggie longed to snatch the photograph out of her daughter's small hands and rip it into tatters. But Kat was already slipping it into the pocket of her pajama top and moving toward the pantry where they kept the cereal.

Once again that sense of irrationality that had plagued her on and off from her first day in the house gnawed in her head and gut. *I just won't give her a frame*, she resolved. *Or I'll sneak in a different one of Tim.* There was no reason to panic.

And frankly, she couldn't afford to panic. She had to get in a productive day of work, despite Kat's appropriation of the weird photo and despite the mild-to-moderate hangover she was suddenly aware she had from all the wine the night before. Once the breakfast dishes were in the sink and Kat was engrossed again in her horse book, Maggie sat down with her laptop and reopened the HMO document.

The third cup of coffee chased away the hangover and jumpstarted her brain. At noon she e-mailed the completed editing job to the HMO. She supposed she should turn to her next task, a ghostwriting project for a Young Adults publisher. They wanted a teen-friendly diet book, and had Fed-Exed a stack of recipes, basic nutrition data, and exercise diagrams the day before her move to Del Mar. The deadline was October 1, but it was already mid-August. And the sooner she finished the book, the sooner she would receive the balance of her fee.

She created a new Word Document, intending to draft an outline. But instead she found herself typing

optical illusions

She stared at the words, thinking. About the face in the trees in the graduation picture. About the shape she *almost* saw near the foot of the staircase yesterday afternoon. About the old fedora that had turned out to be a shadow. Meaningless

chimerae, too literally insubstantial, to make her question either her vision or her sanity.

On the other hand, she hadn't been to the optometrist in three years. She was

probably overdue for a new prescription for her contact lenses, especially given the long

hours she spent at the computer.

She deleted the two words and typed instead *Outline: Lose Weight, Look Great!*

Banner Books 2005.

She took a break at two to fix Kat some lunch and replenish the coffee. Kat was

understandably antsy. "Can we go to the beach, Mommy?"

"Let me work a couple more hours, honey. Then we'll go." It would be a relief

when school started and Kat would begin making new friends. Of course, she already

seemed to like Lauren's daughter Brittany. Maggie would have to call Lauren and

schedule a weekend play date for the girls.

She inserted the DVD of *Black Beauty* into the player for Kat, then returned to

work in the study. She was making progress on the teen diet book, though a part of her

heart ached at the thought of lonely, pudgy, perhaps even bullied adolescent girls

scavenging for a miracle diet that would bestow instant popularity. Maggie had always

been slim, but as the smartest kid in her class and one of the few Latinas at her tony all-

girls Catholic school in Newport Beach, she'd endured her share of teasing and

ostracism. Happily everything changed in college; she made friends easily both with

other Hispanic students and with white, black, and Asian ones. Her best friends were

Ryan, a gay white kid from the San Fernando Valley, and Ellen Li, a Chinese-American

from the Bay Area. Ellen had been no straight arrow, but she was genuinely shocked when Tim inadvertently outed his drug problem that tumultuous senior year. She and

Maggie had started to drift apart from that point onward, not because Ellen was

unsympathetic – she wasn't – but because Maggie had felt ashamed, less of Tim than of

herself. How could she expect Ellen not to judge her for being in love with someone so

reckless and self-destructive?

At quarter to four Kat came in to ask if she could change into her bathing suit.

"Yeah, but don't forget your sweatshirt and sandals in case it gets cold."

She took a few minutes to finish a paragraph, after which she closed the document

and went to Kat's room to see if she was ready. Kat was in her pink floral swimsuit and

in the process of strapping on her sandals. Satisfied, Maggie was just about to leave the

room to change into her own beachwear when she spied the graduation picture of Tim

and his parents taped to Kat's closet door. *Damn!*

"I put it there 'cause I couldn't find the frames," Kat explained.

Maggie inched closer to the photo. Something was different. It took her a

moment to realize that the illusory face in the trees was no longer there.

She could scarcely conceal her relief. "Oh, so you found a different one to put

up."

"It's the same one," Kat replied. "Hurry up and change, Mommy."

Maggie glanced again at the photo. Definitely no bizarre old man's face in the

trees. Clearly Kat had chosen another, similar shot of Tim and his parents.

Nevertheless, later in the evening when Kat was in bed, Maggie returned to the

envelope with the graduation photos and searched in vain for the picture with the disturbing face in the trees. There wasn't even another picture of Tim with Jack and Beth in the set.

And for the first time, she fleetingly wondered if the house could be haunted.

CHAPTER 3

The very notion seemed so crazy, so ludicrous, that she didn't even mention it to Ryan, who had, after all, been the one to spot the disconcerting optical illusion in the photograph. Lauren, of course, was out of the question. They barely knew each other, and haunted house talk would likely prompt Lauren to revise her opinion that Maggie was so "down to earth." She toyed with the idea of confiding in Mama, who believed in ghosts and astrology and the healing power of crystals despite her devout Catholicism. Eva would probably convince herself she'd sensed a "presence" in the house on the day she'd brought Kat down from Newport Beach. But what if Mama either nagged her to bring in a priest or to immediately vacate the house and move back in with them?

"It's so stupid," she said to herself on the drive home from Lauren's Carmel Valley house where she'd just deposited Kat for play with Brittany. There were no such things as ghosts or poltergeists; it was all superstition and Hollywood special effects. Moreover, she argued to herself, there was no consistency to any of the odd phenomena. The old man's face that was and then was not visible in the photo. The ordinary child's kaleidoscope that so fascinated Kat. The shadowy hat and almost-shape at the foot of the stairs. And just now she remembered the stomping on the stairs that seemed to be a

waking echo of her dream. Were those stairs somehow significant?

She was tempted to call the property management company to enquire about the

previous occupants. But it was Saturday afternoon, and the managers were likely not

available except for emergencies.

She found herself reluctant to return home, even though Kat's happy occupation

at Brittany's house ensured a guilt-free afternoon of work. On impulse Maggie decided

to stop in at the stables and visit with the majestic Friesian horse Warlock. His gorgeous

physicality was both imposing and calming. And he certainly wouldn't think her an idiot

or madwoman for even idly considering the possibility of a haunting.

And with any luck she might run into Billy O'Donnell again.

The dirt parking area was almost full, with SUVs bearing "I BRAKE FOR

HORSES" bumperstickers; a handful of luxury sedans – including one Mercedes with the

license frame "I'M NOT SPOILED – MY HUSBAND JUST LOVES ME"; a couple of

dust-coated pickup trucks with trailer balls. Virtually all the humans in sight, whether on

horseback, foot, or congregated around the riding school arena where lessons were taking

place, were females, women and girls, save for the Mexican workers who fed the horses

and mucked the stables. Little girls and horses, like little boys and baseball, seemed a

coupling integral to the illusory fabric of white suburban fantasy. How fortunate she

hadn't had a son, for who would toss the ball back and forth with him and take him to

Little League games?

The idea made her eyes mist, and she donned her sunglasses as she got out of her

car. She avoided the riding school crowd and again took the path behind the barn.

Today, the three larger back arenas were in use as well, and in a clearing, a farrier

pounded new shoes onto a patient bay Thoroughbred in the crossties. Nearby two other

horses were receiving baths in the wash rack, one thirstily slurping water from a hose

wielded by its owner. Maggie saw no familiar faces, at least not until she neared

Warlock's stall and the huge horse, spotting her, jogged right over.

"Hello, handsome," she crooned, patting his nose with one hand and fishing for a

treat in her purse with the other. She found a Power Bar and a small apple. "I may have

to check out the tack store for some carrots for you," she said, offering him the apple.

He took the entire red globe in his mouth and crunched into it. Apple juices and

saliva sprayed her as he chonked. Laughing, she brushed the residue off her shoulder.

"Not exactly a dainty eater, are you, Warlock!"

She glanced around before giving him the Power Bar lest Stacey or some similar

busybody would march over and scold her for feeding him people-food, even if the bar

tasted as if it were made of alfalfa. The horses in adjacent stalls all regarded her

plaintively but theirs was the only scrutiny. "So what do you think, handsome?" she said,

feeding Warlock the energy bar. "Is my house haunted or not?"

As he devoured the bar with no less zeal than he had the apple, a familiar voice

from behind said, "Is it?"

Startled, she spun around. "Oh my God, you're quieter than a cat!" she exclaimed

to Billy, who stood three feet behind her in jeans, T-shirt, a Padres baseball cap.

"Nah, I was right around the corner, watching you flirt with the big guy."

"Voyeur," she said, smiling. She was pleased to see him and eager to change to

subject from the embarrassing one of her "haunted house."

He guffawed, easing past her and sliding the bolt on the stall's gate. He stepped inside, and Warlock greeted him with a nuzzle. Billy gave the horse a brief pat before grabbing a mesh blanket that was draped over one railing. "Nicole always forgets to put his fly sheet back on after she's ridden," he explained to Maggie. He tossed the blanket over Warlock's back and began to fasten various straps to buckles.

"Is that the owner? I thought you said he wasn't broken to ride."

"Nicole owns him, and he's not. But she's a kamikaze." He bent slightly to loop a strap under the horse's belly.

"I envy people who are fearless like that."

"There's fearless, and there's crazy. He's a lot of horse for anybody."

"You ride him, though. What does that make you?"

"Neither. I ride him 'cause it's my job." Warlock attempted a playful nip. Billy gave him a light but businesslike whack on the nose. "*No*," he said firmly.

The Friesian's ears twitched and his lively expression turned meek.

"Awwww," Maggie sympathized.

"He can't go around thinking all fingers are treats. Nicole hand-feeds him too, along with everybody else who walks by 'im."

"Discipline isn't my strong suit either, I admit. My daughter trained our dog. He'd probably be a holy terror if I'd been responsible."

"She riding today?" He gave Warlock a conciliatory pat on the rump, then stepped out of the stall.

"Actually, no. I came here to see this horse, believe it or not."

"To tell him your house is haunted?" he teased, brushing his hands together.

It was then that she spotted, to her great dismay, a plain gold band on his left ring finger. *Shit!* she despaired. "Oh, my house isn't really haunted," she said, feeling all the more foolish and now eager to leave the stables and get back to the house, haunted or not.

"So ... what, you were just trying to make conversation with the horse?" His tone was light but he seemed more curious than condescending.

"It's nothing. A place always seems strange when you first move in."

He took a quick look at his wristwatch. "I got about an hour before my next client. Let me buy you a Coke at the tack store and you can tell me about your ghost."

"It's not a ghost," she said with a helpless laugh.

Nor was that damn wedding ring an otherworldly illusion. But she started strolling back toward the store alongside him, reasoning that just because he was married didn't mean they could not be friends.

The "Tack 'n' Snack" was small, a cross between an ordinary convenience store and horse supply emporium, with snacks and sodas on one side, grooming materials, riding crops, and feed on the other. An affable brunette woman behind the counter rang up their soft drinks. "Thought you were done for the afternoon, Billy," she said.

"Hell no. I'm meeting Miss Thang's sugar-daddy about a horse he wants to buy for her brat."

The woman behind the counter made a face, and Maggie had a strong feeling that the "Miss Thang" in question was Tatiana.

"Kim, this is Maggie," Billy said. "Her daughter's taking lessons at Rhonda's."

"Nice to meet you," Kim said warmly. "Your daughter enjoying her lessons?"

"Loves them," Maggie said. "But if she wants her own horse, I'm going to have to start buying lottery tickets."

"You and me both," Kim agreed.

The Tack 'n' Snack was fronted by a shaded plankwood porch. Maggie and Billy each claimed a white plastic chair. "Kim's really likeable," Maggie said, snapping open her Diet Dr. Pepper. "Except for one other mom, most of the women around here strike me as sort of – "

"Phony? Stuck-up?"

"Oh that."

"Barns are that way. You have the real horse people and you have the rich people." He removed his cap, revealing tousled hair, a lock of which he impatiently brushed from his brow.

"I suppose it makes sense. Horses are an expensive hobby."

"No shit. I have four, and they're bankrupting me." He took a deep drink from his Coke.

"Then you must be rich," she jested.

He almost choked on his cola. "Ahem! That's a good one."

She was amused. "But *four* horses?"

"I get a break on the board for training here. And two are leased out."

"People lease horses? I thought the only leases around here were on the BMWs and Lexuses."

He chuckled. "Leasing horses is almost as common. You pay full or half board depending on how often you plan to ride. Owner's still responsible for vet bills, shoeing, et cetera."

"Did you grow up with horses?"

He nodded. "Yeah, in New Mexico. Didn't have my own, though. I worked at a barn in exchange for lessons from the time I was ten."

Her eyes idly followed the ludicrous figure of a dumpy woman talking on her cellphone astride an elegant paint horse that clopped by. "I lived in Albuquerque for a couple of years. Long time ago, when I was first married."

"Albuquerque's not the most exciting town in the world, 'cept compared to Clovis, where I grew up."

"Clovis? Where's that?"

"About four hours southwest of Albuquerque. Literally in the middle of nowhere."

"Ha, near Roswell?"

He gave her a look. "Not really. Why? Do I look like I just dropped out of a UFO?"

"'The truth is out there.'"

"'Trust no one,'" he countered with his own *X-Files* allusion. "And since we're talking about the supernatural, tell me what's strange about your new house. Do things go bump in the night?"

"No. I mean, not really." She studied his face, again seeing interest rather than patronization. And it was a nice face, with its sharp blue eyes, strong cheekbones, rather stubborn chin.

"What, then?"

"It's hard to pinpoint. A few times I keep thinking I'm seeing things, only to look closer and find it's a shadow, or simply nothing." The admission sounded to her own ears mundane, anticlimactic.

"Like what kind of things?"

"A few days ago I thought I saw out of the corner of my eye a long shadow by the stairs. Long enough to be the shadow of a person. It turned out to be nothing, not even a shadow."

He arched an eyebrow. "That's pretty weird."

Because she felt uncomfortable introducing Kat into the borderline-ridiculous story, she chose not to tell him about the photograph. "I'm surprised you find this interesting. You impress me as a very commonsense kind of guy."

He shrugged. "Maybe. But not everybody has the chance to even wonder if their house is haunted."

"Do you believe in ghosts?"

"Never seen any, if that's what you're asking. But I don't not believe, either. Seems to me, though, that if ghosts exist, they probably have more to do with the living than the dead."

She was intrigued. "Ah-ha. So you think my maybe-ghost could be something I'm projecting onto the house?"

"You tell me."

She thought about it. Could it be that her anxiety about Tim subjecting Kat to his drug madness had followed her to the new house? Why not? It had chased her from her rented condo in Manhattan Beach. Perhaps it would have followed her to the other side of the globe. But she wasn't about to get into that with Billy. "I guess anything is possible." She stood up, tossed her empty soda can into a recycling bin. "I should be going. I'm playing hooky from work."

"And from your house," he joked, standing as well.

"Thanks for the Coke and the conversation," she said with a smile. She slung her hobo bag over one shoulder. "Next one's on me."

"You got a deal. Wanna shake on it?"

She briefly clasped the slender but well-callused hand extended to her. "I'll see you around."

"Remember, Maggie. The house is only as haunted as you let it be."

It was a notion she found reassuring. She vowed to *will* those damn mirages away.

Her newfound determination was tested an hour later, when Kat called to ask if she could spend the night at Brittany's house. Lauren assured her it was fine; the plan was to get the kids KFC and a couple of videos. Kat could borrow a pair of Brit's PJs, so there was no need for Maggie to drive over with the child's overnight case. Maggie could hardly object.

She worked until the sun started to set. She took her modest dinner of scrambled eggs and salsa onto the deck. When the last ribbon of light was engulfed by night sky

and ocean, she went inside and poured a glass of wine. God knew there was no
programming fit for anyone between the ages of fourteen and sixty-four on a Saturday
night, and she didn't have HBO. A very long, warm bubble-bath was in order. She
popped a P.J. Harvey CD into the stereo and cranked up the volume.

In the master bathroom she poured foaming oil into the tub. She toyed with the
idea of lighting a few candles, but Thumper had followed her upstairs and she was afraid
the exuberant little dog might knock over one of the lit tapers and set the house ablaze.
She peeled off her clothes and eased into the warm suds.

Downstairs, P.J. Harvey wailed,

Long goes the night

Longer the day

Teclo, your death

Will send me to my grave …

Leaning back in the tub, she closed her eyes and made herself think about Billy.
Double-damn his marital status, although he hadn't once referred to his wife or even used
the first-person-plural pronoun. What if the ring had no particular significance? Oh
come on, her warier, more pessimistic self countered. People who wore wedding bands
were married. It was wrong even to fantasize about him.

Yet her hand slipped beneath the foam to stroke her vulva. She imagined it was
his hand, pressing down, caressing, insistent.

The phone rang, the landline, not her cell. "Fuck," she swore. With Kat away
from home she could scarcely ignore it. She clambered out of the tub and hurried naked
and dripping into the bedroom.

She caught it on the third ring. "Hello?"

"I'm going to beat the living crap out of you," growled an unfamiliar male voice. Then the line disconnected and she heard only the dial tone.

Trembling so intensely her legs could not support her, she sank to her knees on the carpet. She still clutched the receiver. Half-sobbing, she somehow mustered the presence of mind to push Star-69 on the dialpad.

Only a recording informing her that the Star-69 feature could not be utilized.

Maggie struggled for composure, to still her panting. She knew that a single call could not be traced. She tried Ryan's number but got the machine.

Eventually she rose from the floor, toweled dry, and tossed on her robe. Even with the CD still playing all she could do was strain her ears for another, dreadful phone call. She made her way downstairs, switched off the stereo, raided the refrigerator for the opened bottle of Chardonnay, which she took back to the master suite. She gulped down one glass, then another, drinking until oblivion overcame her panic and ensured that if the phone rang again, she would not hear it.

"For God's sake, Maggie. You should have called me."

Lauren had come by two drop off Kat around ten the next morning. Afraid that Lauren might attribute her puffy skin, sunglasses, and careless ponytail to a wild night partying in her child's absence, Maggie proffered an invitation for coffee. While Kat gave Brittany a tour of the house and acquainted her with Thumper, Maggie led Lauren onto the deck. The ocean air soothed her headache.

She told Lauren about the telephone call, though not about the string of peculiar occurrences that had so frayed her nerves to begin with. "I'm sure it was just some random pervert," Maggie said, taking tiny sips from her coffee mug. "But it scared the hell out of me."

"I'd have been totally freaked out too, even if I hadn't been by myself! If it happens again, Maggie, promise you'll call me, no matter what time it is."

"My number's unlisted. Almost nobody has it other than you and my friend Ryan. And my parents. The riding school." An awful thought popped into her mind. What if the charming Billy O'Donnell was actually a psychopath who had somehow obtained her phone number from Rhonda? He alone knew why she was already unnerved by the house.

"Like you said, it had to have been random," Lauren insisted. "Probably some obnoxious teenagers crank-calling on a Saturday night."

"Jesus, I thought that had given way to trolling Internet porn sites," Maggie tried to joke. But Lauren's hypothesis made at least as much sense as her own – that Billy was a closet psycho. She massaged the back of her stiff neck. "I'd better get my wimpiness under control before I turn into a raging alcoholic."

"Maggie, this house is wonderful. What a view! I thought maybe this was the place when you told me the address. I sold the property right across the street a couple of years ago."

With the coffee clearing her head, Maggie thought of something. "Did you ever meet or see the people who lived here while you were showing the house across the street?"

"Yeah, a few times. They were very nice. I assumed they were the owners."

"Who were they?"

"A UCSD professor and his wife, and I think her teenage son. She and the kid were Asian, and he was white, so I assumed he was the stepdad."

The teenage boy likely was the original owner of the kaleidoscope, but otherwise, the information shed no especial light. "They probably hated to be evicted," she simply remarked. "OK, I'm steady on my feet now. Come see the rest of the house."

Lauren enthused about the living and dining rooms, but agreed with Maggie that the staircase was a bit dreary. "Maybe if you ripped out the carpet and put in nice hardwood … " she mused as they ascended the stairs.

They found the girls seated side-by-side on Kat's bed poring over the horse book. "Mom, I want one too," Brittany declared.

But Lauren seemed not to hear her as she gazed at the photo taped crookedly to the closet door. "Is this Kat's dad?" she asked, pointing at Tim.

"Yes, that's my daddy!" Kat piped up proudly.

"God, he's gorgeous," Lauren said sotto voce to Maggie.

Maggie felt awkward. "Well, that was ten years ago," she said shortly. Tim had long since ceased bearing more than a ghost's resemblance to the young man in the graduation picture.

A ghost. Oh God, what if -- ?

Whether Lauren noticed her sudden pallor Maggie could not guess. The moment the front door closed on their departed guests Maggie turned to Kat. "Honey, I need to make some phone calls for work. Will you watch TV down here for a little while? Afterwards we can go to the beach if you want."

"OK." Kat picked up the TV remote and plopped onto the sofa.

In her bedroom – and with her door closed – Maggie grabbed her cellphone and address book. She didn't have Jack and Beth's number on speed dial.

Beth answered in her usual pleasant lilt. "Hello-o?"

"Mom, this is Maggie. I just need to know – is Tim all right?"

A short sigh. "We're not seeing Tim, Maggie. My understanding, dear, was that you felt the same way."

"Believe me, Mom, I do. But if no one's in touch with him, how can we even be sure he's alive?"

"Diana would let us know. She always seems to maintain contact with him one way or another."

While not as dispassionate as her husband, Beth Emerson sounded at least equally resigned. Maggie recognized the feeling. "He still has no idea where we are, right?"

"No, his sister doesn't even know. Jack told Di you'd taken Kat back to Mexico to stay with relatives."

A second-generation American, Maggie fumed at "*back* to Mexico." She held her tongue only because the lie, however informed by a thoughtless stereotype, served her purpose in keeping her whereabouts unknown to Tim. "The farther he thinks we are, the better. But I still worry about him."

"How are you and Katya settling in at the house? Isn't it a charming place?"

"It's great – we're both great."

"Our family had so many happy summers there, with Jack's folks. The kids went to the beach every day."

Beth's tone had turned pensive, and Maggie felt sorry for her. "Yes, Tim used to tell me about those nice summers." Another lie; Tim had never mentioned the Del Mar summers to her, not even before losing himself completely to methamphetamine. It didn't really surprise her. He'd always been candid to her about his feelings for his family: he loved them, he supposed, but except for Diana, he didn't especially like them. He resented Jack's high expectations and the vicarious pleasure when Tim surpassed them as much as the outspoken disappointment when he failed. As for Beth, he viewed her as willfully stuck in a *Father Knows Best* time-warp. Maggie could not recall him ever speaking of either set of grandparents.

She didn't prolong the conversation with Beth. She'd reassured herself at least that her transient, irrational theory about the "haunting" was baseless.

That night, as she showered off the sand and seawater, she thought she heard Kat softly talking on the stairs again. Could it be? Not ten minutes before she'd tucked her daughter into bed. Maggie shut off the shower, but heard nothing except for the steady drip-drop of water from her skin and hair. She peeked out her bedroom door. The staircase was empty.

She was just crawling into bed herself when Kat, Thumper at her heels, padded in. "Mommy? Can I sleep with you tonight?"

"Sure." Maggie patted the pillow beside her. "Did something scare you, sweetie?" She scanned Kat's face for signs of fear or upset.

Kat shook her head. "Uh-uh. I just feel like it." She hopped up onto the bed.

Nothing in Kat's voice or face belied her words. Maggie felt sheepish for being glad for the company. Kat used to sleep with her in her bed a lot after the divorce. It was a comfort then, as it was now.

She gave her daughter a hug, leaned over to dim the adjustable bulb on the nightstand lamp.

"You can turn it off all the way," Kat said, yawning and nestling into the pillows.

"It's OK," Maggie said. She didn't tell Kat that tonight, she probably would have kept a light on even had she been sleeping by herself.

She was surprised to discover she was the co-subject of old-fashioned barnyard gossip at Camino Equestrian when she brought Kat by for her Tuesday lesson. As Kat hurried off with the teacher Sandy to fetch Sugar, a grinning Rhonda said to Maggie, "I hear you've made friends with Billy."

"We've chatted a couple of times," Maggie said, wondering why she was bothering to explain herself at all.

"Lots of people find him hard to get along with," Rhonda continued in her typical chirpy manner.

Tatiana sashayed over to them. "Billy's an asshole but he knows horses. He helped Bernard buy Bianca that gorgeous Morgan." She pronounced "Bernard" with an exaggerated, Pepe La Pieu French accent. "Same day you and Billy were hanging out at the tack store."

"Tatiana, try to watch your language when kids are around," Rhonda scolded.

Maggie was thrilled to see Lauren's 4-Runner pull into the lot. "Excuse me, I need to ask Lauren something."

"Hi Maggie," greeted Brittany. "Is Kat getting Sugar?"

With Maggie's nod Brittany dashed off to retrieve her own assigned horse. Maggie motioned Lauren aside. "This is unreal," she said in a low voice. "I had a soda with Billy, that trainer, in front of the tack store the other day and evidently it's the talk of the ranch."

Lauren clucked. "God, it's like being back in junior high." She took her sunglasses out of her purse. "Now, fill *me* in!"

"There's nothing to tell. We just chatted. And he's married."

"Damn."

"No kidding."

"The good ones usually are."

Maggie half-watched Paul the Bore and Patty, a good-natured woman whose twins were also in the hour's lesson, join Tatiana and Rhonda at the arena-side picnic table. "Well, according to Tatiana and Rhonda, he's not necessarily one of the good ones."

"Rhonda's probably still ticked off that he chewed her out in front of all the parents, and Tatiana's standard for a good man is a high six-figure income."

Maggie smiled as Kat marched by leading the sweet palomino mare, Sandy strolling alongside. Kat confidently guided Sugar into the crossties. "Oh hell, let the hens gossip," Maggie said.

"On another subject, Maggie, any more weird calls? I hope not."

"No, I'm relieved to say. I think I just overreacted."

"Hardly. But I'm glad it's stayed quiet."

"Now to the more immediate crisis – can we stand to spend the next hour in the company of Tatiana and Paul?"

Lauren laughed. "No. Let me just go talk to Rhonda about Brit's makeup lessons – we missed a week last month when we were in Los Cabos – and then we can go hang out with Kim at the tack store. She's the most no-bullshit person out here."

Maggie nodded. "I'll meet you over there." From the tack store porch she'd still be able to keep an eye on the riding ring and lesson. If the picnic table club thought she'd suddenly turned snob, so be it. After twelve years with Tim in her life, she avoided scrutiny, and judgment, as a reflex.

On the Tack 'n' Snack door was a hand-lettered sign: "Be back in 15 minutes. Kim." Maggie took a seat at the same white plastic table she had shared with Billy. Intuitively she cast a glance toward the back arenas. Yes, there he was, with Warlock, snapping a lunge rope to cue for different gaits. She was mesmerized by the massive black horse in motion, long mane and tail flying as his high-stepping forward trot shifted to a full lumbering canter. Warlock seemed almost an elemental creature; he loped as if charging headlong into the air. Another clicking cue from Billy, and the horse broke back down to a trot.

Entranced, she didn't notice Paul approaching. "That Warlock's something else," he commented with a grin, pulling out a chair across from her.

She found his platitudes faintly unctuous. What was keeping Lauren? "Yes he is." She dragged her eyes away from the Friesian.

"Your little girl's turning into quite the equestrienne. My Skylar was the same way. From the first time on horseback she was National Velvet."

Hurry up, Lauren. "Do you ride?" she asked perfunctorily.

"Now and then, but between running my investment brokerage and my drive club, I'm on a pretty tight sked. You're new to Del Mar, right? You should join us for a drive. It's a great way to meet people."

She was confused. "A drive?"

"Just a bunch of really cool folks with a sense of adventure," he said with a wink.

Maggie could not miss the salacious drift. "Thanks, but – "

"Sorry I took so long," Lauren broke in, stepping onto the porch. "Rhonda couldn't find her appointment book. Oh, Paul, Tatiana said she needed to get your advice about something."

Paul took the bait, and Maggie was ready to hug Lauren. "Excuse me, ladies," he said.

The moment he was out of earshot, Maggie exhaled. "You saved me. I owe you."

"You can do the same thing next time he corners me. Look, there's Warlock and your boyfriend."

Maggie groaned. "Life's so unfair. Why is it that Billy's married but Paul's all too available?"

"Paul's married. Haven't you heard him babble about how his wife won *San Diego Home and Garden*'s Interior Designer of the year award?"

"Eww! Unless I'm really clueless, he just invited me to some kind of swingers event."

"No! What a creepo."

"That he's married too makes it even grosser." Maggie was revolted.

"No argument from me. My ex-husband was a serial adulterer and I just have a kind of knee-jerk reaction to cheaters."

"That's only natural," Maggie said noncommittally. "And you upgraded to a better model."

"Thanks. Maybe someday you – "

A child's frightened, high-pitched wail interrupted her. "That's Brit!" Lauren cried, running to the front arena, Maggie right behind her.

Sandy was helping a sobbing Brittany off the ground. The teacher held the reins of the riderless horse with her free hand. The other kids, Kat included, sat astride their still horses, watching somberly.

Lauren unlatched the arena gateand hurried in to comfort her child, who appeared more frightened than injured. Maggie's own heart pounded. What if it had been Kat?

"Brittany's horse spooked when one of the Mexicans went by in the feedcart," Patty, the twins' mother, told Maggie. "There was a piece of plastic stuck to the hay. It's a wonder more horses didn't go ballistic."

"The *workers* should be more careful," Maggie said icily, but the woman didn't seem to catch her emphasis. Did these well-heeled bigots wonder if *she* had a green card?

Together Sandy and Lauren were able to coax Brittany back onto her horse. The lesson resumed, but Lauren was clearly shaken. Maggie tried to reassure her. "See, she's already getting her confidence back," she pointed out as Brittany joined the other student riders in a posting trot.

"Now if only I could."

Maggie squeezed Lauren's arm. "You will. Look, Kim's probably back by now. Let me go get you something to drink. Soda or Snapple?"

"Anything. Too bad Tack 'n' Snack doesn't stock Jack Daniels."

Maggie chuckled. "Be right back."

Billy was just stepping out of the store. "Hope that wasn't your kid screaming bloody murder over there at the mean horseys."

"No, and that's not a nice way to put it," she replied, even though his wry tone made her bite back a smile.

"Never said I was nice." He held the door open for her.

She bought waters for Lauren, Kat, and herself. Billy was still on the porch when she emerged from the store. "How's your haunting coming along?"

She affected a nonchalance she didn't altogether feel. "I got a scary prank phone call the other night, but I'm sure the source was very much of this world."

"That sucks. Have any idea who did it?"

"No – it was probably random." She had an inspiration. "Since you're so interested in the house, why don't you and your wife come over some night for dinner? I make a fabulous tortilla soup."

"My wife's kinda shy – doesn't go out much. But thanks for the invitation."

Her curiosity was all the more piqued. "Well, I'm thinking about having a housewarming party in a few weeks," she improvised. "Maybe your wife would come with you to that. Some shy people actually feel more at ease in a larger group."

"Maybe. We'll have to see."

There was a moment's awkwardness between them.

"I should get back to the riding school," Maggie said. "My friend's waiting. It was her daughter who fell."

"Kid's OK?"

"Yeah, but her mom's a wreck."

"Let's hope she doesn't put her own issues on the kid. Don't you, either. It's not a lot different from falling off a bike."

Their easy rapport had returned. "I'm so glad it wasn't Kat," she admitted.

"Remind yourself that the other kid fell, shrieked her lungs out, and is no worse for the wear. The fuss is usually worse than the fall."

"I bet you raise the roof when you fall," she teased.

"Damn straight. I cuss like a truckdriver and piss off Rhonda, who's more interested in shielding the parents' tender sensibilities than the kids'. Which makes me cuss even more."

"Contrarian!"

"Something like that," he said with a brief smile. "I'd better get back to work."

"See you later."

"You bet – you still owe me that Coke."

She tried not to stare after him as he strode away, just as she tried to keep her heart from feeling lighter simply from having chatted with him again.

CHAPTER 4

Almost a month to the day since she'd first set foot inside the unfamiliar quarters that comprised her new home, Maggie dashed from kitchen to dining room to living room and back, preparing for the housewarming. She had cheated and gotten the enchiladas, chips, and salsa from Pa's La Jolla restaurant, but the tortilla soup that simmered on the stovetop and the assorted, multiethnic appetizers, which included artichoke dip, ceviche with endive leaf scoops, Thai satay skewers, and a chopped antipasto salad, were her own.

Most of her initial, nebulous apprehensions about the house had given gradual way to a comfortable normalcy. Kat was back in school, at St. James's Academy in Solana Beach, enjoying her studies and making friends. She'd protested at the reduction by half of her riding lessons to a single Wednesday afternoon, but the disappointment was allayed by the fact that Brittany too had suffered a like fate. The decreased time at the stables was a good thing for Maggie as well. Billy seemed to have adjusted his own schedule to be free for the one hour a week she was at Camino Equestrian with Kat, and

she was having a difficult time reining in her attraction to him. He continued to speak

only sparingly of his wife, Stephanie, and then because Maggie herself had raised the

subject. And while their conversation tended to stay casual, *non*-personal rather than

impersonal, the exchanges were touched by an unmistakable undercurrent of reciprocal

flirtation.

It was potentially a volatile situation, but she told herself that at least he wasn't a

masher, like the equally married Paul. She also counted on Lauren's vehemence about

extramarital dalliances to fortify her resolution never to pursue her attraction to Billy.

Mostly she and Billy chatted about Warlock and his ongoing, sometimes difficult training

progress, about the assortment of snobs, parvenus, and buffoons frequenting the barn, and

of course, about her "haunted" house.

To him alone she had confided that on two more occasions, both in broad

daylight, she'd again sensed at the foot of the stairs a shape, a presence, which dissipated

as soon as she looked directly at the flicker teasing the corner of her eye. "It's almost as

if I could close my eyes and think hard enough, I could tell you what it looked like. It's

more frustrating than scary." And once, Thumper had spooked her by standing at the top

of the stairs, as still as stone, growling and staring down the stairs either at nothing or at a

threat that only the normally under-vigilant toy spaniel could see. Billy, by his own

admission more intrigued by animals than by people, told her that he'd read about the

purported psychic abilities of dogs and cats. "I believe it, too. My cat Clancy always

hides the day of his vet appointment. The carrier's not out, nothing to tip him off. But he

knows."

Yet none of the more unnerving incidents had recurred – no more threatening

phone calls or creepy images that appeared, then disappeared, from old photographs. The

first she now firmly believed originated with a random malicious prankster; as for the

second, in retrospect it was obvious that she and Ryan, under the influence of too much

wine, had convinced themselves and each other that in the configuration of the trees

lurked a malevolent old man's face.

She still hadn't told Billy about the snapshot, though, just as she didn't admit to

him that ever since the night Kat had crawled into bed with her, Maggie too was sleeping

with the nightstand lamp on low. Or that on those nights when she found herself feeling

reasonlessly ill at ease, reasonlessly certain that something *strange* was about to happen,

Kat would appear almost uncannily at her bedroom door to placidly ask if she could sleep

with her. They would snuggle under the covers, and Thumper would jump up to join

them, and she would be lulled to sleep by the sound of her daughter's even breathing,

calmed by the scent of her soap-scrubbed skin.

Tonight Kat would be sleeping at Brittany's house. It had been Lauren's

suggestion, eagerly seconded by the girls. Although Lauren and her husband Jeff were

coming to the housewarming, she promised Maggie that their babysitter was reliably

conscientious.

The guest list was relatively short, though diverse. Almost none of her invitees

knew the others, a formula either for fascinating banter or a deadly-dull disaster, she

supposed. Ryan was coming, of course, bringing with him Christy Tobias, their old

UCLA classmate and fellow alumnus of the wild times at Dan Ullman's West Hollywood

digs. Lauren and Jeff. Alan and Rebecca Schulman, Maggie's next-door neighbors, whom she had causally befriended. In their mid-forties, the Schulmans were part quintessential, latte-sipping Yuppies and part second-wave hippies from whose back porch the aroma of pot occasionally drifted. Another new acquaintance who would be attending was statuesque Nicole Ludwig, the German-born biotech executive who owned Warlock. Delighted by Maggie's interest in the Friesian, Nicole urged her to "ride him any time you like," scoffing good-naturedly at Maggie's reply that she was not an experienced rider. "A five year old would be safe on him," Nicole insisted. Maggie thanked the generous owner, but had not needed Billy to warn her that Warlock was too young, newly broke to ride, and barely under training. Typically, he had told her so anyway. "Nicole's crazy to be riding him at this stage. I trust you have more sense."

His RSVP was definite, he said, joking about bringing garlic and holy water to ward off the evil spirits. He was, however, noncommittal about whether his wife would accompany him.

Maggie had asked Ryan to come early so they could visit and she could get reacquainted with Christy. The pair arrived at six, an hour before the other guests were due. "Hey, I said no gifts," Maggie laughed as Ryan presented her with a "Dress Me Up George" refrigerator magnet set featuring Bush in his underwear and assorted ludicrous articles of clothing, including a burnoose and a Speedo, in which to attire him.

She hugged him, then, more tentatively, Christy, who had brought a bottle of wine. Christy had always been among the more reserved of the Night People, not really a hugger. She had changed little in ten years, still willowy and wearing her wavy brown hair to her waist, still possessed with a serious, almost old-fashioned kind of prettiness.

But Christy beat her to that particular long-time-no-see draw. "Maggie Flores, you haven't changed a bit."

"Yeah, right. You guys want wine or sangria?"

"Sangria sounds good," Ryan said.

Christy surveyed the living room, the view. "You know something? I've been in this house before."

"Really?" Maggie handed them their drinks.

"Yes," Christy said with a nod. "I didn't remember it until I saw the deck. A Lit professor used to live here. Stanley Rosen. Last year I dated one of his grad students, and we came here for a party."

"Wow, what a coincidence," Ryan said.

They moved to the deck. "Someone told me that a professor lived here before me," Maggie remarked. "With his wife and kid."

"Oh, they were just 'living in sin.' She was one of his graduate students. Their breakup was the talk of all the Humanities departments."

"Details, details," Ryan urged.

"I guess Rosen didn't really get along with the kid. Twelve-year-old boy. This was the first place the three of them had ever shared. According to my ex-boyfriend, Dawn told him that the tension between Rosen and her son kept building until one night, Stanley got plastered and – in Dawn's own words – beat the living crap out of the kid."

"What an asshole!" Ryan exclaimed, but Maggie chilled. *I'm going to beat the living crap out of you.* Could the anonymous caller have been this brutish literature professor? No, that was impossible. The phone company would not have reassigned the same phone number to her …

"His version of the story was that he'd just slapped the kid across the face for mouthing off," Christy was saying. "The truth probably lies somewhere in the middle."

"Talk about a 'lit' professor," Ryan punned darkly.

Maggie was desperate to change the subject before either of them noticed her discomfiture. "That's just awful. Hey, Christy, do you ever hear from Heather Purcell?" Heather had been the aspiring dominatrix of their little subculture, the sweatshirt and jeans she generally wore to classes inevitably replaced by black leather catsuits and stiletto thigh-boots when she was hanging out at Dan's.

"Not in ages," Christy said.

"Dan says she's switched teams yet again," Ryan said. "She's living with a Mormon guy in Salt Lake City."

Maggie and Christy's gasps were simultaneous.

Christy turned a plainly sympathetic eye to Maggie. "I'm sorry you and Tim didn't make it. I hope he puts his life back together someday."

"Thanks. I hope he does too."

Thank God that's out of the way.

Ryan and Christy helped her lay out the appetizer platters on the dining room table and move chairs into the living room. She put the enchiladas in the oven to heat on low. They all chattered about their work and their meager love-lives, Thumper underfoot and begging for treats from the moment of Ryan's tactical error in tossing the dog a strip of prosciutto from the antipasto.

The Schulmans arrived promptly at seven, followed soon by the model-gorgeous

Nicole and her date, an unassuming fellow she introduced as Greg, her fiancé. Next was

Billy, bearing a bottle of "Authentic Extraterrestrial Tequila" from the Roswell UFO

Museum. Instead of the customary mescal worm coiled at the bottom, a miniature plastic

alien lurked. Everyone laughed.

"I love New Mexico," Nicole said in her accented English. "I go to Taos every

year but I've never seen any flying saucers there."

"Only weather balloons," Ryan quipped.

General mirth ensued about UFOs, Roswell, and who was an "X-phile" and who

a Trekkie (Ryan, Billy, and Maggie self-identified with the first category, Nicole and the

Schulmans with the second, and Christy with both). Soon little subgroups formed:

Nicole and Rebecca Schulman; Alan Schulman and Greg, who were both attorneys, as it

turned out; Billy, Ryan, and Christy. Maggie did her best to circulate among them, but

by 7:30 she was wondering what could possibly be keeping Lauren and her husband.

What if there was a crisis involving the kids? Maggie was just about to excuse herself so

she could phone Lauren when the couple showed up. "Sorry we're late," Lauren

apologized. "My fault. I forgot to gas up the car this afternoon and there was a huge line

at the Shell station."

Her husband Jeff, tall, balding, and ordinarily as genial as his spouse, forged a

caustic little smile. "Always something," he said, pointedly mock-jovial.

Maggie introduced them around and got them drinks. The sangria seemed to

relax them both. In a few minutes Lauren was singing Warlock's praises to a beaming

Nicole and Jeff was discoursing on North County property values with the Schulmans.

Maggie stole into the kitchen to check on the enchiladas.

"Need a hand?" Billy.

She lifted the foil-covered Pyrex out of the oven. "Nope. Oh, you could get the sour cream out of the fridge. It's in a little black bowl."

"So you, Ryan, and Christy all went to college together. That's cool that you've stayed in touch."

Maggie brushed a strand of hair from her eyes. The cheese on the enchiladas was bubbly-hot and liquid; best to let them cool for a few minutes. "Well, tonight's the first time I've seen Christy in years. But Ryan and I've stayed pretty close."

"I never went to college. Hated school," he said matter-of-factly.

She took a sip from her sangria. Her third one. She'd better slow down a little. "So? Some of the world's biggest creeps or --" (Tim's word) "-- fuck-ups have advanced degrees. Want a case in point?"

"Why not?"

She repeated to him Christy's account of the previous lessees and the bizarrely coincidental echo of last month's malicious prank call.

"That is fucking weird. That was the wife, or girlfriend's, exact phrase?"

"So Christy says. A chill ran down my spine."

"You tell 'em about the call?"

"No. I've only told you and Lauren."

He leaned back against the counter and crossed his arms. "Maybe what happened with those tenants is what you've been sensing here. They say intense shit like that can leave a kind of imprint in a place, like a photographic negative."

She thought of the strange image first there and then not in the photo of Tim and his parents. "How come you know so much about this stuff?"

He smiled ironically. "My mom, God rest her soul, was really into it. She was more Irish than the Blarney Stone. One of her life's biggest disappointments was that she never saw a ghost."

"My mother completely believes in them, too. Guess we're the skeptical generation."

"Looks like."

"But your theory -- that the odd things in this house could be like echoes of what the previous residents were going through – that makes a sort of sense to me." The notion, while unconventional, was somehow more mundane and manageable than the idea of ghosts. "I'll have to ask Christy if there was an age difference between the professor and his girlfriend."

"Why?"

She'd spoken before thinking, before recalling that she hadn't told him about the photograph. And damn Ryan – he'd put Alice in Chains on the stereo, Tim's favorite band and the soundtrack to his addiction.

"Bury me softly in this womb

I give this part of me for you

Sand rains down and here I sit

Holding rare flowers in a tomb ... "

Obviously reading her expression, Billy remarked drily, "This is real cheery music."

"My ex-husband's a drug addict – a worthless piece of crap," she blurted out.

He looked taken aback. "Christ, that's ... awful."

Maggie's hand flew to her lips. "Oh my God, I can't believe I just said that!"

"Why, if it's true?"

She pushed aside her sangria. "OK, no more for me." She felt as if she'd just inexplicably ripped off her clothes (*or had them ripped off*) in front of him.

Ryan poked his head into the kitchen. "Want some help?"

"No, thanks," she said, too grateful for his interruption to ask him to change the music on the stereo. "The enchiladas will be ready in a few minutes. How are we doing on the appetizers?"

"Fine. Do I have time before dinner to give Christy a tour of the second story? The view from the upstairs balcony is even better than the deck's."

She gave him a knowing look. "Ryan, I'm sure no one will call the DEA if you light up a joint down here."

"It's not that. I don't have enough to share with everybody and get any of us a decent buzz. Want to join us, Billy?"

"Pass. I can't string together more than two words when I'm stoned. But I appreciate the offer since you're triaging."

"I'd better return to my hostess duties," Maggie said. She grabbed two potholders and picked up the enchilada pan. If her guests burned their mouths and sued her, it was still preferable to dealing with any fallout from her almost unwitting declaration to Billy.

In the living room, Rebecca Schulman was holding merry court. "Our son's only three, but he notices when Alan and I are cursing and groaning at CNN every time Bush appears on the screen. So we're trying to make it a learning experience for Trevor."

Alan Schulman picked up the narrative. "If Bush comes on, we don't call him an asshole anymore. We point out to Trevor, 'That's a chimpanzee!'"

Maggie joined in the laughter. "Ryan calls him a chimp too." But Ryan and Christy had already gone upstairs.

"And if it's Cheney," Rebecca went on, "we tell Trev, 'That's Satan.'"

"Perfect," Nicole complimented. "What about Rumsfeld?"

"'Monster,'" Alan replied. "Condi's the 'Wicked Witch.'"

Maggie thought that Lauren and Jeff's amusement seemed forced. Republicans, she surmised, and strove to shift the topic. "Enchiladas and salad are on the dining room table, amigos. Grab a plate and help yourselves."

As the guests moved toward the dining room, Maggie eased Lauren aside. "Are you sure everything's OK?"

"It's fine. Jeff bitches but he's used to my lateness. He even calls me 'the late Lauren Byers.'"

Just as most of the others were returning to the living room with their enchiladas and antipasto, Ryan and Christy reappeared in the dining room. "That looks fantastic," Christy said, picking up a plate.

"Maggie, can you believe we got lost upstairs?" Ryan said. "We ended up in Kat's room and I saw that creepy graduation picture on the wall. I showed it to Christy."

"That is the weirdest freaking thing – the face in the trees," Christy added. She slid an enchilada onto her plate.

Maggie was puzzled. She had convinced herself weeks ago that the face in the trees was a transitory product of tipsy imaginations. "That must be some damn good pot you smoked."

Ryan, evidently assuming she was reluctant to discuss the image in front of Christy, shrugged. "It's nice and mellow."

Maggie realized that Billy had remained in the dining room with them. "A face in the trees?" he asked Christy.

"To me it's really obvious, but maybe Maggie doesn't think so," Christy said. "In the pattern of the branches and breaks of light, there's an outline of an old man's face."

"Or not," Ryan said. "It's probably like a Rorschach ink blot – one person sees an old man, another might see a rhinoceros."

"Can I see?" Billy asked Maggie.

By now the subject was making her extremely nervous. She set down her plate and poured another sangria, after all. "OK. It's in my daughter's bedroom upstairs." She wasn't about to fetch the photograph and circulate it like a vacation souvenir among all the guests, whether that image was still there and she'd just willed herself not to see it, or Ryan's recollection was influencing Christy and his own perception. She felt bad enough as it was for what she'd blurted out about Tim to Billy.

No one paid any special attention as she led Billy upstairs. Ryan had left the overhead light on in Kat's room. "It's just a shot of my ex-husband and his parents from graduation," she said, pointing to the photograph on the closet door. She meant to give the photo only a cursory glance. Instead, she found herself staring as if she were seeing it

for the first time.

The face had returned.

"Man," Billy breathed behind her. "Either I'm crazy, or your friends aren't

simply stoned."

Unable to speak, she kept staring at it. No amount of willpower could have

induced her to miss the image in the trees over the last month. It had come back.

"Didn't you see it before?" Billy asked quietly.

"Ryan and I both saw it about a month ago, while we were going through old

pictures." Her voice was barely more than a whisper. "Kat wanted it, and I was really

upset because of that thing in the trees. But I swear to God, Billy, from the moment she

taped it up on this door, the face – that image, optical illusion, whatever the hell it is –

wasn't there anymore."

"Jeez."

"By now you probably think I'm certifiable."

"I believe you." He continued to scrutinize the picture. "Is that the first thing that

made you think the house was haunted?"

"Yeah. I didn't tell you because it was just too bizarre. And I didn't want to

bring Kat into it, or Tim."

"He looks like Mr. Big-Man-On-Campus." His tone was rather acid.

"Then that's the real optical illusion," she half-snapped.

She had no intention of elaborating, but there was no opportunity for him to press

her when a chorus of shrieks and shouts erupted from downstairs, followed by thumping and banging as if people were hurling furniture at one another. The dog's earsplitting whine rang above the din like a siren.

Maggie and Billy raced downstairs. In the living room, amid spilled food and several upturned dining room chairs, Alan Schulman and Ryan pinned a dazed and panting Jeff Byers against a wall. On the sofa Nicole, her date, and Christy huddled over a softly weeping Lauren. Her face was swollen and blood streamed from her nose. By the fireplace Rebecca stood talking soberly into her cellphone.

Billy's eyes flashed. "What the fuck? Did this son of a bitch -- ?"

"He backhanded her across the face," seethed Alan. "Rebecca's talking to the cops."

"Please," Lauren begged through sobs. "Don't call the police." She held a cloth napkin to her nose.

"Do you have an ice bag?" Nicole asked Maggie.

Maggie was beyond shocked. "Upstairs in the master bathroom."

"I'll get it," Christy offered, rising.

Maggie took Christy's place next to Lauren. "My God, I can't believe he did this to you. How can I help?"

Lauren cried but didn't answer.

"I think her nose is broken," Nicole fretted, stroking Lauren's hair. "We should take her to the hospital."

"Cops are on their way," Rebecca announced, dropping her cellphone into her purse.

"No," Lauren again protested.

"Let's move this asshole outside to wait for the cops," Billy said to Ryan and Alan. Jeff's chest was still heaving and his eyes remained glazed but he didn't struggle as the other men dragged him out the front door.

"He's gone now. He can't hurt you again," Rebecca said firmly.

"He just had too much to drink," Lauren said. "This isn't how he is!"

Christy returned with the ice bag and Maggie hastened into the kitchen to fill it with cubes. She also poured a small snifter of cognac, which she gave to Lauren along with the cold compress. A large purple bruise was forming from her right cheekbone to her nose. The bastard had really smacked her. "You don't have to explain anything right now, honey," Maggie said, patting Lauren's knee.

"Dear lord, the kids!" Lauren moaned.

Maggie certainly didn't want her daughter anywhere near Jeff Byers on the all too likely chance that Lauren declined to press charges. "As soon as we see you off to the hospital, I'll go get them and bring them here."

"No – Brit will know something's wrong. Just call Sara and tell her we'll be a little late."

The other women exchanged glances. "Your husband's going to be spending the night in jail," Rebecca declared. "Do you want your kid around when he comes home tomorrow pissed off?"

"He'd never hurt her."

By the time the police arrived, the women had at least convinced Lauren to have the babysitter take Brittany to Lauren's mother's house 20 minutes north in Carlsbad.

Maggie would pick up Kat. Lauren refused to allow any of them to accompany her to the hospital.

Two uniformed officers, one a woman, entered to talk with Lauren. They assured the other four women that they had already taken witness statements from Alan, Greg, and Ryan. The men were drifting back in, Jeff Byers presumably handcuffed in the backseat of a squad car.

Maggie ached for Lauren, for the terrible humiliation that had accompanied the injury. She understood why Lauren wanted to go to the hospital alone.

The cops escorted Lauren out. The remaining guests congregated in the kitchen. "I hope she throws that bastard out for keeps," Nicole said.

"Amen to that," Rebecca replied.

Christy, Ryan, and Billy began bringing in platters, plates, and glasses from the other rooms. "You guys don't need to do that," Maggie tried, but they ignored her. Soon the others were pitching in. The Schulmans even volunteered to pick up Kat, but Maggie feared her daughter would be alarmed if the couple showed up for her. "Then go on and get her," Rebecca insisted. "We'll have everything spic and span by the time you get back."

Maggie picked up her purse. "I'm so grateful to all of you. I'll have to throw another party to thank everybody."

"Sorry – I have other plans," Ryan joked, breaking them all up.

At the Byers's Carmel Valley home, the babysitter told her that Lauren's mother was already en route. Evidently Lauren had managed to contact her mother from the hospital. Maggie had no idea how much the babysitter knew about the sudden change in plans, but Brittany, who tended to be a whiner, was wailing. Kat, her jacket thrown over her pajamas, clutched her little overnight bag. She was grave but calm, no doubt because she was accustomed to domestic upheavals. Maggie felt a pang of remorse.

On the drive home, Kat said, "It was his fault, Mommy."

Maggie was fleetingly annoyed with Lauren; from Kat's remark it was clear that she had witnessed Jeff Byers's brutishness toward his wife on some prior occasion. The last thing Kat needed was yet more exposure to family turmoil. "I know it, sweetie. But it's going to be OK." She reached over to clasp her daughter's hand.

Only Ryan and Billy were still at the house, seated at the now bare dining room table nursing beers. No visible evidence remained of the uproar. Kat greeted both of them, adding to Billy, "You should have brought Warlock!"

He smiled. "It's way past his bedtime."

"And yours, too," Maggie said to Kat. "Go on up to bed. I'll be there in a minute."

"Come on, Thumper," Kat said. The little dog followed her out of the room.

Maggie dropped her purse and keys onto the kitchen counter. "What happened to Christy?"

"Nicole and what's-his-name gave her a ride home. They don't live far from UCSD," Ryan said. "Christy used to be in an abusive relationship, and I think she was more freaked out than she let on."

"Oh no. Don't tell me it was Corey, the guy she dated in college."

"OK, I won't tell you."

Maggie was disgusted. "I always knew he was a pseudo-intellectual windbag, but I never would have guessed … Shit, at the very least he was six inches shorter than Christy!" She sighed. "I never would have guessed about Lauren and Jeff either."

"I should be on my way," Billy said. "I just wanted to make sure you were all right."

Maggie waved him back into his chair. "Please – stay a little while longer. Both of you." She wasn't merely being polite. She was nowhere near ready to be alone yet.

They agreed, and she excused herself to go upstairs and tuck Kat in. She found Kat sitting cross-legged on her bed, petting Thumper with one hand and holding the kaleidoscope in the other. For once Maggie didn't cringe. Because Kat had convinced herself the kaleidoscope was a gift from her beloved Daddy, the toy likely served as a kind of security blanket, a way of coping with change. "Under the covers, muchacha," Maggie directed.

She kissed Kat goodnight. As she straightened her gaze drifted, almost against her will, to the photograph taped on the closet door.

The image of the face was gone again.

"'Night, Mommy," Kat yawned.

"Goodnight, me hija," she replied, struggling to suppress the tremor in her throat. She gently shut the door behind her, then flew down the stairs past the elongated shadow she *almost* saw waiting by the bottom step.

Ryan and Billy looked up at her in concern. "What happened?" Ryan cried.

"You guys," she gasped. "You won't believe this. The picture – the one of Tim – the face in the trees has disappeared again."

"Jesus Christ!" Billy said, helping her into a chair.

Ryan too had turned ashen. "'Again'? You mean that face-thing comes and goes?"

"We need to keep our voices down – I don't want Kat to overhear."

"Let me get you a beer," Billy said.

"God, yes." A moment later a cold Corona was in front of her. She took a gulp before disclosing to Ryan how the image had simply vanished from the day Kat had taped it to the door until earlier this evening – just before Jeff Byers had attacked his wife.

"When your daughter was out of the house," Billy mused. "She comes home, and it's gone again."

Maggie shivered. "If whatever is in this damn house is somehow fixated on Kat, to hell with it, we're leaving."

"Slow down," Ryan said. "It's just a coincidence."

"Even if it is, that thing in the picture is still too creepy," she argued. "And combined with everything else, I can't risk exposing Kat to something in the atmosphere here that's – not right."

Billy leaned over and placed his hand on top of hers for a moment. "Ryan is right. You shouldn't make any snap decisions right now. It's been a bitch of a night."

Slightly calmer, she took another quick swig of beer. "Or ... what if it's all connected to that picture? Maybe if I just got rid of it everything would be OK."

"Maybe," Ryan said. But he sounded as if he was humoring her.

"I think the picture's not cause but effect," Billy said. "If you ask me, the thing in the trees, the weird phone call, and that fuckhead pounding his wife all tie back to what we were talking about earlier."

"What weird phone call? Maggie, you don't tell me anything."

She recognized the futility of holding back with either of them. "About a month ago I received a threatening prank call. A man saying he was going to 'beat the living crap' out of me. The same words Christy said the professor's girlfriend used to describe what he did to her son."

"Oh my fucking God."

"It's my view," Billy explained, "that those people left a kind of kinetic residue in this house. Leftover psychic energy."

Ryan nodded slowly. "Not ghosts, because they aren't dead. Just … energy."

"Then how on earth do I get rid of it?" Maggie wondered aloud. "Obviously it's not harmless if it could affect Lauren's husband like that."

"I bet that wasn't the first time he's popped her one," Billy said. "The house, or the energy, might have been the catalyst. But he was probably susceptible to start with."

Maggie recalled how tense the couple had seemed from the moment of their late arrival. "What about the face in the picture?"

Ryan ventured a theory. "That's not just a picture of Tim – it's a picture of Tim with his parents. That professor resented his girlfriend's son. And you said yourself that there was friction between Tim and his folks even back then."

"I'm going to burn that picture. I never should have let Kat take it in the first place."

"Are you sure that's a good idea?" Billy said. "Your daughter seems to have a neutralizing effect on it."

"Oh great," Maggie said with a groan. "I don't want Kat to have any kind of effect on it, or vice-versa."

"And getting back to Maggie's other point, how *do* you exorcise energy, assuming your hypothesis is on target and this isn't really a ghost?"

Billy's lips twisted. "I have no fucking idea."

"How about inventing a pretext for luring that professor over here? Maybe his negative vibes will reattach themselves, like a shadow. Or a fungus, for that matter," Ryan proposed. But before Maggie could object, he added, "Just kidding."

"Or you could try Googling the problem," Billy said.

"Exorcism in the Internet era. Where's Beetlejuice when you need him?" Ryan said.

Maggie glared at both of them. "Come on, you guys. This is serious."

"Look, Maggie, what happened tonight was awful," Billy said levelly. "And the picture thing is a fucking mystery. But we could all be getting carried away."

By "we" she guessed he primarily meant her. "Easy for you to say. I have to live alone here with my daughter."

"Kat hasn't sensed anything?" Ryan asked.

"No, unless she's not telling me. She's actually loved the house from day one."

"See?" Billy said. "House can't be all bad."

Even though they hadn't requested more beers, she got up and fetched two more. She hoped that at least Ryan would decide he'd had too much to drink and opt to sleep on the sofa again. "I wish you were my roommate," she said a bit grumpily to him, grumpily because she knew he would turn down the offer.

"Shit, I'm not living in this haunted house!" he teased. "Seriously, though. Rufus would terrorize your dog. And this neighborhood's a little too suburban for me."

"Some friend you are," Billy said.

Maggie sighed again. "No, I get it. You have your own life, and I need to handle this on my own."

"Not tonight you don't," Billy said. "At least one of us should stay over. Let me call my wife. I'm sure she'll be cool with this under the circumstances."

When he chose the relative privacy of the living room to make the call, Ryan didn't hesitate to mouth to Maggie, "Wife?"

She nodded, touching her left ring finger.

"Yeah, I saw," Ryan whispered. "But they must not be close."

She pantomimed bemusement with two upraised palms.

Billy rejoined them. "It's fine. You should stay too, man."

Ryan stood up. "Unfortunately, I can't. I have an all-day seminar tomorrow. But I'm glad Maggie won't be alone."

She suspected that this departure was strategic. Ryan likely thought that she and Billy were planning to sleep together. But she was not about to cap off the night by having sex with a married man.

Which was not to say, however, that she wasn't perplexed by his odd marital arrangement. Once Ryan had left and they were seated more comfortably on the sofa with their Coronas, she remarked, "Your wife is extraordinarily understanding."

"Anyone married to me'd have to be."

She scoffed. "You don't strike me as such a pain in the ass as all that."

"If you'd known me when I was drinking nearly a quart a day of Jameson's, you'd think otherwise."

The off-handed admission made her sad. Not that he'd had a drinking problem, but sad anew about Tim. "Your wife stuck by you. I tried for years to stick by my husband."

"Every situation's different. Plus in your case, there's a kid. I grew up with a stepfather who was a drunk, and I wouldn't wish that on anybody's childhood."

She studied her hands. "I know. But I still feel guilty – for staying when I should have left, and for leaving when I should have stayed."

"No one can help somebody else get sober. Any more than you can force 'em to."

"How did you stop?"

"Well, as you can see," he said, raising his beer bottle, "I didn't stop altogether. But it's only beer now, and only on weekends. Twelve-Steppers would still call me a drunk, but trust me, they never saw me when I was really boozing either."

"Tim could smoke pot or have a few drinks and never get out of control. But hard drugs were – are – another story."

"Anyway, you asked how I quit that kind of drinking. I scared myself. Got into a fight with my wife. She was trying to wrest the bottle from me, and I – " He winced.

She swallowed hard. "You hit her?"

"Christ, no – if I had I could never have lived with myself. This was bad enough. I yanked the bottle out of her hands with such force that she fell. And she cried. And man, I could never deal with her crying. That was it for me."

He no longer sounded nonchalant. Bitterness had crept into his voice, and she realized that he had yet to fully forgive himself. "I'm glad for both of you, Billy, that you turned things around."

"My wife's a saint. As for me, I'm just lucky."

"I'd like to meet her."

He was predictably noncommittal. "Maybe. Like I said, she's shy unless she knows someone pretty well."

"She never comes out to the stables?"

"Not often. She doesn't drive, and we live way out to hell and gone in Fallbrook. Lower rent district than Del Mar."

"You should introduce her to Warlock. He'd put anyone at ease."

"He's a big flirt, that one."

"I suppose he taught you everything you know?"

"Hey, I'm not a flirt," he pretended to protest.

"Um, OK."

Now they were both smiling. Unbelievable, given the night's events. She uncurled the leg she had tucked beneath her. "Thank your wife for letting me borrow you. And thank yourself for being here." She got up. "I'm going to attempt to get some sleep. But if something weird happens, I'm coming to get you."

"You got a deal."

The extra pillow and blanket were in the hall closet, and an unused toothbrush in the downstairs bathroom's medicine chest. She climbed the narrow staircase, feeling no ghosts, no unearthly energy. Just a wistful regret that Billy was not coming to bed with her, coupled with an equally wistful certainty of the honor of resisting temptation.

She dreamed she was riding Warlock, clopping happily along the Manhattan Beach Strand amid the pedestrians and rollerbladers and tourists pushing kids in strollers. None of them registered as the least extraordinary the presence of the massive Friesian. Nor was she afraid to be riding him, despite not having been on a horse in years.

Suddenly she was aware of a police cruiser moving on the sand right alongside her. The vehicle stopped, and somehow she knew enough to "whoa" Warlock. Out of the squad car stepped not a uniformed cop but a mean-looking old man in a baggy trenchcoat and fedora. He was monochromatically gray, his skin as well as his clothing the sickly color of cigarette smoke.

"I'm going to beat the living crap out of you," he growled, taking one heavy step toward her.

Warlock reared, neighing furiously. Terrified, Maggie clung to his long mane.

She woke up, quaking in fear.

This time when she heard the *stomp stomp stomp* on the stairs, she knew it was no dream-hangover.

She sat up in bed, listening. The stomping continued for perhaps another ten or fifteen seconds. Then it simply stopped.

She waited to see if it would resume. But the silence stayed unbroken. Her heart raced and her hands were clammy, but she made herself get out of bed and throw on her robe. She had to know if Billy had also heard the stomping.

Stepping out into the hallway, she saw faint light downstairs. Billy must have switched on a lamp in the living room. She tiptoed down, half-surprised to feel no unnatural chill nor alien presence. In the living room Billy, clad only in his boxer shorts, sat up on the sofa, all alertness. "Thank God it's you," he said in a low voice.

"It wasn't me before, though."

"No shit. At first I thought it might be Kat. But it stopped as soon as I turned on the light."

"I heard it my first night here, but not since until now. Could it have been pipes?"

She knew his answer before he gave it. "No way. It was too rhythmic. It sounded like a kid running up and down the stairs."

She sank into an armchair. "I sure hope you're right and it's just a psychic echo or whatever. I can't bear to think it's the ghost of a dead child." She bit down on her lip.

"I know it's creepy as hell, Maggie. But I'm sure that's all it is – an echo, like you said. We know there were problems between that professor and the girlfriend's kid."

"You make it sound so rational."

"I'm not a skeptic but I do try to use common sense. Just 'cause we don't understand something doesn't mean a reasonable explanation doesn't exist." He rubbed his palms against his knees.

"You must have driven your poor, ghost-believing mother crazy with that attitude," she said with a flicker of a smile.

"Christ, yes. Now that she's gone, I wish to hell I'd just played along with her."

They stayed up the rest of the night, talking, picking at leftover food, drinking strong coffee. The housewarming and the harrowing incident that had brought it to a premature conclusion seemed as if they had taken place weeks before. She no longer even felt odd sitting with him in the kitchen with the sun coming up, she in her pajamas and he shirtless, jeans over his shorts. They might as well have been perched in front of the Tack 'n' Snack on an ordinary afternoon.

With dawn in full bloom, however, he drained the last of his coffee. "I really gotta go."

"Don't you want to take a shower?"

"Nah. I'll have one when I get home."

She walked him out to his pickup truck. La Amatista Road was perfectly still. Folded newspapers rested unopened on doorsteps. West down the hill, the ocean's dull silver had yet to deepen into blue. "I can't thank you enough for staying, and keeping me sane."

His eyes twinkled. "Actually, it was pretty cool hearing those steps and everything." He reached for the truck door handle.

She was just backing away when he pulled her to him and kissed her. Yet even as she relaxed into him, savoring his taste, the feel of his mouth, he broke the embrace. "I'll see ya."

Pleasantly bemused, she watched him leave.

CHAPTER 5

She was inspired to make Kat pancakes, her favorite, for breakfast. Afterwards they took Thumper on a 20-minute walk through the neighborhood. She hoped to provide Kat with ample opportunity to bring up the subject of Brittany and her parents. But Kat seemed more interested in speculating as to whether Thumper would get along with a rabbit. Taylor, her classmate at St. James's with whom she had a play date later that day, had two lop-eared bunnies, "*plus* a dog and a cat!"

Maggie didn't miss the broad hint. "You wouldn't want to make Thumper jealous, would you?"

Kat gave it some thought. "He's used to being the only one," she conceded.

Nearing their house, Maggie saw Rebecca Schulman emerge from her garage in sweats and running shoes. Maggie allowed Kat to take Thumper and go inside ahead of her.

"Have you heard from Lauren?" Rebecca asked, jogging over.

"Uh-uh. I'm trying to decide if I should call her or wait for her to get in touch with me."

"I have a creeping fear she's taken him back. Women are always giving the assholes the proverbial 'one last chance.'"

Maggie looked away. "I guess I'll give it a day, and call her tomorrow if I haven't heard from her yet."

"Good idea. She's probably in a lot of physical pain. Her nose was definitely broken."

Rebecca went along on her morning run. Mood a bit dimmer, Maggie went back inside.

Kat was settled on the carpet in front of Saturday morning cartoons. Maggie moved her laptop downstairs, thinking to do some website editing while Kat watched TV. "*An animatronic cat, an animatronic cat,*" trilled a cartoon jingle to the tune of "Ta-Ra-Ra-Boom-De-Yay."

Maggie logged on to the Internet. She remembered something, and without even checking her e-mailbox she went to Google and typed in, "haunting explanations."

"*A reachy and climby cat,*" the jingle went on.

Kat laughed. "Reachy and climby aren't even words," she informed the TV.

Maggie no longer heard the silly jingle. She'd gotten thousands of hits on her broad search terms. She began to scan cites that referred to scientific explanations. Apparently Billy's "theory" was not especially unusual, but reading about it on the Internet reassured her he'd not been merely humoring her. Here the term employed was "residual haunting," referring to the very notion Billy had described of psychic phenomena born not of supernatural beings but instead past experience, usually of the emotionally intense variety, that had become somehow inscribed in a house's atmosphere. She was amazed to find several of the phenomena she had perceived – footsteps on stairs, corner-of-the-eye glimpses of something, even dogs growling into thin air—listed as fairly common "residual haunting" events. She gleaned from investigating only the first page of Google hits that supposed experts seemed to have widely divergent opinions as to the origins of residual phenomena: low-frequency sound waves, electromagnetic fields, psychokinetic energy. Most of the sites dealing with residual haunting also assumed the reality of the traditional spirit-entity visitation and poltergeists, but Maggie was confident that the house's peculiarities were definitely of the terrestrial species. In fact, her house seemed a textbook example.

But one piece of information was less than comforting. Since residual hauntings involved not ghosts but rather physical (if not entirely explicable) phenomena that replayed like a scratched phonograph record snagged by a needle, there was no restless spirit to attempt to appease – or to exorcise. The pages she viewed primarily advised those with residually haunted houses to learn to live with the disturbances, which, however unsettling, were thoroughly benign.

Could she learn to live with them? She wasn't sure. Knowledge – such as it was – about what the disturbances were and how they might have come about made them seem less frightening, more akin to such nuisances as leaky faucets or noisy pipes. And most importantly, Kat remained either unaware or unbothered by the phenomena. She glanced at her daughter still lost in the adventures of the Animatronic Cat on TV. Kat really was happy here, almost as if she had finally come home. And why not? She'd spent the first eight years of her life in a series of small apartments, with Daddy sometimes there, just as often not. Here she had a regular house, with an upstairs and downstairs, a yard and a view, horses and the beach only minutes away. What child would not embrace such a home? Perhaps that was what Tim's grandmother had had in mind, knowing that he was in no position to provide any like haven for his daughter.

Nevertheless, once Kat was safely deposited at Taylor's house a mile away, Maggie stood in the center of the living room and literally dared the "energy" to make its presence known. "I'm not afraid of you," she called out, though she certainly felt foolish. "Run up and down the stairs, or cast a shadow."

Now Thumper was circling her feet, thinking she was addressing him. Maggie strained her ears but heard only the dog's excited sniffing and panting. Nor did she spy any suspicious shadows near the foot of the stairs.

Of course not. It wasn't a ghost with its own free will to come and go as it pleased, but a mindless aggregate of atmospheric conditions.

And then she heard it, and so did Thumper. It seemed to be coming from the hall closet where just a few hours ago she had replaced the pillow and blanket Billy had used.

"Sssshhhh! Sssshhhh!"

She froze, and Thumper started to growl, although he didn't approach the closet from where the shushing noise was emanating. It sounded so human that for a moment she thought frantically that a neighborhood child had somehow sneaked inside to play a prank.

"Sssshhhh!"

Finding his courage, Thumper darted over to the closet, still growling as menacingly as a toy spaniel was capable. He sniffed the closet door jamb, then, to Maggie's surprise, simply trotted away. He jumped onto the sofa and proceeded to lick himself.

She supposed the dog's behavior was reassuring, but allowed five minutes of quiet to elapse before even considering taking a peek inside the closet. What if the shushing, despite sounding so human, came from a snake? Should she run next door to see if Alan or Rebecca would provide backup?

On the horrible chance that the interloper was a prowler, she pretended to call 9-11. "Yes, police?" she said loudly. "Please send an officer over right away. There's an intruder here!"

She waited another five minutes for some sign or sound from within the closet. When none came, she braced herself, got a sharp paring knife from the kitchen just in case, and inched open the closet door.

Except for the pillow that had slipped down from the top shelf above the coat rack, nothing appeared amiss. Her coats and Kat's, unworn since the previous winter, hung undisturbed. Nor did Thumper's carrier, the vacuum cleaner, or the three cardboard boxes of books for which she'd run out of shelf space betray any sign of trespass. Reaching up to shove the pillow back into place atop the folded blanket, she noticed what appeared to be a broad square panel on the closet ceiling. She stretched for it, but her fingertips were still a few inches short. She stepped up onto one of the book boxes, tapped at the panel. It pushed in.

Although she feared the distinct possibility of rodents, she was hopelessly

intrigued by what she might find. She retrieved a flashlight from the kitchen, boosted

herself back on the box and pushed the panel again. Managing to ease it aside, she shone

the flashlight into what appeared to be a crawlspace, either a construction defect or

designed for extra storage.

Even with her makeshift stepstool she had to crane her neck to see further into the

crawlspace. It smelled of dust and cedar. She could make out two boxes, not heavy

moving cartons like the one she perched atop, but plain, lidless grocery-store boxes such

as might have originally contained cases of wine or even produce.

She yanked the nearer of the two boxes toward her. It was fairly light. Inside she

discovered strands of tangled Christmas lights, the old-fashioned kind with the big

teardrop-shaped colored bulbs. They were caked in dust and heaped on top of a folded

but moth-eaten red felt tree skirt. Evidently a previous resident had forgotten, or

deliberately abandoned, the shabby and outmoded holiday décor.

She pushed the box farther back in the crawlspace and reached for the remaining

one. The carton was just beyond her grasp. She hooked its edge with a hanger and drew

it forward. From the feel of it this box was slightly heavier than the first.

She lifted it down with both hands. On first glance it appeared to hold a mélange

of odds and ends, including a travel iron, a set of kitschy penguin salt and pepper shakers,

an old heating pad. Clutching the box, she stepped out of the closet to inspect its contents

in the afternoon light that streamed into the front hallway.

Stooping down on her knees, she removed the iron, the cheesy Sea World

penguins, and the heating pad. Underneath lay a creased leather baseball mitt. She picked it up as gently as if it were fragile bone china. It seemed impossible that the mitt could have been Tim's. More likely it had belonged to the unfortunate little boy whose violent conflict with his stepfather was at the heart of this "residual haunting." And how many other kids might have lived here over the past ten years, even before the literature professor?

But reason notwithstanding, she cradled the mitt in her lap and continued to inventory the box's contents. Some plastic dinosaurs. A handful of Legos. A half-rusted Slinky. Three children's books – *The Marshmallow Ghosts*, *Dr. Seuss's Happy Birthday to You*, and *Danny Kaye's Stories from Around the World*. Irresistibly she leafed through the smallest book, *The Marshmallow Ghosts*. As the title implied, the story was more whimsical than portentous. In simple text accompanied by sweet cartoon illustrations, the narrative told of a family of ghosts who became visible upon eating marshmallows, enabling the child apparitions to masquerade as ordinary trick-or-treaters on Halloween night. She glanced at the publication date: 1960, 13 years before Tim was even born. Of course, the book might have been purchased used, or handed down intergenerationally. Neither *The Marshmallow Ghosts* nor the other two books were marked by a childish scrawl of ownership.

She thought about her childhood, and how she and her older brother Juan-Gil had loved books. They would play "library" by pasting donation envelopes swiped from church inside their books' covers, into which they'd insert slips with their own or each other's name, along with imaginary due dates. With libraries now all employing computerized scans and bar codes, she doubted that children of Kat's generation played similar games with beloved books.

Had these books been beloved? Was there somewhere a child, or former child, who remembered these books and puzzled over what had become of them? She wondered too if these books and baseball glove had belonged to the same child as the kaleidoscope with which Kat was so enchanted.

She reached up to put the iron, heating pad, and penguin shakers back into the crawlspace, but carried the box of books and toys upstairs. Before secreting the box in her bedroom closet, she lifted the mitt briefly to her lips and kissed it.

She had virtually forgotten the mysterious shushing that had led her to the crawlspace in the first place.

It was clear by mid-afternoon the next day that Lauren was not going to call. Making sure that Kat was outside in the side yard playing with Thumper, Maggie dialed Lauren's number.

Jeff answered, and Maggie fought the temptation to disconnect. "Is Lauren in?"

"She isn't taking calls."

"Is she OK?"

"She's fine. We're working things out in private, if you don't mind." And then he hung up on her.

Maggie was stunned. Was Jeff really speaking for both of them, or merely screening calls without Lauren's knowledge? Had his violent behavior escalated?

With Tuesday came Kat's riding lesson. Neither Lauren's 4Runner was in the lot nor Brittany in the crossties grooming her horse. Perhaps Lauren was simply running late again. At the picnic table Paul was talking at Geri, another soccer mom whose daughters

Sydney and Ariel had recently joined the lesson. Geri drove a Prius, a fact alone that predisposed Maggie to like her.

Despite her aversion to Paul, Maggie joined them at the table. She hoped that Lauren and Brittany would arrive soon. Billy's Ford truck was also absent from the lot. Damn, if he were now avoiding her too she was going to forswear stable socializing from hereon in.

Geri tossed her a subtly grateful look. "How are you today? Is Kat riding Sugar again?"

"Of course. She loves that palomino as if –"

"Maggie, I was just telling Geri about the barn Halloween party last year," Paul oozed. "All the kids dressed up and put their horses in costume too. It's the cutest darn thing you've ever seen. One girl came as Cruella deVille and put black plastic polkadots on that white Arab, Charger, to make him a Dalmatian."

An SUV cruised into the lot, but it was a Mercedes dropping off another little girl.

Kat led Sugar into the crossties, planting a kiss on the horse's nose as she hooked the chains to either side of the faded purple halter. Maggie was already setting aside some of her freelance earnings to buy Kat her own English saddle and velvet riding helmet for Christmas. It was all she could do to discourage her parents from buying Kat her own horse.

Paul continued to gab about the equine Halloween party. The four children with their horses lined up at the mounting block; none of the girls was tall enough to mount from the ground without assistance. Maggie glimpsed Rhonda in the tack room and excused herself.

"I was wondering, Rhonda, if Lauren and Brittany were coming today."

Rhonda busily penciled in names of horses and riders on the large handmade chart

that served as schedule. "Brittany has the flu. Her mom called this morning and

cancelled. I hope the other kids don't get it," she replied in her usual, impersonally

cheery manner.

Maggie's heart sank. "Me too. Thanks."

"By the way, Maggie," Rhonda added, "Billy's over at Helen Woodward picking

up a horse that colicked last week. He should be back soon. I thought you might want to

know."

Maggie was appalled by Rhonda's nerve. "Helen Woodward?" she echoed.

"The animal hospital in Rancho Santa Fe."

"Well, I'm glad the horse is doing better." Maggie beat a fast retreat from the

tack room and the insinuation.

Geri was alone at the table, but Maggie's relief was short-lived, for Paul was

sauntering over from his Chevy Blazer, clasping an envelope. "I've been meaning to

give you this," he said to Maggie. "I just haven't run into you until today."

It was true; he wasn't typically at the stables on Tuesdays since the start of school.

Maggie took the blank envelope from him with trepidation. "What is it?"

He winked. "Read it later."

Her skin crawled. "I just remembered that I need to make a call to my editor."

Billy or not, she made her way to the tack store. After buying a soda and chatting

with Kim, she went outside to the porch and plastic table. Although she was confident

that the envelope's contents would be prurient, morbid curiosity got the better of her and she opened it. Four stapled pages of computer-generated text listed in mock-contractual form "DRIVE CLUB RULES."

All she had to skim the first couple of pages to catch the rules' drift. The "club" involved men and women driving around as a group to various points in the county, and urinating, defecating, or (for men only) ejaculating in designated spots. There was an elaborate point system depending on where and what type of "deposit" was made. On the last page was a line for the new member to sign and date.

Maggie considered herself reasonably sophisticated, but she couldn't have been more shocked than if the document had included illustrations.

Billy's truck, hauling a horse trailer, rumbled in. He jumped out of the cab and waved. "Give me five minutes."

Nodding, she watched dumbly as he jogged around to the back of the trailer, opened the doors, lowered a wooden ramp. He vanished inside the trailer, and in moments a bay gelding emerged, backside first, Billy guiding it down the ramp. Clearing the trailer, the horse reared up and whinnied, but a swift yank on the lead rope settled it down. Billy led the now docile animal into the barn.

Maggie was so disgusted by Paul's lewd missive that she wasn't sure she wanted to discuss it with anyone. But Billy plainly gleaned her distress. "What's wrong? Is it the house again? Your friend Lauren?"

Before she could answer he grabbed the stapled pages in front of her on the table.

"Oh God, don't read that. It's beyond gross," she said.

He scanned the pages. "What the *fuck*?" he exploded.

"Hey, keep it down out there or Rhonda will have your ass!" Kim called from within the store.

Outraged darkened his face. "Where the fuck did this come from?"

"That sleazy man Paul. Just throw it away and burn it. Please."

"Like hell." He threw the papers back on the table, turned on one boot-heel, and stomped toward the riding school arena.

Maggie hastened after him, fearing an ugly confrontation. "Billy, please don't make a scene. The kids – "

"Screw the kids. Or maybe that's exactly what this pervert's thinking."

She tugged his arm but he jerked free. "Hey, asshole!" he shouted at Paul, flanked by Geri and Patty at the picnic table.

Paul looked startled, as though he had no clue as to why Billy was addressing him with such hostility. "Chill out, buddy."

Inside the ring, Sandy instructed her students to halt their horses. Rhonda charged out from the tack room. "Billy, get away from my riding school!" she shrieked.

Billy seized Paul by the front of his green Izod polo shirt and rammed a fist into his jaw. Paul tumbled backward onto the dirt.

Geri and Patty screamed, and one of the girls – Paul's daughter Skylar – began to cry. "I'm calling the police," Rhonda thundered.

"Billy, come on," Maggie pleaded but it was as if he didn't hear her. He stood over the collapsed man, fist still drawn.

"You keep your perverted shit to yourself, asshole!" he warned. "You read?"

Paul, blood tricking from his split lip, managed a stiff nod.

"You better," Billy spat. He turned to Rhonda, who clasped her phone to her ear. "Tell the cops I'll be in front of the tack store."

He stalked off, but Maggie was too shaken to follow. Rhonda and the other two women helped Paul to his feet. He had certainly gotten what he deserved, but Billy's violent outburst and Paul's bloody face recalled all too painfully Jeff Byers's assault on his wife only a few nights before. Maggie's own father had a temper but was all bark, and she'd never so much as dated someone who was a brawler. Even at his most drug-addled, Tim fought only verbally, his violence self-directed. Unaccustomed to physical fights, she was unsettled by her proximity to two violent incidents in less than a week. And this most recent one she could not attribute to "residual haunting."

She waved Kat, astride Sugar, over to the railing. "Are you OK, sweetie?"

"People shouldn't hit," Kat said somberly. "Not even Billy."

"That's exactly right."

"It breaks them in two."

An odd comment. Maggie searched her daughter's face. Kat looked sad but calm.

"Come on, girls!" urged Sandy. "Back to posting trot!"

All alertness, Kat set Sugar trotting, her small hips rising and falling in perfect cadence with the horse's stride.

Rhonda had taken Paul into her tack room where she was ministering first aid. Maggie was surprised that little Skylar, eyes red-rimmed but dry, was continuing with her lesson.

Geri touched her arm. "Jesus, what was that about?"

"Paul's a creep and Billy's a hothead." Maggie didn't elaborate.

She didn't want to face Billy or witness the police's arrival. With Paul's gross "rules" presumably still on the porch table and Patty and Geri available to give their accounts of the melee, Maggie trusted that her presence would not be needed. Just in case, however, she told Geri that she would be visiting with Warlock if anyone wanted to speak to her.

The big horse stomped in pleasure at the sight of her. "Hello, handsome," she said, petting his nose. "What a fiasco that was."

Like a big dog he licked her palm.

"Let me see if I have a treat for you." She found a couple of peppermints in her purse, which he ate in two happy crunches, his liquid black eyes fixed on her in affection. She'd never realized before how expressive horses could be. "What a nice boy you are," she crooned, even as she pondered Kat's peculiar remark. *It breaks them in two.* The statement would have struck her as uncharacteristically babyish and imprecise were it not for the kind of rueful certainty with which Kat had uttered it.

"Oh, Tim, what have you and I done to our child?" she sighed.

Warlock nuzzled her sleeve and she stroked his cheek. "Nice boy," she repeated. Her dream the other night and Nicole's invitation notwithstanding, she had no intention of ever riding him. Billy, a lifelong rider, admitted that Warlock had thrown him twice already. But wouldn't it be cool, she daydreamed, just to own Warlock and keep him as a pet? No; horses needed regular, vigorous exercise, especially a young, big horse like Warlock. "Thou art too dear for my possessing," she whispered to him. "But you're about the best friend I've made since moving here."

She stayed with her "best friend" another twenty minutes, even after the novelty of her presence waned and he alternated visiting with her at the rail with munching from his feed bucket and nosing at the occasional horse and rider that passed by his stall. At four she trudged back to the riding school area. The kids were dismounted and out of the ring, brushing their horses in the crossties. No sign of either Rhonda or Paul, but a pencil-thin woman with dark bobbed hair was helping little Skylar untack her horse. The child's mother, perhaps, the unfortunate wife of Paul.

Maggie didn't care to hear what had transpired in her absence, but Geri told her anyway. "The police came and went. I guess Paul didn't want to press charges, for whatever reason."

Maggie was glad, for Billy's sake, though she marveled inwardly about people's apparent unwillingness to involve the police in more or less "minor" cases of assault. Paul's refusal to press charges was certainly more understandable than Lauren's; he obviously didn't want his perverse "contract" to become part of any record. Did Lauren somehow believe herself to blame for being struck? And was Maggie's own anger with Billy less because he attacked Paul than because it reminded her own her helplessness about Lauren's situation?

"I hope the rest of your lesson turned out OK," she said to Kat as they buckled themselves into the Honda.

"I got Sugar to do a flying lead change!"

"That's wonderful, sweetie," Maggie said, though she had no idea what such a feat entailed.

"She has the best canter, Mommy. She's so smooth and fast."

Maggie wasn't especially thrilled about the "fast" part, but she was pleased that Kat displayed no lingering upset over the Billy-Paul contretemps. "I'm sorry I missed your flying canter, honey."

"Flying lead change," Kat patiently corrected. "And your eyes get all scared when you watch me."

Maggie winced. She hadn't realized her nervousness was that visible. "I'll try not to be such a worry-wart. I was like that with Daddy, too, when he used to play baseball. If the batter hit the ball anywhere near him, I had to cover my eyes."

Kat smiled, as she often did when Maggie mentioned Tim. "I bet Daddy wasn't scared. Not then."

"Not then?" Maggie echoed uneasily.

"Not like kids get scared."

Maggie chuckled. "And mothers!"

She was putting a chicken into the oven when the doorbell rang. Kat, busy with homework at the dining room table, called, "Can I get it?"

"Better let me, honey," Maggie said, setting the roaster on the countertop. The caller was likely UPS with a work assignment for her.

It was Billy. "Can I talk to you for a bit?"

Warily she widened the door. Kat peered out from the dining room. "Hi, Billy," she said pleasantly.

"Hey, princess."

Kat went back to her homework. Outside on the redwood deck, it was cool enough for Maggie to justify closing the sliding glass door behind them along with the screen. "I know it must have looked as if I was avoiding you," she fumbled. "I guess I was. I don't even know why – that creep deserved it."

"Most women hate it when guys fight."

She managed a crooked smile. "It wasn't actually much of a fight."

"I guess your old man wasn't one to get in barroom brawls."

"Oh no. The only time I ever saw him fight was when he'd hit somebody with a ball and then all the guys raced out of the dugout to throw their fists around like a bunch of schoolboys."

"He played baseball?"

"Yes, in college, and for a couple of years in the minors. He never made it to the major leagues."

"That's still pretty impressive. He was a pitcher?"

"He was."

"Lefty?"

"How did you guess that?"

"I dunno. I suppose 'cause the guy sounds like he was Mr. Perfect until he blew it all on dope."

She bristled slightly at his sardonic tone. "Addiction's a disease, not a weakness."

"Maybe. I have bad temper, as you saw today. Is that a disease or a weakness?"

"You tell me," she shot back.

"I fought all the time in my heavy boozing days," he admitted, sounding less cocky. "Believe it or not, Maggie, I regret flooring that pervert, though man, it sure felt good."

"Why do you regret it?"

"'Cause it upset you, and it could've spooked the horses and ended up hurting some kid. It was fucking stupid of me."

The awful thought of the horses spooking hadn't occurred to her. "I know that thing Paul foisted on me was offensive and disgusting. But why ... ?"

"But why did it set me off like that?" he finished for her. "Got any more beers, Maggie? I could sure use one."

"Yeah, some Coronas in the fridge." She started for the door.

"No, I'll get it," he said.

He went into the house. She clutched her shoulders, her eyes on the ocean but her mind churning at the possibility of an imminent, dark revelation.

Soon he was back, holding two Coronas. "Your daughter asked me not to tell you she and the dog are sharing a Krispy Kreme."

Maggie accepted a beer. "She'll spoil dinner for both of them."

Billy took a long gulp of beer. "Four years ago, my wife was raped."

"Oh my God. How awful."

"We were living in New Mexico. She was a waitress. The fucking scumbag who raped her was a regular customer."

"That's horrible. Did they catch him?"

He nodded. "Talk about regrets. I wanted so bad to get to him first. I would've killed him. Happily. Still wish I had."

"No," she snapped. "You'd have gone to prison." She blinked back tears at the dreadful words.

"Nah. Southeastern New Mexico's more like Texas than Taos. I'd have gotten a slap on the wrist."

"You can't be sure of that."

"Whatever. He went to trial, and as usual, he tried to say it was consensual." His eyes narrowed. "Thank God the jury didn't buy it, especially not after his ex-girlfriend testified he was a full-on pervert, too. Whips, chains, golden showers. Maybe Steph was lucky all he did was fuck her and make her suck him off at knifepoint."

"I can't tell you how sorry I am, Billy. For both of you." She tried to give him a quick hug, but he brushed her off.

"Don't feel sorry for me. I wasn't raped. She's been stronger than I could imagine anyone being, but – you ever heard of agoraphobia?"

"A fear of open spaces."

"That's what she has. She can go out into the yard, and be with the horses. But other than that, she won't – she can't – leave our property."

"My mother had a friend like that. She couldn't set foot outside her house. I assume your wife had gotten counseling?"

"She was in a group right after it happened. It wasn't until after the trial that the agoraphobia came on. I thought that moving to a totally different place might help. But it didn't."

"Has she tried medication?"

He took another swig of beer. "Nope. She doesn't want to. In a bizarre way, she's content. It's like after the trial, she decided the outside world hopelessly sucked, and closed the door on it for good."

Maggie wasn't sure whether he found the situation oppressive or simply a norm to which he'd become resigned. "Do you two ever have friends over?"

"Sometimes."

"I'd like to meet her."

He gave a short, humorless laugh. "Not a good idea, Maggie."

She flushed. "I'm not sure I understand."

He regarded her directly. "I'd never cheat on her. That doesn't mean I'm not tempted."

Flustered anew, she broke the gaze. "I'm attracted to you too. Maybe we're playing with fire, Billy, spending so much time together."

"No. There's a safety valve I haven't even mentioned."

"What?"

"You're still in love with your ex-husband."

CHAPTER 6

With Halloween approaching, Maggie's life in Del Mar settled into a comfortable

mid-autumnal ordinariness. As the days shortened her workload increased incrementally,

a seasonal upsurge due to the academic calendar superseding the Roman one.

Abstracting scholarly articles on both English and Spanish literature was not particularly

exciting labor, but the work was regular throughout the schoolyear and she supposed it

kept her up to date on the latest trends in feminist and queer theory, postcolonial studies,

post-Marxism, and the moribund flickerings of poststructuralism and deconstruction that

had been so fashionable when she was in college.

Even the residually haunted house was falling into familiar rhythms. Occasional

running sounds on the stairs, silvery jangling, warning growls from Thumper as he

looked down from the landing at nothing. She had not heard the strange shushing sound

again, which made her consider the possibility the noise had simply been the result of

items naturally shifting in the hidden crawlspace. Similarly, the menacing face stayed absent from the photo in Kat's room. She continued to be grateful that Kat never seemed to be near when any of the house's peculiarities made its presence known.

The one phenomenon that still unnerved her was that corner-of-the-eye shadow intermittently teasing her peripheral vision near the bottom of the staircase. Her nightmare that followed the interrupted housewarming had convinced her that the transient shadow was that of a man – the same old man in the fedora and trenchcoat who had menaced her in her dream.

Not a ghost but an impression from the past. Only inanimate "energy."

The ripple effects from the fateful housewarming were still making faint circles. Lauren remained absent from the stables and unavailable to take her calls; the answering machine picked up every time Maggie called her number. She missed Lauren, although she guiltily conceded to herself that even before the housewarming she was spending much of her time at the ranch with Billy.

Their agreement to maintain their relationship in a kind of limbo state had deferred rather than doused their mutual attraction. Except for the occasional goodbye kiss that slipped from friendly to perilous, she might have viewed him merely as a platonic friend. She cooked dinner for him every Monday, which was his wife's book club night. Kat, too, liked him; she'd evidently either forgiven or forgotten the ugly incident with Paul. As for Paul, amazingly he was still a regular at the stables.

Fond though she was of Billy, she was slightly irked by his penchant for terse, contemptuous remarks whenever she casually mentioned Tim. She sensed that Billy was jealous, not because he believed she was still in love with Tim, but rather because he felt Tim had wantonly squandered every precious opportunity Billy had never had – college, a professional athletic career, a comfortable upper-middle-class family life. Once he

even said as much, after she'd made a benign comment about a major meth bust near

Billy's house in Fallbrook. "If you ask me, your husband's biggest problem is that he

was spoiled," he remarked. She'd refused to acknowledge the comment, but privately

resolved to avoid even the most oblique references to Tim.

On this Sunday afternoon, the first, already darkening one of the return to

standard time, Maggie was occupied with helping Kat put together her costume for the

riding school's Halloween party scheduled from 4 to 6. Kat was going as Little BoPeep,

and three huge bags of white batting and a pair of improvised black felt ovine ears would

transform Sugar into one very large lost sheep. The sight of Kat in an old-fashioned

pinafore, frilly pantaloons, ballet slippers, and straw bonnet tickled Maggie. "Sweetie, let

me get the camcorder." Her parents, whom they'd visited the previous weekend, had lent

her their video recorder for this precise purpose.

"Abuelo and 'Lita said it was for the Halloween party," Kat warned.

"Don't worry, I'll use it there too. Now, stand in the middle of the living room

and make believe you're looking for your lost sheep."

"That's dumb, Mommy," Kat said, but obliged. "Sheepie, where are you? Where

are you hiding?" She pantomimed scanning an imaginary meadow. Thumper, excited by

the performance, yapped and danced at her feet.

"There's your sheepdog," Maggie chuckled, running the camcorder a few more

moments.

They arrived at the ranch just after 3:30. Costumed children and a few adults too

were busy dressing up their horses. Rhonda and Kim, from the tack store, were setting up a cooler with soft drinks and paper plates of assorted Halloween cookies on the picnic

table. One child, dressed in a gold graduation gown and mortarboard, affixed pipe-

cleaner eyeglasses and a pointy dunce cap on a Welsh pony. A teenage girl with bright

fuchsia hair had fashioned her horse's mane into a giant Mohawk. Maggie spotted

Nicole Ludwig, in green Peter Pan tunic and tights, leading Warlock over to the crossties

where Kat diligently pasted the cottony white batting onto Sugar's mesh flysheet.

Warlock wore a pair of filigreed wings and a silver sequined tutu taped to his massive

chest. "He's Tinkerbelle!" Nicole trilled. "Doesn't he look cute?"

"A cross-dressed horse – I love it!" Maggie aimed the camcorder at Nicole and

Warlock.

"You know she's just wearing that costume to show off her legs," sniped one

mother to another under her breath.

Maggie pretended not to hear and Nicole was already parading Warlock before

Rhonda and Kim.

Sugar stood patiently as Maggie and Kat fastened her fleece around her, poodle-

like puffy cuffs to her fetlocks, and the felt ears with double-sided tape. "Baa ram ewe,"

Billy quipped, striding up.

Kat laughed at the *Babe* allusion. "Doesn't Sugar look good as a sheep?"

"Sure does. You could practically make a sweater from her."

Kat led Sugar into the ring in preparation for the promenade of costumes. Rhonda

had forbidden anyone to ride, given the number of horses and the spooking potential of

cumbersome frippery. "Where's your costume?" Billy teased Maggie

"I might ask you the same thing."

He grinned. "Hell, I came as a redneck sumbitch." Then he frowned, regarding Nicole who was now astride the incongruously costumed Warlock in defiance of Rhonda's admonition. "What the fuck's she up to?"

"I know. Rhonda's going to have a hissy-fit."

"Screw Rhonda. I meant, what is that shit she's got on the horse?"

"He's Tinkerbelle," Maggie replied.

"Like hell he is – he's a gelding, and one that thinks he's still a stallion!"

She was amused by his umbrage. "I'm sure he doesn't realize his masculinity's being impugned."

He scowled. "Don't bet on it."

Once all the horses and their human chaperones were in the ring, Maggie switched the camcorder on again. Kat looked adorable leading her "sheep," and the other costumes were clever as well, bound to entertain Pa and Mama. In addition to the "punk" twosome and the little professor and equine dunce, a child in safari gear accompanied a faux zebra, a haloed angel a demonic mare, and Tatiana's brat Bianca played Cinderella to her prize Morgan's crepe-paper pumpkin. Nor was Nicole atop Warlock the sole adult participant. A large woman had cleverly dressed her roan gelding as Vegas Elvis with a jet black wig, white satin fringed blanket, and giant sunglasses. And a fortyish woman in braids wore an "IMPEACH BUSH" shirt, her bay quarterhorse unadorned except for a giant picture of George W. Bush taped to its rear end. "Ryan will adore that," Maggie said to Billy. "What a brilliant idea."

"Risky in this neck of the woods, too," he agreed. Suddenly gleeful astonishment splashed across his face. "Look at Warlock!"

Once she looked it was impossible to avert her eyes – Warlock, unbeknownst to Nicole, had "dropped," his fully extended penis bobbing like a good foot and a half of black garden hose.

Rhonda, at the center of the ring, turned redder than the "devil" horse's costume. Most of the onlookers muffled chuckles lest they alert the innocent youngsters to Warlock's unabashed display of maleness. Billy opted for no such subtlety. "Looks like Tinkerbelle's got his magic wand," he said loudly, all but doubled over in laughter.

A couple of the parents shot him dirty looks. Maggie giggled irrepressibly and kept filming. "I guess you were right about Warlock still thinking he's a stallion."

"Never been so proud of a horse in my life," he replied.

Glimpsing Maggie and Billy, Warlock left his place in the circular procession to jog over to them at the rail, Nicole tugging the reins futilely. "Good boy," Maggie said, petting him.

"Don't let him do that, Nicole," Billy said. "Keep him moving along with the other horses. You gotta let him know who's boss."

Rhonda pointedly "ahem'd." "Attention, everybody! It's time to give out some prizes!" She held up some black and orange ribbons. Of course, every participant "won" something – cutest costume, scariest costume, funniest costume, most colorful costume. Rhonda seemed to assign the awards arbitrarily, although Kat looked thrilled to receive the "most creative" ribbon.

Billy wasn't about to let Rhonda pretend Warlock's embarrassing display had never happened. "Hey, Rhonda, you didn't give Warlock a prize!" he called.

Her broad smile became forced. "The prizes are for the kids."

Nicole, still unaware of her horse's spotlight-stealing gesture, chimed in. "But you gave Marco and Valentine ribbons," she pointed out, referring to the Elvis and Bush-as-horse's-ass entrants.

"How 'bout 'best Peter ... Pan'?" Billy suggested.

"Fine," Rhonda said through clenched teeth. "Best movie characters."

At last Maggie lowered the videocam. "You are so bad," she said to Billy, feigning disapproval.

"Damn, you have the whole thing on film. I want a copy!"

Maggie looked at the camcorder dubiously. "It's the old-fashioned kind. How do you duplicate a videotape?"

"It's easy. I'll bring my VCR over tomorrow night – you need two to dub. And we can watch it ... " He burst into renewed gales of laughter.

"Tomorrow's Halloween, remember?"

"Yeah. Why? You have plans other than taking Kat trick or treating?"

"No, but – I thought maybe your wife wouldn't want to be alone with all the kids ringing the bell and everything."

"Book club's coming over, same as always. They're all reading something by Anne Rice for the occasion."

"OK. Taylor's mom is taking the kids around the neighborhood, so you can help me answer my door and scare away the frat boys trying to pass themselves off as sixth-graders."

She had another reason, one she to which she didn't give voice, for being glad he was coming over as usual. Childish though she felt for thinking such a thing, she didn't want to be alone, even for the hour or so that Kat would be out trick or treating, in her

residually haunted house.

Because Kat deemed the "BoPeep" costume nonsensical without a sheep, for

Halloween proper she dressed as one of "The Incredibles." Taylor's mother Claire

swung by just before five. The plan was to take the girls around the neighborhood, then

on to the mall for an organized Halloween party. "I'll have her back by seven," promised

Claire.

Kat skipped off with Taylor, who was clad as one of the "Sky High" kids. Taylor

was Kat's current "best friend," and she seldom mentioned Brittany. Perhaps that was

natural, since Taylor and Kat were classmates at St. James's Academy. Or maybe Kat

was simply accustomed to people suddenly disappearing from her life.

Billy showed up, VCR in his arms, simultaneously with the first trick-or-treaters.

a little "Shrek" and two vampires. "I thought for a moment you'd spawned," Maggie

joked, waving him in and dropping miniature Snickers bars into the kids' sacks. She and

Kat had carved their pumpkin the night before. and it glowed benevolently atop a planter

on the doorstep.

"Thanks but no thanks," Billy replied. Upstairs, Thumper yipped from behind

Maggie's bedroom door. She didn't want to worry about him getting out every time she

answered the door.

Billy set the VCR on the coffee table. "I'll hook it up in a couple minutes. Have

you watched the tape yet?"

"No, I wanted to do it when Kat wasn't around. I know I'm going to die all over again."

He guffawed. "That'll teach Nicole to dress Warlock like a sissy."

The doorbell rang. Maggie hastened to "treat" the callers. Shutting the door on thm, she remarked, "Now I'm wondering if we shouldn't wait to watch the tape until later, after Kat's in bed. Or will that make for too late a night for you?"

"Nah. That's a good idea."

The bell chimed again. Billy peered over her shoulder as she offered candy to a solo trick-or-treater, a little boy of Kat's age,with long taffy curls, who wore a child-size Dodger uniform. Maggie had to smile at the uncommonly pretty child with the rather serious little face that somehow reminded her of Kat's. "Here you go, sweetheart."

"Number 34," Billy read on the child's jersey. "Who're you supposed to be?"

"Fernando," the little boy said.

Maggie thought nothing of the reply, but Billy looked puzzled.

"Thank you," the little Dodger said, and trod off into the night.

"Isn't it terrible to worry about kids running around alone on Halloween?" Maggie said, assuming that was why Billy looked so perplexed. "When I was a kid, my brother and I would trick-or-treat all over by ourselves."

"Fernando Valenzuela was number 34, wasn't he?"

"I don't know, was he?"

Billy shrugged. "Kid's dad must be a Dodger fanatic, that's all."

"Yeah, I understand that's anathema here in San Diego. I hope the kid isn't attacked by a pint-sized Padre."

"No shit."

"Let's go grab the guac and some cervezas before the bell rings again." She nodded toward the kitchen.

"They ought to invent an automatic candy dispenser so people can just ignore the doorbell."

"Misanthrope."

"Got that straight."

Once more the bell sounded. "I see your point," she granted, putting down the basket of chips and heading back for the foyer.

By seven the trick-or-treaters were tailing off. Soon Kat was home as well, her bag crammed full of candy. She was happy but tired, and from her relative indifference to the homemade lasagna Maggie served the three of them, no doubt Kat had been dipping into her cache of treats.

"Why don't you hook up the other VCR while I help Kat get ready for bed?" Maggie said to Billy, who was clearing away the dishes. Useful fellow; his wife had trained him well, she thought ironically.

"Mommy?" Kat stifled a yawn, drowsier than ever after a quick, warm bath.

Maggie folded down the comforter and blanket, and patted the bed. "Hop in, muchacha."

Kat crawled beneath the covers. "Is Billy your boyfriend?"

"No, sweetie. He's a good friend, but not a boyfriend. Why?"

"Taylor asked."

Probably on behalf of her affable but somewhat nosy mother, Maggie suspected. At least she hoped so. Kat and Taylor were too young yet to be talking about anyone's "boyfriend." Or were they?

She was nonetheless struck by how relieved Kat looked. Maggie could only trust that when and if the time came for her to become seriously involved with a man, Kat would not feel it a betrayal of her father.

Billy had the VCRs ready to play and dub when she returned downstairs. She handed him the videotape from the camcorder. "It needs to be rewound," she apologized.

He slid the cassette into the slot of her VCR, pushed manual rewind. They sat down on the sofa and waited for the click to signal the rewind was completed.

"Ha, here we go," Maggie said, pressing "play" on the remote.

Snow, then Kat posing in her costume calling "Sheepie, where are you?"

"Let me fast-forward this." Maggie picked up the remote again.

"Wait," he said urgently, waving her hand away from the remote control. "Somebody's on your deck."

"Oh God, right now?"

"No – on the tape. Rewind it again."

Kat's BoPeeping had already given way to Nicole in her Peter Pan outfit.

With a trembling hand Maggie hit "rewind," then "play."

"Watch," Billy said, his voice tense.

Kat prancing and calling for her sheep in front of the sliding glass door. And over her shoulder, on the deck, was a tall figure, back turned, in a dull gray coat and fedora.

Maggie barely suppressed a scream. It was him, the menacing old man from her dream, the smoky chimera near the foot of the stairs.

Billy froze the tape, staring intently at the image. "What the fuck is that," he breathed.

She couldn't stand to look at it any longer. "Get rid of it," she whispered frantically. *"Please."*

He pressed "stop" and the television screen went to cobalt blue. "Maggie, could somebody have actually been out there?"

"No," she said, shaking her head emphatically. "That's the man I keep thinking I see out of the corner of my eye. Fuck this 'residual haunting' theory – that's an honest to God ghost!"

"Shit."

"Who could it be?" she fretted. "Tim's grandfather? Someone who lived, or died, here before the professor and his family? Whoever he is, Billy, he's not good. Can't you feel it?"

"Well," he said, swallowing hard. "I think who he is – or was – is less important than getting rid of him."

She regarded him as if he were insane. "What do you suggest – calling in Ghostbusters? Or, God forbid, an exorcist?"

"No. But there's gotta be something in between the two."

"It's too crazy. And I can't have any weird mumbo-jumbo going on around Kat."

"Didn't you say she hasn't been bothered by any of this strange shit?"

"Yes, but … " Should she take minor comfort in the fact that the apparition was looking away from her daughter on the videotape? She recalled as well how the sinister face amid the trees had reappeared in the graduation photo only when Kat was away for the evening.

"But what?"

"It's leaving her alone for now. I can't count on that."

"So you either get rid of it, or move."

She sighed. "She's been so happy here. I can't just keep uprooting her like this – it'll make her more neurotic than the things I'm trying to protect her from." She got up to grab a bottle of wine from the dining room buffet. "Of course, if we stay here I'm going to end up an alcoholic. I haven't drunk so much since I was in college."

"Maggie, that thing is *trying* to scare you out of your mind. Now's not the time to start Twelve-Stepping yourself."

She uncorked the bottle of Cabernet, poured them each a glass. "Maybe I'll tell Kat the house has to be renovated, and we can take an apartment near here. That way she can still ride and go to the same school."

"Don't you want to at least attempt to get rid of it before throwing in the towel? You don't seem like a quitter."

"I quit on Tim," she said acidly.

"No, you quit on letting him screw up your life, and your kid's. That takes a lot more guts than keeping somebody company in hell."

"What if your wife had thought that?"

"Maggie, I said she was a saint. I didn't say she was especially – courageous."
His expression was unhappy.

"I'm sorry. I shouldn't have said that."

"Whatever. But speaking of my wife, one of her book club friends is a practicing
Wiccan. Maybe she'd have some ideas about how to chase off this damn ghost."

"I guess it wouldn't hurt to ask. But what if she's some crackpot?"

His lips twisted. "You want a referral from the Better Business Bureau?"

"All right, all right. Besides, she's likely to think we're the ones who are
crackpots."

"Nah. Crackpot would be boarding up the house and running for the hills without
taking a stab at solving the problem."

His remark made her glean that he was far less at peace with his wife's decision to
lock out the world than she evidently was.

Nonetheless, she declined his offer to spend the night on the sofa. "No, I'll be
fine, and tomorrow's a school day."

"You sure you're OK?"

She stole a quick glance at the stairs. "Yeah. Whoever or whatever he is, I don't
believe he has the power to do much more than scare me." And she didn't want to spark
Kat's "boyfriend" curiosity by having her awaken to him sleeping on the sofa again.

She sent him home with a hug and a promise to let him watch and dub the
Halloween party segment of the videotape the next time he came over. She certainly
wasn't going to send the tape, as it was, to her parents. He told her he would splice out
the eerie prologue on his next visit.

She resisted the temptation to shut her eyes and run blindly up the stairs. Instead she ascended at a normal pace, eyes wide though her pulse raced, slowing only when she had reached her bedroom. She felt sheepish for wishing that Kat would decide that this was one of those nights she felt like sleeping with her mother. So much for her "courage."

But fatigue and wine were seeping into her consciousness; indeed, she was feeling pleasantly sedated. With great effort she undressed, not even brushing her teeth or washing her face before falling into bed. She surrendered to the oddly soothing drowsiness, almost hearing *"Sssshhhh!"* again, but the sound was indistinguishable from the hazy dream into which she drifted. The shushing was coming, as before, from the downstairs coat closet, only this time, when she opened the door she found the strikingly beautiful child in the baseball uniform within, holding a finger to his lips and fixing her with his grave brown eyes.

She knelt down to embrace the little boy. Her arms closed around nothing.

"OK, this chick is gonna call you. I hope you don't mind I gave her your number."

"The Wiccan?"

Maggie fed Warlock apple quarters as Billy vigorously curried the handsome horse. The ranch bore no traces of the Halloween party two days earlier, no errant orange or black crepe streamers, no paper jack o'lanterns in the window of the tack store. November was settling over the stables, and at three p.m. the day was already fading.

"No, not the Wiccan. A friend of hers who's supposed to be something of an expert in this department."

"An expert! There's actually a demand for this sort of service?"

He stooped to lift one if Warlock's shaggy fetlocks, scraping at the bottom of the huge shod hoof with a pick. Maggie eyed Billy's backside appreciatively.

"Probably more people think they have ghosts than really do," he said, straightening a moment before moving to Warlock's hind fetlock.

"So I'd imagine. I'm glad you got on this so quickly."

"I lucked out. The book-clubbers were just breaking up when I got home."

"They must have loved hearing about a real-life haunted house." She was no less curious about what any of the literary ladies thought of their hostess's husband spending Monday evenings with another woman, haunted house notwithstanding.

He shot her an impatient look. "I didn't just charge in and announce it. I took Alison, the Wiccan, aside and gave her the Readers Digest condensed version."

"Does Stephanie know about it?"

"Oh yeah. She thinks you're brave for even staying there."

There was that word again of which she felt only marginally worthy. And his casual reference to his wife's thoughts about her situation made Maggie feel awkward and guilty. Awkward because it indicated that he really did view their relationship as innocent, and guilty because a part of her didn't. "Is this woman a medium or psychic or … well, I don't know what? When do you think she'll contact me?"

"In answer to all your questions, I have no idea. Alison said the woman's name is Darlene."

"Darlene?" she echoed dubiously.

"What were you expecting – Endora?" he joked, giving Warlock a playful slap on the rump. He reached into his tack box and handed her a large plastic spray bottle marked Show Sheen. "Want to do his mane and tail?"

She inspected the bottle. "Do I just spray this on him, like conditioner?"

"Yep. And then brush him out."

She looked at Warlock's curtain of black mane. "That sounds fun," she said, smiling. "As long as he doesn't kick me when I brush his tail."

"Nah, not even his ground manners are that bad." He placed the brush in her free hand. "I'm gonna grab a Coke."

She ducked under the crosstie chain and reached up to stroke his mane. He seemed even larger from this proximity, but his kind eye reassured her. She sprayed a timid amount of Show Sheen on the mane, sprayed more when he didn't flinch. As silky as his mane appeared, the hair was coarse, and she brushed carefully through the tangles.

Billy returned with his soft drink. "Nice job."

"It does look pretty," she agreed, admiring her glossy handiwork.

"Next time you can pick his hooves."

"I trust you're kidding – they're the size of hubcaps and I bet they weigh ten times as much."

She turned her attention to Warlock's tail. It reached almost to his shoes and was infinitely thicker than his mane. She sprayed the tail liberally, began brushing it in small sections. Absorbed in the task, she barely heard Billy's idle conversation with Kim, who had stepped outside the store for a cigarette.

Maggie felt an inordinate satisfaction when at last the brush passed through every segment of Warlock's tail without resistance from knots or tangles.

Kim clapped lightly. "Bravo!"

Maggie stepped back, still holding the brush. "Just look at that beautiful tail!"

"I am," Billy teased, pointedly eyeing her buttocks.

She made as if the scowl at him and Kim pretended to slap him.

The merriment was interrupted by Rhonda on the march toward the tack store. "Kim, I need to buy some fly spray," she reproached.

Kim crushed her cigarette with her boot heel. "I'm on my way back in."

Maggie petted Warlock's neck and waited until the tack store door shut behind the two women. "At first I thought Rhonda was so sweet, but lately she seems like the barnyard scold."

"That's the real her," Billy said. "The Mary Poppins act is just for the benefit of the crotch-droppings and their parents."

"Please," she groaned, though the crude epithet was one of his favorite for children.

"Come on, you know I don't put your kid in that category."

"Still."

Rhonda stomped back outside with her purchase. "Maggie, can I have a minute with you? It's about Kat's lessons." The ersatz cheeriness had returned to her tone.

Maggie planted a quick kiss on Warlock's nose. She caught up with Rhonda on the stroll back to the riding school arena. "Kat's doing so well, I wonder if I could put her in a smaller group of more advanced riders," Rhonda said. "Or even private lessons, if you want to do that."

Maggie watched Kat lope easily on Sugar in the ring. Private lessons were an additional $65 a month, she knew; they could probably swing it, but she wondered if the group lessons weren't simply more fun for her daughter. "Maybe private lessons after the first of the year. Let's stick with the group for the time being."

Inside her tack room, Rhonda surveyed her schedule. "Let's see, what about Monday at four? There are only two other girls in that group, and they're both intermediates."

"That should be fine."

Rhonda penciled Kat's name in the Monday column. "Oh, and Maggie? I hope you don't take this the wrong way, but people are talking about you and Billy. You wouldn't want that gossip to get back to Kat."

Annoyed, she supposed she ought to have seen this coming. "Billy and I are friends, and Kat knows that. I can't be responsible for what busybodies are going to think or say."

Rhonda wouldn't back down. ""Maybe if you'd spend more time with the other parents watching the kids, people wouldn't be jumping to the wrong conclusions." She emphasized "wrong," as though to underscore her own skepticism.

Maggie bristled at the implication that she was more interested in Billy than in her own daughter. "As I said, Rhonda, I can't and won't concern myself with what a bunch of 'Mommier-than-thou' hens with too much time on their hands are saying behind my back," she said coldly. "Thanks for your concern."

She hastened out of the tack room before she lost her temper and blurted out something that could jeopardize Kat's continued participation at the riding school. For the same reason, she didn't return to the crossties by the tack store and report the incident to Billy. With his hot temper, he'd surely storm over to Rhonda and make matters worse.

Fortunately the lesson was just breaking up. Kat was thrilled to hear that Rhonda thought she belonged in a more advanced class. "And now I only have to wait until Monday," she reasoned.

"I'm really proud of you, Kat. Your daddy would be too."

Kat's smile widened. "I know."

Her certainty was touching – or so Maggie struggled to convince herself.

She was preparing dinner when she received a call from a woman identifying herself as Darlene Zarlengo. "It's difficult for me to talk right now," Maggie said quietly. "My daughter's in the next room."

"That's OK, I understand. Do you want to meet for coffee some time tomorrow, when your child's in school?"

Maggie was both taken aback and relieved by the woman's level, no-nonsense manner. Darlene Zarlengo might as well have been setting up a dental appointment. "That'd be great," Maggie replied.

"Is there a Starbucks near you?"

"Yes, over in the Del Mar Highlands shopping center."

"I'll see you there at noon."

Darlene Zarlengo was striking, if not the least otherworldly, in appearance. She was a rather large, auburn-haired woman with bright brown eyes and a creamy complexion. She was dressed in black, but the simple long tunic and leggings seemed designed more to minimize her weight than to mark her as a Goth. Her jewelry was expensive and tasteful.

She and Maggie took their coffees outside to the one bistro table in front of Starbucks not occupied by business people on cellphones, skinny Botoxed blondes in low-slung jeans, the random computer geek in horn-rimmed glasses and techno T-shirt. "Maybe we should have met at my house," Maggie said, casting a nervous glance at all the noontime coffee-breakers.

"Don't worry, these people are all into their own issues. Besides, I don't want to go into your house before you've begun the cleansing ritual."

"I take it that's not simply a comment on my housekeeping," Maggie tried to jest.

"In a way it is," Darlene said, picking up her coffee with one perfectly manicured hand. "It's really important to give the house a top-to-bottom scouring before we even think about ritual purification. But first things first. Tell me about your ghost."

The woman's brisk, practical style made Maggie feel less self-conscious as she recounted the various strange phenomena – the unexplained noises, the face that came and went in the photograph, and the shadowy old man in the coat and hat, sensed by the stairway, seen on the videotape. "It was the video that convinced me that this wasn't what I guess is called a residual haunting."

"Really? I can't say for sure until I've been in your house, but everything you've told me actually is quite consistent with residual haunting."

Maggie was skeptical. "But the man on the tape looked so real, so – embodied."

Darlene Zarlengo seemed to consider it. "Figures glimpsed out of the corner of the eye – they're sometimes called 'shadow people' – are more common than three-dimensional apparitions," she granted. "But spiritual entities, or ghosts, tend to try to interact directly with the living. Residual images and sounds, while scary, don't really *do* anything. Remember, they're simply the other things you capture on film or tape, recordings of people and emotions and sounds, not the things themselves."

Maggie frowned, thinking. "But that shushing noise did seem directed toward me. As if it wanted me to find the crawlspace and the children's books."

"And one of the books was a ghost story, you say?" Darlene prodded with the dispassionate professionalism of a reporter from the local paper.

"Yes, but it was a kids' book, not even nominally scary."

"Well, there I have to agree that it sounds more like an entity haunting. It's not unheard of to have elements of both in the same house."

Maggie was absurdly pleased to have convinced the woman to revise her initial diagnosis, such as it was. "Can you help me get rid of this, whatever it is?"

"I'll do my best. But first, you need to do some homework along with housework."

"Ok ... "

"Most entity hauntings are caused by the spirit of someone who's died in that place – maybe this old man – and either doesn't realize he or she is dead or simply doesn't want to leave the home they loved. They're harmless, but they need to move on."

She might as well have been referring to a family of squirrels that had taken up residence on the roof. "Go on," Maggie said.

"You need to find out who's died either in that house or shortly after being in it."

Maggie tensed. "My husband's grandparents lived there until about ten years ago. It must be Tim's grandfather."

"Maybe, maybe not. Who lived there after them? Can you find out?"

"A college professor and his family, but I think they were only there for the last couple of years. And my impression is that they were in their 40s, if that."

Darlene neatly reattached the plastic lid to her empty paper coffee cup. "Find out. They might have had an elderly relative who visited. What about before them?"

"That I don't know. But I'm sure I can find out through the property management company that took care of rental and maintenance for the last ten years." Absently she gnawed her lower lip. "I didn't realize that you'd need all these specifics."

"Honey, the more specific knowledge we have, the better our chances are of persuading whoever it is to leave." She reached into her oversize leather purse for a notepad and pen. "I'm going to write down some instructions for you when you do the cleaning. Or hire someone else to do it. I hate housework myself." She started scribbling. "Oh, one more thing. Are you religious?"

"I was raised Catholic but I don't practice."

"Unless you have a strong aversion to it, as a lot of ex-Catholics do, I'd advise you to go get some holy water from the font in a church. A quarter cup or so is all you need."

"Oh God, what if the priest catches me and thinks I'm some kind of Satanist?"

"Just tell him you need it to bless your house – which is the truth – and give him a ten buck donation. Once you get the holy water, dip your fingers in and sprinkle a few drops everywhere in the house you've seen or heard a manifestation. Obviously, don't do this until after you've finished cleaning. But if I were you, I'd make my top priority finding out who has lived and died there in the last ten years. That's crucial to focusing our energies when we actually perform the banishing ritual."

Maggie wasn't sure whether Darlene was intending to include her in this rite – she sorely hoped not – or merely employing the editorial "we." Or perhaps she worked with a partner. She let it pass for the time being. "I'm really grateful for your help. And relieved that none of this will involve Ouija Boards or people going into trances."

Darlene clucked. "Those things are worse than useless – they can be dangerous. You're trying to get an entity to leave, not beckon more in."

"Now I have a really dumb question. What, ah, do you charge?"

"Nothing," Darlene replied emphatically. "No honest witch or Wiccan does. Just as none of us can guarantee success. But I'll do my best for you, Maggie. You don't deserve to be haunted."

Maggie smiled but with no humor. "That's another story. I just want to take care of the house."

The woman at the property management office seemed eager to help Maggie with her fabricated predicament: several unlabeled boxes of personal possessions discovered in a crawlspace that she wanted to return to their owner. Juan-Gil had taught her when they were children that the most effective lies always contained an element of the truth.

"Let's see," the woman said. "Stanley Rosen leased from 2003-2005."

"Yes, I know about him. I'm sure I can reach him at UCSD."

"Before him it was the same family for nearly 7 years. Mrs. Emerson gave them a little break on the rent because she figured they would be stable." A decided note of disapproval had crept into the woman's voice.

"Weren't they?"

"Well, half the time the rent was late. I think the woman drank. She was a divorced mother of two, and she was always complaining in the filthiest language you can imagine about the heat not working or the gardener being too noisy." She sighed. "Some tenants are like that – never satisfied."

"What was the family's name?"

"She was Judy Showalter. I think the kids were Scott and Andrea. They moved when the older of the two kids went off to college and they no longer needed three bedrooms."

"You wouldn't have a forwarding address or number, would you?"

"You bet! She was nagging us for months to return the entire security deposit, even threatening to get a lawyer. And they left the place a pigsty." She read Maggie a number with a 619 area code, San Diego proper. "Of course, I can't promise she hasn't moved again. I wouldn't be at all surprised if the boxes you found were hers. She wasn't exactly Martha Stewart as a housekeeper."

"Who is?" Maggie quipped.

She thanked the woman for her efforts, hung up the phone. She felt vaguely sad. Both families who had lived here before her had included sons, decreasing the likelihood that the baseball mitt and the children's books she'd found had once belonged to Tim.

For a few moments it was as if she almost believed her own false pretext for contacting

the property managers, and she had to remind herself of the actual reason in order to snap

out of her fleeting melancholy.

It was certainly plausible, she mused, that either the Judy Showalter or Stanley

Rosen household might have had an elderly male relative. But how on earth would she

go about trying to unearth that information? She hadn't confessed to Darlene Zarlengo

that she'd gladly swallow a box of nails before pressing Jack Emerson about his late

father. But if neither Judy Showalter nor Stanley Rosen turned out to have hosted an old

man, now deceased, at the house, she would then have to assume by process of

elimination the apparition to be that of Tim's grandfather.

The idea made her shudder. She didn't want to consider the possibility that the

shadowy figure was related to Tim, to Kat. A flurry of doubts washed over her. Maybe

she should abandon this ludicrous notion of trying to banish the entity. After all,

everyone seemed to agree that the ghost, if that was indeed what it was, seemed

powerless to do more than momentarily frighten her. And Darlene had reminded her that

the shadow man was still consistent with a residual rather than sentient haunt. As for the

hushing sound, that might well have been an echo from past experience too, and her

discovery of the crawlspace and forgotten boxes coincidental.

"House, what do you want?" she asked aloud, scanning the living room and

beyond it, the deck, for some clue or response.

Only stillness, silence. Not even Thumper, snoozing in front of the fireplace,

twitched an ear.

But that was how the house was. Its peculiarities came and went according to no pattern, seemingly of their own accord. How could a mere ritual drive them out?

Her eyes drifted back to the deck. That was where *he* stood, the shadow man embodied only after the fact on film, no more than three or four feet from Kat. That he'd faced the opposite direction was of little comfort. The thought was enough to convince her that she had to try, with whatever means were available, to free the house of its strangeness, regardless of its origins.

Suddenly fearless, she dialed the number she'd scrawled down for Judy Showalter.

Two rings, then the machine message: "You have reached the Henchy residence. Please leave a message at the beep."

Had Judy Showalter remarried? "Hi, my name is Maggie Flores, and I'm trying to contact Judy Showalter." She left her number, hung up.

Intuition told her that the number had been reassigned. She located her slim SBC white pages and flipped to "S." A handful of listings, but no "J" or "Judith." She dialed information for the 619 area code. Again, no Judith or Judy, but there was a Scott, which Maggie recalled was the name of the woman's son. It was worth a try.

"Yeah?" a male voice answered.

"Hi, is this Scott Showalter?"

"Speaking."

"My name is Maggie Flores, and I live in the Del Mar house I believe you and your family used to rent. On La Amatista Road."

"Oh yeah. That was a great house."

As the ex-wife of a drug addict, she slipped easily into improvisation. "I've found some items in the house that seem to belong to an elderly person – heating pad, arthritis medication, some very old books. Could they belong to a relative of yours?"

"The meds could've been my mom's. She was hooked on Darvocet."

She chilled at his detached tone; it reminded her too much of Jack Emerson's. "I think the prescription bottle had a man's name on it," she contrived.

"Look, my mom died from a drug OD two years ago. Where she got her dope is anyone's guess. If I were you, I'd flush that crap down the toilet and donate the rest of the stuff to GoodWill. I've gotta go."

The line went dead.

Maggie felt as if she'd been struck, only the blow was self-inflicted, the just consequence of charging thoughtlessly into a stranger's life in pursuit of chimerae – or how to rid herself of them. She stumbled over to the stairs, which looked merely homely and dim, and sank down on the bottom step, crying.

She wasn't really crying for Judy Showalter, though the dead woman and her family certainly merited tears. No, she cried now, as ever, for Tim, who was bound to come to the same eventual fate as Judy Showalter.

At once a powerful, almost *alien* wave of anger seared her from within, and a wild hatred consumed her grief. "Bastard! Spoiled rotten bastard!" she screamed, the curse bursting from her throat with such violence that her vocal cords felt singed.

Thumper trotted over and froze two feet in front of her. Ears and tail down, he stared at her as if she were a stranger, muzzle curled up, his teeth bared.

The sight of her lovable, eight-pound dog snarling at her and poised to attack shocked her out of her fugue of wild rage. "Thumper, it's me, muchacho," she cooed, but didn't offer a hand to him.

His posture relaxed and tail wagged, and he came over to be petted. "Good boy," she said, scratching behind his ears.

And then she got the hell away from the staircase.

CHAPTER 7

"Jesus, Maggie, I thought *my* life was complicated!" Ryan refilled each of their

mugs from the pitcher of beer on their table.

"I'm sorry. All I've done is talk about myself." With Kat spending the night with

Taylor, Maggie had jumped at Ryan's invitation to dinner at Bully's, a casual steakhouse

and bar on the old coast highway in the Del Mar village. Although determined to give

herself a break from her terrestrial and otherworldly concerns, she'd launched into her

report on the house's latest eerie events the moment she'd climbed into his car.

"Trust me, I have nothing to top a haunted videotape, a pissed-off psychic, and

barnyard gossip about you and a married man whose bones you want to jump."

His humorous recap of her woes cheered her. "I told you, Darlene Zarlengo isn't

technically a psychic, and she's not technically pissed off, either. She's still going to

perform this 'banishing ritual,' but she seems less hopeful it'll work without establishing

definitively who the old man is."

"Want to split an appetizer?"

"Sure. Crab-stuffed shrimp?"

"Perfect." He motioned the waitress over, gave her the order. After she left, he said, "I still think a séance could be interesting."

"Oh no. If we did that then Darlene would dump me as a client. She says they're very dangerous."

"I don't think the Ouija Board's ever fully recovered from *The Exorcist*. But there's something kind of cool about a haunted house, as long as your ghost's not Son of Chucky or some out-of-control poltergeists."

"I know the type of crazy occurrences you see in movies don't really happen. But Ryan, that old man I sense, and now have seen, is malignant. I can feel it. I don't want it around me or Kat."

"What if this ritual doesn't work?"

"I don't know," she replied candidly. "I can't uproot Kat again when she's so happy here in Del Mar. I guess I'll lease out the house and rent us an apartment."

"Maybe I'll find myself a sugar daddy who'll rent it for me."

"I wouldn't rent it to you," she said, although aware he was joking. "The house seems to bring bad luck to whoever lives in it. I think the old man is Tim's grandfather and he doesn't want anyone else living there. Or maybe he's looking for his wife."

Ryan was silent for a moment or two. "I remember Tim's parents as pretty uptight. I guess you wouldn't want to ask them about it."

"God no. They've always seemed to expect me to reveal myself as 'Magdalena, the Mexican spitfire.' That'd just confirm it."

"Living la vida loca. Have you told this theory to your psychic or witch or whatever she is?"

"Yeah, but without proof, she thinks it's no more or less plausible that the old man is one of the renters' dead relatives."

"Christ. For a psychic she's sure a wet blanket."

Maggie barely heard his quip. At the entrance to the small restaurant, Lauren and Jeff Byers, suntanned and smiling, hovered by the hostess's stand.

Ryan followed the direction of her gaze. "Wow. Looks like they've patched things up."

Their waitress bounced over with the appetizer. Blocking their view of the entry, she lay the platter between them, centered their bread plates, and topped off their beer mugs. "Enjoy!"

She strode off. The view was clear again, but Lauren and Jeff seemed to have vanished, unless they had gone into the bar. "They must have seen us," Maggie said, her heart sinking.

"Yeah, they left. They were probably just embarrassed and didn't want to deal."

"They looked so ... happy." A new, unpleasant thought entered her mind. What if Lauren and Jeff had always been happy, and it was the house, the old man, that had compelled Jeff to assault his wife?

No, it couldn't be. After all, Kat had indirectly confirmed that she'd witnessed altercations between the Byerses. It was his fault, she'd said.

Not Mr. Byers's fault. Kat had simply said *his*.

"Don't brood, Maggie," Ryan said gently. "Lauren will probably reach out to you once enough time's passed that she can pretend it never happened."

"Jeez, I'm being such a pill tonight!" She felt bad for him. She took a gulp from her beer and reached for a shrimp. "Come on, let's have a good time."

"You Mexican spitfire."

They finished the appetizers and ordered Bully-burgers along with another pitcher of beer. By the time they paid their bill both of them were fairly lit. Ryan proposed a walk on the beach, just a block away. "That way if we stagger we can blame it on the sand."

"That's an excellent idea," Maggie said with a laugh.

It was a chilly night and the beach was mostly empty. But the salt and the smell of the ocean calmed her frayed nerves as much as the beer, and the cool sand was a balm to her bare feet. "Remember that party – I think it was Julie's, when she was living in Venice? Christy was hammered and went for a romantic walk along the shore with that geeky sociology grad student – "

"Yeah, and someone stole their shoes," Ryan chortled. "Why didn't they carry them instead of leaving them right on the beach?"

"Presumably, they wanted their hands free for other things."

Ryan sidestepped a mound of kelp. "Sometimes all I remember of my junior and senior years is one long party. When I think of all the wild sex I could've been having if I hadn't been too shit-faced to get off that sofa in Dan's apartment ... "

"That fuzzy red sofa! The stuffing was coming out and it had that baseboard piece, with nails, that kept falling down."

"But you can't deny it was comfortable."

She locked an arm in his as they strolled crookedly along the dark shoreline. "What was that 'Lies, Lies, Lies' song they played constantly on KROQ that used to crack us all up?"

"I don't remember who did it, but it had that sort of Japanese-style riff that we all laughed at like it was the punchline at the end of *Some Like It Hot*. That had to be the crystal."

"I know. Because I can hear the song in my head, and I can't figure out why we thought it was so hilarious." She brushed a strand of wind-whipped hair from her face. "And speaking of wild sex, are you having any?"

"As a matter of fact, yes. But it's gotten knotty."

"Naughty?"

"That too. But I meant complicated. Stephen's a great guy, but he wants to be a couple. I just want to fuck."

"How very male of you."

He snickered. "Are you insulting me as a gay man or just as a man?"

"The latter."

"Oh, come on. You and Tim were the least commitment-phobic couple I ever knew."

"He was the exception that proved the rule. Once upon a time I dated other guys, and they just wanted to fuck too." *Bodies and pleasures*; Tim's wired, ironic allusion to Foucault echoed in her brain.

"This is why it's so insane for the right-wingers to fight gay marriage," Ryan grumbled. "You'd think they'd want us all in, quote, 'committed relationships' instead of having purely animal, lip-smacking-good wild sex."

"No, they don't want anyone to be having sex. In which case they highly approve of me."

"Maybe Billy's wife is his way of avoiding commitment. And yours."

"No, it's our way of avoiding sex. And – to be honest – it's been years and years since I've had sex without being emotionally involved."

"Would it be rude to ask *how* many years?"

"Yes, but I'll tell you anyway. Twelve."

He whistled. "So it's only been Tim for the last twelve years."

"Isn't that strange? When we divorced I swore I was going to truly start over. I even had this brief fantasy of living like the poorer Latina relation of the *Sex and the City* women – cosmopolitans, Manolo Blahniks, and fun, casual sex." Drunk though she was, the admission still embarrassed her. "Isn't that stupid?"

"No way. I could've been your urbane gay sidekick – the cute one, not the bald nebbish with all the money."

"I just could never really break off with Tim. Not until last summer, at any rate. If only my house wasn't haunted, and Billy wasn't married." Then she pictured the used needle and scorched spoon on her kitchen counter in Manhattan Beach. "I guess things aren't so bad after all."

"Yep, you're one pair of stiletto heels away from your own sitcom on HBO."

She patted his arm. "So what are you going to do about Stephen?"

He shrugged. "Put off making a decision. You know what a procrastinator I am."

"Yes, you're downright Hamletic."

"And you're not?"

"I can make decisions – I just can't stick to them."

"That could be a virtue if you're looking to get laid by a certain married cowboy."

She glared. "I'm not."

"*Why* not, though?"

In her dream, she was back in therapy, only her therapist wasn't soft-spoken, humorless Francine but rather, the old man. He no longer looked the least sinister. A warm twinkle shone in his gray-blue eyes, the craggy lines on his weathered face were as genial as a bloodhound's, and even the trenchcoat and fedora seemed a charmingly quaint throwback to the bygone era when a gentleman still dressed up.

"Because, doctor, he's married and it would be wrong."

"What's wrong is that you're saving yourself for the other, like a virgin for her wedding night."

It was impossible to take offense at his avuncular teasing. "No, I'm not. I swear I'm not."

"Honey, you're just afraid of the new. That's normal," he sympathized. "But you'll never be free of the past unless you commit to the present." He leaned closer, folding his hands atop his tidy desk. An old-fashioned wedding band, platinum with an intricate pattern of interlocking grapevines, graced his left ring finger.

"What a pretty ring," she said.

He winked. "Ginny chose it, of course. We men have no taste."

"I still love the cheap one Tim bought me in Vegas."

"That's the problem. You're less concerned about betraying Billy's marriage than about betraying your own. He already betrayed it, Maggie, not only with Big Ed but with a little tramp named Crystal Methamphetamine. It's time to move on."

He was still smiling paternally at her, but now his face was starting to peel off like onion skin, layer by layer, until all that remained was not a skeleton but blackening, burnt-orange pulp like the rotting insides of a jack o'lantern.

Maggie woke, trembling yet still a little drunk. Even as she strained her senses for waking echoes and images, the vivid dream was rapidly dissipating into only a vague unease. Within moments she remembered little more than that the old man had been talking to her about something, and that he'd actually been rather pleasant. She had no recollection of what had frightened her awake.

With Kat away for the night, Thumper snored lightly at the foot of the bed, undisturbed. Soon she drifted back to sleep, and dreamed benignly and erotically of Billy.

She called Darlene Zarlengo the next day. "I'm ready for you to do the ritual."

"That's great," replied the now-familiar, no-nonsense voice. "Your place is all cleaned and everything?"

"Yes. I'm going to get the holy water and sage smudge stick today. I already have an abalone shell."

"When's a good day for you to do it? I'm guessing you want to make sure your little girl's not at home."

Maggie was a bit flustered. She'd assumed the ritual had to be performed at night, and during a particular phase of the moon. "You mean, any time is all right?"

"Well, I'm kind of booked for the early part of next week. How does Wednesday morning sound?"

"Fine. Could I ask a friend to be here too?" She hoped that Ryan could get the morning off.

"Only if he or she is open-minded," Darlene cautioned.

At last the woman was acknowledging the arcane nature of the business at hand. "Of course," Maggie said.

"Bad vibes can really derail a ritual. The person doesn't have to believe, per se, but it shouldn't be someone who's going to be biting back laughter the whole time."

Maggie wasn't sure she could promise the same for herself. Sincere though she was in her hope that Darlene could rid the house of its disturbances, a part of her was still reeling at the absurdity of the situation.

So, too, was Ryan, evidently, for he declined her invitation to attend. "Maggie, I know I'll laugh, and then you'll be stuck with your ghost forever. I always laugh at solemn occasions – weddings, funerals, you name it."

"Tim's that way too. Or was."

"Besides, didn't you say Billy's the one who hooked you up with this Darlene woman? Why not ask him?"

"Yes, but ... " Asking Billy seemed somehow inappropriately intimate, akin to asking him to be her date at a wedding.

"Do you have to have someone else there, or is it more for moral support?"

"Don't underestimate moral support," she said wryly. "I'll think about asking Billy."

To her mild surprise, Billy volunteered to be with her for the ritual without her needing to ask. "I think it'll be interesting to watch," he said, sponging suds over a patient Warlock in the stable's wash rack. Others were bathing their horses as well, taking advantage of the unexpected Santa Ana weather – hot, clear, and drier than dust – that had swept overnight into Southern California.

To Maggie, the sudden heat wave compounded the surreality of the impending ritual, now just two days away. But she was more certain than ever of its necessity. For the last two nights she had slept well, but Kat, uncharacteristically, had been disturbed by nightmares – nightmares about her daddy. Unable either to recall or to articulate the precise nature of the dreamt horror that had befallen Tim, Kat bravely brushed away tears but insisted on sleeping with Maggie for the remainder of each night.

Kat's night terrors also doubled Maggie's resolve to keep her daughter out of the house for as long as possible Wednesday. Darlene speculated that the banishing ritual would not take more than an hour or so, but the scent of burning sage might linger, and Maggie wanted to air out the house. While it seemed unlikely that Kat would infer witchcraft from a strange smell, Maggie wanted the house completely returned to normalcy by nightfall.

Taylor's mother Claire didn't hesitate when Maggie asked if Kat might spend the after-school hours at her friend's house. "I have an appointment with my OB/GYN for a checkup, and Wednesday at 3:30 was the only time I could get." Maggie figured that Claire would probably suspect a salacious reason for the supposed appointment, but that would make the fiction all the more credible.

"I know how that goes. We'll look for you between five and six."

It was a good thing, too, that she had allowed herself a lot of leeway with time. Darlene Zarlengo, due at nine a.m., didn't show up until closer to ten Wednesday morning. "Sorry I'm running late," she said to Maggie and Billy. "It's this goddamn heat wave. I think half the county's playing hooky and heading to the beach." She was dressed as before in an innocuous, oversized black tunic, leggings, and short boots, hugging her expensive tote bag.

"I put the dog outside and the phone off the hook," Maggie said, clasping and unclasping her hands nervously.

Darlene took a quick glance around the living room. "This house is definitely haunted," she declared.

"Well, that's why you're here, right?" Billy rejoined. Maggie shot him a look.

But Darlene didn't pay his remark any especial note. "Where can I set up an altar? Do you have a dining room table?"

Her demeanor brought to mind a Mary Kay sales rep. Maggie escorted her to the dining room.

From her bag Darlene removed a box of long matches, a thick white decorator candle, and a jewel-studded silver ornamental dagger. "You have the smudge stick and abalone shell?"

Maggie gestured to the items on the buffet. "I sprinkled the holy water all over the house this morning, going from left to right like you said."

"Why left to right?" Billy asked.

"For white magic," Darlene said. "Trust me, you don't want to screw up and go the other way."

"What do you need us to do, or not do?" Maggie asked.

"OK, after I draw the pentagram and the circle, I need to light the smudge stick and walk around the house. You guys have to sit her quietly – no talking or whispering – and keep your eyes on this candle's flame. Try to concentrate on the flame, but if your mind wanders, don't worry about it. Just do your best not to look away, and definitely don't talk." She struck one of the long matches and carefully lit the candle. "You might want to get a plate or something so the wax doesn't drip on your table. It's supposed to be a dripless candle, but the last one I bought was a piece of crap."

Maggie found an old Corningware plate, which probably dated back to her college, second-hand days, and placed the lit candle on it.

"Let's get started, then," Darlene said. "Thank God you have air conditioning. We'd all be sweltering."

Maggie and Billy took seats opposite each other at the table, but Darlene remained standing. Facing east, toward the kitchen, she took up the dagger with one elegant hand. She seemed to make a sign of the cross with it, uttering strange words –

"Hertha … Cernunnos … Azarak … Amelak" – as she lightly touched the point to her brow, her abdomen, right, then left shoulder. "So mote it be."

Next, she slowly drew in the air the recognizable shape of a five-pointed star, again intoning strange words: "Herne … Aradia … Cernunnos … Habondia."

Her "drawing" of a circle was a similar ritual, although this time the names she invoked were somewhat more familiar-sounding. Adonai, Michael, Gabriel, Uriel. This was followed by a repeat of the sign of the cross ceremony with which she had begun. Riveted, Maggie was taken aback when Darlene set down the dagger and addressed them in her usual matter-of-fact manner. "I'm going to light the smudge stick now, so you've got to be quiet until I come back into this room. If the candle blows out, just relight it."

Focusing on the candle was harder than Maggie had anticipated. She heard Darlene moving about the house, heading up the stairs, walking around the second floor. No incantations this time. The smoldering sage had a strong, woody fragrance; as soon as the ritual was over, she'd need to throw open every window in the house. Billy, across from her, watched the flame but bore a distant expression as if he was thinking about things completely unrelated to the house, the ritual, herself.

She could not gauge how much time had elapsed when she heard Darlene come down the stairs, open the front door, close it a few moments later. Presently she returned to the dining room, holding the abalone shell now lightly dusted with ashes. "Maggie, say a silent prayer and blow out the candle."

Just let everything be all right. Let my daughter be all right.

"OK, we're done," Darlene said. "I sprinkled a line of ashes across your doorstep and at the top of the stairs. Try not to sweep or vacuum for a week."

"What about the dog?" Billy asked, suddenly looking very relieved.

"Don't worry about it. It's not like a sidewalk crack that you're not supposed to step on. Just don't get rid of the ashes for a week."

Maggie nodded. "Kat and I always come in through the kitchen. And that stairway is so dark I'm sure no one would even notice the ashes."

"Yeah, there's been a lot of spirit activity on and around those stairs, which is very common. Doorways, stairs, places of comings and goings. Sometimes entities get confused by them, literally not able to tell if they're entering or leaving."

The words evoked a naggingly familiar image. "Or stuck entering and leaving at the same time," Maggie said slowly, chilling as the image took on clarity in her mind – a tattooed image of Tiresius, the blind seer, doomed to walk the inferno facing the past.

And at that moment she knew that Tim was dead. Either his parents themselves didn't know it or else they were deliberately not telling her.

"Jesus Christ, Maggie, what's wrong?" Billy leaped up to help her back into a chair. It was only then she realized she'd been standing there swaying.

Darlene Zarlengo patted her shoulder. "It's OK, Maggie. What you're experiencing is probably your own sense of the entity's departure. It's a good sign."

"*Good* sign?" Billy challenged. "She's ice cold and the color of chalk!"

"No, no," Maggie said. "She's right, Billy. It's over. Finally over."

Darlene suggested Maggie have a glass of wine to calm her nerves. "That's ridiculous – it's not even noon," Maggie protested.

But Billy was already pouring some Chianti into a goblet. "Pretend you're in Italy."

"Call me any time if you have questions or experience any residual phenomena," Darlene said, wrapping the dagger in a velvet cloth and tucking it back into her bag. "I hate to run, but I have a hair appointment at one and as you know, I'm a little behind schedule today."

Maggie clasped her hand, fighting back tears. *Over.*

"Drink that wine," Darlene advised. "I can see myself out."

When she left Billy poured himself a glass. "That whole thing was … fucking bizarre. Let's hope it works."

Maggie sipped her wine. She couldn't bring herself to tell him of her sudden conviction that Tim was dead, or to hear her own voice saying as much. "I guess it was more draining than I expected it to be."

"I assume she doesn't guarantee her work?"

"No, but how's that any different from a priest or minister promising to save your soul?" Another two sips of wine; she was growing impatient for sedation. *My sweet darling Timmy.* "I wonder if the college professor who lived here was an alcoholic. I'm betting he was."

"'Cause this house drives people to it?"

"Think about it." Finally a tingle of relaxation in her bloodstream. "Tim spent time here as a kid, and grew up to be a drug addict. Judy Showalter was one, too. And – " She nodded at her wine glass. "Hit me again, amigo."

"You don't strike me as a raving drunk," he said, refilling her glass. "Take it from one with first-hand knowledge."

"Yeah, and you're drinking with me at eleven o'clock in the morning. I almost feel as if we're holding a two-person wake."

"Irish wake for sure," he said with a grim smile. "I suppose in a way we are. Maybe that old guy's been sent on his way to his reward, whatever that might be."

"'*Enfer ou ciel, q'importe?*'" she quoted. "I tried to do a Spanish translation of that poem my junior year. I made a holy mess of it. Not unlike my marriage."

"Hold on there. From everything you've told me, it wasn't you who did the messing up."

"I did my share of drugs the first couple years we were together. Not as often as he did, but I look back and it's so clear that he had a problem. I should've tried harder to get him to stop before he reached the point of no return. But then we would've both had to grow up, let go of the parties and the craziness that seemed so – damn it, still seems so innocent."

"Now it sounds like you're the one who doesn't know if she's coming or going. Don't do it, Maggie. Who thinks of the future at twenty-two years old? Or if you do, it's a future so completely different from the one that actually happens to you you're ashamed you were ever that dumb and naïve." He sat down in the chair next to her. "In the future everybody wins the lottery." His warm, callused hands folded over hers. "I gotta get to the barn."

"No, please don't go yet." She clutched the hands he had tried to ease away. "Please, not yet."

This time when they kissed, neither of them moved to break the embrace.

It should have felt alien, or at least awkward, sex with the first man other than Tim in twelve years. It should have felt like cheating. But welcoming him into her bed, into herself, she felt only the desire to be filled up with him. To be less bereft.

No ghosts in the bedroom with them. But when their bodies eventually parted she felt more alone than she ever had in her life.

"I wish you could stay." she murmured against his shoulder.

He stroked her hair. "Me too. But I better go."

"I'll come by the ranch tomorrow, after I drop Kat off," she said, watching him dress.

"Call tonight if you find yourself missing your ghost – or not."

They kissed goodbye. The moment she heard the front door close downstairs the sobs she'd been suppressing for hours burst through, convulsing her like death throes.

She was still struggling to compose herself hours later on the drive to Solana Beach to pick up Kat. Kat was sensitive and might well glean that something was amiss. Or was it amiss or just … different?

Her daughter's presence brought her back to the familiar. "I love you, sweetie," she said impulsively as Kat, still in her little Catholic school uniform, strapped into the Accord's passenger seat.

"What did the doctor say, Mommy?"

"I'm just fine. Did you get a snack at Taylor's or are you up for pizza?"

"Let's have Taco Bell!"

Maggie groaned good-naturedly. "Abuelo would never forgive us. Shall we go to Armando's so we can tell him how good it was?" In truth, she would have gladly gone to Taco Bell, but she wanted to delay going home for as long as possible, irrationally certain that Kat would know about her and Billy from the moment she stepped inside.

Being in one of Pa's restaurants felt safe and familiar too. Located in the University Towne Center area of malls and high-rise hotels and condos likely priced well out of the range of the college community the development ostensibly served, Armando's La Jolla boasted, like its brethren, standard Cal-Mex décor, with lots of dark woods, piñatas and ornamental sombreros, bright red tablecloths and napkins. Though she had gotten the enchiladas and chips for her fateful housewarming at the restaurant, she had yet to dine in at Pa's newest "baby."

Even on a Wednesday night the bar was three-deep in Happy Hour patrons, but Maggie and Kat were seated in the dining room immediately. It was still early, but she decided she would lie and tell Pa they'd had a twenty-minute wait to reassure him that business was flourishing. The young waitress, in her uniform of embroidered peasant blouse and flouncy red and green skirt, promptly brought them warm coarse tortilla chips and the chunky salsa fresca for which the chain was known.

"You seem sad, Mommy," Kat observed, reaching for a chip.

"I'm not, honey. Just a little tired. You gonna have tacos?"

"Tacquitos."

Though Maggie wasn't hungry, she was loath to further concern Kat, so she ordered a chicken quesadilla and forced herself to eat it. Kat saved half a tacquito for Thumper, taking pleasure in the literal use to which she put the doggie bag.

The impromptu outing eased Maggie's tension. Pulling into the garage, she refused to think, to reflect. It's going to be OK, she told herself sternly.

"Thumper!" Kat greeted the barking spaniel. "I brought you a treat." She reached into the paper bag for the cold tacquito.

"Here, sweetie, let me chop it into a few pieces." She switched on the kitchen light, illuminating a reassuring sameness. Getting away from the house for a couple of hours had been a good idea.

With Kat eyeballing him in satisfaction, Thumper gobbled up the pieces of fried tortilla and shredded beef. Maggie could still smell a faint burnt aroma, but Kat appeared not to notice.

She helped Kat complete some homework started earlier with Taylor, led her upstairs for a bath. The sage odor was stronger on the stairs, and Kat's button nose wrinkled. "It's stinky up here."

"It's from the air conditioning. It'll be gone by tomorrow." Maggie vowed to respray the stairs with Glade before retiring for the night.

Turning down Kat's comforter and blanket, she couldn't deny that the overwhelming panic and grief of a few hours before was receding as surely as most of the burnt sage scent. The sudden intuition that Tim was dead now seemed irrational and remote. And her guilt over sleeping with Billy was giving way to a kind of excited uncertainty, a throbbing *what happens now?* sensation teasing her consciousness. It was a feeling she had long forgotten.

She tucked Kat in, kissed her goodnight, and headed into the study to check her e-mail. Just as she clicked on the AOL mail icon she was startled by Kat's scream of mortal terror.

Kat was still screaming when Maggie burst into her room. Kat clutched the kaleidoscope, shrieking and sobbing. "He's gone! He's gone!" Her anguished face was the color of butcher paper. Thumper whined frantically at her feet.

Maggie wrapped Kat in her arms. "What is it, baby? A nightmare?"

Kat kept screaming. "We have to find him! Hurry, hurry, Mommy!"

Her child's hysteria shattered her. "Katya, baby, it's OK. It's OK." She rocked Kat back and forth in her arms.

"No!" Kat cried, her slight frame wracked with sobs. She still clasped the kaleidoscope. "He went away!"

"Who, sweetie?" Something cold was creeping into her veins.

"The little lost boy!" Kat's tears were finally ebbing, replaced by heaving so convulsive Maggie feared she might hyperventilate. "We have to find him."

"We will, muchacha, I promise." She was considering an emergency call to Kat's pediatrician. "Tell me about the little lost boy, Kat."

Kat shook her head violently. "He said not to."

Maggie chilled, realizing that Kat had been far more aware of the house's paranormal phenomena than she'd ever suspected. "But sweetie, I can't find him if you don't tell me who he is," she attempted to soothe.

The distraught child seemed to accept her reasoning. "We have to find him, Mommy," she hiccupped.

"We will. But tell me about him, so we can start looking."

"I see him in here," Kat said, holding up the kaleidoscope. "He visits and we talk."

It was all Maggie could do to mask her horror. "Who is he, honey?"

"He's hiding from the mean old man. If the mean old man catches him he hits him hard." Kat's heaving breaths were settling into a light panting.

Oh my God, there are two. Or were. Maggie prayed the ritual had driven out both of them. "Kat, maybe if the little boy is gone, it's because he's found a new, better home where the old man can never get to him."

"No!" Kat insisted with renewed passion, tears streaming again from her swollen eyes. "No, Mommy! He needs to be with Daddy!"

"Sweetie, you're not making any sense – "

"Find the little lost boy, Mommy! *Find Daddy!*"

To her undying gratitude, Dr. Bowerman was possibly the last physician in the county – maybe even in the state – willing to make emergency house calls. He had come to them highly recommended by Kat's pediatrician in LA. "I just can't seem to calm her down," Maggie said to him upon his arrival. She'd brought Kat downstairs with her down comforter and bundled her up on the sofa. All she'd told Dr. Bowerman on the phone was that Kat had suffered a shock and was hysterical.

"Hi Kat," Dr. Bowerman greeted Kat in a pleasant, nothing's-out-of-the-ordinary tone. Clad in jeans and a University of Kansas sweatshirt, he was slim and boyish looking, with light brown hair and kind blue eyes.

He sat down beside Kat and proceeded to take her temperature and measure her heart rate. "Her pulse is really racing," he said. "No fever, though."

Kat tossed desperate looks at her mother. "We have to find him, Mommy!"

"We will, sweetie," Maggie repeated, caressing her daughter's curls.

"I'm going to give her a mild sedative," Dr. Bowerman said, reaching into his medical bag. "She'll sleep through the night. Call me in the morning to let me know how she's doing, and we'll take it from there."

He administered the injection, and in moments, Kat was asleep. "I'm going to sleep with her tonight," Maggie said, readjusting the comforter around Kat's shoulders. *We'll have to sleep in her bed because I didn't have time to change my sheets. Oh God.* "I can't thank you enough for coming, Doctor."

"What gave her such a scare?" he asked gently.

The truth was likely to convince the doctor that the mother, not child, was crazy, but she couldn't risk holding back with her daughter's well-being at stake. "You're probably going to think I'm nuts, but weird things have happened in this house. Unexplainable things."

The pediatrician tilted his head, but his expression betrayed no judgment. "Really? What sort of things?"

"Paranormal things. I'm not talking about *Poltergeist*-like bells and whistles – it's more like impressions of some kind of presence." *Or presences?* "I've been aware of them almost since the day we moved in, but I was positive that Kat was oblivious to them until tonight."

"Kids are a lot more perceptive than they sometimes let on." He regarded Kat thoughtfully. "She probably picked up on your anxiety. Whether or not she saw a ghost, she may believe she did, and that could account for the acute anxiety episode."

Maggie supposed it would be irrelevant to clarify that it was the ghost Kat *didn't* see that had sent her into hysterics. "What do we do, Doctor, if she wakes up and she's still this agitated?"

"Let's cross that bridge when we come to it. Usually these episodes are transient. She's never had a reaction like this before?"

"No, though she's certainly witnessed her share of upheaval. Her father and I had a very difficult relationship."

Dr. Bowerman looked concerned. "Domestic violence?"

"Oh, no, never. We just fought verbally a lot, and he had – has – a drug problem, so his presence in Kat's life has been pretty erratic." Her lower lip trembled. "I know it's been harder on her than she lets me see. She adores him."

"Counseling might be helpful for her. I can recommend a first-rate child psychologist just down the 5 in the Golden Triangle."

Maggie nodded. She realized she probably should have put Kat in therapy long ago.

Dr. Bowerman patted her arm. "I'll give you her name and number when you call me tomorrow morning."

She saw the pediatrician to the door, then swept Kat up and carried her upstairs into her own bedroom. Kat's breathing was regular and her skin warm. Maggie eased her between the covers. Thumper jumped up on the bed to snuggle with Kat. "You better be prepared to make room for me," Maggie whispered to the spaniel. It would be a tight squeeze in Kat's twin bed, but on this night, she couldn't hold her daughter close enough.

She kissed Kat's cheek. Rather than leave her alone for even a minute, Maggie stepped out of her jeans and undid her bra, deciding to sleep in her T-shirt and panties. She was about to slip into bed next to Kat when she spied the kaleidoscope on the pillow.

Irresistibly she picked it up and, squinting one eye, peered inside with the other.

The old man's face, craggy and malignant, glowered back at her. The visage outlined in the trees above Tim's graduation was lucid, vicious – and animate.

Hurling away the kaleidoscope, she clamped both hands over her mouth to stifle a scream.

Unlike the little lost boy, he hadn't been driven out at all.

Not long after dawn Kat's eyelashes began to flutter. Maggie tried to comfort her back to sleep. She had slept little herself. She'd made up her mind that they would not spend another night in this house. Once she could be reasonably sure that Kat was all right, she'd attempt to figure out their long-term plans. In the interim, she would drive them up to Newport and her parents' home this morning, so long as Kat felt well enough to endure the hour-long drive.

"Mommy?"

Maggie cuddled her against the pillows. "I'm right here, sweetie."

"We have to find the little lost boy."

The statement seemed all the more urgent for the drowsy gravity of Kat's tone. The little girl sat up in bed and looked at Maggie directly, albeit under heavy lids. "Mommy, you have to find Daddy."

Maggie entwined her fingers in Kat's. "Is that how we'll find the little lost boy?"

Kat nodded somberly. "He has to be with Daddy."

Maggie got it, though she prayed Kat did not. The little lost boy *was* Daddy. It was whatever part of Tim he had left behind in this house, terrorized by the old man's cruelty. The part of Tim so brutalized it had broken off from him like a rotting limb, leaving him forever psychically maimed and unfinished. And she had driven away the child-Tim but not his tormenter, driven him away as much through her physical union with Billy as through Darlene Zarlengo's banishing ritual.

She was sure of it.

"I'll find Daddy," she told Kat, pulling her close and kissing the crown of her head. Perhaps telling Tim of this, explaining the connection to him, would heal him at last. At the very least, she hoped that finding him would heal their daughter.

"*When*, Mommy?"

"As soon as I can, Kat. I need to make some calls, then we're going up to Abuelo and Lita's. Are you up for that?"

"OK. But then you have to go find Daddy."

"I need to get my phone so I can call Dr. Bowerman, so you and Thumper stay snuggled here until I get back." A thought came to her. "I have some books and a baseball mitt that were Daddy's, probably when he was about your age." She could no longer doubt they were his, or that she had been deliberately directed to them. Had the shushing sound come from the strange child entity?

"Can I see them?"

"Yes, I'll bring them back with the phone. Sit tight, sweetie."

In her bedroom she grabbed her cellphone and opened the closet to retrieve the

books and glove, which she placed in Kat's hands. "Here they are."

"Cool," Kat breathed, inspecting the mitt.

Keeping an eye on her, Maggie called Dr. Bowerman at his office. She was

surprised he answered; it was not yet seven. "Kat has calmed down, though she's still

bothered by her experience," Maggie said in a low voice. "I'm going to keep her home

from school for the rest of the week."

"Good. Let me give you Dr. Rehberger's number. Got a pencil?"

She located a Magic Marker and jotted the information down on the inside cover

of a coloring book. She'd call for an appointment later today.

"I'm going to phone in a prescription for Valium for her at the lowest dosage, just

in case the agitation returns," Dr. Bowerman said. "Give her half a tablet if she needs it.

Is the Longs Drugs by your house OK?"

"That's perfect." They could pick up the prescription on the way to Orange

County.

Kat, the mitt in her lap, was leafing through *The Marshmallow Ghosts*, a slight

smile curving her lips. "The little boy told me about this story."

Tim. Maggie was relieved that Kat had not made the connection. "It's a really

good story. Why don't you bring it downstairs while I make us some breakfast?"

"I'm not hungry."

"I know, but let's see if we can eat some cereal. The sooner we finish breakfast, the sooner we can get on the road."

"What if it's hard to find Daddy?" Kat fretted.

"Well, I'll just keep looking until I do." Her mind was already gnawing at the challenge. The last time she'd seen him, he said he was living in his car. But his mother had said, however dismissively, that he tended to stay in touch with his older sister Diana. As soon as she had Kat settled in with her parents, she would begin her search with a call to Diana.

After breakfast, she skipped a shower and quickly packed their overnight bags. They put Thumper in the side yard long enough for him to do his business. Five minutes later they were piled into the Accord and backing out of the driveway. Maggie cast one last, wary look at the house as she shifted into drive.

CHAPTER 8

Just over the Orange County line, where a light coastal fog indicated that the hot Santa Ana was over, her cellphone rang. Billy. "Hey, I was thinking about stopping by on the way to the barn."

"I'm on my way to my parents' place," she replied carefully. Next to her, Kat looked worried and preoccupied. "Something's come up."

"Shit. Does it have to do with the house?"

"You bet. Can I call you back later? I don't like to talk on the phone while I drive."

"So you're the one. OK. Call me later. Take care of yourself, Maggie."

She dropped the phone back into her purse. "That was Billy," she said to Kat. "He just wanted to say hi."

"Maybe he can help you find Daddy."

Maggie tried not to wince. She could hardly explain to Kat why that wasn't such a hot suggestion. Everything about Billy – her attraction, her confusion, her guilt – had to be held in suspension, like a film image frozen by the "pause" mechanism.

She hadn't called ahead because she didn't want to explain to her mother or father in Kat's presence the reasons for the unscheduled visit. The security guard at the affluent gated community above Newport Harbor recognized her and waved her into the complex. She hoped her parents were at home, but if not, she still had a house key on her ring from last summer.

As it turned out, they were just finishing breakfast. "What a surprise!" her father boomed, hugging first Kat and then Maggie. "How come you aren't in school, chiquita?"

"Mommy and I have to find Daddy," Kat replied gravely.

Seeing her father darken and her mother frown, Maggie interjected. "Don't you two go flying off the handle. I promised Kat I'd go find Tim, and she and Thumper are going to stay here until I do."

Her mother caught her ominous look, but Armando still looked to be on the verge of an eruption. "Tranquilo, tranquilo," Eva tried to calm him.

"Pa, will you take Kat and Thumper into the family room and find something good for them to watch on TV?" The Floreses had a state-of-the-art home entertainment center, including a huge plasma-screen TV that always fascinated Kat.

"Mommy, you have to go find Daddy," Kat said nervously, even as her grandfather, a compact yet sturdily built man of sixty-two, swung her up in his arms.

"I will, sweetie. I'm just going to visit with 'Lita for a few minutes, and then I'll get back in the car and go to LA to look for Daddy."

Kat didn't look especially appeased, but she meekly allowed her grandfather to carry her toward the family room.

Maggie followed her mother into the large, airy kitchen with its granite countertops, sparkling stainless steel appliances, and travertine floors. "Bless you, you have fresh coffee," she said, pouring herself a cup from the machine's carafe.

"Magdalena, what on earth is going on?"

"Mama, don't give all the details to Pa, but our house in Del Mar is haunted."

Eva's expression registered a blend of concern and grim recognition. "I knew it. I could tell the day I brought Katya down that something felt wrong. Of course, I didn't want to tell you about it."

At least there was no chance her mother would think her declaration lunatic, Maggie thought ironically. "Kat believes a spirit there wants me to find Tim, and she won't rest until I do."

"Oh no, me hija. It might be a devil trying to mislead you into doing something terrible!"

"Mama, she's completely distraught over this. I even had the doctor come out last night. What choice do I have?"

"La pobrecita," Eva clucked. "I hope you're not going back to that house."

Maggie was caught off-guard, so sure had she been that her mother was going to say "going back to *Tim*." Well, in either case, her answer was the same. "Of course not. As soon as I've found Tim, and he can reassure Kat that he's all right, I'm going to take an apartment in Del Mar so she can stay in school and riding lessons. I may need help

from you and Pa, Mama – security deposits and all – until we can get the house leased

out."

"You don't need to ask, Maggie. We wish you'd let us do more." Her mother lay

a smooth, ringed hand on her cheek.

She glanced at her watch. "I'd better hit the road. Kat will get upset if I linger.

Try to keep her distracted, Mama – take her to a movie, or to the park with Thumper."

"You know I will."

She took a last gulp of coffee. "I'll call to check on her in a few hours."

"Be careful, mi niña. Some of Tim's friends are … not the best."

"You don't have to tell me. But I'm going to contact his sister and see if she can

put me in touch with him without having to scour every drug den in LA County."

Her mother walked her to her car. "I'll tell Papa that Kat just had a very bad

dream and wants to see her daddy."

"Good. If you start talking ghosts he'll disown both you and me."

Supernaturalism, like speaking Spanish at home, belonged in the barrio, according to

Armando.

They hugged goodbye. Maggie set off again on the 405 north.

Out of habit, she took the Rosecrans exit for Manhattan Beach. She knew there

was a Starbucks in the Bed Bath & Beyond shopping center just west of the freeway

where she could grab another coffee and call Tim's dad for Diana's number. She would

have preferred to call Diana directly, but couldn't recall if Tim's sister had taken her

husband's surname.

She really needed the extra coffee, too, for after virtually no sleep and almost two hours on the road, she was feeling borderline punchy. She purchased a tall coffee, used the Starbucks restroom, and returned to the car to call Jack Emerson's office. "Jack, this is Maggie. I need to contact Tim. Could I possibly have Diana's number?"

"I suppose she'd know if anyone would," he replied with a hint of impatience. "I'll give you her home number. She's still on maternity leave."

"She had a baby?" Leave it to Tim's parents not to inform her that Kat had a new cousin.

"A beautiful boy, born three weeks ago yesterday." The words suggested pride but his tone was as clinical as if he'd been referring to a patient.

"That's wonderful. Congratulations."

"How is Katya?"

"She's OK," Maggie lied.

She dialed the number he gave her the moment Jack hung up. A woman answered. "Diana?"

"Yes?"

"This is Maggie, Tim's ex-wife."

"Maggie!" Diana sounded relieved. "Is he with you?"

Maggie chilled. Diana didn't know where he was, either. "No, but I really need to find him. Your parents have said he kept in touch with you."

Pause. "Are you in Del Mar?"

"No, I'm actually here in LA. Diana, it's extremely important that I find Tim."

"Oh God, is Kat sick?"

"Physically she's fine. But she's desperate to see Tim. It's a complicated story."

"So is mine," Diana said with a dry laugh. "Maggie, can you come over? I'd feel better talking face to face. And there's something I want to give you. It might help us find Tim."

Maggie's hopes revived. "Absolutely."

Diana directed her to an address on North Vermont, in Los Feliz, "just down the hill from Griffith Park." Maggie knew the area; she'd gone to several rock concerts with Tim at the Greek Theater. Los Feliz was woodsy and old-money, close enough to Hollywood but traditional rather than glitzy. Diana and her husband, both physicians, no doubt fit in well.

But Los Feliz was also clear across town, and the web of freeways that would take her there from Manhattan Beach were invariably congested, even at 11 a.m. Maggie feared the trip would take at least an hour. Diana's cryptic reference to "something I want to give you" stirred both her curiosity and dread.

No surprises; the traffic was dense, at times slowing to a crawl on the Harbor Freeway, stopping intermittently on the 5 north. She almost wept with relief when she finally approached the Los Feliz Boulevard off-ramp.

A couple of miles north of blocks of marginally rundown stucco apartment buildings, gas stations, a grocery store or two, Vermont Avenue turned green enough to merit its eponym. It became a street of thick shade trees and large but not ostentatious two-story homes. Diana's was a traditional white clapboard colonial with dark green shutters and eaves. A black BMW sedan was parked in the driveway in front of a detached garage with an upstairs "granny" unit.

Maggie pulled up behind the BMW and hurried to the door. She hadn't seen Diana in several years but recognized her at once. Diana had changed little, and even postpartum she seemed to have regained the slender, athletic figure Maggie recalled. Diana had played competitive tennis and volleyball at USC, her father's alma mater; like Tim, she was tall, and her honey-colored hair was virtually the same hue as Kat's. "Come on in," Diana said after a brief hug. "Was the traffic a nightmare?"

The entry was old-fashioned and welcoming, with dark hardwood floors and a carpeted, sweeping staircase, open and with banisters, that contrasted with its dreary Del Mar counterpart. "The traffic was bad, but I'm so glad to be here. And congratulations – your dad told me about the baby."

Diana's drawn expression gave way to a broad smile. "Thanks. Kat has a cousin now. His name is Brandon Timothy."

Tears sprang to Maggie's eyes. "I'd love to see him."

"God, Maggie, don't start crying or you'll get me going too," Diana said, voice trembling. "He's down for his nap, but I'll introduce you as soon as he's up. Come on into the family room. Or I guess we call them 'great rooms' now."

Touching her elbow, Diana led Maggie down the central hall to the back of the house, into a spacious, oak-paneled room with plush boxy chairs, a deep green overstuffed sofa, a spinet piano, and brick hearth whose mantle was adorned with framed photographs. "Have a seat. Can I get you something to drink?"

"No, thanks. Your home is beautiful."

Diana grabbed a bottled water from the coffee table. "Thank the nice folks at Ethan Allen. Wes and I just told them what we didn't want, and they took it from there." She sat down next to Maggie on the sofa.

Maggie could hold back no longer. "Diana, when was the last time you saw Tim?"

The tautness returned to Diana's face. "Four days ago. Maggie, he's been in rehab since mid-August. But the night before last, he just left. Walked out, didn't tell anyone why he was leaving or where he was going." Now tears spilled down her cheeks. "He was doing so well. It was like having my baby brother again, for the first time in years."

Maggie was stunned. She squeezed Diana's hand. "Nearly three months in rehab? Of his own free will?"

Diana swiped at her tears. "Just about. Once he realized you'd left your place and changed your number, he was beside himself. The meth fed into his obsession. 'Where are they?' Pretty much 24/7, at least when he wasn't off buying drugs."

The obsessiveness Diana described was unnervingly reminiscent of Kat's insistent "We have to find him, Mommy."

"My folks would've thought me downright insane," Diana went on, "but I let him stay here, in the in-law apartment above our garage. He had nowhere to go, and I was afraid he'd end up back in jail, or worse. I had one rule – no drug dealers on the property."

"That was so generous of you," Maggie said softly. "So very kind."

"I'm his sister. And I'm a doctor – I help sick people. My dad obviously has a different conception of the Hippocratic oath when it comes to Tim." She sighed. "Tim was really sick. He was going into methamphetamine psychosis. He thought the CIA had kidnapped you and Kat because you don't like Bush. He thought they were monitoring his calls. The whole paranoid shebang."

Maggie's very being ached. "How in God's name did you get him into rehab?" For surely it had been Diana. How she regretted not staying in touch with her former sister-in-law. Maybe their combined efforts could have helped Tim sooner.

"You helped, too, without knowing it. I had no idea my grandmother had left the Del Mar house to Kat, or that you guys had moved down there. But one night, Wes and I were having dinner with my parents, and Mother let it slip. Dad was going to San Diego for a conference and she said something like, 'why don't you check in on Maggie and Katya when you're down there?' My dad was so irritated. Mother was wringing her hands. Moments like that remind me of why I'm a feminist."

"I know. When my mother defers to my father I want to scream."

"Ah, the old 'defer to dad.' Sometimes I think that's the entire root of my family's problems." Diana exhaled. "Anyway, Dad told me in no uncertain terms not to breathe a word about your whereabouts to Tim. He said you wanted it that way, and I believed him. I understood. I'd already made up my mind that Tim would have to go once Brandon was born. You just can't take chances when you have a child."

Maggie nodded. "But you got him into rehab before the baby came."

"Mother's slip-up gave me an idea. When Wes and I got home that night, I went out to the garage and told Tim I'd found out exactly where you and Kat were. And that

I'd tell him only if he completed six months as an inpatient in rehab. I'd foot the bill. I was hoping that an extended treatment program would be more effective than the compulsory 28-day stints he'd done before. That's barely time enough to detox."

Maggie was moved and amazed. "And he went. You're an angel, Diana."

"No – if you and Kat hadn't disappeared, he'd have had no incentive. I just seized the opportunity. I drove him to this place in the Valley that's got a great reputation. I've known some doctors with pill problems who've gone there to get clean. It was going so damn well, Maggie. By the second month he was starting to look – and sound – human again. He was so determined to see it through."

Something puzzled Maggie. "If you drove him there, how could he have left?"

"I have no clue. Walked. Caught a bus. Called someone to come get him. I've been praying that he somehow found out where you and Kat were and went down there."

"You didn't tell him?"

Diana shook her head firmly. "No. I wasn't going to until he'd been there six months. And of course, my folks never even knew he was there. Tim insisted on that."

The hope that had fluttered within Maggie's chest upon hearing of his seeming progress evaporated. It was impossible not to conclude that he had fled rehab in order to relapse. No doubt he'd hate himself all the more for having gone nearly three months clean, only to surrender once again. "Maybe he'll come back here, Diana. You took him in before."

"I hope so, but for the last few weeks he kept insisting that he wasn't going to let me down. I told him that his getting well had nothing to do with me, but he carries such a burden of guilt. It breaks my heart." She took a deep breath. "I never realized until yesterday how much guilt and pain he's been masking with the drugs. And damn it! I should have realized."

"Yesterday? But you said he left rehab two nights ago."

Diana got up, strode into the adjacent dining room, returning with a spiral notebook. "This is the thing I mentioned on the phone. It's Tim's rehab journal, with the draft of the personal statement every patient has to present in front of the group. They gave it to me yesterday when I went out to collect his stuff and ask the staff if they had any inkling where he'd gone. I started reading it, and Maggie, I couldn't finish beyond his childhood. Did he ever tell you how my grandfather used to beat him?"

Maggie felt the color drain from her face. "No, never. But I figured it out through the house. So did Kat. I'll explain that later – let me see the journal."

Diana still held onto the notebook, stroking its cover absently. "I was Granddad's favorite. He treated me like a little princess. But he seemed to relish what he called 'beating the crap' out of Tim. And my dad deferred to his dad, and my mother did nothing – Shit." Her eyes were streaming again.

Maggie had a thought. "Do you have a picture of your grandfather, by any chance?"

"Ugh, these postpartum hormones," Diana groaned.

"Oh yes, I remember."

Diana strode over to the mantle and picked up a framed 5x8 picture. "Here we are, three generations of Emersons. One big dysfunctional family." She handed the picture to Maggie.

It was the old man, all right, genial and smiling as he'd been in that almost-forgotten dream, standing alongside a mild-looking older woman, a much younger Jack and Beth Emerson, in front of them a teenage Diana and perhaps ten-year-old Tim. But it was Tim who made her gasp. A beautiful child with taffy-colored curls, wearing a little Dodger uniform with a number 34 on the jersey – it was the little boy who had come trick or treating on Halloween night, just like the ghosts in the children's book.

"What?" Diana cried.

Maggie couldn't speak. She simply lifted the picture to her lips and kissed Tim's image.

And the details of that dream, with the old man as psychologist and advising her to forget Tim, came rushing back to her as well. Her voice returned to her. "Was your grandmother's name Ginny?"

"Yes, it was Virginia. You probably saw it on the house's title."

Diana was likely correct; nothing paranormal there. "OK ... did your grandfather wear an unusual wedding band, platinum with grapevines or something?"

Now Diana appeared startled. "I'd forgotten that. Yeah, they both had wedding bands like that. Antique filigree. I imagine they were buried in them. Jeez, how did you know that?"

"I dreamed it," Maggie said flatly. "I dreamed all sorts of things in that house."

"Good lord, Maggie. How horrible."

"I'll tell you more – there's so much more. But let me read Tim's journal first."

Diana placed the notebook in her hands. "It's really long. But it explains a lot. And maybe you'll find some clue as to where he's gone. I'm going to run upstairs and check on Brandon. Shall I put on some coffee? You look exhausted."

Indeed, Maggie was so tired that her entire body felt leaden, but her brain snapped into hyper-alertness as she flipped open the notebook. Paperclipped to the inside cover was a Polaroid snapshot of Tim probably taken the day he checked in. His hair was disheveled, almost reaching his shoulders, and his eyes and cheeks were so sunken his face seemed devoid of flesh. She chilled; it was obvious that he would have died had Diana not intervened with her "deal."

The first few pages seemed a jumble of fragmentary phrases and words, as if he had been taking notes from a lecture or discussion. *"Triggers – blah blah blah."* *"Retraining the brain."* *"Fucked up pleasure receptors???"* An occasional doodle – a sinewy cat, a stick-figure palm tree. Her eyes lingered on the scrawls, the familiarity of his hand, an almost arbitrary mix of block and lower-case letters, cursive and print.

She soon came to the first full page of apparently expository writing, with "PERSONAL DRUG HISTORY" printed in the upper margin. In the left margin he'd scribbled, between brackets, *"Too long – condense."* Hoping that he hadn't, she leafed ahead without reading the body of the text. It was indeed quite long. Here and there in the margins he'd scrawled other notes to himself to shorten or delete, but it didn't appear he'd blacked anything out.

She took a deep swallow of air as if to prepare for a plunge into a bottomless black lake.

* * *

TIM'S JOURNAL

I'm Tim, and I'm a drug addict. Crystal's my drug of choice, but I also use heroin, OxyContin (gross, the Rush Limbaugh drug), crack, X. I've pretty much done them all.

This is really hard for me, because I've had to do this three or four times before, at other rehabs and in prison group therapy. And all those other times, I was there only because I was forced to be and I lied and left a lot of major shit out. Dark shit that was nobody else's fucking business, not even my wife's – well, my then-wife. She and my daughter are major reasons why I want to get clean, why I want this time to be different. But even if they can't forgive me or let me try to make it up to them, I'm so tired of hiding in and from the darkness. To cop Jim Carroll's line from one of my favorite books, *The Basketball Diaries*, I want to be pure. And the only way I can be pure is to deal with all the ugly shit that has made me feel contaminated most of my life.

I was born 32 years ago, here in LA. My dad's a sports medicine doctor and my mom's a homemaker, totally of the "stand by your man" school. My sister Di is six years older than me, and she's a doctor too, an OB-GYN. Our parents, especially my dad, had extremely high expectations of us. He could be a real drill sergeant. He never hit us, but if we fucked up, it wasn't pretty. We'd lose whatever privileges kids usually have and get a hell of a blistering lecture. Diana and I both did well in school and in sports – like I said, it was expected of us. Diana didn't fuck up very often; she's always been calm and rational, even as a kid. I, on the other hand, fucked up a lot. Nothing major – I tended to mouth off, and in my teens I was careless about curfews, refused to go to Sunday Mass, and got caught coming home drunk a couple of times. All of this pissed my dad off

royally. I can only imagine how he'd have reacted if he'd found out that by the time I

was 16, I was smoking pot most weekends and occasionally did Ecstasy and acid.

By then, I was my high school's ace pitcher, and a couple of major league scouts

had come sniffing around. This thrilled my dad, and he was convinced I'd end up in the

majors after college. He obsessed over coaching me, which he did from Little League on.

I was a fastball pitcher, even then addicted to speed and to throwing as hard as I could.

My dad helped me develop a decent change-up and slider, not just to keep batters

guessing but so I wouldn't throw out my arm by the time I graduated from high school.

He even helped me with hitting. I think he'd have done the same thing if I'd ended up

playing tennis or soccer or basketball, the other sports I loved playing as a kid. But when

I was 10 I decided that I liked baseball the best, and Dad focused his energies on honing

my skills. He insisted I learn to pitch and hit as a lefty, though I'm naturally right-

handed. My dad knew that southpaws are a hotter commodity in the majors. He

designed an entire physical regimen for me, and by the time I was 12 I felt like I'd been

pitching with my left arm from the very start.

But I'm getting ahead of myself, probably on purpose. It's just so goddamn hard

to go back to that part of my childhood that looked and felt nothing like the fucking All-

American dream my family seemed to resemble from the outside.

I chose baseball for my sport, at 10, as I said, because I knew Little League would

put an end to those long summers spent at my grandparents' house down in Del Mar.

That was where we went for most of every summer from about the time I could walk.

Put plainly, my grandfather – my dad's father – used to beat the holy crap out of me whenever the urge struck him. I mean, not just over my typical fuckups but even if he

didn't like the expression on my face. And what really made him go ballistic was when

I'd run up and down the stairs instead of taking them one step at a time. He beat me with

his buckled belt, with their dog's choke chain, or with his bare fists. And nobody did

anything about it. Or even mentioned it. My grandmother was a kind-hearted person but

she was so deferential to her husband that she made my own mom seem like Gloria

Steinem by comparison. As for my dad, I don't know whether this was how his old man

treated him when he was a kid or if he secretly thought I deserved it, but he just allowed

it, and my mom followed his lead. Actually, Diana hated it, though he never hit her.

She begged him to stop but he ignored her, told her how good she was and that good little

children never were struck. She worked in vain, to try to help me find ways to forestall if

not escape the old man's anger. Until I got too big she'd lift me up into this crawlspace

under the stairs where he couldn't find me.

I remember him beating me so hard that I'd throw up, and get beaten again for

that. I remember the lies I'd tell my summer friends in Del Mar about bruises on my

arms, sometimes on my face. I remember how difficult it was not to cry, but I knew if I

cried he'd somehow have "won." I don't know why it didn't occur to me that the

beatings themselves were already proof he'd won, though I did wonder what would

happen to him if he tried this shit once I was big enough to fight back. I'm glad I never

found out, because I'm fairly certain to this day I would have killed him.

Little League intervened, along with Diana's summer job, and we quit going to

Del Mar. We still saw them at Christmas, but at my parents' home the house rules were

different, and my grandfather never so much as raised his voice to me. He died of a stroke when I was 22. I didn't feel anything at all, not even relief. I'd long since put him out of my mind and I didn't even mention his death to my wife, for fear she'd start asking me about what he was like. Needless to say, I skipped the funeral.

My grandmother moved into a retirement community; I have no idea whatever happened to their house. All I knew was that I'd never have to see that old motherfucker or step inside that dark house again.

But back then, I felt my real liberation had come well before his death, when I left home for college, even if it was only across town. I'd won a baseball scholarship to UCLA. The pro scouts were now talking to me in earnest, but I never entertained the notion of going from high school right into the minors. With my dad a doctor and my mother an honors graduate in art history from Mount St. Mary's, there'd never been any question about Di and me going to college. And I wanted to. I liked school, liked learning. And I wasn't about to miss out on another few years of getting high and meeting and fucking hot babes. I was something of a horndog in those days. I dated cheerleaders, surfer chicks, prom queen-types in high school, never staying with any one girl for long. Give up more of that for A-ball in the middle of nowhere? No way.

My first two years at UCLA went by fast – a whirl of baseball, partying, and screwing. I pitched a no-hitter my sophomore year and was named to the All-Pac-10 team; I maintained a 3.9 GPA; and while I'd yet to have my first taste of crystal, I partook in weed, beer, and cocaine any chance I got. Most of my friends were jocks, baseball guys, whose idea of partying was pretty tame – keg parties, maybe a little pot. By the time I began my junior year, I was restless for newer and different highs. My old roommate, who'd been somewhat straitlaced, had dropped out to go into the minors.

Luckily, my new roommate, a football scholarship guy, had an adventurous streak. One

night not long after the term started, he said he felt like scoring some crystal meth, knew

where he could probably find some, and asked if I wanted in. I was all for it. We headed

out from Westwood to West Hollywood, where Scott said a stoner named Dan lived, a

dude he knew from a shared sociology class the previous spring. "There's always

craziness going on in his apartment," Scott said enviously. "Great weed – chronic, not

the pussy frat-boy shit. Usually crystal, and the people, man, are something else."

Upon our arrival I saw what he meant. Even though it was after nine, and a week

night, eight or nine people, not counting Dan himself or Scott and me, were hanging out

in this tiny apartment, drinking, smoking cigarettes and grass, passing around a blue glass

pipe, and listening to KROQ. There was a drag queen in a flowered dress and high heels,

and a couple of very hot actual women – one dressed like a dominatrix in black leather

and the other tiny, olive-skinned, with huge sparkling brown eyes and dark hair that

looked so silky I just knew it would smell nice. But the dominatrix was busy helping the

drag queen with his bra and the little brown-eyed girl looked to have a date, some guy I

think might have been in my huge freshman Intro to Philosophy class. In fact, I'd

recently declared a philosophy major, partly to bug my dad, who thought it completely

impractical, and partly to contradict the stereotype that jocks always picked "soft"

majors. Maybe that first-year philosophy class could be the ice-breaker to wheedle me an

introduction to the guy's girlfriend.

Dan was a big, friendly blond guy, and he welcomed me like a longtime friend.

Again luck was with me, because the first people he introduced me to were Brown Eyes

and her escort, only they were named Maggie and Ryan and weren't a couple after all, since Dan teased Ryan about having ditched his boyfriend Eric for the night. Maggie and I got to talking, and I was floored by her. She was so damn beautiful but also smart and funny and spoke her mind. She was a Comp Lit major and didn't give a fuck about sports. But we really hit it off right away. So, too, did meth and I. From my first hit off the glass pipe I experienced a rush so goddamn exhilarating and electric it was almost enough to make me forget my attraction to Maggie. I left that night with her phone number and a little plastic bag of white powder.

My life hasn't been the same since that night. Maggie and I got together as a couple on our first date, and we were crazy in love the way you are at 20. She didn't especially like crystal; she did it a few times with me but at Dan's she usually stuck to wine or grass. I loved tweaking, though, and couldn't fathom how I'd gotten by without it. For the rest of my junior year, I used at least a couple times a week. I believed, and part of me still believes, that crystal actually enhanced my academic and athletic performance. I finished that year with my 3.9 intact, nearly pitched another no-hitter (goddamn that bloop single in the bottom of the ninth – it still hurts), and was named an Academic All-American on the NCAA baseball team. The baseball scouts were pestering me constantly trying to cajole me into their farm systems. But while I still loved the game and took pride in my pitching and even my not-bad-for-a-pitcher hitting, baseball was sliding down on my priority list. I wasn't about to leave Mags, the love of my life. And I hate to admit it, but I was just as determined not to forsake my other love, crystal.

That summer, I bypassed an invitation to play semi-pro ball and took a boring, undemanding job at a campus bookstore, the kind of work that allowed me to be high pretty much 24/7. Maggie finally put her foot down, told me she was tired of never

seeing me in an un-altered state, and threatened to dump me if I didn't quit doing meth. I

took her seriously – we were planning to move in together in the fall, Scott having

flunked out and transferred to a Cal State college. So I promised her I'd quit, really

meaning that I'd cut back to my once or twice weekly routine. But in mid-August, Dan's

connection disappeared and meth was scarce for a couple of weeks. After my third day

on compulsory cold turkey, I was praying for death. Imagine the worst hangover you've

ever had – the headache, the nausea, the simultaneous anxiety and depression – and then

magnify that about a thousand times. Maggie wanted me to go to a doctor, but instead I

managed to get Dan to bring me about a mountain of Valium. Then it wasn't so bad – I

pretty much slept off the rest of withdrawal.

      I'd learned a valuable lesson. Not to give up tweaking, but how to deal with

either enforced or voluntary withdrawal.

      It still amazes me, though, that I was able to go back to regular if not yet daily

meth use and function so well as a student, athlete, teammate, and boyfriend. Everybody,

me included, figured I was a shoo-in for a Major League Baseball career. Maggie and I

continued to fight a lot over my using, breaking up a few times about it, but we always

seemed to find our way back to each other. And then I'd cut down for a while, and then

my habit would creep back up on me and we'd fight again, break up again, and so on.

All our friends thought we were the biggest drama queens. In retrospect, we probably

were both somewhat hooked on the drama. Otherwise, I can't imagine why she kept

coming back. She had so much going for her, not the least of which was a 4.0 GPA and

the hopes of one day supporting herself as a writer.

But Maggie and I had a real crisis about midway through our senior year. During Christmas break Maggie realized she was pregnant, and we both knew a kid was so not in our immediate plans. She had an abortion and we were both pretty torn up about it. For one, we'd both been raised strict Catholics and we had all that guilt going on. We didn't tell anybody – our families would have freaked and it wasn't exactly something we felt like sharing with either our "night people" friends at Dan's or our more conventional acquaintances from the team or the *Daily Bruin*, respectively. I was determined to be there for Maggie, so I decided to get off crystal for good – and ended up OD'ing on about 50 Xanax and one last huge snort of meth, and having to be rushed to the hospital. I had a little crystal in my pockets too, so needless to say, I was outed as a drug user. My dad somehow talked the cops into charging me with only misdemeanor possession, but he didn't wait for me to be released from the hospital to tear into me for what was at the time my biggest fuckup to date. He called me stupid, spoiled, selfish, and so on; he raged about how I'd let down my family, my teammates, and myself. But when he demanded to know if my, quote, "Mexican girlfriend," unquote, had gotten me mixed up with drugs, I lost it. I tried to shout every cuss word in the book at him but my voice was raspy from the tube that had been shoved down my throat. My mom got all flustered and somehow found the gumption to tell us both to calm down.

But things were never the same between my dad and me. Where I'd once looked for – and sometimes found – pride in his expression, now I saw at best only suspicion.

The consequences didn't end there. I was suspended from the baseball program for my entire, pivotal senior year. It even got mentioned in the *Times* sports page, though buried fairly far back, as my dad pointed out. The whole thing freaked me out enough that I didn't do anything stronger than pot for the rest of my senior year. Maggie was

devastated too. She'd finally gotten what she'd wanted – me off crystal – but not exactly

how she'd hoped it would happen. And given her persistent Catholic guilt over the

abortion, she was almost as depressed as I was. We clung together like a couple of old

people or a couple of total nerds, rarely leaving our apartment except for classes, staying

home most nights to work on our respective honors theses: hers on Octavio Paz and mine

on Kant. Once in a while we'd rent a movie. We pretty much stopped having sex during

that period. Instead we'd sleep knotted together in silence.

Things started to look up for us as graduation drew closer. It wasn't just that the

old man croaked, a fact that, as I said before, I kept to myself. I still ended up being

drafted in June, and by the Dodgers, no less, but in the third round. They were a little

wary of me now, too, and they offered me a relatively modest contract with their Double-

A team in San Antonio, the Missions, instead of the dazzling, six-figure deal with Triple-

A that I'd hoped for before my OD. I was due to report to San Antonio on the first of

July, and Maggie had accepted a year's internship at the *Times*. We realized there would

be no more carefree summers for us, and on impulse, we decided to drive to Vegas and

get married. This way, even if we had to suffer a long-distance relationship for a year,

we'd be doing it as husband and wife.

It was a great weekend in Vegas, maybe the last pure happy time I can remember.

We had the ceremony at some Elvissy chapel that had us fighting laughter the entire ten

minutes. Then we just wandered from cheesy theme-park hotel to hotel, drinking

champagne and commenting on all the weird people we saw. Most of the time we spent

in our generic hotel room at the MGM Grand, fucking our brains out like we hadn't in months. All the hopes for the future that I'd thought I'd killed for good now seemed

within grasp again. I made up my mind to pitch my fucking heart out in San Antonio,

work like a dog to get back to top playing form, and then how could I fail to get called up

to LA before the next season had even begun?

When we got back from Vegas and told our families, my dad was predictably

pissed but kind of backed off from the usual tirade; I think he somehow realized it was

unseemly to dress down his now-married son as if I were still a teenager who'd broken

curfew. At least he no longer blamed Maggie for my problem with drugs. My mom and

sister, along with Maggie's folks, seemed surprised but more or less happy for us. We

offered an olive branch to our parents by agreeing to have our marriage blessed by the

Church the next weekend. It was a small, dignified ceremony – especially compared to

our glitzy Elvis one – though I still wanted to laugh during the priest's solemn

intonations. Afterward, Maggie's dad turned over one of his restaurants for a reception,

where everyone – including our friends we'd barely seen since my OD – drank too many

margaritas and danced to a salsa band. My parents, even Dad, actually looked like they

were having a good time.

Maggie's folks had always liked me, and had felt sorry for my recent misfortunes,

which they attributed to stress over trying to juggle too many oranges at once. Of course,

that's exactly how Maggie had explained my overdose to them, but they doted on her and

had no reason to doubt her version of events. They were more old-fashioned than my

parents – who aren't exactly bohemians – and they kept saying that Maggie should go

with me to San Antonio, since she was now my wife. I wouldn't hear of it – the *Times*

internship was a fantastic opportunity for her, and anyway, this was the 1990s, not the sexist era of our parents' generation. I wonder, though, if things might have turned out

differently had Maggie been with me my first year in the minors. Probably not. Maybe

subconsciously I was looking forward to being able to do real drugs again without fear of

upsetting her. Maybe I was subconsciously hatching that plan ten years before I

knowingly put it into play. I wasn't even near being over meth. I viewed my OD as

simply a freak accident rather than as an inevitable consequence of my dependence on

crystal. Plain old bad luck, and so were the repercussions.

In short, none of the bad shit that had happened in January was my fault.

I was, though, relatively clean my first couple of months in the minors. Mainly I

drank with the other guys. But I missed Maggie and UCLA, and I really wished I knew

how to score some crystal. A few of the guys did greenies, and of course, lots did

steroids, but I didn't have much interest in either. Greenies were so mild compared to

meth, not packing much more punch than a cup of strong coffee, as far as I was

concerned. Plus, I knew I was under the microscope because of my senior year

suspension at UCLA. I worked hard to get my arm in shape and my stamina up, and soon

I was pitching middle relief, doing OK if not yet up to my old college form. Maggie flew

out weekends or sometimes met up with me when we were on the road. The separation

was hard on her too, and she kept reminding both of us that before we knew it October

would arrive and I'd be back home in LA.

But as the summer drew to an end I got lucky, or so it seemed at the time. I was

having a beer with one of my neighbors on a rare off-night – better than holing up in my

practically empty apartment – and somehow the subject of drugs came up. This neighbor

was sort of a character, an old hippie type of guy in his late 40s, and through him I found out where I could get some crystal. I met the dealer in a shitty bar in the seediest part of

town, and I bought a lot of meth, about $500 worth. I didn't want to risk being spotted

with this dude on a regular basis, I rationalized. The minute I got home I snorted some –

I preferred snorting to smoking, until much later when I began shooting it – and it was

almost like my first time tweaking. Figuring I was smarter now, I tried to pace myself.

None of the guys on the team seemed to notice – fuck, half of them were doing 'roids or

greenies or both. The following weekend, when I saw Maggie, she asked me outright if I

was using again, and I lied and said I was taking legal supplements like Ephedra. She

bought the lie, probably because she wanted to so badly.

We found a new apartment in West Hollywood, not far from Dan's, though he

        The season ended and I was back in LA. I was somewhat disappointed I hadn't

been called up to the Dodgers or even to Triple-A Albuquerque, but the team brass told

me it was a strong possibility for next year. If I worked hard in the off-season maybe I'd

even make the big league roster after spring training. The team said I could improve my

chances by playing winter ball in the Mexican leagues, but that interfered with my plans

to use crystal, for the first time since my OD, without fear of detection that could once

again cost me my baseball life. I told them I couldn't ask my wife to make still another

sacrifice so I could play winter ball, and they called me pussy-whipped but didn't really

press the point.

        We found a new apartment in West Hollywood, not far from Dan's, though he

was off hard drugs and most of our other doper friends had either dispersed for post-

graduation jobs or just drifted away. Maggie was working long hours at the newspaper

and was usually tired when she got home. Without school or baseball I was bored and

alone during the day, though I swallowed my pride and worked with my dad twice a week on my arm, my delivery, all sorts of ergonomic shit that he said would help me with my pitch location, which tended toward the inside.

It didn't take me long to find a new drug supplier once I learned Dan was no longer running. Soon I was using several times a week again. Even though he's a doctor and already held me in low regard for my OD, my dad didn't notice either. He was actually impressed with my focus, my seemingly endless energy during our workouts. Maggie was another story. She figured it out fairly quickly, and she was pissed, really pissed. Just like old times. We'd fight, I'd clean up my act, and then I'd sneak and start using again. She caught me off-guard when she announced she would come back with me to San Antonio if I didn't make the LA roster after spring training. She was finally catching on to my tricks.

I had a really lousy spring training, though. My concentration was shot from tweaking, and the pitch location problems that had started to improve when I was working with my dad returned with a vengeance. In Vero Beach, Florida, where the Dodgers train, it was all hot rain and frustration with myself. I was clean but this time, my body wasn't rebounding the way it always had. I was the skinniest guy there, a beanpole at 6'2, and people were practically begging me to beef up with 'roids to increase my strength and stamina. I became depressed, ready to quit baseball entirely, but Maggie and some of the coaches told me to hang in there. Even a couple of veteran pitchers – guys whose names you'd know – stepped in and tried to encourage me. I had the talent, they said; I just needed to work on my discipline and conditioning.

Maggie was the only one who knew the real source of my lackluster spring training, and she suggested I try therapy. She thought if I understood why I was so compelled to keep using crystal despite knowing it could ruin my career, our relationship, and my life, that maybe I could finally quit for keeps. Well, I sure as hell didn't want some shrink prying into my life or trying to dredge up bad memories I'd never even shared with my wife. I flat-out refused, and she cried but let it go.

I was, however, reassigned to the Albuquerque Dukes, a bump up to triple-A. Maggie found a job easily with the newspaper there, unlike the *Times* a regular writing job doing restaurant and occasional book reviews. Having her there did help me, at first, keep away from crystal. My game also began to shape up and in June of that year I won my first start, giving up only four hits and an unearned run. About a month after that Maggie got pregnant again, and this time there was no question about keeping it. We were both walking on air, and while I'd secretly begun taking a few of those greenies to curb my meth cravings, I was determined that my crystal days were behind me. My career prospects were looking up, my wife and I were expecting a kid, and I really wanted to be a good father, even more than I wanted to make it to the majors.

I finished the year with a so-so record of 4-5, but an ERA just under 3. More important to me and certainly to Mags, I'd played an entire season without crystal, and I didn't miss the greenies when I stopped taking them. I still thought about meth every day, but with Maggie living with me I was less prone to impulsively seeking out a new connection.

I did a fair share of cocaine on the road, though, with a couple of other guys on the team. Coke was a lot easier to run across than crystal. But it was fucking expensive, and its rush, while a hell of a lot more potent than greenies', was relatively short-lived. Both factors kept me from getting hooked, along with my reluctance to do anything to upset Maggie. She really liked her job and wanted to work as close to her due date as she

could, so we decided to stay in New Mexico instead of going back to LA at the end of the

season. Our families were disappointed, but we placated them by returning for

Thanksgiving and Christmas. By then we knew the baby was a girl, and we chose the

name Katya because we liked it and thought it sounded Dostoevskian.

On those short trips to LA I did some coke – which I'd convinced myself I didn't

like – with some old friends from UCLA, but as long as it wasn't meth I could rationalize

that I was more or less clean and sober. Unfortunately, the Albuquerque cops didn't see

it that way in January, when I was pulled over for speeding on my way home from

buying a big bag of coke off one of my teammates. Like my senior year overdose, my

arrest brought major consequences. Maggie was so beside herself that her obstetrician

ordered her to bed for two weeks. My lawyer arranged a plea deal that assessed me

$10,000 when we could least afford it, and both the court and the team management

insisted I check myself immediately into rehab for a minimum 28 days. Not only did I

miss the start of spring training, I damn near missed the birth of my daughter and had to

beg for the court's permission to leave Drunk Camp for Maggie's eight-hour labor. Our

joy over Kat – she was so pure and perfect – was tempered by my miserable situation.

Thank God Maggie's parents flew over, because I had to leave them – my wife and infant

daughter – to head back to complete the remaining two weeks of my rehab stint.

There against my will, I was sullen and cooperated only enough to keep from

being tagged a hopeless case. I aped what they wanted to hear about twelve steps and

denial and the moral inventory; I daydreamed during the endless, infantilizing group

sessions and high-schoolish "Just Say No" videos; and fought sleep during the equally endless "drug-alogues" and "drunk-alogues." Mine should have won an award for

fiction. I said I'd had a normal childhood, had done great at sports and in school, and that

I'd only picked up the cocaine habit in the minors out of loneliness for my wife and LA.

The main thing I got out of Drunk Camp was another addiction, to cigarettes. I'd never

smoked tobacco, but rehab was so boring and depressing, and our only freedom from the

incessant anti-drug, anti-booze indoctrination was the intermittent twenty-minute break

period where we inmates would go outside, talk about nothing, and smoke cigarettes.

They wouldn't even allow caffeine in there, yet every patient was almost

immediately pressured to go on one antidepressant or another. I had no interest in any

drug that provided no buzz, but I was afraid a refusal would look bad to my probation

officer and the team. I gamely signed on for Zoloft, which made me kind of irritable but

otherwise had no effect as far as I could tell. I stopped taking it the day I was discharged.

That same day, Maggie informed me she was going home to California to stay

with her folks. She was exhausted, not just from the baby, but also the stress of my arrest

and exile to rehab. She didn't think she could handle my road trips once I rejoined the

team. I'd never seen such dark hollows under her eyes; it almost looked like she was

wearing the eyeblack grease some players use as a sunblock. She insisted that she wasn't

leaving me, that she still loved me, and that soon we'd all be together as a family. But I

knew she was running away from me, and having achieved a new level of fucked-

uppedness, I couldn't exactly blame her. But even I knew better than to drown myself in

drugs to blunt the pain. One more fuckup and I was likely to lose not only my family and

my career, but my freedom.

The guys on the team were sympathetic, but I was rusty as hell, back in the bullpen and struggling to make up for lost time. I'd missed all of spring training, and I was half-surprised not to have been demoted still further down the farm system food chain.

Because I had to pee in the drug-test cup on a regular basis, I couldn't even have a beer. Being this alone with myself was torture. I couldn't sleep more than two or three hours a night, and I was reluctant to call Maggie too late; she was so tired and sleeping poorly herself. All those dark hours between midnight and dawn, wanting my wife and kid, wanting to sleep, and most of all wanting to get high. I couldn't concentrate to watch TV or movies. I played hour after hour of computer solitaire or poker. I chainsmoked cigarettes. Sometimes I'd go for a long walk, studiously not thinking about anything except the hollow sound of my footsteps, the tired rhythms of my breath, against all that darkness.

Amazingly enough, though, I was starting to regain my previous season's form. Maybe it was because my mind welcomed a concrete focus, an absorption in a self-contained system outside of which nothing else of my life outside of baseball existed. At the beginning of May, one of our starters was called up to LA and I got his place in the rotation. The pressure I put on myself was intense. I kept thinking, if I pitch really great, maybe I'll be the next one called up, and Maggie and Kat and I can all be together. I was rocked my first start, so obsessed with not walking anybody that almost everything I threw was 98 miles an hour and right over the plate. But my second shot, coming five days later, started out like a dream. I had a no-hitter going into the fifth, and I was in the zone – calm, completely focused, in total control. The catcher signaled for a changeup. I wound up, focused, and released. I heard a sharp crack as the bat made contact, and for a second I thought, fuck, there goes the no-no. Then I was overwhelmed by such fierce pain that I collapsed on the mound, clutching my left elbow. The agony was so intense that it wasn't until later I realized what had happened – not the ball, but a huge piece of the broken bat had struck me with the velocity of a supersonic missile. If it had hit me in the face it could've blinded or even killed me. My reflexes had always been good, and I prided myself on my defense; Greg Maddux was one of my idols. Sometimes I still wonder if drugs had somehow slowed my reaction time, even a millisecond, but time enough to have ducked that broken bat coming at me.

What a way to finally get some drugs. The pain was bad enough to merit morphine. The injury was worse than I'd expected. I needed immediate surgery to patch together my shattered elbow with a bunch of rods and pins. I was so stoned that it didn't really sink in when the doctor told me it would be half a year before I could even begin rehabbing my arm. I do remember exaggerating my already considerable pain so they'd give me more morphine, and I remember making all sorts of bad puns whenever the doctor mentioned my humerus bone – "I see nothing humorous about it" – stupid shit like that.

Hospitals don't usually send you home with morphine unless you're dying of cancer or something. Flying home to LA, mildly stoned on Demerol and my arm in a cast, it was dawning on me what a totally fucked-up predicament I was in. Rehab or not, mine was the kind of injury that ended pitching careers. A goddamn freak injury. Without baseball, what was I going to do with my life? How would I support myself, much less my family?

I was paralyzed with self-pity, but not to the extent of burying my head in the sand. I knew I could count on my dad to give it to me straight, no false hope or Horatio Alger pep talks. He examined my arm, looked at the X-rays, and told me dispassionately I'd never pitch again.

I was still under contract and drawing a paycheck, but I was consumed with anxiety over my uncertain future. Maggie didn't pressure me. She'd started doing freelance writing and editing from home so she could be with Kat, and she didn't mind me just hanging around the house, getting to know my little girl who was the only light in my gloom of self-pity and painkillers. We rented a little house in Hermosa Beach. I forced myself to run on the beach every morning because the exercise, combined with the drugs, helped me not to think.

It wasn't long before meth was creeping back into my life. I ran into an old druggie friend from college, Andy, at a club in Redondo Beach. He was a systems analyst for TRW, very white-collar yuppie, and for him crystal was simply a way of sustaining eighty-hour work weeks and a horndogging social life. Once my cast came off I began surfing most mornings with Andy. Surfing and tweaking at the same time became my new obsession. I was tapering off the painkillers, using them mainly when I needed to conceal from Mags how wired I was.

Remember on *The X-Files*, how alien abductees were said to suffer from "lost time"? Whole blocks of time that just seemed to have vanished from their consciousness? That's kind of what happened to me for the first couple of years out of baseball. I know rationally that Maggie was losing patience with me and we were fighting a lot. I want to remember, but don't quite, my little girl taking her first steps, saying her first words. I'm sure that my dad was giving me shit, my mom was clucking

meekly, and Diana was trying to get me to go to graduate school. But the memories are

hazy and feel twice-removed, as if I'm remembering someone telling me about all of this

rather than my own experiences. I got off meth when Andy lost his job and had to move

to the Valley. I managed to track down another former acquaintance from "the Dan

days" who turned me on to heroin. It took Maggie a while to realize I was using junk

because its effects are so different from crystal's. To humor her, I was going to therapy

once a week. The shrink was low-key and I just fed him a lot of bullshit about being

depressed over losing baseball, having no direction, blah blah blah. I pretended to take

his suggestions and pretended to both him and Maggie that I was taking the

antidepressants he told me to get from my GP. It was easy, then, to blame my lethargy

and spaciness on the Zoloft. I assured Mags that the doctor said eventually my body

would adjust and I'd be less zoned out. Man, I was so devious. If I'd applied half the

energy I expended on getting drugs and trying to conceal the fact from my wife to a

Ph.D. program, I'd have an endowed chair in Philosophy right now. If I'd spent half that

energy trying to beat the odds and developing my right arm, my natural throwing arm,

maybe I'd have a Cy Young right now. But that's all water under the bridge, just more

shadows.

When Maggie finally did find out about the heroin – and the lies – she threw me

out. I was pretty much flat-broke, and for a while I slept on the living room floor of

Brian, my drug dealer, occasionally running for him in return for room, board, and meth.

I'd gotten bored with smack and the lethargy. Brian put me in touch with a quack who

rapid-detoxed me, again in return for running some drugs, and soon I was back on the meth rollercoaster. On the rare occasions I had my wits about me, Maggie let me see

Kat, though always with her supervision. On even rarer occasions still we'd end up in

bed together, and she'd beg me to get clean and I'd promise to try. Once, I made it an

entire month, and we discussed my moving back in. Then I fucked up again, and that's

when she filed for divorce.

Funny; the divorce really didn't change things that much. I still saw Maggie and

Kat when I was more or less lucid, but the intervals between were growing longer. My

parents were totally fed up with me and told me I wasn't welcome in their lives until I got

my act together. I was so broke that I took a job at an all-night convenience store in

Hollywood. One thing about tweakers, we're great on the late shift. I reconnected with

Andy, my old surfing and tweaking buddy, and moved into a rundown little house in

Silver Lake with him. He was in almost as desperate shape as I was, working at Kinko's

and living off a small trust fund enough to keep him in crystal but not much else. He was

developing a bad case of meth mouth – his teeth were coming loose – and he was all

paranoid about it, convinced his dental X-rays had been tampered with by the DEA. My

teeth stayed in great shape, since by this time I was slamming it right into my veins.

We got our crystal from our neighbors right across the street, a biker couple who

were the middle-men, so to speak, for a big meth lab out in Chatsworth. They were very

businesslike about it. But one day they said the Chatsworth lab had been busted and the

well was dry, at least temporarily. Andy and I were almost completely out of meth

ourselves, and we'd become so dependent on our source across the street that we

panicked.

It was my idea to break into Pete and Vicky's house to scour the place for meth. Being tweakers themselves, they were sure to have set aside some of their wares for personal use. Andy was all for it, but he chose to serve as lookout from our garage rather than come along. Ten minutes after we watched Pete and Vicky zoom off on their Harley, I crept across the street, jimmied open a back window, and began rifling through their house. I wanted to make it look like a random burglary, so I threw open and emptied drawers and ransacked the kitchen, which was where I came across a nice clean bag of crystal, at least a good gram of it, along with a wad of hundreds. Pete and Vicky hadn't used a lot of imagination in picking a place to stash the stuff; the drugs and cash were in a plastic tool chest, tossed in with screwdrivers, nails, and bolts, under the sink. I really didn't want the money but took it, as well as their boom box, because as I said, I hoped they'd think this was a chance rather than planned burglary.

None of this mattered to the two uniformed cops who greeted me, with drawn guns, at the backdoor. All I could think was why the fuck hadn't Andy called me on my cell the moment the cops drove up? Later I learned that Andy, in his paranoia, freaked out at the first glimpse of the prowl car and ran inside to barricade himself in the bathroom.

I mean, I was busted, and this time the cops were a lot less cordial than the ones in Albuquerque had been. Then they'd treated me like a dumb minor-league ballplayer with a little coke. Now I was garden-variety scum, charged with felony breaking and entering, caught red-handed. I spent three days in LA County Jail, up to then the most harrowing experience of my life, before Diana came through with the bail money and a decent lawyer. On his advice I checked right in to another 28-day rehab facility. I really needed help detoxing – in jail I'd scratched my speed bugs bloody and begun to hallucinate – but

as before in New Mexico, I merely went through the motions with the therapeutic

aspects. It just didn't make sense to me, connections between my drug use and my own

psyche. Nor had a lack of self confidence or peer pressure, other things the counselors

stressed, ever been factors in my addiction. The way I saw it, I got high because I loved

the way it felt, and I saw no point in psychoanalyzing it.

  None of this is to say I wasn't scared shitless by the prospect of going to prison.

My lawyer kept requesting continuances, hoping to frustrate the hard-ass DA into cutting

me a deal with no jail time. You can bet I was clean during this. As soon as I got out of

rehab I moved back in with Maggie, who was now living with Kat in a rented condo in

Manhattan Beach. It blew my mind that she still loved me, and she was as frightened as I

over the possibility of my incarceration. We were too stressed out to be happy, but it was

the first extended time I ever spent sober with my wife – ex-wife – and daughter together.

Kat loved me the way Maggie did, without reservation. Kat was my light, and Mags,

whom I'd burned more times than I could count over the years, was my ballast. "Come

hell or high water you're going to get through this," she said, always adding, "as long as

you stay clean." She made me believe it too. Sober, I loved her and Kat so profoundly it

was almost painful. I tried, too, to patch things up with my parents, although my dad

repeatedly declared that he felt a prison term would be the best rehab program for an

addiction as "stubborn" – his word – as mine. The ultimate Tough Love. Ha, little did he

know.

  As it turned out, he got his wish. My case pled out, but the judge was as hard-

assed as the DA, and I was sentenced to a year in the Cal State prison system, of which I had to serve nine months. I went into emotional autopilot. Maggie was being strong for

both of us. She promised to visit me every chance she had, and we even discussed

remarrying so I could have conjugal rights. We were going to remarry, I vowed, but not

under these circumstances. And I forbade her to ever bring Kat to see me in prison. I

wouldn't have that blistered into her memory. I entered the state prison at Lancaster

determined to survive through self-willed numbness to what was happening to me.

It didn't work – not the "self-willed" part, anyway. I was gang-raped in the

showers my second day in the pen, fucked and beaten by a bunch of guys whose faces I

never saw. I've had two HIV tests since then, and miraculously, they've both been

negative. At the time, the prison guards saw it all and did nothing except transfer me to

another cell block. Maybe not coincidentally, my new cell mate was this big, muscular

tattooed guy serving out the second half of a two-year sentence for armed robbery and

possession with intent to sell. Heroin. He acted as if some part of him felt genuinely

sorry for me, but he was also an opportunist. "Look, dude," he said, "a pretty boy like

you is just fresh meat in here. You need to buy yourself some protection." I was so

shell-shocked I didn't catch his drift. I told Ed that I didn't have any money. But what I

really wanted to know was if there was any chance of scoring some drugs in here. He

seemed amused I was even asking. "OK, you need protection and dope," he said. "I'll

provide both to you. In exchange you're my punk." He was kind of the kingpin on this

block, he added; the other cons both needed and feared him.

I had only one question. Could he get me some crystal? Sure, he said, crystal,

smack, weed, you name it.

An hour later I had my crystal. That night Ed cut me some slack and insisted only on a blowjob for my first installment on his payment plan. I was high and the whole encounter seemed unreal.

The prison grapevine is no fable; by the next day word was out that I was Ed's bitch. The other cons snickered and shit, but didn't come near me. Maggie visited me that afternoon. I told her the bruises were from a minor fistfight in the rec yard, and that I was doing as well as could be expected. I was a little reluctant to kiss her, because I kept thinking about where my mouth had been the night before and I didn't want it to touch hers. I forced myself to give her a brief, close-mouthed kiss before she left. The crystal was wearing off and I was shifting rapidly into panic/depression mode. But just like a wish-granting genii, Ed drew me aside and gave me another really nice line. This meth was a higher grade than yesterday's, and I was bouncing off the walls. And when the door locked us into our cell for the night, I was so horny from the speed that I probably would have fucked the very crew who'd attacked me in the showers. Mostly what I remember now is the sound of panting, heavy guy-breaths, and how I concentrated on those sounds because they seemed so incongruously private in this place where a big part of the punishment is the active denial of privacy. I remember thinking about Foucault and the panopticon. And I remember wondering if I'd get used to this.

God help me, but I did. It's an aspect of what they call "prisonization." I knew my goddamn Foucault and I still got "prisonized," gradually swallowed by and incorporated into the culture, the surveillance, the prisoners' hierarchy. My big mistake had been going in thinking I could decide the terms of my survival. Not my decision to make, any more than it was Ed's or even the guys who'd raped me. We had all become

cogs in the prison machinery.

Because I was college educated, I was assigned to work in the prison library.

Talk about slim pickin's. But even in my debased and drugged out state, I was moved

every time I checked out a book to a fellow con. Any book. There's something

humanizing about reading a book. Someday I'd like to volunteer as a tutor for a prison

literacy program.

Ed could always get me drugs, but not always meth. Sometimes it'd be heroin or

crack. It was kind of fortuitous, because the arbitrary nature of my supply kept me from

getting physically addicted to any one drug. That, in turn, helped me maintain the

charade with Maggie, who visited at least once a week. Not that I painted everything as

jack-dandy, but the main thing we discussed, at my request, was her life and Kat's, lives

that now seemed to me to be playing out in a parallel universe so remote from my own it

might have been a dream. When I allowed myself to think about her reaction should she

find out the truth of my prison existence, I became suicidal. Seriously. I'd try to pick

fights with the gangstas or the neo-Nazis, and only Ed's clout kept me from getting my

throat slit.

I believe that Ed saw me as not only his punk but his project. He scored me my

drugs in return for a nightly fuck, but weirdly enough, he seemed to want to take care of

me, and that creeped me out even more than the sex. When he heard we were due to be

released within a couple weeks of each other, he told me he'd keep me in crystal for as

long as I wanted if I'd move in with him once we were both free. Taken aback by the suggestion, I kept stalling because I was afraid if I turned him down he'd stop supplying me with drugs.

But as time passed and my freedom was actually in sight, I began to freak out. Mags would come to see me with hope splashed across her face, talking about our future as a family, expressing such faith in me, such respect for having apparently weathered my ordeal. God, I loathed myself for all the lies I'd foisted on her, and for the lies I'd inevitably feed her again if we reconciled. The only way I'd held on to my sanity, if you even want to call it that, was through getting high. And I knew the only way I'd be able to endure the memories of how I'd gotten through prison was to keep using until it killed me. A few weeks before my release date, I snorted some meth before going to meet Maggie in the visiting room, because man, I needed my courage for one last gargantuan lie. I told her that Ed and I'd been fucking the entire time I was in prison and that I was going to shack up with him when we were both out – both of which were true. The lie, the one I knew she'd never forgive, came in the form of my informing her I was in love with Ed. I hadn't miscalculated. The life seemed to literally drain out of her, leaving a ghost with huge holes of eyes, eyes black with disbelief, disappointment, betrayal. That image of her eyes will stay with me forever. When I think of it now it reminds me of Virgil's description of the way Dido looked at Aeneas in hell.

But at the time, all I could think was that I'd finally lost her and it was for the best.

Now I really had nowhere else to go. Ed got out ten days before I did, but since he still had contacts in the pen, no one bothered me and I was at least able to get some weed. Ed's house was a real dump in Echo Park that he kept in his ex-wife's name so that neither the cops nor the lawyers could get their hands on it. His ex-wife was an

alcoholic who lived in Bakersfield, and evidently they were still on decent terms. I had

no idea if he was habitually gay, bi, or whatever. But something changed from the day I

moved in with him. In the pen he'd really been into the power and dominance dynamic

with me – not S&M, exactly, but he made our roles clear. On the outside, he started

acting like, what, we were boyfriends or lovers. At first I put up with his hand-holding,

and his almost – courtly – behavior. I was just so relieved to be out of prison and free to

slam crystal into my veins for the first time since my time at Andy's in Silver Lake. I

was still pissed at Andy for blowing it as my lookout and I didn't care if I ever saw him

again. But I'll say one thing for him as a roommate – he kept to his own bed and didn't

want to make out with me in front of the World's Strongest Man competition on ESPN2.

Ed was leery about being busted again, but he was a dealer by trade and quickly

resumed his business relationships with some very hard-core Mexican smugglers who

trafficked crystal as well as smack. Man, did they have great shit. My first couple of

months in Echo Park raced by in a fast-forward crystal meth blur. But by my third month

I was growing convinced that there wasn't enough meth on the planet to get me to

tolerate Ed's bizarre sentimentality toward me. I mean, he was telling me he loved me

and shit. I planned his moment of disenchantment with a hell of a lot more calculation

than I had Maggie's. One day when he was down in San Ysidro to meet with one of his

suppliers, I deliberately left his front door wide open, which in this neighborhood was

tantamount to posting a big sign reading "Rob Me." Then I drove around in the old

Toyota I'd left at Diana's during my prison stint, high out of my mind and blasting Alice

in Chains. After several hours I went back to Ed's house.

Whoever helped himself or themselves to Ed's unintentional bounty had really

done a job on the place. His guns were gone, his drugs were gone, his computer, stereo,

and TV – all gone. Even the Jack Daniels and beer were gone. Ed had beaten me home,

and he was in a state of complete rage. Obviously he couldn't report the burglary to the

cops. He may have thought he loved me, but I knew that what he really loved most in the

world was his stuff. He missed his shit in prison more than he missed freedom. I

pretended to have forgotten to lock the door, but at last he was thinking with his head

instead of his dick. He shouted at me to get the fuck out and never come back. I took no

chance he might cool off and change his mind, and of course, I'd appropriated all the

crystal in the house myself along with some pills, leaving small amounts of crack, heroin,

and weed for the neighborhood scavengers. I got out of there as fast as I could, almost as

relieved to be free of him as I'd been to be let out of the pen. But like crystal this was an

artificial, temporary high. When I came down the next morning I was tempted to crash

my piece of crap car with me in it into the nearest concrete wall. I wanted Maggie. I

wanted my daughter Kat. I wanted back the vision of us she had conjured again and

again during her prison visits.

I drove to Manhattan Beach but for two days I was afraid to call or stop by. I

used the showers and bathroom at the beach, forced myself to eat a meal a day at Jack in

the Box, and slept, when I could, in my car. I'd pop a couple Oxycontin and just zone

out for a few hours.

I finally found the nerve to stop by Maggie's condo. Not surprisingly, she was

still pissed at me, pissed and disgusted. It was her disgust that made me lose it; I broke

down and cried like a baby. I was so ashamed of myself. I told her Ed had kicked me out but not how I'd staged it, which I suspected would sicken her further. It was clear

how appalled she was at the whole thing, how betrayed she still felt. I begged her to at

least let me look in on Kat, who was sleeping, and she grudgingly agreed. But something

about looking at our sleeping daughter together must have softened Maggie a little,

because she told me I could stay the night if I swore I'd go back to rehab the next

morning. We ended up having incredible sex, which had always been our lifeline, and

for the duration I meant everything I promised. I wanted to get clean so I could be with

her and Kat, so I could be myself again. But by the next morning I was shooting crystal

again, and I forgot and left the needle on the kitchen counter, where Kat could've spotted

it. I don't think she did. I hope to hell she didn't. Maggie saw it, though, and that was it.

She ordered me to get out and stay out, threatening to call the cops if I ever showed my

face there again. She was beyond angry, even beyond disgusted. This was far from the

first time she'd told me to get permanently lost, but she'd never sounded this cold, this

done with me, before.

          Yet – and it kills me to admit this – the keen self-hatred and despair I felt that

morning were soon overshadowed by a much more urgent desperation: I was running low

on crystal and virtually penniless. Crawling back to Ed was not an option, not even as a

last resort. I decided to let bygones be bygones and drove over to Andy's house in Silver

Lake. He wasn't home but his new roommate was, a skinny red-haired guy named Neil

whom I quickly came to think of as "NBC" – for "Neanderthal Bozo the Clown." NBC

told me the biker-dealers whose house I'd robbed no longer lived across the street, which

was a damn good thing. Maybe they'd gotten busted too, for having the meth I'd tried to

steal from them in the first place. NBC spotted me a couple lines of crystal and I waited for Andy to get home from Kinko's. He wasn't as strung out as he'd been last time I'd

seen him, and he claimed to be tapering off. He repeatedly apologized for getting me

busted, and I asked him to prove it by lending me $500. I was sort of surprised by how

fast he agreed. Either he had a guilty conscience or feared retribution should he refuse.

Or maybe Andy just wanted to be buddies again. I'd become so dishonorable by

that point that I suspected everyone's motives were as base as mine. Everyone except

Maggie's. I wished with all my soul I could rewind the tape and not have left that

goddamn needle and spoon on the counter.

I ended up crashing with Andy and Neil for a few days, slamming speed and

drinking vodka. It used to be that drinking and tweaking at the same time made me sick,

the proverbial wide-awake drunk. Now I was both wired and emotionally all over the

map. It was the vodka, not the meth, that gave me the courage to call Maggie, and when

the recording told me that number was no longer in service, I freaked. I must have tried it

a dozen more times, but always got the recording. I leaped to the worst conclusions. A

serial killer had slaughtered them and their gutted bodies were lying in the apartment

rotting, like Layne Stayley of Alice in Chains, who OD'd and wasn't found for a week. I

drove like a maniac to Manhattan Beach, saw that her car wasn't there, and waited like a

stalker for ten, twelve hours in hopes she'd return. I just knew their corpses were in

there, stinking. Totally wigged out, I rang the next-door neighbor's bell and asked the

guy if he knew how I could reach Maggie's landlord. I said I was her husband. The guy

replied yeah, he'd seen me around last year. But Maggie had split, he said, just a couple

of days ago. Loaded a bunch of suitcases into her car and just drove off with the kid and

the dog. Far from feeling relieved they hadn't been butchered by a crazed intruder, I got it into my head that either a kidnapper had been hiding in the backseat or that the FBI or

CIA had "disappeared" them because Mags had an anti-Bush sticker on her car. Either

way, something really bad had befallen them. And my mind was consumed by one

thought that pounded in my head like a bad drum solo. *I've got to find them. I've got to*

find Maggie and Kat. I've got to find them.

     Kierkegaard wrote that purity of heart is to will one thing. By his standard I was

purer than ether. I had to find them. I wound up at my sister's house in Los Feliz,

intending to hit her up for the money to hire a private detective to locate them. Diana

was so hugely pregnant I almost didn't recognize her at first. She heard me out and

agreed to retain a PI – only since I was so fucked up, she said she'd better be the one to

talk to the guy. She was humoring me, of course, but at the time I took her at her word.

She conditioned her offer on one thing, though: I had to move into her garage apartment,

let her or her husband Wes, also a doctor, check on my health periodically, and have none

of my druggie pals on the premises. She pointedly didn't include in these house rules a

stipulation that I not use. I suppose she knew I wasn't able to abide by that condition, but

I did my best to cooperate with the other ones. She and Wes made sure I ate at least one

meal a day, and even gave me money when they knew I was likely going to spend it on

drugs.

     But my obsession didn't go away. I bugged Diana constantly about the private

eye, and she assured me he was checking out a number of leads. The days and nights

were running together again. Finally one morning, Di came out to the garage and told me

that our PI had located Maggie and Kat. I was elated. Where were they? Were they

OK? She said they were fine, but that she'd disclose their whereabouts if and only if I went back to rehab and stayed there for a minimum of six months. I initially refused –

no, I'd go to rehab *after* I saw my daughter and ex-wife. Di wouldn't budge and she

wouldn't bargain. Don't you want your life back? she asked me. At that I started crying,

not just over her question but also the way she'd posed it, with no judgment, no

impatience, no disgust. It was hard to believe she was related to me. All I'd known –

from my dad and myself – was judgment, impatience, and contempt for my behavior.

Passive disapproval from my mom. How had Diana grown up in the same family and

ended up so compassionate?

       With no particular optimism I let Diana bring me here, and here's where I've been

for two months. I have no idea whether I'm making any kind of progress. I'm getting to

know myself again, and that, frankly, has been unnerving. Maybe "again" is the wrong

word. I still can't connect what I was before to what I am now, or what happened to me

as a kid, or in the pen, to much of anything. I wish I believed in the concept of a soul, if

only as a rubric, some kind of metaphysical glue to hold all I am and all I've done

together. But I don't know how to turn my brain off outside of getting high, and my

brain's hard-wired me to be a strict materialist. How can I think about a "Higher Power"

when my concept of power is as this impersonal mechanism of subjugation? Ugh.

"Forget Foucault." I can detoxify my body but if I detoxify my brain, what if there's

nothing left? It scares the fuck out of me.

       I am struggling to keep my goals concrete and short-term – get clean, learn how to

stay clean, see my ex-wife and daughter again (assuming Di didn't invent the whole story

about finding them as a way to get me in here). But even if I've lost them forever, I would like eventually to be the kind of man my daughter would be proud of if she ever

gets curious about her dad. That's something I can control, and something to live for.

* * *

The journal appeared to have reached its natural conclusion. Maggie was drained,

devastated, as she tried to digest it all. Automatically she flipped the page, expecting to

see blank blue lines and pristine margins.

Instead, huge black letters had been pressed into the paper with sufficient force to

tear right through it:

"NO! LEAVE ME THE FUCK ALONE!"

CHAPTER 9

"Maggie, are you OK?"

She startled, realizing only then that Diana was sitting in the old-fashioned rocking chair across from her, cradling her baby. "Oh my God, Diana, how long have you been there?"

"Almost twenty minutes."

"He's beautiful." She thought to get up from the sofa, but a spell of dizziness forced her to stay seated. The room spun. The impact of Tim's journal combined with worry and sleeplessness to make her fear she was on the verge of passing out.

"Maggie, why don't you stretch out there on the sofa? You look exhausted."

"No, I have to find Tim – "

Diana, balancing the pink, swaddled infant on a hip, had already arisen to reach for a crocheted afghan folded along the back of the sofa. She tossed it to Maggie. "Rest.

I'll put on some coffee and then you can tell me if you learned anything from what he wrote."

"Coffee would be great," Maggie murmured, stretching out her legs that she'd held curled beneath her. She reclined against the down-filled back cushions, deciding it couldn't hurt to rest her eyes just until the coffee was ready.

When she reopened them the room was dim, almost dark, all shapes and shadows. For a moment she thought she was in her own bed. Another moment of panic as she realized she was not. Then she remembered. She bolted up to switch on the silhouetted lamp on an end table.

The burst of light made her squint. She glanced at her watch. Ten minutes to five. "Diana?" she called out, upset by the lost time. No answer.

She found her way to a downstairs half-bath, used the toilet. When she emerged Diana was descending the sweeping staircase. "I was just putting Brandon down. Come to the kitchen and I'll get you that coffee."

"I shouldn't have slept so long," Maggie said, stifling a yawn.

"If you slept it was because you needed it."

The kitchen, like Eva's all marble counters and stainless steel, was clearly not the house's original one. Maggie gratefully accepted a mug of coffee. "I need to call Kat once I wake up."

"I'll give you some privacy, then."

"No, no, it's not necessary. Now, what did I do with my phone?"

Diana nodded at a telephone on a land line atop a corner butcher block. "Use ours."

Maggie spoke briefly with her mother. According to Eva, Kat appeared calm but extremely preoccupied. As for Kat, she didn't even say hello before asking, "Have you found Daddy, Mommy?"

"Not yet, sweetie. But I have some good ideas where to look for him. I'm with Daddy's sister, your Aunt Diana." She met Diana's eyes across the room. "She's helping me find him."

Diana gave her a silent nod.

Kat sounded heartened. "Call as soon as you've found him, Mommy."

"I will, I promise. Be good for your abuelita and abuelo. I love you, Kat."

"Please just find Daddy."

"I'm going to, Kat. Bye-bye for now."

She hung up. "She's so obsessed with finding him. God, I pray I can."

"Did his notes give any hint about where he might have gone? Like I told you, I couldn't bear to read beyond his description of those horrible summers in Del Mar."

Thinking of the *stomp-stomp-stomp* on the stairs and the secret crawlspace, Maggie shook her head. Poor Tim. Poor little Tim.

Diana misinterpreted the gesture. "Damn it, Maggie. No clues at all?"

"Oh, I'm sorry, Diana. I did get a couple of ideas. Especially if Andy Chase is in the phone book. He's someone we knew in college. Tim hooked up again with him a few years ago. He's also a tweaker."

"Did you get any sense at all why he left rehab? Or was it just the addiction?"

"I don't know," Maggie said thoughtfully. "The last thing he seems to have written is 'no, leave me the fuck alone' in huge letters. I suppose that could mean the cravings were rearing up again."

Diana looked melancholy. "Damn it. I was hoping against hope that something else made him go AWOL."

"Same here. But even if he has relapsed, Diana, everything else he wrote in that notebook seemed so lucid, so determined to stay clean. And you say that's how he struck you too. If I can find him in time, maybe we can get him back in the program before the drugs make him forget the progress he'd been making."

A distant, muffled ringing sounded. Maggie realized it was her cellphone inside her purse in the family room. "That's mine," she said, hurrying toward the ringing. She'd forgotten to give her mother Diana's number.

It was Billy. "Maggie, I've been going nuts. What the hell's happening?"

"I'm in LA and I've got to find Tim."

"Fuck. Kat's bad off?"

She kept her voice low. "Billy, the old man's still in the house. It was Tim – or some fragment of him from his childhood – that we drove out."

A long silence. Then, finally, "The little kid on Halloween in the Fernando Valenzuela uni. That was him."

"Yes. I don't know if Kat quite understands, but she's beside herself. She keeps insisting, 'You've got to find Daddy.' And in fact, Tim is missing."

"Hold tight. I'm coming up to help you look."

Maggie gripped the phone, disconcerted. "I don't think that's a good idea."

"Maggie, given where you're probably gonna have to look and what you might end up finding, I want to be there with you."

"Your wife needs you more than I do."

"My wife's not planning to wander into God knows what kind of meth houses to look for an MIA junkie. No offense, Maggie – I can feel you bristling. But it's not safe."

She was about to protest. But it struck her that he was probably right. Especially if, God forbid, Andy Chase was of no help, leaving her with no choice other than to attempt to somehow track down Ed. Although the idea of it sickened her, she was willing to risk her own safety and sanity. But she had to think of Kat. "All right. It'll probably take you over three hours to get here. How well do you know LA?"

"Not well, but I have a killer sense of direction. Where are you?"

"I'm in Los Feliz, but I'll meet you between nine and ten at Musso and Frank's restaurant on Hollywood Boulevard." Ridiculously, Musso's was the first landmark to pop into her head. She was reluctant to have to explain her relationship with him to Diana, and Musso and Frank's held pleasant memories. In college it had been the favorite "special occasion" restaurant of all the "night people," a place so retro it was chic, with pricey a la carte steaks and classic hash-house entrees, like liver and onions and spaghetti and meatballs, world-class martinis, all served by curmudgeonly, red-jacketed waiters who looked as if they'd worked there since the 1940s.

Billy promised to meet her, and she returned to the kitchen. "That was a friend of mine. He's insisting on playing bodyguard for me when I start hitting the dens of iniquity."

Diana was setting a block of Irish cheddar and some crackers on a rustic cheese board. "That's smart. My experience with hard-core druggies is that they don't like people snooping around asking questions, whatever the reason." She lay the cheese board on the kitchen table.

"I may need to track down the guy Tim lived with right after he got out of prison. You think his parole officer might have the number or address?" She assumed Tim had to have been assigned a probation officer.

"Possibly, but I'm not sure we want to tip off the P.O. that Tim's missing," Diana said. "Refill your coffee and have a snack. Wes won't be home until after seven."

"I'm meeting my friend at Musso's around nine."

"Good for you – I love that place. But you know, I hope, that you and your friend are spending the night here."

"Oh, Diana, I couldn't – "

"Yes you can, and the same goes for your friend. We have two extra bedrooms. Plus the garage apartment, if you want more privacy. We're early risers."

Maggie's resolve wavered at the promise of spending the night where *he* had, and she forgot about the complication of Billy's lodgings. "Thanks. With any luck I'll have a real lead on Tim, if not Tim himself, tomorrow. And how could I be so stupid to have thought of calling the probation officer?"

"We told the P.O. that he was going into rehab not because he'd slipped, but because he feared he was about to," Diana explained, slicing off some cheese with a small silver wedge.

Maggie was puzzled. "Wasn't he required to be drug-tested? Was he just not showing up?"

Diana's mouth twisted. "You know how my dad claimed that prison would teach Tim a lesson? Seems one of the things he learned in there was how to beat drug tests."

"God. I don't want to know." There had to be another means of locating Ed, if need be.

"Maggie, what were they – the bad dreams in that house?" Diana asked quietly.

"If you'll find me your phone book so I can see if Andy's listed, I'll tell you. According to Tim, Andy lives in Silver Lake." With caffeine and a bite or two of food in her system, her mind was switching back into high gear.

Diana twisted around in her chair toward a small pine étagère crammed with what looked to be mostly cookbooks – *The Joy of Cooking*, *Chez Panisse*, *The Art of French Cooking*, *The French Laundry*. From the lower shelf she drew out the SBC white pages and passed the directory over to Maggie.

Maggie flipped to the "Cs," found a "Chase, Andrew J." in Silver Lake. "Maybe we'll get lucky," she hoped aloud, picking up the phone and pressing in the numbers.

"Hello?" came a groggy male voice after the third ring.

"Hi, is this Andy or Andy's roommate?" She couldn't remember the guy's actual name noted in Tim's journal. And something told her the roomie didn't answer to "Neanderthal Bozo the Clown."

"This is Neil. Who's asking?"

"I'm Tim Emerson's ex-wife Maggie. Have you or Andy seen him lately?"

"Fuck, I haven't seen Tim in ages. He went to live with his sister or something."

Maggie grimaced. "Do you know if Andy's heard from him?"

"I don't think so, dude. Andy's working tonight at Kinko's. Want me to tell him to call you when he gets home?"

She almost asked which Kinko's before remembering Diana's admonition about druggies' aversion to too many questions posed by strangers. Chances were that Andy worked at a Kinko's near or not far from his own neck of the woods. "No, I'll just try him again later." She hung up. "I hate to be a pest, but can I have the Yellow Pages now?"

Diana hefted the thicker phone book onto the table. "Maggie, is that house in Del Mar haunted?"

Maggie studied Diana's expression, found it serious. "Yes," she said softly.

"My grandparents?"

Maggie hesitated, then answered, "Your grandfather. And – some piece of Tim."

Diana shuddered visibly. "That's so ... beyond horrible."

Maggie was surprised by her former sister-in-law's acceptance of the haunting. Diana, for all her sympathetic nature, was a doctor, a woman of science one would expect to be supremely skeptical of all things paranormal. "I'm so glad you don't think I'm some kind of hysteric."

"I'd never think that. I just had a feeling when Mother accidentally spilled the beans about you two living there that it was *wrong*. Wrong for you and Kat to be living right where Tim had been so terribly abused. If I didn't know my parents and their own addiction to denial, I'd have accused them of sadism for letting you guys move into that house without telling you what had gone on there." A flintiness came to her eyes. "Denial can be a form of sadism, now that I think of it."

Maggie squeezed Diana's hand. "That makes us all culpable. I kept telling myself that Tim would eventually outgrow the drugs."

"We don't know yet that you're not right." Diana chuckled grimly. "Is that hope or still more denial?"

Maggie felt for Diana's longstanding guilt over not having been able to stop her grandfather or protect her little brother. But they had little time to spare for recriminations. "Woo-hoo, there's a Kinko's on Vine, not far from Musso's," she said, touching the Yellow Page entry with a fingertip. She drained the last of her coffee. "I'm going over there, Diana. I may go to Musso's from there, depending on how long it takes with Andy."

"Let me give you a key in case you're late. And call me if you hear anything about Tim."

As she drove to Hollywood, daring to hope, she reflected on Tim's narrative. Her chest tightened. It was *him*, not some drug addicted shadow of him, inscribed in desperate blue ink on cheap lined paper. Yes, the more familiar self-pity and confusion were there, too, along with an occasional, unnerving amorality of which she'd never believed him capable. But for the first time in years, he was also fully present, the old Tim, the real Tim, alternately anguished and introspective. Some part of him had stirred from the dead, and she prayed she could find him before it was extinguished permanently.

The old Tim would have chided her good-naturedly for even thinking in such terms. There was no authentic "self," he'd have argued, only contradictory and constantly shifting "subject positions." In college he'd been so enamored of poststructuralism, his honors thesis a Derridean critique of Kant's categorical imperative. She used to wonder if what he most liked about poststructuralism was its intellectual gamesmanship, strategies of maneuver and play not unlike those he engaged while pitching. Now she suspected that he'd been drawn to the notion of a fragmentary self because it provided a theory for his own sense of dissociation.

Hollywood. Wilting monuments of bygone show-biz glamour – the Pantages, the garish pink and gray art deco of Frederick's of Hollywood, the Capital Records building with its dated stacked-record architecture, juxtaposed with tacky wig shops, tattoo parlors, cheap souvenir stands. Even on a chilly November weeknight tourists paced the sidewalks, hookers preened on curbs, and slow-moving traffic clogged Hollywood Boulevard. All the night people – Tim and herself, Ryan, Christy, Julie, and Dan – and yes, sometimes Andy Chase too – had been drawn to the seamy carnival. Upper-middle-class college kids thinking themselves oh-so-tragically hip for faking an occasional walk on the wild side. Naïve, yes, but no less poseurs and dilettantes for flirting with depravity as an amusement, a pose, like the eighteenth-century aristocrats who entertained themselves with tours of Bedlam.

She found Kinko's easily, but a parking space was another story. She finally settled for one two blocks down Vine. She wished she'd worn a warmer jacket instead of the light sweater she'd thrown over her shoulders this morning in Del Mar.

She briskly walked the two blocks and into the brightly lit, bustling Kinko's. Every copy machine was in use, every computer terminal occupied, and six or seven customers formed a FAX line. She scanned the over-bright store, spotting a number of young men and women in Kinko's vests, but no one resembling Andy Chase as she recalled him. What if his spaced-out roommate had lied, or been mistaken, about Andy's whereabouts?

She was ready to seek out a phone book and call Andy's number again when she spied a wiry fellow with center-parted brown hair who crouched beside a copier fixing a paper jam for an impatient fat woman in a pink warmup ensemble. It was Andy all right; she hadn't seen him in years but recognized that stupid middle part and the cleft in his square chin. He straightened up, grinned at the customer, showing his perfect white teeth that bore no sign of the ravages of the "meth mouth" Tim had described. Andy must have found one hell of a cosmetic dentist.

He was heading back toward the counter, and she stepped directly into his path. "Can I help you?" he said. Up close his skin was blotchy and his watery eyes blinked rapidly. Tweaking. His plastic Kinko's nametag read ANDREW CHASE, ASSISTANT MANAGER. The aspiring high-tech whiz-kid had obviously settled for more modest occupational goals.

"Andy, it's me, Maggie Flores," she said sternly. "I need to talk to you about Tim."

"Oh Christ. Is Tim dead?"

She pulled him aside, toward a copy machine topped with a "not in service" sign. "I don't know if he's dead or alive. When was the last time you saw him?"

Apparently relieved she'd not come bearing bad tidings, Andy wiped his mouth with the back of one scab-dotted hand. "Wow, let me think. Right around the time he was looking for you. Beginning of August, I guess."

"You haven't heard from him recently?"

"No. Have you tried his sister? He was crashing at her house for a while."

"Damn," she muttered.

"Sorry." Andy started to move away.

"Wait a minute," she stopped him. "Do you know this guy Ed, Tim's friend in Echo Park?"

Andy tossed her an impatient look. "I don't know any Ed. Look, Maggie, we're really busy tonight, as you can see. If Tim shows up I'll tell him you're looking for him. The two of you ought to form a tag team."

"Please, one last thing," she said, dropping her voice as well as its sharp tone. "Andy, this guy Ed's a dealer, and he might know where Tim is. I don't want to cause any trouble – I just need to find Tim."

Andy's brows knit together. "You don't know this dude's last name?"

"I've no clue."

"I know someone in Echo Park who's probably heard of this Ed. Meet me behind the store in fifteen minutes and I'll give you this other person's address."

Given the darkness and the unpredictability of the neighborhood, Maggie waited exactly fifteen minutes before exiting Kinko's and heading to the back. Andy was already there, lighting a cigarette. He handed her a slip of paper with a name – Alma

Gomez – and an address. "She's always changing her cell number and I don't know what it is," he apologized. "Just go over there tomorrow and say I referred you."

"Thanks." As an afterthought, she added, "Is she a dealer?"

"Weed. Small-time. She's no one scary, Maggie. Tim would kick my ass if I sent you into some crack house."

At once she felt rather sorry for him. "I really appreciate your help, Andy. I hope your life gets better."

He guffawed, though with little humor. "Hey, my life's not that bad. Not exactly what I planned, but hell, whose is?"

"Very true."

He snuffed out his cigarette on the pavement. "I better get back to work. Good luck, Maggie. See you around."

She left Kinko's just past seven. It would probably take a miracle for Billy to reach Hollywood by nine given the guaranteed rush-hour traffic throughout San Diego, Orange, and Los Angeles counties. She drove to the Hollywood at Highland shopping center, one of the city's more recent attempts to jumpstart urban renewal on Hollywood Boulevard. Except for some Cecil B. deMillean pillars topped with elephants and an "awards show" red carpet, it was a fairly generic multilevel mall with the inevitable Starbucks for which she was hoping.

She wished Billy weren't coming, despite the good sense of his rationale that Diana had heartily endorsed. Certainly seeking out Ed was potentially a far riskier enterprise than corralling Andy at Kinko's had been. But sex with Billy had complicated their relationship at the precise time she couldn't deal with any more complications.

Nothing was important except for finding Tim – for Kat, for herself, and for him. "Purity

of heart is to will one thing," he had ironically quoted from Kierkegaard. The line was

unfamiliar to her, but she could guess at the Danish theologian's general context;

presumably he was referring to the will to know God. Will elsewhere directed had by

definition to be impure, debased. She grimaced as she sat down with her coffee and

cookie in front of Starbucks. Kierkegaard wasn't Catholic, but damn, with that kind of

thinking he might as well have been.

At eight she called her mother again, was relieved to learn that Kat was already in

bed sound asleep. "Pobra de ella, estaba muy cansada," Eva said. Maggie reminded her

mother to keep an ear open should Kat have a nightmare or wake up agitated, and not to

hesitate to give the child half a Valium to settle her down if need be.

She decided that if she had any more coffee she'd end up almost as wired as if she

were the one tweaking, not to mention acquainting herself with every ladies room in the

mall. She had Starbucks validate her parking slip, bought a stuffed Dumbo for Kat at a

souvenir store, and left Hollywood at Highland for the restaurant. At least Musso and

Frank's had a pay-parking lot. She locked the stuffed toy in her trunk, glanced around

the lot for Billy's truck. No Ford pickup with a trailer ball amid the Mercedeses and

BMWs.

She passed a couple of smokers in the small patio, descended down old-fashioned

iron stairs into the restaurant. In the main dining room, all of the leather booths and seats

at the long counter were occupied by typical Musso and Frank's patrons – a motley of

old-timers who likely remembered when Hollywood Boulevard really was glamorous;

industry players in hip haircuts and expensive eyewear; arty twenty- and thirtysomethings in black clothes to contrast with defiantly artificial hair colors. It was noisy, like most LA "scene" restaurants, but that was OK. She wasn't up for deep conversation when and if Billy got there.

She asked one of the famously surly maitre d's to tell her friend to look for her in the bar, which was in the adjacent room along with more tables. She lucked onto a barstool and ordered one of the legendary martinis. She sipped it with care, though; she had no appetite but resolved to order at least a salad or sandwich once Billy arrived.

She was surprised not to have a long wait. Looking harried, he appeared at around twenty after. She was even more surprised by how glad she was to see him. "You are truly heroic," she said, hugging him.

He ordered a Heineken. "Jesus Christ, it feels good to be out of that goddamn traffic. How do people up here stand it?"

"You just get used to it. Shall I put in our name for a table? You must be famished."

"I already did." He took a long drink of beer. "Now, tell me what happened, from the beginning."

"It's been such a long twenty-four hours I'm not sure I even remember the beginning."

A grumpy looking waiter marched up. "Your table is ready."

"That was quick," Maggie said.

"Well, do you want it or should I give it to somebody else?" the waiter challenged in that characteristic Musso and Frank's insolence that she could never be quite sure was purely in jest.

They followed him back into the main dining room and a comfortable booth. He handed them long laminated menus, a busboy brought them water, and then they were let be.

Maggie pretended to study the menu. She gave Billy credit for not exclaiming over the a la carte prices. "Shall we order first before getting into it all?"

"No – tell me what happened."

She drew a deep breath, and recounted to him what had occurred when she and Kat went up to bed the night before.

He actually flinched on hearing how she'd seen the old man's snarling face in the kaleidoscope, but said little until her story was finished. Even then, he paused several moments before speaking. "I'm not sure I see how finding Tim's gonna fix things."

"What matters is that Kat believes it will. That's why I have to track him down somehow."

"And when you find him and he's out of his mind on meth? That's gonna help Kat?"

She was mildly irritated. "You need to understand, Billy. Kat loves him no matter what shape he's in."

"You may hate me for suggesting this. But maybe subconsciously Kat wanted you to find her dad anyway."

Was he implying the same of her subconscious as well? "Kat's subconscious didn't make me see Tim's bastard of a grandfather in that kaleidoscope," she said coldly.

"I'm not saying that. And see? You are pissed."

The waiter reappeared. "Ready?"

Maggie, who *was* pissed, welcomed the interruption. She ordered a Caesar salad and another martini, Billy a cold prime rib sandwich. "For the sake of argument," she resumed once the waiter strode off, "let's grant your point. My daughter still won't be all right until I bring him to her."

"I guess that's true," he conceded. "So the ex-roommate at Kinko's was a bust? What next?"

"Something I'm really dreading," she admitted. "It's someone Tim knew in prison and stayed with when he first got out." She couldn't bring herself to go into details. His written words – *I knew my goddamn Foucault and I still got prisonized* – sprang to mind and she winced.

"Well, that's why I'm here. You won't have to walk into the belly of the beast without backup."

She was suddenly overwhelmed by exhaustion, a sense that she was insufficient to the task that lay ahead of her. But mingled with fatigue was gratitude to him, not just for having driven three hours for her at a moment's notice, but equally for being canny enough, kind enough, to act no differently with her than he had two days ago, before they were lovers and before she discovered they had driven out the wrong ghost.

She touched his hand. "You're the best."

"Nah. Just not the worst. Don't mistake that for being a good man."

Over her protests he picked up the dinner tab, but he demurred when she told him that Tim's sister had offered them lodgings for the night. "Thank her for me, but I'm gonna get a motel room."

They stood in the dark, now half-empty Musso and Frank's parking lot, where it was too dim for her to read his expression. Could she have, would she have deciphered guilt, regret, uncertainty – or perhaps merely the practical recognition that their time had come and gone? She was glad she couldn't see.

"I'll call you first thing in the morning," she said. They kissed briefly; their close embrace lasted a little longer. She drove back to Los Feliz, pensive, worried, and impossibly tired.

It was eleven; Diana had gone to bed but her husband Wes was still up watching the local news in the family room. A suntanned, animated man in his mid-forties with crinkly laugh lines and salt-and-pepper hair and mustache, he greeted her with a hug.

She hugged him back warmly. "You two have been so good to Tim."

"We love him, Maggie. I'm sure we can find him before he's too far gone." He picked up his snifter. "Can I offer you a nightcap? Cognac?"

"I'd love one but I'd better pass. I'm so tired that I'm afraid one sip would knock me out."

"I hope you at least treated yourself to a martini at Musso's," he said with a chuckle. "Let me show you upstairs to the guest room."

"Wes, I know this sounds silly, but could I sleep in the garage apartment? Where Tim stayed?"

He shrugged. "I don't see why not. It's pretty bare-bones out there but it's got a kitchenette and a sofabed."

He found the key, switched on the outdoor lights, and led her up a flight of exterior stairs to the studio above the carriage-house style garage.

The small apartment was indeed simply furnished, but the plump sofa looked comfortable enough to sleep on without even rolling out the hide-a-bed. She felt vague disappointment at no immediate signs of Tim's brief residence until Wes pointed out the boombox, stack of CDs, and a few books on the kitchenette counter. "Those are Tim's. Di took him to Tower and Book Soup one day and bought him those as an early birthday present."

Maggie smiled. "His birthday's not until February." But she understood Diana's motives. Diana had bought him these gifts to remind him of the self he'd lost, and which she hoped he would somehow rediscover.

"Di's terrible with dates," Wes played along. "You all set, Maggie? I think there are some sodas in the little fridge but not much else."

She almost asked what they had done with the drugs and paraphernalia Tim had surely left behind, but stopped herself. Wes and Diana had followed their hearts and even their Hippocratic oaths in helping Tim, but perhaps not the letter of the law. Better for them not to tell her, and better for her not to know.

Wes bade her goodnight, and she got a second wind as she set about inspecting the CDs and books. The titles of the former, of which there were a good dozen, she might have guessed: Alice in Chains, Nirvana, Nine Inch Nails – music haunted by drugs and death. A few of their old, mutual favorites: The Cure's *Disintegration* and *Pornography*, REM's *Fables from the Reconstruction*, X's *See How We Are*. She turned her attention to the soft-cover books. Foucault's *Discipline and Punish* and Kant's *Critique of Pure Reason* were no surprise; nor, for that matter, was Charles Barkley's *I May Be Wrong (But I Doubt It)*. But *The Confessions of Saint Augustine* and a selection of poetry in interfacing English and Spanish by St. John of the Cross took her aback. At once she began to cry.

"We love him, Maggie." That was Wes's simple explanation for his and Diana's generosity. Her sadness turned to anger at the pop psychologists who sermonized about "women who love too much," at the therapists who called her "co-dependent" and an "enabler," even at her parents and friends who had told her to dump him and get on with her life. Her problem had not been that she'd loved him too much, but rather that she hadn't loved him nearly enough.

Leaving his drug paraphernalia in Kat's view was inexcusable. But it was not a sin but a symptom. She'd cast him out as rashly as she'd cast out the spirit of the frightened, abused child he once was, using their child as a justification for her own failure of empathy, courage, love. She'd behaved, far more than Diana, like Jack Emerson's blood daughter, refusing to understand, unwilling to probe beyond the effects to their cause. It wasn't tough love – it was emotional and moral cowardice.

She wept for him, for the prison rape he had suffered and the tragic light it shed on his subsequent relationship with Ed. He had been unable to tell her the truth because the truth lay in the part of him severed and suspended in timeless purgatory in the house in Del Mar. Being raped under any circumstances inflicted a singular psychic trauma, as Billy's wife proved; for Tim's fragile psyche, no less tenuously patched together than his shattered left arm, the sexual assault had to have been catastrophic. Indeed, for all his self-destructiveness, his references in the journal to explicitly suicidal feelings had all narratively followed the attack in prison.

How could she have failed him so profoundly? What if Diana and Wes hadn't stepped up to the plate? If Tim were now irrevocably lost to all of them, how would she ever explain her own complicity to Kat?

She had no answers. All she could do was give herself over to heavy, dreamless sleep.

The rainy morning to which she awakened was as welcome as the oblivion of sleep it had interrupted, even if it did recall to her the nightmare about Tim's funeral not long after she had forsaken him.

Despite the weather she wore sunglasses to conceal her swollen eyes from Billy, who arrived to pick her up at nine. Wes had already departed for work at Cedars-Sinai and Diana was feeding Brandon, precluding any introductions awkward or otherwise.

"Who is this you've got to see first?" he asked as they set off for Echo Park.

"This woman named Alma Gomez. She lives just off Sunset. Andy's sure she'll know how to find Ed."

"And these are both dealers?"

She nodded.

"I should've brought my gun," he remarked, switching the windshield wipers to high speed.

"You don't have a gun."

"'Course I do. Told you I was a redneck."

"Well, let's just hope you don't need it. I mean, Ed's an ex-con, but how threatening can this woman be?"

She started to wonder the moment they pulled up in front of the dilapidated stucco

duplex in what appeared to be a heavily Hispanic neighborhood yet to be gentrified in the

half-bohemian, half-working class community. As had occurred the previous decade in

Silver Lake, gritty blue-collar ethnic was slowly being recast in Echo Park as seedy-chic

"authenticity."

Neither Maggie nor Billy had an umbrella, and they hurried to the front door of

the duplex marked by the number Andy had written down. There was no bell. Their

knocks were presently answered by a scrawny brown woman of indeterminate age. She

wore faded jeans and a tank top, her hair cut in a messy bob. "What do you want?" she

said, sounding neither wary nor particularly interested. She reeked of stale beer.

The woman's face was so haggard it was almost fascinating, Maggie thought, like

a death mask. Her leathery skin stretched over hollow eyes, cheekbones, jaw, her teeth

yellowed, the whites of her eyes venous. It was a face that looked at once ageless and

mummified. "Are you Alma Gomez?" Maggie asked, trying not to stare.

"Who's asking?"

"Andy Chase referred me to you."

"Oh, OK. Come on in."

Maggie and Billy were both soaking, but Alma didn't object to their dripping

clothes or wet feet. Small wonder. Her living room was dark, with cheap stained carpet,

overspilling ashtrays, and haphazard piles of fast-food wrappers. There was a faint

ammonia smell of cat urine. "You got cash?" Alma said, folding her arms in businesslike

manner.

"We're not here to buy," Billy replied. "Andy said you knew where we could find this guy Ed."

Alma fumbled for a cigarette. "Fuck, I shoulda known. Who else but tweakers would show up in a goddamn rainstorm at the crack of dawn?"

Maggie disguised her relief that Andy had not steered her wrong. "I really need some crystal. Realmente lo necesito," she said. "I'm starting to crash."

The woman snickered, exhaling smoke. "Chill, senorita. Save it for the boyfriend." She looked at Billy. "Twenty bucks finders fee." She clearly assumed Billy, as the male, was in charge of disbursals.

Maggie quickly found a twenty in her purse. "Aqui, senora." Billy shot her a glare but she guessed that it would soon occur to him hers was not a perverse feminist gesture but rather a way of ensuring he stayed on guard. Alma struck her as an opportunist who wouldn't hesitate to take advantage if he was distracted.

"La senorita es muy independente," he quipped, and from his tone Maggie knew he'd gleaned her purpose.

Alma shoved the bill into her jeans pocket. "Ok, I'm gonna call Ed first to let him know you guys are coming," she said, grabbing a cordless phone. "He gets fucking paranoid when strangers stop by without a head's up first." She snickered again. "And if you guys are narcs, well, may God fucking help you."

She thumbed in a number. "Hey, dickwad. Get your ass out of bed – I'm sending some people over. Dude and chick in wet clothes." She then set down the phone. "OK, I left a message. You tell Andy he owes me one."

"Are you sure Ed's home?" Maggie pressed.

"Where else would he be? He never picks up the phone," Alma snapped. "Christ, you tweakers get on my nerves."

She gave them Ed's address but didn't see them to the door.

"Nice lady," Billy said grimly, helping Maggie back into the truck.

"Yes, charming." She pulled the shoulder belt across her wet sweater.

He climbed into the driver's side. "Now, how do I get to Big Ed's Crystal Cathedral?"

"It's less than a mile away, assuming this is the right address,"

They found themselves on another unprettified block, in front of a rundown bungalow with a high chain-link fence and an ominous "Beware of Dog" sign posted on the gate. Maggie struggled not to picture Tim living here. "If a rabid pit bull comes racing out from around the corner I trust you to do the gentlemanly thing," she warned Billy.

He cautiously opened the gate. "Only if you admit then you wish I'd brought my gun."

But Ed's guard dog seemed as elusive as whatever cat had left the urine stink in Alma's apartment. Maggie pressed the rusty doorbell, heard its tinny buzz from within, followed by footsteps. The door flung open, though not the screen behind which stood a strongly built man who looked like he'd been working out with weights for years. He had dark hair clipped close to his skull, small eyes and a lantern jaw, and his thick arms bore intricate veins of tattoos from his wrists to biceps beneath his T-shirt. "What can I do for ya?" he said gruffly, making no move to open the screen door. Still no sound of barking, and Maggie now suspected the sign was but a decoy.

If she'd had to force herself not to stare at the ghoulish Alma Gomez, she was wholly unable to tear her eyes from this frightening-looking man. "My name is Maggie Flores," she started tentatively.

Now he was gaping at her. "Shit, I'll be damned," he said, abruptly yanking open the screen. "It *is* you. Little Maggie of the Flowers."

She felt faint but couldn't show it; it would be like betraying fear to a vicious dog, although in truth he sounded more astonished than hostile. "This is my friend Billy," she stammered. "I need to find Tim."

He shrugged them inside. Apparently he'd replaced the personal property stolen as a result of Tim's improvised neighborhood giveaway. The dingy living room boasted a plasma TV, expensive stereo system, and deep red leather sectional couch.

"Where's the dog?" Billy asked with a tinge of irony.

"With my ex-wife in Bakersfield," Ed said flatly.

"How did you know who I was?" Maggie all but whispered.

"He always had your picture with him." His manner remained direct, neither suspicious nor familiar. "So he's missing? He sure as hell ain't here."

"You haven't seen him in the last few days?" she tried.

"Sweetheart, I ain't seen him since the day last July he forgot to lock the door, and cost me about fifty grand worth of shit. I always figured he went back to you." He grabbed a Tecate off the scarred coffee table. "Have a seat. Want a brew?"

She was very much surprised that Billy answered in the affirmative. He looked studiously inscrutable.

It took Ed only a moment to return with the beer for his guest. "Yep, I was pissed as all fuck he left the house open like that. There's a tweaker for ya, I said. Now I wonder if maybe he did it on purpose."

Maggie said nothing.

But her expression must have betrayed her, for Ed continued, "And that's still a tweaker for you. They get off on betrayal like they get off on crystal."

"Yeah, whatever," Billy said. "Who gives a shit what makes this guy tick? Do you have any idea where he might be?"

"*I* give a shit," Maggie snapped. She looked back at their stone-faced host. "He hasn't been with me. He's been in drug rehab the last few months. And now he's gone and I don't know where he might have gone. I was hoping you would."

Ed frowned, appeared actually to be considering it. "He wouldn't show his ass here, not unless I had the last eight-ball of crank in LA, and that's sure as shit not the case. The dude was like a ghost – in the slammer, out of the slammer, he just passed through without ever really being there."

Maggie saw her own shock at the fumbling analogy mirrored in Billy's eyes.

"What?" Ed demanded.

She shook her head. "It's nothing – it's just that your description was really on point."

"I can't blame you for thinking me a faggot and a scumbag all this time," Ed said. "But I felt sorry for him. From day one in the pen he was a mark, with that pretty face and college-boy way of talking. Hell yeah, there was something in it for me. But I felt sorry for him." He spoke slowly, unemotionally, save for the barest hint of regret.

Maggie felt exceedingly awkward. "Billy's right – this is not the time or place to psychoanalyze Tim. Just promise me, Ed, that if he does show up, or if you hear anything about him, you'll contact me right away." She scribbled her cell number on the flip side of the same paper scrap on which Alma had scrawled Ed's address.

He accepted the paper. "Hang in there, Little Maggie of the Flowers," he said, escorting them out. To Billy he added, "Be good to this sweet lady, dude."

"Oughta keep that dog on a leash," Billy advised.

Maggie entertained the possibility that she was dreaming. Soon she'd wake up in the strange sofabed above Diana and Wes's garage, ill-rested but anxious to resume the search for Tim. What had just taken place with Ed could only have unfurled in her subconscious.

Evidently Billy shared in the sentiment, for he was silent until they had driven out of Echo Park and back into Hollywood. "That was surreal. Wanna get some coffee?"

She nodded, not yet persuaded she wasn't dreaming.

It was somehow comforting that he pulled into an IHOP rather than a pseudo-chic generic chain like Starbucks or The Coffee Bean. The fluorescent lighting and crayon-hued vinyl booths of this decidedly unhip coffee shop served to confirm to her she had been fully awake for hours now. So did the standard-issue white coffee cups and saucers that the waitress placed before them. She took a sip. Nothing fancy, but strong and hot, and that was good enough for this strange morning. "It's hard for me to believe ... that Tim actually lived with someone like Ed," she said, guessing that Billy had inferred the details she'd pointedly omitted.

"Not having been in prison – through the grace of God, I might add – I don't judge the choices people make when they're in there."

"But you have that stern brow."

"Do not."

"Liar." She sighed, belatedly opening a plastic tub of half-and-half, which she stirred into her coffee. "But now I'm at a loss as to where to look next."

"I can't help you there, Maggie. But I do have a hunch about one thing."

"What?"

"Just a hunch. But I don't think he left rehab to go back on drugs."

Hope made her glance up from her coffee, but it evaporated when she saw his gravity. "You think he went somewhere to die. Or that he's already dead."

"Whoa. Don't jump to conclusions. Thanks to that house of yours, I do believe in ghosts. But I'm not trying to be metaphysical here. Just the opposite."

"How so?"

"Logically, if he cut out on rehab to score some meth, why wouldn't he first go to people he knew for sure would have it? Especially if the craving was so intense as all that."

Her welling panic ebbed. "But if not for crystal, why did he leave?"

"To run away from himself, I'd guess."

No judgment in his voice or brow this time. Indeed, she thought she detected, for the first time, a note of sympathy toward Tim. "That's why I have to find him and explain to him about the house and the lost child. So he can stop running." She remembered that "NO! LEAVE ME THE FUCK ALONE!" inked with such fierce desperation he'd torn through the paper. Suddenly, she realized she was wrong – she had read it wrong. "Oh my God!"

"Jesus, Maggie!"

It wasn't desperation at all. It was a possibly lethal determination. "I have to get back to Del Mar. I think he's been trying to get to the house."

"He's been missing for three days. What's he been doing, walking to San Diego?"

Her heart raced with both fear and certainty. "I don't know … maybe he doesn't remember exactly where it is. He hasn't been there since he was a kid." She pulled her cellphone out of her purse. "Let me at least run this by Diana."

To her mild disappointment, Diana was only slightly less skeptical than Billy. "You're right – I'm sure he wouldn't remember how to get there or even what street it's on. I don't, and I was eighteen the last time I was there, not twelve like Tim. But why wouldn't he have called me if he were still clean? And where's he been for the last few days?"

Maggie had no answers other than her unwavering intuition. "All I know is that I've got to get home right away."

"What about Kat?"

"I'm leaving her with my parents until he shows up and I can see for myself what kind of shape he's in."

"Oh Maggie, I'll keep my fingers crossed that you're right about this."

"See you in a few minutes."

As she tucked her phone back into her purse, she noticed that Billy was eyeing her in open concern. "Aren't you forgetting about something?"

"No, didn't you hear me tell Diana about Kat?"

He stood with her, tossing a five onto the table. "I mean the old guy."

She tossed back her damp hair. "I'm on to him now. It's not us he's after. It's what's left of Tim."

"Maybe the old guy's not so easily outsmarted. I don't like the idea of you there by yourself."

"Well, frankly, I'm not crazy about it either, but it has to be. Come on, Billy. I want to be on the 5 south before the lunch-hour rush."

CHAPTER 10

Speeding out of Los Angeles County, she explained on the phone to Kat that she'd not found Daddy yet but was positive she would very shortly. Kat seemed to take heart from her certainty. "Call me when you find him, Mommy."

"You know I will, sweetie. Prometo, me hija." No more habitual "deferring to Dad," as Diana put it, about speaking Spanish in the home, even as a thirty-two year old mother herself. Once this ordeal was over, all of them could finally be whole again.

The rain, though somewhat lighter than this morning's, followed her to Del Mar. She pulled into her driveway and felt her courage falter. In the wet gray afternoon, the house looked even less inviting than Alma Gomez's seedy duplex in Echo Park had. She'd declined Billy's offer to meet up with her here, but now she was second-guessing her decision. No Kat awaited within, no Thumper. Only him, the Shadow Man, awaiting not her but Tim.

The thought of Tim steeled her. She retrieved her satchel from the trunk and went inside.

It was dim, almost dark, though it was not quite three. She switched on a pole lamp in the living room. Beyond the sliding glass door and redwood deck, the sea and sky might as well have been smoke. Smoke. That was it – she would build a fire, even if all she had was a Dura-Flame. How foreboding could a house be with a blazing fire in the hearth?

Prefab though it was, the Dura-Flame log was fragrant. She poured a glass of wine and curled up on the sofa, listening to the rain, gazing at the dance of flames in the fireplace. She too was waiting.

"I'm not going to let you have him, you old bastard," she said aloud. "You stole part of his life, but you didn't destroy him." She gave full voice to her anger. "Is that why you refuse to die, you son of a bitch? You broke him in two – " (and from months back Kat's voice echoed, *People shouldn't hit people. It breaks them in two*) "— yes, you broke him in two, but you didn't kill him! And you're not going to!"

Stomp stomp stomp down the stairs.

And then there was Tim.

He looked horrible, worse even than in the ID Polaroid paperclipped to his rehab notebook, more gaunt and sunken than Alma Gomez. Soaking wet as if he had spent not just hours but days in the rain, and – uncharacteristically – he smelled bad, of mildew and filth and something else awful, something fetid and rotting.

Maggie leaped to her feet and recoiled, despite herself. "Oh my God, Tim! I've been so worried – "

She broke off. He was smiling now, crazily, showing stumps of broken black teeth. He offered a skeletal hand as if inviting her to dance.

It was not him.

"All the king's horses and all the king's men, couldn't put Timmy together again," the thing croaked, stepping closer as she backed away. She hurled her wine glass at the creature, striking it squarely in the face whose skin was peeling away before her eyes to reveal an older, wizened visage that, however distorted, she recognized. "Get out," it snarled. "Don't interfere or you'll be sorry, you little whore. *Puta.*"

"I won't leave him to you!" she screamed, even though instinct was urging her to flee, to escape by any means she could.

Having shed the remnants of the illusive Tim-shape, the Shadow Man let his hideous face glare out beneath a gray fedora, the chimerical old sweatshirt and jeans replaced by a trenchcoat. "*Puta,*" he hissed at her. "Baby-killer. That was a baby boy just like Timmy that you two murdered. You didn't think you'd have to pay the piper for killing that baby, *puta*?"

She flinched as if she'd been shot. She clamped her hands over her ears, squeezed her eyes shut, but it was useless. She still heard him, saw him.

"You'll pay for messing with me, too, you little greaser whore. Baby-killer," he taunted.

"Mags!"

She spun around toward the front door. "Tim, *go!* Get out of here!"

Dripping wet, his long hair plastered to his skull, he froze in the front hallway, his eyes transfixed and unblinking and locked on the gray figure at the bottom of the stairs. She could no longer see it, but she knew it was still there.

She ran to Tim, grabbed his arm and shook it. It was even his bad arm, but he remained motionless, eyes burning and sightless. "Don't listen to him, Tim," she pleaded. "I know about the little lost boy. Don't, Timmy. Don't let him finish the job."

Eerily he touched an index finger to his lips. "Ssh. Ssh."

"You don't have to hide from him any more, mi querido."

"Ssh." A little more insistent.

She could see the apparition again, still in the coat and fedora, but now in its benign, avuncular guise from her dream, from the family photograph that Diana had shown her. "Just take the stairs one at a time, Timmy. That's all I ask," it wheedled. "Is that to much to ask?"

At once Tim's deep brown eyes lost their glaze. He reached into the pocket of the damp, ill-fitting bomber jacket he wore and produced a plain wooden cross about ten inches tall. "Go to hell," he said quietly, lifting the cross to the specter's face. "Go ... to ... hell."

"You little shit, you don't talk to me like that," wheezed the shape. It refused to cower but its skin was starting to peel away again. "The time's coming to pay the piper, for you and the Mexican bitch and the brat – "

Tim pressed the cross into what was rapidly becoming burnt yellow pulp. Chunks of the glob stuck to the cross. And then it was gone, all of it – the coat, the hat, the nauseous pulp.

Only then did Tim lower the cross and casually set it on the mantle above the dwindling fire. "You OK, Mags?" he asked, sounding tentative, as if he'd interrupted an otherwise innocuous afternoon.

She fell into him and held him as tightly as she could. "I love you so much. Te amo tambien, mi querido."

And then the corner of her eye caught a waft of smoke shaped like a man in a hat and coat floating at the foot of the staircase.

She passed out in her ex-husband's arms.

"Yeah, Kit-Kat. I can't wait either."

Maggie eased an eye open. Tim perched on the side of her bed, considerably drier, the phone to his ear. How fine he looked, with clear eyes and skin. He was still too thin but no longer haggard. Had he ever looked so well?

"Mommy's resting now, but she'll call you when she wakes up. I love you to pieces, baby."

Maggie sat up, motioning for the phone, but he was already hanging up. "Hey, lie back down," he said, twisting over to readjust the comforter over her shoulder. "Di said you need to keep your feet elevated, too." He propped her ankles up on his denimed thigh.

"You're as shaggy as Warlock," she said, reaching out to stroke his nearly shoulder-length hair.

"Who's Warlock? And you don't dig the Johnny Damon hair?"

""Who's Johnny Damon?"

They both smiled.

"How long was I out?" The last thing she remembered was the glop on the wooden cross.

"Only a couple minutes. I called my sister and she told me what to do. And that Kat's with Armando and Eva."

"Tim, hand me the phone, sweetie. I've got to call Kat back so she won't worry about me."

"She's cool, Mags. Said she was so happy she and Thumper were going to go play in the puddles. Presumably the ones outside."

She threw an arm over her eyes, chuckling. "Don't make me laugh. I have so much to ask you. And to tell you."

He looked thoughtful. "Same here."

She folded back a corner of the duvet. "Get under here and snuggle. It's chilly in here."

"I'm still pretty damp."

"Aqui, muchacho." She patted the sheets.

Once nestled into him, she said, "Did Diana tell you we've been living here?"

He shook his head. "I know she was trying to get me clean, but I wish to hell she had told me. Jesus fucking Christ, to have you and Kat in this house, with … "

He was growing emotional. She caressed his chest, over his banging heart, to soothe him. "It's OK. Maybe this stuff should wait."

"No." He heaved a deep, deliberate breath as if to steady himself. "It all needs to be out in the open, Mags. I can't believe the violence I've done to you and Kat and everybody by trying to bury myself in the dark."

"Not to us, Tim. It's the violence that you've done to yourself that's mattered all along."

He winced. "Don't be so damn forgiving."

"Nothing to forgive."

He arched an eyebrow. "OK, let's table that discussion. You have any food downstairs? You look weak, baby, and I'm starving."

"First, tell me – what made you leave rehab and come here?" When he looked hesitant, she added gently, "I read the notebook you wrote in rehab."

He passed a nervous hand through his hair. "Oh man. Well, fuck. I guess that just means I don't have quite as much to explain."

"Honey, don't cry. I was just so amazed by your courage."

He gave her a quick kiss before swinging his long legs out from under the comforter and getting up. He cleared his throat. "I've gotta get us something to eat. I know I'm supposed to emote and all that nice healthy shit, but it's still a little hard for me." He hurried out of the room.

Five minutes later he was back with two Diet Cokes and a peanut butter and jelly sandwich. "Half of that's yours." He set the plate on the nightstand.

Sitting up, she rubbed his back, rested her cheek against his shoulder. "Kat sent me to find you."

"Yeah, she told me."

"Did you sense somehow that we needed you? Is that why you left the clinic?"

He shifted, clasping her to his chest and leaning back against the headboard. "No," he said, balancing his chin on the crown of her head. "I thought I was losing my mind. I kept hearing him taunting me. He wouldn't stop. I knew he was dead and I just wanted to make his voice stop."

"That's why you came back here to the house?"

"OK, why not?" he said, with a faint note of exasperation.

"All right," she relented. "Go on."

"My second month in rehab I met this Catholic priest. Jesuit. An alcoholic, pretty far gone by the time he got into Drunk Camp. Not one of your garden-variety altar-boy gropers, but he'd had problems with his bishop because of his politics. The more he drank, the more pissed off and outspoken he got. In Mass, he'd use the homily to rant and rave about how Bush was fucking up the country."

"Bless his heart. One of God's lefties."

He smiled. "Oh yeah. *Catholic Worker*, liberation theology, all that cool stuff." He patted his T-shirt pocket, found his hard-pack Marlboros. Maggie moved the untouched sandwich from the plate to a paper napkin so he'd have an ashtray.

He took a deep draw from the cigarette. "Anyway, this guy was brainy. I liked talking to him. Not about our addictions – God, you get so damn tired of talking about your addiction. We talked, you know, about ideas."

She thought of the unlikely religious books in the garage apartment, realizing his search had begun even before he'd agreed to go back into treatment. She was curious as to whether he'd overcome his hostility to religion, and she wondered what, if any role, the Jesuit had played in Tim's acquisition of the wooden cross he'd wielded against the

monster. But she decided to let him proceed with his story at his own pace.

"He checked out a few weeks ago. When I started hearing the old man, I knew I

had to come down here and find him. I had no memory where the house was, but I knew

he'd be here. Not dead or alive but dead and alive."

Again their eyes met, and she knew he referred to himself as well. "Since you've

already chastised me for interrupting you, maybe I'd just better nod," she teased.

He tweaked her nose. "Sorry about that."

"So how did you get down here? Your car was at Diana's."

"I hitchhiked. I remembered that Father Bob's parish was St. Thomas Aquinas, in

Carlsbad – how could I forget a name like that? The Seven Proofs of the existence of

God, and the Scholastics. That shit's scarier than Hobbes. But if Bob had been with

some generic Holy-Mary-Mounting-Joseph church it never would have stuck in my

mind."

Something told her that wooden cross and friendly left-wing priest

notwithstanding, he hadn't changed his views about Catholicism in particular and religion

in general. She was secretly relieved. "You located Father Bob, I presume?"

"Yeah. I told him about the voice and that I was afraid I was losing my mind.

He'd been in group therapy the day it was my turn to do the dog-and-pony show, so he

knew all about the old man. Mags, he didn't think I was crazy." He mashed out the

cigarette on the plate. "I'm sure he had no idea that *thing* has been here all along – fuck,

neither did I, really – but he thought I needed to confront my demons, at least

symbolically. He let me borrow his car and I drove up and down every goddamn street in

Del Mar between the coast highway and the 5 until I recognized this house. You know the rest."

"Your grandmother left this house to Kat in her will. We've been living here since August. I'm sure she must have meant it as a peace offering."

He grimaced. "Yeah, right. It kills me to think of Kat here, with him. Jesus!"

"You protected her, Tim. From day one you protected her from him." And she told him about the kaleidoscope and the little boy apparition in the Fernando Valenzuela uniform.

This was, evidently, more than he could bear. He wept openly, his fingers tangled in his hair. "Ah, shit," he gasped. "Shit."

She guided his head to her lap. "It's finally over, Tim."

"It's not that easy, Maggie. I can't ask you and Kat to put up with me rebuilding myself from scratch."

"Whether you ask or not is irrelevant."

"Marry me again?"

"I will," she said with a smile. "Either with another fake Elvis officiating or in a white dress with a train three blocks long."

"Ugh. Which one of us has to wear it?"

How she had missed his quick, offbeat wit over the lost years. At last he was back.

"You and Kat have to move out of this house. If it's hers, it's hers. Who knows what the old lady was thinking? But I won't have any of us living here."

He's not sure the Shadow Man's really gone for good, she realized. She was glad his face still rested in her lap lest he note her rekindled apprehension. "Agreed. But Kat loves her school and she's taken up horseback riding at a ranch not far from here."

He sat up. "Really? How cool. Can't wait to see her cantering around."

She smothered the unsettling picture of him and Billy face to face. *Oh my God, these are the same sheets!* It was all she could do not to spring off the bed and drag Tim with her. *Puta.* "Sweetie, would you mind terribly going back downstairs and bringing us both a glass of wine? Or shouldn't you have it?"

"I'm fine with it. Wine sounds great, in fact. Be right back."

Frantic though she was, she feared he'd definitely think something amiss if he returned to find the bed stripped. Blame the dog, she told herself, yanking off the top and fitted sheets and tossing them in a corner.

"I just discovered that Thumper left a little gift on the bedding," she said as he came back into the room with two glasses of white wine.

"Solid, liquid, or gas?"

"Oh God, don't ask!" She accepted the glass from him, savored the reassurance as much as the oaky Chardonnay flavor of the first sips. "We'll go get Kat tomorrow and take it from there."

He eased the glass from her hand and set it along with his own on the dresser. Framing her face with his hands, he kissed her mouth leisurely. At length he raised his head. "Hm, what are you thinking?"

"I'm just wondering what made him so cruel."

"Does it matter? Fuck it, Mags, I've given up wondering. What difference would it make if he'd been a drunk or psychotic or beaten to a pulp by his own father or grandfather? Or if my own father had been too bullied by him to intervene? None of it matters. I can't have him – or this house – as my referent any more."

She was about to speak, but the house seemingly chose that moment to spring first one, then another almost simultaneous leak in the roof right over their heads. "Shit!" she squealed, brushing at the raindrop that struck her forehead.

They dashed downstairs in tandem for pots to collect the rainwater. Maggie left a message with the property management office asking for a referral to a roofer, and Tim left one for Father Bob. She finished her wine, and then they leaped into her car to drive north to join their daughter.

CHAPTER 11

The huge black horse snorted and groaned, his cart-sturdy musculature straining with each heavy anapest beat of the canter. Mane and tail flew like silk banners in the wind. The rider was one with the strong horse's locomotion as they traversed the rails of the large all-purpose arena.

"Look how beautiful, " Nicole Ludwig marveled, proud of her horse – or so Maggie hoped – commenting to the handful of holiday revelers who had stepped away from the center of the ranch's New Year's day party to watch Katya Emerson's dad ride Warlock.

Kat, for whom the spectacle had lost a little of its novelty, tugged Maggie's sweater. "Mommy, can I go ride Sugar?"

"Sweetie, who don't you give her the day off like Rhonda's giving the other school horses?"

Kat smiled. "Because she's not a school horse any more, remember? She's mine."

Maggie silently cursed her parents for buying Sugar for Kat as a Christmas present. Armando and Eva were already helping them out with money; to have thrown Sugar and her accompanying expenses into the mix only compounded Maggie's worry that her little family would never get back on its feet.

Rhonda, in candy cane earrings, strolled over. "When are we going to see you on a horse, Maggie?"

When hell freezes over, Maggie wanted to reply; watching Tim ride made her almost as nervous as watching Kat. "It's my New Year's resolution," she lied.

In truth, her resolutions were both more modest and daunting. Keeping her family together, balancing Kat's needs, Tim's needs, and her own, trying to help them all adjust to a normalcy that was utterly alien. With the house leased out again as of this day, family finances were bound to improve, but they'd likely still need some assistance from both sets of in-laws with rent. Their two-bedroom apartment in Solana Beach was small, but the rent was outrageous, considering they had no view, no in-unit washer and drier, and no garage. Tim hated the handouts from family even more than she; his relationship with Jack and Beth Emerson remained strained, despite his sobriety and reconciliation with his ex-wife and child. At least Diana and Wes were happy to run interference, and their new baby had gone a ways toward easing Emerson family tensions. Diana and Maggie had undertaken their own species of intervention with Jack over the Christmas holiday, virtually ordering him not to start pressuring Tim about future employment or educational plans. For the foreseeable future, they warned, Tim's full-time job had to be re-learning how to live drug-free.

It was hard enough keeping Tim from beating up himself. He hated feeling as underfoot as Thumper when Kat was at school and Maggie working at her computer. He wanted to take a part-time job, and Maggie'd had to enlist the support of his friend Father Bob, a passionate, energetic man of fifty, to convince Tim to limit himself to daily NA or AA meetings and church-related volunteer work for the time being. Tim's involvement with the church both amused and perplexed her. By his own admission he didn't believe in God and thought the Pope had no more moral authority than Bug Selig, the Commissioner of Major League Baseball. But Tim didn't seem to mind helping with the parish newsletter or carting around canned goods for food drives, and Kat was delighted that her father willingly ushered during Sunday Mass.

What he especially loved, though, was accompanying Kat to her riding lessons. He was openly proud of his daughter's equestrian talent, which endeared him to the barnyard biddies already a-cluck over his apparently out-of-the-blue materialization in Maggie and Kat's lives. When Nicole, upon their introduction, tossed out her characteristic blithe invitation to ride Warlock, Tim promptly took her up on it, much to Maggie's consternation. Not only had it been years since he'd ridden a horse, but she also knew that the situation would not sit well with Billy. He and Tim were polite, but seemed instinctively to mistrust one another.

A jagged part of her missed Billy, their easy friendship and casual intimacy that probably would have survived that one afternoon of mad misguided sex. Maybe someday she'd tell Tim, maybe some part of him already knew. But socializing with Billy as before was out of the question. She and Tim didn't do much socializing anyway, save for an occasional dinner and DVD with Ryan, or a weekend visit with Maggie's parents or Diana and Wes. Maggie struggled mightily against the urge to circumscribe

their world too closely. God forbid she turn all three of them into agoraphobics like

Stephanie O'Donnell. After all, it had been shadows, not the outside world, that had

threatened to destroy them. She did her best not to think about the Shadow Man, not to

wonder if he still cast a hazy silhouette at the bottom of those stairs, just as he still did at

night in her dreams, shapeless yet somehow unmistakably gloating. She didn't tell Tim

about the dreams – he had his own nightmares to deal with. And if she managed to drink

just enough wine to feel a little tipsy, she either didn't dream at all or didn't remember if

she had.

Tim had slowed Warlock to a jog, and Kat beckoned him over to the rail. "When

do I get to ride Warlock?"

"What if Sugar gets jealous?" he queried.

"But Nicole says … "

Reassured that Tim was going to tow her line about the big horse's unsuitability

for Kat, Maggie wandered in the direction of the refreshment tables set up on the porch of

the Tack 'n' Snack. She peered into a cooler. The only beverages were soft drinks and

bottled water. Damn it. She placed a few Christmas cookies on a paper plate to share

with Tim and Kat.

Starting back toward the all-purpose arena, she caught sight of Billy across the

way, using the crossties at the riding school to curry a big chestnut gelding easily as tall

as Warlock if not so heavily built. She wandered over to them. "Hey, there. How come

you're not back by the tack store making merry?"

He tossed aside the curry comb, taking up a soft brush for the horse's large head. "I'm not big on office parties," he said, gently rubbing the brush along the horse's muzzle.

"Who's this?"

"Name's Westcott. He's an Oldenburg – gonna make a great hunter/jumper someday."

She patted the horse's broad neck, offered him a cookie, which he accepted daintily. "He's a very handsome boy."

"He's as smart as Warlock but with better manners. Don't give him more than one, though. I'd like to keep it that way." He rubbed the gunk from the corner of the horse's eye with a soft rag. "So – how's life?"

"It's good. Challenging, sometimes. But things are going fine."

"Don't miss your ocean view?"

"The view, yes, but not the ambience."

"Can't have everything, I guess."

She turned around at the approaching, heavy clip-clop of hooves. Tim, on Warlock. Damn if he didn't have a sixth sense.

"Here you are," he said, easing back the reins to stop Warlock. "I thought maybe you were hiding from David Coprophile."

"That's what Tim calls Paul the Pervo," Maggie explained.

"Clever," Billy said.

"So, what do you think, man?" Tim said levelly. "Isn't it about time we get Mags up on a horse?"

"Not that horse," Billy replied, eyeing Warlock rather than Tim. "If you want to risk your neck on a horse that's barely green-broke, that's up to you." He looked at Maggie. "You should ride, though."

Afraid the exchange was becoming too awkwardly metaphorical, she felt herself flush. Dear God, she wanted a drink.

She *needed* a drink.

"Sweetie, can I talk to you in private?" she said to Tim, although it was almost as if the words were speaking her and not the other way around.

They stepped away from Billy and the Oldenburg. Tim started to dismount but she waved for him to stay on the horse. "Timmy, I think I'm getting my period. I'm just going to dash over to Rite-Aid and get some tampons." Her period wasn't due for another ten days, but no matter; she'd tell him later it was a false alarm. Because men knew next to nothing about women's periods, they were easy to fool about the same.

At the drugstore she bought a bottle of inexpensive, twist-off-capped chardonnay, another, plastic bottle of Diet 7-Up, and a plastic kitchen funnel, throwing a box of Tampax into her cart to appease her guilty conscience. She drove around to the most deserted end of the shopping center, by a "Closed For the Holidays" Barnes and Noble's. She dumped most of the 7-Up out the window, then used the funnel to refill the green plastic bottle with wine. She took a deep gulp, followed by two more. Her breathing and the pressure points at her temples relaxed. She topped off the plastic bottle again before recapping the remainder of the wine and tucking it under the crumpled, seldom-used car cover in the trunk. In her purse she found one of the peppermints she often carried there to give to the horses, popped it into her mouth, and drove back to the Happy New Year celebration at Camino Equestrian.

Part Two: <u>Tim</u>

"What can I know? What ought I to do? What can I hope?"

Immanuel Kant

CHAPTER 1

The little patio off the dining area had been his smoker's haven, his thinking spot, from the day they'd moved in nearly four months before. These days, when he doubted she cared any longer if he smoked inside or out, it was still his haven.

He'd quit doing irony along with meth; now he realized irony was just a hipper form of self-pity. He had no self-pity. The situation was what it was. No time for the Big Picture, either. All the "one day at a times" and "easy does its," Twelve-Step mantras that had always sounded so facile and Stuart Smalley-esque (*I'm good enough, I'm smart enough, and doggone it, people like me*) now swirled about him like a cloying miasma, mocking the scorn he'd once heaped upon them. At no other time in his life had he so longed for the manic energy and present-fixation that crystal brought. And at no other time in his life could he less afford even to fleetingly acknowledge as much to himself.

He lit another cigarette, listened to the quiet, listened for the muted rote of the surf across the street. They really ought to have moved further inland, east of I-5; cramped though it was, this little apartment on busy Sierra was a block from the ocean and they were paying dearly in rent for the proximity. He wondered how she had ever managed on a freelancer's wages to support Kat and herself, before the fateful windfall of the trust and the house and the old man. The windfall had probably saved his life, but was it at the too-high cost of hers? They were adamant about taking no more from the trust than covered Kat's expenses, not their own, and even that still felt opportunistic and mercenary. Kat deserved better than two parents forced to support her through the largesse of a dead woman she'd never known. But again, the situation was what it was, and he supposed they should be grateful for a source of income not dependent on the fruits of their own labor.

He'd assumed most of her freelance obligations with none of her clients the wiser. She'd told him what the work required and as always, he was a good student, a quick study. Sometimes when she felt up to it she helped him, or made the phone calls necessary for keeping up the pretense. When she couldn't, his years of easy, practiced lying came to their rescue. He'd even told one client the week before who was seeking a face to face meeting that she had Epstein-Barr, and too compromised an immune system to leave the apartment.

Because he, of all people, should have noticed the crisis creeping up, he questioned his own motives for not doing so. Alcohol and marijuana had never been a problem for him, and although – or perhaps because – he knew it was in defiance of AA and NA's strict admonitions against any kind of intoxicant, he truly saw no harm in having a few beers with her, with Ryan, sharing the occasional joint when Kat was

spending the night with a friend. Neither booze nor weed ignited that insatiable *more!*

within his being that meth did. Sometimes he'd join her in wine with or after dinner,

other times he'd refrain. Fuck, in Europe they drank it with lunch, too, every day, and

they were the healthiest people in the Western world. And when she'd begun to drink a

bottle of wine most every night he had actually thought it good for her. She never really

got drunk, and she was under so much stress, worrying about him, about Kat, about

money. But did a part of him recognize what was happening and somehow feel

vindicated for her weakness given all the years ruined by his own? Or was his refusal to

see born of habitual blind faith in her strength, in her being the one who held things

together? Worse still, was his subconscious filing away her frailty for future reference to

justify a relapse of his own?

　　　　She was so proud; she'd always tried so hard to present a perfect façade to the

world. Not for him, because for years he'd monopolized the role of family fuckup. He

knew she suffered keenly from a sense of having failed everyone, even though he was

fairly certain that almost no one among their family and friends suspected the extent of

her problem. The only person he'd told about her excessive drinking was Father Bob,

and then only after he'd discovered in mid-January that she was drinking during the day,

too, camouflaging vodka in Coke cans and with breath mints. Predictably the priest had

recommended inpatient treatment and AA, both so instrumental in his own recovery. But

he didn't judge Tim for refusing, for admitting he couldn't humiliate her by confronting

her with what she already knew and agonized over. Besides, he'd added, she wasn't an

alcoholic; it was the goddamn house and the old man that had done this to her. How insane and naïve of them to have believed the house's virulence, its toxicity, was so

easily subdued. "He did this to her because she made sure he couldn't do it any more to

me."

Though a priest, Father Bob was a man of reason and attempted to dissuade Tim

from this line of thinking. Alcoholism was a disease, not a supernatural stigma; who

knew better than he himself? But then, Father Bob hadn't witnessed their battle with that

awful thing at the foot of the stairs, heard its mocking voice or smelled its putrescence.

Though the priest hadn't said as much, Bob plainly attributed Tim's account of the

bizarre encounter with the malignant ghost of his grandfather to an overly excited

imagination.

"Daddy?"

Behind him Kat, in her flannel pajamas, was slipping through the screen door to

join him.

"You should be in bed, baby." But he eased her onto his knee and wrapped his

arms around her slim waist.

"I can't sleep."

He knew she missed her mother. Maggie tried to keep up appearances with Kat,

but the child was too astute and, unfortunately, too experienced with having a parent

simultaneously there and not there to accept the charade. "Things'll get better, Kat," he

said, smoothing her hair. "Look at me. I got better and Mommy's not half as sick as I

was."

"I don't want her to go away, though."

"She's not going to. She's gonna be OK. We all are." Of course, he didn't believe a word of it but hoped she would.

"I wish we were all in our old house."

"Hm, back in LA?"

She shifted in his lap to face him. "No, silly. Where Mommy and I lived before you came home. We shouldn't have left."

Tim hoped that the darkness shielded his revulsion. "There were leaks in the roof, Kat. We couldn't stay."

"I liked it there until the little boy left. Then when you came home I didn't even miss him anymore."

He tried not to shudder, just as he tried not to consider the possibility that Kat, too, had been infected through her brief exposure to the house's malignancy. "Someday we'll have a really cool house," he improvised. "As nice as Aunt Di and Uncle Wes's, or your abuelos' place." Eva and Armando were another worry. How long before they sensed that their daughter wasn't *quite right*? He hoped that if they did, they would blame the stress of his own peculiar circumstances. And maybe he was being hypervigilant, but he thought Eva was starting to sound skeptical about his various excuses why Maggie couldn't come to the phone.

Maggie would cry and cry every hungover morning, begging him not to tell anyone – that is, after she begged him to bring her just a little glass of something to get her past the nerves and shakes. Lately she'd begun to suffer from acute anxiety attacks, drunk or sober, if she set foot outside the apartment, a circumstance that put him in the

position of having to be her supplier. That would really break him up if he let himself
think about it.

Thus it was that Tim Emerson, onetime student philosopher and recovering meth
addict, did his best these days not to do much thinking at all.

Morning. He hoped that Kat had managed to sleep after he let her stay up an
extra hour to watch reruns of *The Simpsons* on one of the local stations. Today was a
riding lesson day on top of school, and he didn't want her taking jumps on less than a full
night's sleep. Reckless though he was about his own riding of Warlock – yes, to that
extent that asshole Billy O'Donnell had been right – his solicitude about Kat's safety had
increased exponentially with her mother's incapacity.

Maggie still slept that fake sleep induced by alcohol. He kissed her hair lightly
before hopping into the shower. When he emerged from the bathroom she was just
beginning to stir. "I'll make Kat breakfast," she mumbled against the pillow, her swollen
eyelids fluttering.

"I got it, Mags."

The muffled sound of her crying followed him out of the bedroom. He carefully
clicked the door shut behind him so Kat wouldn't hear.

He let the dog outside into the patio whose small patch of grass served as
Thumper's latrine, went around to the front door to retrieve the LA *Times*. Had to keep
abreast of Bush's abundant fuckups. He glanced at the headlines as he put on coffee,
grabbed cereal bowls and a box of Cheerios for Kat and himself. She'd informed him

that only Thumper liked his scrambled eggs, and he wasn't about to apply his limited

culinary skills to the dog's breakfast.

"How'd you sleep?" he asked when she appeared neat and combed and pretty in

her Catholic school uniform.

"OK." She let Thumper back inside. "Can he have some sausage?"

"If you eat some. I'm not playing fry cook just for Thumper's benefit."

Maggie came into the kitchen. Wrapped in her robe with her hair tied back, she

looked almost as tiny and fragile as Kat. "I'll make the sausage," she said, and the

relative steadiness of her voice told him she'd had the hair of the dog it took for her to get

out of bed.

He saw as well the tears streaming down her wan cheeks as she took the box of

sausage links out of the freezer. He stepped between her and the open freezer door and

planted a kiss on her chapped lips, subtly swiping at the tearstains in hopes that Kat

wouldn't notice them.

The ploy must have worked, for Kat laughed and said, "That's gross. Who wants

to kiss first thing in the morning?"

Maggie strained to smile. "Only your father and Thumper, I think." She moved

away from him to put a few sausages into a frying pan, which she splashed with a little

water from the tea kettle before covering the skillet.

He knew her routine. She'd be all right for the first couple of hours, sipping wine

or vodka mixed in a tumbler with Diet 7-Up. By midmorning she'd need a nap.

Sometimes she asked him to make love to her, but he sensed the request was motivated

less by desire than a need to appease him. She never came nor seemed bothered that she didn't. Then she'd sleep maybe another hour, wake up again, refill her tumbler, and take a bath. Afterwards she'd usually curl up on the sofa, dully watching TV while he worked at the laptop at the dining room table. Occasionally she'd respond to his request for advice regarding a project; other times she would simply look at him helplessly and shake her head.

Damn good thing that Kat had the stables, that Armando and Eva had overridden Tim and Maggie's initial objections and bought her the little school palomino. Kat rode after school most days, with her evenings devoted to homework and some television. Unless Ryan was visiting, Maggie had generally retired for the night by the time Kat got home from Camino Equestrian. Loath to have her daughter see her inebriated, she opted instead to retreat behind the closed bedroom door.

Ryan, of course, was aware of Maggie's dependency – on two recent occasions she'd called him in a state of panic, pleading with him to bring her some wine, because Tim was either at the barn with Kat or had taken her to a movie. But Ryan told Tim he believed that Maggie's excessive drinking was only a temporary aberration. "I went through a similar thing a few years ago after Eric and I broke up. I almost lost my job and ended up in the ER with alcohol poisoning. But then I just sort of clawed my way out of it."

Maggie's behavior was so uncharacteristic that Tim might have bought Ryan's take on the situation – if only it hadn't been for that goddamn house.

"Are you gonna ride Warlock today?" Kat asked on the drive to school. Busy with her job and her new marriage, Nicole was happy to have Tim ride her horse as often as he liked during the week.

"Maybe. Maybe I'll just watch you ride instead." That she was already learning show-jumping was a source of tremendous pride for him, although Maggie was terrified by it and couldn't watch even before the anxiety attacks made leaving the apartment a considerable feat.

"Warlock couldn't jump, could he?"

"Uh-uh. He's not built for it. It'd be like asking an elephant to use a trampoline."

She giggled. "We call Sister Pius the old elephant. She made a little boy cry yesterday."

"No. That's bad."

"His name is Zack, and she kept saying to him it was Zachary. He cried."

"Jesus. I thought they phased out that kind of nun with the eight-track tape."

"What's that?"

"Well, what I mean is that I thought nasty nuns like Sister Elephant were what Mom and I had to deal with when we were your age. Now they're supposed to be nicer."

"Sister Pius is old. I think she's, like, a hundred."

He bit back a smile. Nothing, not even the grim circumstances at home, could dim the joy his daughter gave him.

He dropped Kat off at Saint James's and drove on to the morning AA meeting in Carlsbad he preferred to attend because it was Father Bob's usual group. His feelings remained radically mixed about the dogma of Twelve Step programs; their hybrid disease/spiritual-sickness paradigm struck him as contradictory, and given his Catholic upbringing, he really didn't need a self-help group to exacerbate his already acute sense of guilt. But there was, he admitted, something calming about the nonjudgmental

company of other addicts, now more than ever.

The value of such camaraderie had only started to sink in during what he hoped

was his last stint in rehab, maybe because he'd gone in under no legal duress, maybe

because he'd at last "hit bottom" after literally losing Maggie and Kat. Hearing of other

lives at least as screwed up as his own, if not more so, of the destruction of families,

promising futures, and physical and psychic health, eroded his conviction of a doom as

personalized as a vanity license plate. On occasion he wondered how many of those

fellow travelers were still clean. Certainly Father Bob was, but there had been casualties,

defections, even before Tim had walked out that night last November. A beautiful, deaf

woman, Hannah, who had a Masters in education and two small children whose custody

she'd lost due to her crack addiction, had just vanished one day from the program, and

when she tried to re-up forty-eight hours later she failed the pee test and was turned

away. He'd felt awful about her. An expert lip-reader, she had been especially kind to

him, sharing his irrepressible cynicism about some of the more inane treatment protocols

such as high-schoolish peer pressure videos and therapeutic field trips to the Universal

Studios theme park. Then there were others who were so gung-ho, so desperate to

embrace every orthodoxy of the rehab philosophy or "Hazeldenia," as he'd dubbed it,

that either they were bound to annoy everyone out of their lives not already alienated by

their addiction or to return to earth with such a precipitous thud that only that forbidden

drink or drug would cushion the disillusionment. Successful treatment outcomes were

like batting averages -- .300 was considered good, and meth addicts were lucky to hit the

Mendoza line – and it seemed hubris to think one would be in the minority to achieve permanent sobriety. "It's like the doctrine of the elect," he'd once complained to Father

Bob. "Only a handful of us are going to be saved, and the rest are just screwed no matter

how hard we try." Not unexpectedly, Father Bob offered a less Calvinistic interpretation

of the long odds against lasting recovery. The high failure rate didn't account for the

vicissitudes of human motives, the more-or-less sober, or those who had fought and

conquered their chemical demons in privacy. Amused, Tim thought it highly Jesuitical of

Bob to base his counter-argument in statistical error.

Father Bob was already inside the meeting hall adjacent to a Lutheran church,

chatting with a few other AAs by the coffee machine and pink bakery boxes of doughnuts

on a table at the back of the room. As was his wont, he didn't wear his clerical collar to

meetings, agreeing with Tim that recovering addicts had enough guilt as it was,

regardless of religious affiliation. Tim filled a Styrofoam cup with the sludge that passed

as coffee and took a seat in one of the back rows. It wasn't simply that he disliked being

called upon to read AA rules or prayers. But as a tall man, he sat in the back as a matter

of habit.

Leading today's meeting were two regulars, a diminutive, salty woman in her

seventies named Norma with a cigarette-smoke voice and a no-bullshit manner, and a

younger woman, with hair dyed a glossy black and more tattoos -- up and down her arms

and peeking above the top of her low-rise jeans -- than half the guys in prison had

sported. Her name was Carol, and like him, she was a recovering meth freak. With AA

meetings far more numerous than NA ones, you could always count on a good number of

drug addicts among the drunks.

Another such was this little chick Sara, who promptly sat down next to him. Sara had punky blue streaks in her dishwater-blonde hair, and always wore chunky platform shoes and skimpy tops that showed off a suspiciously voluptuous bustline for a girl who maybe weighed ninety pounds. Twenty-one years old and a veteran of multiple rehabs, she had an obvious crush on him that made him rather uncomfortable. Not because he wasn't accustomed to female attention – he'd taken his good looks for granted since sixth grade – but because despite a generic empathy for her as a fellow addict, he didn't much like her. She was from an extremely wealthy Rancho Santa Fe family, and every experience she recounted in meetings, no matter how sordid, was couched in the language of entitlement and privilege.

"How can you be so wide awake at nine in the morning?" she said, touching his knee. "Are you sure you're not tweaking?"

He knew she was kidding, but he was glad that Father Bob took the chair on his other side so he could pretty much ignore her. "How's it going?" Bob asked, not too pointedly, for Sara's proximity precluded any specific discussion of the situation with Maggie.

"Comme ci, comme ca," Tim said, a habitual evasion that Kat had for years thought was Spanish.

"Ahem!" Norma growled, calling the meeting to order.

A couple of Scripture-like readings from the hallowed Big Book, Twelve Steps and Twelve Traditions, then Carol introduced the morning's general topic. "I've been thinking about this whole Thirteenth Step thing," she began.

"Always a popular topic," someone joked from the first row, and everyone laughed. "Thirteenth-stepping" referred to the much-debated, unofficial AA rule against romantic entanglements, especially between group members, during the first year of sobriety.

"Hush up, you hooligans," Norma pretended to scold. "Go on, Carol."

"I had a really cool time with my old boyfriend the other night," Carol said. "We went bowling, if you can believe it. I think he may want to get back together, and I feel like I'm ready, even though I only have eight months. I just want to hear what you guys think."

A pudgy fellow in his thirties stood. "I'm Josh and I'm a doubly diagnosed alcoholic," he declared.

"Hi Josh," came the unison response.

"Carol, is your ex in the program?" Josh asked, sitting down.

"No. He drinks a little beer. But he has no use for addicts. That's why we broke up. Being back together would be great motivation for staying clean."

"Hi, I'm Barb, and I'm an alcoholic and drug addict." A nicely dressed and coiffed women near fifty now stood.

"Hi, Barb," echoed the congregation.

"Carol, it sounds to me like you might be thinking of this ex-boyfriend as a crutch. What if things don't work out? You have a built-in reason to relapse. Why not wait for your one-year anniversary of sobriety before leaping back into a relationship?"

Here Sara rose to join the discussion. "I think the whole Thirteenth Step taboo sucks. What about people who are already hooked up? No one's telling them to break up with their partners for a year."

"We're talking about new entanglements, Sara," Norma reminded her acidly. "Those of us lucky enough to have someone stick with us through the worst of our sickness have our own amendments to make. And let me tell you, it's a full-time job." She grabbed her canvas totebag. "And I'm going to take a cigarette break."

"Me too," Tim whispered to Father Bob.

He followed Norma out a side door to a narrow walkway between meeting hall and church. She was just snapping open one of those quaint, old-ladyish vinyl cigarette sleeves. "Some of those people in there are such goddamn babies," she complained, letting Tim light her cigarette. "Can't go a year without getting their ashes hauled, poor things."

Tim laughed. "Where does that expression come from, anyway?"

"From old foofs like me," she retorted, wheezing a chuckle. "How's your little girl, handsome?"

"She's good. Looking forward to Easter break in a couple weeks."

"She'll spend it all with her horsey, I bet. When I was a kid in New Jersey, my daddy used to take me to Aqueduct. I never rode, but boy, I loved watching those racehorses. Could pick a winner, even at all of five years old."

He puffed his cigarette, listening to her reminisce. You could always depend on Norma's inveterate raconteurship. She'd politely ask you about your own family, but the old lady's field of expertise was holding court, not listening. Mags would have called that a very "male" trait.

Eventually they went back inside, where the debate had shifted to general issues of sobriety and making amends. Father Bob was talking about the Eleventh Step and St. Francis's prayer, and the importance of forgiving without expectation of forgiveness, understanding rather than seeking to be understood.

After the meeting concluded with what Tim regarded as a painful hand-holding group recitation of the Lord's Prayer – he'd take the squishier but less Biblical Serenity Prayer any day – he asked Father Bob about his comments as they walked toward their cars. "What you said in there – it's what I'm trying to do with Maggie. I'm trying to be compassionate and understanding and forgiving, the way she's been for me."

"That's not the same as being passive, Tim." Bob opened the trunk of his old sedan, tossed in his AA handbook. The car's bumper sported "Jesus Was a Liberal" and "War Is Not the Answer" stickers.

Tim scowled. "Being confronted with my own fucked-uppedness only made me feel I was so worthless that I had to get high to keep from killing myself."

"Deconstruct *that* binary," the priest advised. "There are options other than passivity or confrontation."

"Oh yeah? Name one. And I'm not being passive. The way I see it, I'm doing what my sister did for me – standing by her until she's ready to get help."

"Is that it?" Father Bob rejoined amiably. "So you've given up the notion about the house being cursed?"

Tim was silent.

Father Bob pantomime-punched his arm. "Gotta lose that determinism."

"And then think that Maggie's drinking because she can't deal with me back in her life?" It wasn't as if the idea hadn't crossed his mind.

"I'm not a psychologist, Tim. But – "

Sara clomped up to them in her exaggerated platform wedgies. "Tim, could I hit on you for a ride home to Rancho? My dad's giving me shit for needing rides while my car's in the shop." Her car was a cherry red vintage Mercedes convertible that she dismissively called a hand-me-down.

"Yeah, fine. Talk to you later, Bob."

He suffered through Sara's self-involved chatter about what a piece of crap her car was and how Eminem, though a genius, was in danger of selling out. On and on. Like Norma she was a monologist, but unlike that feisty old bird, she had nothing of interest or even passing entertainment value to say. Hell, Kat was a more sophisticated conversationalist.

He let her out in front of a sprawling Mediterranean house in "the Covenant," brushed off her overly effusive thanks, and headed west on Lomas Santa Fe back to Solana Beach. At home he found Maggie, with her tumbler of wine, in bed but awake, talking on the phone to her mother. "Mama, I'm OK. I've just had this damn cold I can't shake … no, the doctor says it's not mono. Just a garden-variety cold."

He dropped the car keys on the dresser. She glanced up at him nervously. "Tim's home, Mama. I've got to go." She hung up the phone.

He sank down on the bed next to her. "Ah, Mags, he sighed, enfolding her in his arms.

She squirmed free. "Please, Tim – stop being so fucking understanding!" she hissed.

"Why? How would you like me to be?"

"I don't know! But when it was you I was so heartless ... "

Here came the waterworks. "No you weren't. I was a much bigger pain in the ass than you are."

"Tomorrow, sweetie, I'll quit drinking. I've got some Restoril left – enough to help me just sleep it off, don't you think?"

He pretended not to have heard it before. "Be careful, honey. 'Member where that tactic got me in college."

A crooked smile. "I always want to laugh when you call me 'honey.'"

"For the same reason Kat laughs when I walk Thumper? Nice to know I keep everybody in stitches around here."

"No, not for the same reason. It just sounds so husbandy." She gulped from her tumbler. "Mama wants to know when we're getting married again."

"Like I've said for months, Mags – you name the date."

"Tomorrow, sweetie. Manana. A demain."

"'K. In the meantime, why don't you come with me to the barn today for Kat's lesson? Everybody's always asking about you." He entwined his fingers in hers.

"Like who? Those stuck-up busybodies?"

"Yeah, them. And your pal Billy."

Her eyes narrowed and he wanted to kick himself for indulging in a moment of sarcasm. "What do you tell him?" she demanded.

"What I tell everyone – that you're really busy with work. Only he gives me a look like he thinks I've got you buried in the backyard."

"I'm sure he doesn't. That's just his way."

You slept with him, didn't you? challenged his instinct. He swallowed hard as if to force it back down into his gut. "Well, why don't you come along and shut everybody up?"

"Maybe I will … after my nap," she said, and he knew that was that.

As bad luck would have it, Billy was the first person he ran into at Camino Equestrian, inside the tack store. Kat had run off to get Sugar from her stall. Kim, the earthy storekeeper, was nowhere in sight, though he could hear her call from the adjoining stock room, "I know I've got another case of Betadine, Billy."

Billy, waiting at the counter, nodded to Tim, who returned the gesture as he slid open the refrigerator case to grab a Dr. Pepper. "How's Maggie?" Billy asked.

"Fine. Busy." He made a mental note to finish copy-editing that boring "How To" e-book on home businesses tonight after Kat went to bed.

Kim bounced out clasping a box of equine antiseptic scrub. "Hey there, good-looking," she greeted Tim. "Want that Coke on your tab?"

"I think I can scrounge up 80 cents today." Their "tab," which covered Sugar's feed, board, and Kat's supplies, was footed by Armando Flores.

He paid for the soft drink and stepped outside, but Billy was right behind him. "Gonna ride Warlock?"

"No. Just watch my daughter."

"I'll turn him out then." Billy started away, but stopped and looked back at him squarely. "Something's wrong with Maggie. You're pretty transparent, dude."

Tim maintained a poker face. "What I said. She's just busy. Freelancers don't work nine-to-five."

"How come when I asked Kat the other day she said her mom was sick?" Billy challenged.

Now Tim was getting pissed. "You leave my kid alone. She has enough to deal with."

Billy cocked an eyebrow. "Like I said, man, you're really transparent." He strode away.

Mostly angry with himself, Tim was tempted to go after Billy. But for once, the Twelve Step indoctrination got the best of him, and he forced himself to let it go.

Later that evening, however, while he was changing what seemed to be an infinite number of "company/they"s to "company/it"s, he pondered first Billy's cross-examination and then Father Bob's chide about his passivity. He was trying to protect her, he argued with himself. What did Bob recommend, a big judgmental room of interveners to chastise and browbeat her into the shame that he knew would make her long for death? A group that included Armando and Eva, who thought she was perfect, and Billy, her probable ex-lover? Should Kat, too, participate, to fix her serious brown eyes on her mother and tell her how she'd let her down?

Fuck. He decided to dash off an e-mail to Bob in defiance of the unspoken advice. He signed in to the Internet not with his personal screen name, BuryMeSoftly9999, which alluded to an Alice in Chains song, but with the more generic one, FloremersonSD, they used mostly for work. Bob may not have been a shrink, but Tim didn't want him psychoanalyzing what some might have viewed as a drug reference.

He clicked on the "write mail" icon, typed in Bob's e-mail address. But barely past the subject line – "Thoughts" – an IM box intruded on the screen from HotAddict858. "Hi!"

Could it be Sara? How would that idiotic bimbo have obtained his and Maggie's e-mail address? It had to be a coincidence. He clicked on the "X" corner of the IM box, resumed typing.

The IM reappeared. "Hi Tim. Guess how I found you."

Distracted as well as suspicious, he swore under his breath. "Hacker?" he typed back.

A smiley face icon. "☺"

"Good for you," he typed. "Goodbye."

"The Shadow Man has your lady. You'll never get her back."

He stared at the words, his fingers frozen over the keyboard.

Another smiley emoticon. "☺ -- Night-Night!"

He furiously typed in, "What the fuck are you talking about?" but received the message "Member not logged on."

He tried sending the same question via e-mail but it was bounced back. Jesus Christ, what was happening?

Chill, he ordered himself. It was just a spoiled, stupid little girl playing with his head. *The Shadow Man has your lady. You'll never get her back.* Coincidence or hallucination. Chronic meth use caused irreparable neurological damage. Everyone knew that. Why would he have escaped? He logged off, hurried to the master bedroom expecting to find her crashed out, dead to the world. Instead, she was sitting up in bed, clutching the glass with both hands, as if waiting for him.

"Oh, Maggie." He swept her up, spilling her drink in the process. She mewled an objection.

He hastened to pour her more from the half-empty bottle of cheap Livingston Cellars chardonnay on the floor next to the bed. She gave him a drowsy smile. "Tomorrow."

"I know it, babe. Gimme a kiss."

She did. "Just take off your clothes and lie next to me, OK?"

"Sure." He stripped off his clothes, wishing he could be inside her without a condom. His HIV tests were negative, but to his knowledge she wasn't using the Pill.

"Love you, Timmy." She curled her body into his.

"Tambien, querida. Always."

Tangled together, they fell into separate oblivions.

The nebulous feeling of irritability and frustration with which he awakened came to a head when he saw Sara outside the meeting hall the next morning. "What were you IMing me about last night?"

She bristled. "I don't know what the hell you're talking about."

Seeing nothing coy in her reaction, he thought *neurological damage.*

Hallucination. He backed off. "You weren't IMing me?"

She rolled her eyes and pegged into the hall in her Frankenstein shoes.

Norma shuffled up to him in her customary jogging suit and ladies Keds. "Why

don't you lead today, Tim?"

"Oh man, Norma. I'm not good at that."

"Think of it as a favor to an old lady. I'm sick and tired of hearing these girls go

on about whether they should sleep with their boyfriends."

"I don't know what to talk about."

"Fake it," she replied gruffly, and he could hardly refuse.

Thus he took a reluctant seat next to Norma behind the table at the front of the

meeting room. He studied his hands as Norma recited AA announcements and appointed

Father Bob to read the Twelve Steps.

Then it was his turn. "I'm Tim and I'm a drug addict," he said perfunctorily,

receiving the equally perfunctory greeting from the congregants. "Norma roped me into

this – " Laughter "—so I'm not really sure what to say. I guess I want to focus on this

idea of wreckage we talk about all the time. We talk about making amends, but what

about things that can't be fixed? I mean, I did crystal pretty much nonstop for almost

thirteen years. Those years are lost." He hesitated briefly. "I worry I have brain

damage. I need to be responsible for my family and my life, but I don't know if I'm up to

it. So ... " He shrugged. "Any thoughts?"

Josh, the voluble "doubly diagnosed" fellow, stood up. Introduction, chanted

greetings.

("The Lord be with you."

"And also with you."

Dominus vobiscum."

"Et cum spiritu tuo.")

Too young to have remembered the Latin Mass, or so he thought, Tim frowned, barely hearing Josh's remarks.

"—it's like re-learning basic life skills, and you have to stay humble, man. Ask for help."

Tim noted Father Bob's raised hand. "Bob?"

"I think our shared commitment to 'one day at a time' is key," the priest said. "It also seems to me, Tim, that if you can wonder whether you're brain-damaged, you probably aren't."

Tim's eyes drifted to Sara, who looked bored. A stocky man was waving his arm. "Uh-huh?" Tim said, not recognizing him from other meetings.

"Hi, I'm Dean, and I'm an alcoholic." He stood, yanking up his left pants leg to reveal a skinny steel prosthetic calf. "You wanna talk wreckage? I crashed out on a railroad track in Sorrento Valley, and here's what I got to show for it."

Tim nodded, longing for a cigarette and silently cursing Norma.

"See this leg here?" the guy went on. "It's a blessing. Talk about a wakeup call. My wreckage reminds me of the gift of sobriety. I love my leg for it. I even have a name for it. I call it Charley, like in Charley-horse."

Genial group chuckles. Tim, finding the moment surreal, fumbled for a comment. "That's really cool." But it wasn't. He imagined himself an amputee, dealing with a stump instead of a leg every cold morning after dreams of still being whole. He felt mildly sick to his stomach.

Things got worse. Two women led in one of the "regulars," a very elderly lady named Ada, who was obviously drunk as well as infirm. "My motherfucking husband and my faggot son stole my money!" Ada raged, thin frail arms struggling against the bracing clasps of her escorts.

Father Bob leaped up to assist the staggering trio. Norma muttered something about Ada's venal caretakers. Amid the craning assembly, Sara was conspicuous for her indifference, pill-rolling with her perfect, blue-tipped acrylic nails.

The old lady started to vomit, spewing liquory-smelling streams of amber onto herself, the floor. Tim felt his overall helplessness magnified a thousand degrees. He yanked Norma up and extended his other arm to the nearest person, in this case the chatty Josh. "God grant me the serenity," Tim began, "to accept the things I cannot change … "

The Shadow Man has your lady.

CHAPTER 2

Her sleep was fitful; she woke each time she shifted in bed, fumbled for a crushed
pillow, pawed for her water bottle on the nightstand. But the dream, however interrupted,
maintained its insistent narrative. Back in the house. Mama and Pa and Juan-Gil were
there, along with Kat and Tim. Everything was all right, except that the kitchen was on
fire and she somehow had to get all of them, plus Thumper, out of the house as the flames
licked at her heels.

She tossed, stretched, against the rumpled blankets. He was lying next to her, but
from his shallow breaths she could tell he wasn't asleep. Poor Timmy. She started to
open her eyes, but they ached and her lids were so heavy. She was so tired.

Her heart began to race. She was no longer tired, but panicked – panicked over
how much time she'd lost, panicked over the mess the apartment had to be in (Tim's
notion of housekeeping was limited to running the dishwasher), panicked over her
neglect of Kat, of work, of her increasingly suspicious parents.

And panicked most of all over the emptiness of all the wine bottles Tim had likely already taken outside to the recycling bin.

She wished he would leave. She had her secret stash, her *just-in-case* bottle of vodka, stowed inside of the small, lidded wicker laundry basket never used for that purpose because it was too small to accommodate the clothing of three people and it served better as an additional nightstand for issues of *The Nation* and the LA *Times* Book Review they'd not yet caught up with. Not to mention countless yellow legal pads with work drafts and "to-do" lists. "I just need to sleep," she whispered, thinking, *Go.*

A kiss on her bare shoulder, then he left. She waited a minute or two before hoisting the legal pads and magazines and expired coupon pages from the top of the laundry basket. Inside, amid old T-shirts preserved as cleaning rags and odd socks irrevocably estranged from their mates, was the bottle of off-brand vodka.

The first desperate swig made her shudder. Not so the second. Calm trickled into her veins. Another hearty gulp fortified her out of bed, into the shower. Hot spray and fragrant body wash. Nice. Now, she had to invent a pretext for getting Tim out of the apartment long enough for her to make a dash for more wine to the Longs Drugs a few blocks away. Her anxiety attacks kicked in only after the initial buzz wore off, so her window of opportunity was narrow.

"Sweetie?" she said, toweling her hair dry. He was working with pen and paper at the dining room table, and from the stack of scholarly journals in front of him she guessed that this week's abstracting assignment was a hefty one.

"'The Political Implications of East Asian Postage Stamps,'" he grumbled. "I'm gonna die."

"Special issue?"

"Uh-huh. And nobody knows how to write a thesis paragraph."

She nuzzled him. "Thank you for doing my homework for me."

"De nada."

"Want a break?"

His eyes lit up and she realized he'd misunderstood. Sex would take too much time, leaving her too nervous to drive to the drugstore. "Not that," she amended, trying to sound saucy. "Why don't you go get us Chinese food for dinner at that place, Ming's Whatever, on Carmel Country?"

"It's only one thirty, Mags. I'll get it on the way home from the barn with Kat."

Difficult. Sweet though he was in recovery, he was difficult.

Their eyes met and the pretense withered. "OK, I'll go get the wine. But you've got to come with me," he said, pushing away the tedious political science journals.

"I'll come along but wait in the car."

"No, you have to come inside with me. You don't have to stand in line, but you've got to be in the store."

"You're so difficult," she complained. "Let me get dressed." Another shot of vodka, and maybe she could get through the ordeal.

Resentful, she couldn't resist observing as he pulled onto Via de la Valle, "Billy O'Donnell's wife has agoraphobia. She hasn't left their house in years."

To her satisfaction, his jaw tensed. What she didn't know was that a dozen irritable rejoinders leaped to his mind – *So he says. And you aspire to be like Mrs. Billy*

O'Donnell? Why don't you just admit you fucked him? "What a drag," he said, with considerable effort.

Despite the vodka her nerves were fluttering. "I don't think I can go into the store with you, Tim."

"Sure you can," he said, reaching across to squeeze her hand. "It's going to be OK."

Despair fell over her. She lifted his hand to kiss it. "Tim, why can't I quit drinking? Should I go to one of those meetings?"

"If you want, Mags. You know I'd be there too, bucking you up."

"But you make such fun of them," she pointed out.

He swung into the Albertsons center. At every freeway exit in North County, it seemed there was a supermarket-anchored mini-mall, with designer coffeehouses, a UPS Store or Postal Annex, fast food, and a host of other specialty boutiques that offered nothing in particular to buy. A Macy's or Nordstrom short of a real mall, these centers boasted all of the parking congestion with little of the impulse-purchase temptation. Suburban blight.

"Yeah, I make fun of them, but I go," he said, steering into a parking space. "For the discipline."

"And 'punish'?" she teased, gleaning a Foucault allusion.

"Well, yeah, the 'punish' is having to sit through 'em." He shifted into park and looked at her directly. "It's the habit, Maggie, of having to show up clean every day. It kind of comes to replace the habit of getting high. You tune out all the platitudes and navel-gazing, and it's still about showing up, being straight, and wanting to stay that way."

"Maybe I'll go with you day after tomorrow. I just need some wine now, querido. I just need to get through this nervous phase."

She was annoyed that even with this concession, he still insisted she accompany him into the supermarket. Her heart banged and knees wobbled. The store felt grossly overheated. She wanted to run. She leaned against their cart like an old person using a walker. He tossed in a couple of big bottles of wine, a six-pack of beer for himself, fruit, sandwich stuff, and cookies for Kat, dogfood for Thumper. She reminded him about the paper towels and napkins, which ordinarily he seemed to treat interchangeably. But when he pushed their cart into the checkout line, her panic crested. She squeezed past him and the shopper ahead of them in line to escape through the automatic doors.

"Maggie! Where have you been?" Geri, the affable "supermom" of two of Kat's fellow riders, was approaching from the parking lot in her usual oversized pink T-shirt and shorts. She was one of the friendliest, least pretentious people out at the barn, despite buying her daughters expensive horses and five-day-a-week lessons.

Hurry up, Tim, please, Maggie thought. "Geri, it's so nice to see you." She prayed that the Lifesaver mint she'd sucked on the drive over was sufficient to mask the vodka on her breath. She regarded the commonplace that vodka had no scent as an urban myth.

"Tim says you've been swamped with work," Geri said. "I hope this means lots of money."

"We're doing all right." *Hurry up, Tim!*

"I wish Gordon was half as interested in Sydney and Ariel's riding as Tim is in Kat's," Geri smiled. "He's so adorable, Maggie. All of us horse-fraus are madly in love with him. What a catch."

I bet you wouldn't think he was such a catch if you'd seen him before, a meth skeleton with a needle in his arm and a tattooed convict's –

The unbidden thought appalled her, made her dizzy.

"Are you feeling OK?" Geri asked, alarmed, reaching out to steady her.

"Maggie's had a bear of a cold," came Tim's calm voice as he wheeled up the cart. He clasped his free arm around her shoulder.

Maggie looked at him with guilt and gratitude. "Yes, I'm so lucky to have Tim back with me."

"I'd count myself lucky if Gordon volunteered for the civilian space program," Geri joked. "Good seeing you, Maggie. Don't be a stranger at the barn."

"Oh my God," Maggie said, sinking into the passenger seat. "That was awful."

"It was nothing. Buckle up or I ain't moving this heap."

She dragged the shoulder strap across her upper body. "Geri's going to tell everyone I'm a staggering-around lush."

"No way. You smell like a peppermint."

How much she loved him. How could she have thought such a cruel thing about him in silent response to Geri's praise? She felt suddenly compelled to atone. "Tim, we should have another baby someday."

"Someday," he said, his tone measured. "When we're both well and we can afford it."

His studied lack of enthusiasm upset her. "I wouldn't drink if I were pregnant! And what about the baby we *killed*, our senior year?"

Yellow light. He slammed on the brakes, sending their bodies straining against the shoulder straps. "Fuck."

He was angry, and she was afraid to say more, at least not until he veered right onto Sierra and its rows of condos and apartments on either side. "OK, it was just an abortion, and it was the right thing to do."

"Don't," he warned, eyes on their complex's parking lot. "Don't go all Catholic on me. We lucked out with one kid coming out normal, with me on drugs. You think we could've taken care of two?"

They rolled into their designated space. "I didn't mean it," she said.

He popped open the trunk and she hurried around back to retrieve her wine. Clutching the bag, she hastened into their apartment, into the bedroom, to drink back the wall between them.

He rode Warlock hard, harder than usual. The big horse heaved and groaned as Tim pushed him forward into a lope across the tomato fields, crushing plants and a path where there wasn't one before. Over his shoulder, afternoon freeway traffic crawled north on the 5. He slowed the horse down to a trot, swung the reins back toward the ranch.

"Good boy," he said, patting the horse's heavy, damp neck. "Good boy." Thanks for putting up with me, he added silently. What a good horse.

Warlock's sigh shook his entire massive body. He slowed to a stroll.

Tim exhaled with the horse, urged him across the tomatoes, dirt, and brush up toward the uneven white fencing that bounded the stables.

In the jumping arena, Kat, her taut body one with Sugar, glided over horizontal poles. Perfect.

The palomino cantered gracefully around half the ring, cut inside, floating back toward the jump.

Perfect.

"Quit watching!" Kat laughed, bounding around the ring.

"Yeah, knock it off, Dad!" Sandy called good-naturedly from the platform perch just outside the jumping arena gate.

"Yeah, yeah," he groused, but he urged Warlock in the direction of the crossties. Nicole Ludwig's big Range Rover cruised up right behind the crossties next to a fogeyish white Olds Cutlass. Startled, Warlock lunged forward and neighed. "It's OK," Tim soothed.

Nicole climbed out of the vehicle, her long yellow hair ponytailed, her even longer legs stretching out beneath running shorts, although it was only in the low 60s. "How's our handsome boy?" she greeted, dancing around to the crossties to pat the horse.

"I'm great," Tim couldn't resist replying.

"Not you, Mr. Conceited," she smiled, rubbing her face against Warlock's head.

As was his habit around women, Warlock dropped his huge penis. The fine horse apparently had no idea he was a gelding.

"I should have named him Dirk Diggler," Nicole chuckled, tucking a horse cookie into his eager mouth. "He was good today?"

"He was great. He loves trail. Take him out this weekend if you can." He found himself staring into her deep blue eyes. Had they always been so blue?

She noticed his gaze. "Colored contacts! Do they look too fake?"

"They look – cool," he admitted.

"My husband doesn't like them," she shrugged.

He unstrapped the cinch, hoisted off the blanket and saddle he'd bought used at Bits. Warlock had worked up a good sweat, and Tim took a curry comb to the lathered coat.

"Tim, I would like to sell you Warlock. I've been riding Halo on trail – "

" – and yeah, she's as completely insane as you are," he teased. "But Nicole, there's no way we can afford Warlock. I wish there were."

"Maybe we can work something out? He loves you so much, Tim, and you're so good with him."

"Let me think about it, OK? If there's any way we can swing it, I'll let you know." He didn't know why he was stalling. Warlock was at least a $20,000 horse, and his feed and board would require half of what they paid in rent.

Nicole stuffed an apple quarter into Warlock's drooling maw. "Greg and I are flexible. We just want him with someone who really loves him."

"Well, that I sure do."

"We'll work something out, then." She touched his back.

Ah, don't do that. His penis stirred against his jeans.

Kat's lesson couldn't have ended at a more propitious moment. "Hi Daddy, hi Nicole," she said, expertly dismounting from the palomino.

"Wow, I saw you take that three-foot jump," Nicole complimented. "I want to jump Halo."

Nicole, like his daughter, was fearless. "You should!" Kat encouraged, ushering Sugar into the crossties.

"I leave jumping to the fleet of foot," Tim remarked. "Let's get our horses untacked and groomed, Kat. Then I'll take you for an ice cream." By this time Mags was probably out-and-out hammered; there was no point in rushing home.

They went to Rite-Aid in the Highlands center, because the drugstore featured one of those retro ice cream fountains where customers could purchase cones of not especially high-quality frozen desserts in a host of conventional flavors. Kat made no such snobbish distinctions, ordering a double-fudge cone. Tim was not big on ice cream, but when he saw pistachio, artificially green and dotted with nuts, he began to laugh. "A single pistachio," he managed to request.

The uniformed clerk gave him a wary look, and Kat, already holding her cone, tugged his arm. "What's so funny?"

"I'll tell you in a sec," he said, paying the clerk for the treats.

They strolled outside. "You think Starbucks will boot us if we take one of their tables?" he asked Kat. Starbucks was a couple of stores down, with wrought iron tables in front, only one of which appeared to be occupied by a bespectacled sixtyish woman with ginger hair who was speaking into a cellphone.

"Maybe you should buy some coffee," Kat said dubiously.

He was touched and saddened by her desire to play by the rules. "OK. You hold our table and my ice cream – " Just looking at the melting green round atop the sugar cone made him want to chortle. "I'll be right back."

No line in Starbucks. He bought a House Grande and a brownie in case Maggie felt like eating anything later that night. Thin though she was, she could seldom resist chocolate.

"Daddy, this is melting. It's gross," Kat said, returning the dripping pistachio cone to him.

Tim licked the spillage. "Want to hear why this makes me laugh?"

"Duh!"

"Well, when I was around your age, my dad used to take Diana and me out for ice cream, maybe once or twice a month. At Baskin-Robbins."

She frowned at him, impatient but not uninterested. "Mommy and I used to go there in Manhattan Beach."

"OK, there was one like that in Pasadena, where I grew up. Pistachio was my favorite flavor. One time I was carrying my cone out to the parking lot – " He burst into laughter, hoping Kat wouldn't think him insane.

She was laughing too, albeit in confusion. "Was there, like, a bug in it?"

"No, but I licked the ball of ice cream right off the cone and it fell on the pavement."

Her face fell. "Daddy, that's sad."

"No it isn't. Ha, I thought my dad would get mad at me, so I sneaked and put the ice cream back on the cone. My dad said, 'Give me a taste.' And Kat, he ate this whole big bite of gritty ice cream and never knew the difference."

She squealed. "Daddy, that's so mean!" Her eyes danced.

He winked at her. "Yeah, it was, wasn't it."

Her expression turned somber. "But sometimes it's not funny to be mean."

Christ, what message had he just conveyed to his child by indulging a moment of nostalgic spite? Mags, I need you so much. "No, baby. Most times it isn't funny."

"Why are some people mean about Mexicans?"

A brief wild fury that someone had been cruel to her about her heritage swiftly gave way to a desire to protect her by helping her to understand. "Your mom is Mexican American, which means you are part, too. That's something to be proud of, Kat."

"Why, when people hate Mexicans?"

Fuck the horses, fuck Maggie's alcoholism – I'm moving this whole family to Canada, he seethed inwardly. But showing his anger wouldn't explain anything to her. "California used to be part of Mexico, Kit-Kat. But then there was a war, and I hope you've learned in school, most wars suck and happen for the wrong reasons. So this country took over a part of Mexico, and at the same time tried to make Mexico seem bad. That way, they could pretend stealing their land was a good thing." God, California History for Beginners, and even he gave himself a failing grade. "Is this making any sense?"

She nodded tentatively. "So you act like other people don't deserve being nice to?"

"Yeah. Same's true with black people, Kat." Did kids her age learn about the Civil War? He doubted it. "We took them away from their countries and forced them to work as slaves. And when they were freed, we kept treating them badly because we didn't want to face how wrong we were."

"I read about Harriet Tubman," she said knowledgably.

"Good girl."

Then she threw him for a loop. "Why are people mean to gay people? Did they take their land?"

Having no clue as to what she knew about sex from school, classmates, her mother, he was truly at a loss. Ryan was a regular visitor and Kat adored him – but did she even realize he was "gay"? "Um, they're mean about gay people," he fumbled, "because they don't understand them." Tautology, he scolded himself. "What do you think about gay people?"

"Guys who marry guys and girls who marry girls."

Good – safe and generic. "Right. Which is fine. People who love each other should get to marry each other."

"Uh-huh. So could Ryan, like, marry Billy?"

He longed to howl. *Ryan could do better.* At least she hadn't asked how gay couples – or straight ones, for that matter – had babies. With a great deal of effort he opted for restraint. "Billy has a wife. But hopefully one day Ryan will find someone who's much, much better."

They were finished with their ice cream. Tim picked up his coffee and the bag containing the brownie. "Ready to hit the road?"

It was only when they stood that he noticed that the red-haired woman had set down her cellphone and was glaring through her stylish tortoiseshell glasses at him. More than glaring, really – hers was almost a look of bald hatred. Most unnerving of all, there was something familiar about that look, if not about the woman herself.

He averted his eyes lest he call Kat's attention to the stranger's inexplicable hostility. Fuck the bitch, he thought; she was probably just some Jesussy bigot affronted through her own eavesdropping.

Crazy times, these, when trying to teach your kids empathy and tolerance was viewed as an act of moral turpitude.

The car parked next to his – oddly enough, another white Olds Cutlass just like the one at the barn – bore a metallic fish decal on its trunk. He'd bet money that the car belonged to the evil-eye harpy in front of Starbucks.

He didn't realize until he and Kat walked into the apartment how portentous the strange woman's glower actually had been. Maggie, her eyes red-rimmed and her hair mussed, awaited with folded arms. "You son of a bitch!" she raged, seemingly oblivious to Kat's presence. "How long have you been fucking Nicole behind my back?"

Tim was stunned. "What?"

"Don't fight," Kat implored, tugging at her mother's hand.

"Kat, go to your room," Maggie barked. "Mommy's *very* mad at Daddy right now!"

Kat dashed off to escape, and Tim lost his temper. "And Mommy's shitfaced drunk and out of her mind! What's this bullshit about me fucking Nicole?"

"One of the people at the stables saw the two of you today and called me – thank God, or I'd still be in the dark! You hypocrite – no wonder you've been so sweet and understanding about my drinking!"

He could hardly believe what he was hearing. "Nicole and I were talking about the goddamn horse! And who was the asshole who called you – O'Donnell?"

"No, it was not Billy – if he'd seen you, I'm sure he would've kicked your ass before making any phone calls!" With a wave of one furious arm she shoved the books, ashtray, and her own familiar tumbler off the dining room table.

Her flailing gesture was so pathetic that he rediscovered his composure. "Mags, I'm not fucking Nicole, or anybody else. Whoever called you was just trying to make trouble."

She sank to her knees on the floor, weeping while she mechanically gathered up scattered cigarette butts. "I don't blame you for cheating this time … look at what a mess I am."

He stooped down next to her and drew her to his chest. "I swear to you, I'm not cheating. And you're not a mess. You're just – "

(The Shadow Man has your lady)

" – going through a hard time. Tell me what I can do to make it better." He shut his eyes briefly, adding, "Would it help you if I left for a while, went to stay with Diana or something?"

She flared again. "So you can be with Nicole?"

"No. So you can have your own life back. You and Kat were getting along all right before."

"Are you serious?" she spat. "We were living in a haunted house, or have you forgotten?"

Far from it. "You're not anymore."

She clutched his shoulders. "I don't want you to leave. I'd die if you did. I've missed you every day you weren't with me from the moment we met."

He was ashamed by how relieved he felt by her words. "I don't want to leave either. And I won't."

"Promise?"

"Yeah, I promise. Just call me Velcro." He kissed her, tasting red wine. He supposed it was better than vodka.

As if reading his mind, she broke the embrace. "Will you have a drink with me?" Her tone was both plaintive and challenging.

"OK." He helped her to her feet.

"I think there's some white in the fridge. Unless you want red."

"Either one's fine."

Watching her slosh the white wine into two stemmed glasses, he wondered who the fuck had taken upon himself or herself to call Maggie with a patently spurious report of the fleeting flirtation with Nicole by the crossties. He feared that pressing her about the caller's identity would reignite the unfortunate topic. And though he hated to concede as much, he agreed that goddamn O'Donnell was more the type to confront him in an overblown display of machismo about the alleged dalliance. He tried to recall who else he'd seen at the barn this afternoon. He couldn't believe that either Kat's teacher Sandy or Kim from the tack store would dabble in such malicious bullshit. Maybe the caller had been one of the hoity-toity teenage girls who frequented the stables – except how would they have obtained this unlisted number? And Rhonda, while something of a snoop, seemed genuinely fond of Kat and thus unlikely to engage in vicious rumor-mongering certain to distress the child.

Vicious. The word brought to mind the scowling witch outside of Starbucks. Could that old-fart-mobile Cutlass in the Highlands Center lot have been the same one by which Nicole had parked behind the crossties?

It couldn't be, he reasoned, absently sipping the wine Maggie handed him. The strange woman was no more likely to have their phone number than the teenage equestrians were, even less so given the remote possibility an older girl had conned the number out of Kat. He was just being paranoid, probably yet another lingering after-effect of crystal that he hadn't anticipated.

Maggie was refilling their glasses when she raised the subject herself. "I bet it was that stupid whore Tatiana who called," she said abruptly. "She and Nicole had a falling out over Nicole not inviting her to the wedding."

"The caller didn't say who she was?"

Maggie looked flustered, and he realized she couldn't remember.

"It doesn't matter," he assured her. "You've always said that place is teeming with busybodies." The ditzy Tatiana seemed as likely a suspect as any, especially since the caller's motive may have been to stir up trouble for Nicole as well.

"I'm sorry I didn't trust you, sweetie." Her words were starting to slur.

"No big deal. Ninety percent of our time together I haven't been especially trustworthy."

"I'm 'nna take a little nap, and after maybe we can be the ones doing the fucking."

She staggered toward their bedroom, and he knew that unless he and his hand got reacquainted, there'd be no fucking in this home tonight.

CHAPTER 3

Irrational though he knew it was, he made it his business the next afternoon at the stables to attempt to find out who might have owned a white Oldsmobile Cutlass. "I think I accidentally dinged its bumper on my way out yesterday," he said to a predictably curious Rhonda.

"I don't know an Oldsmobile from a Chevrolet," Rhonda said. "But I'm pretty sure none of the parents whose kids ride with me drive a white sedan. It probably belongs to someone riding with Dennis or Gail." Dennis and Gail ran their own equestrian academies at the stables, and Rhonda always seemed to be feuding with one or the other of them over whose riding school was allowed to use which arena.

The abrasive Gail was leading a lesson in the all-purpose arena, but Dennis, whose white thatch of hair, deep tan, and dark sunglasses suggested a side gig as impersonator of Bob Baffert, the famous Thoroughbred trainer, was ambling leisurely toward the Tack 'n' Snack, whistling for unknown reasons the "Addams Family" theme.

Goddamn it, now I'll have that stupid song stuck in my head all day, Tim thought, stepping into Dennis's path.

Perennially hail-fellow-well-met, Dennis declared that he didn't think people even drove Olds Cutlasses anymore. Certainly he hadn't noticed such a car at the stables. "Maybe one of the kids was bringing Gramma out to see the ponies."

"It's definitely an old person's car," Tim agreed. On the other hand, Sandy drove a beat-up Buick Riviera. Some people below the age of retirement didn't give a shit about what kind of car they drove, as long as it got them where they needed to go. Hell, he'd been driving his '96 Toyota for a decade now, though he wasn't exactly one to brag about the fact.

Gail's response to his inquiry was, if possible, even less helpful than Dennis's had been. It was considerably more offensive. "I bet it belongs to one of the Mexicans," she said. "They wouldn't give a crap if you hit their beaner mobile. Did it have a Baja license plate?"

"I dunno – what kind of car do you use to cart around your fat ass?" Tim said.

She gaped at him. "Go screw yourself," she snapped, punctuating the imperative with a stiff middle finger and stomping away.

Snickering in back of him. "You know, dude, I don't like you much, but that was a good one."

Tim ground his teeth and turned around. "'Hic et ubique,'" he said haughtily. O'Donnell was fucking ubiquitous. But could he afford not to grill O'Donnell about the car, even if the guy was a complete asshole? "Someone out here made a malicious call to Maggie yesterday. It might have been whoever owns an Old-mobile Cutlass."

Billy looked concerned, which annoyed Tim all the more. "I wasn't out here yesterday. What makes you think it was someone from here? It sure as hell wasn't before."

"Before?"

"She got a threatening phone call when she was still at the house. We all assumed it had something to do with all the weird shit going on there."

Tim was unnerved. He'd long suspected Maggie had given him a highly selective account of "all the weird shit" that had occurred in that accursed house; no doubt she saw no reason to share every unpleasant detail, especially since they'd initially (*stupidly*) believed its otherworldly horrors had been subdued. "What did the call say?" he asked.

"Just some strange shit. Something like 'I'm going to get you.'"

"'And your little dog too,'" Tim mocked. "You're lying, man. What exactly did it say?"

"Ask her. I can't recall it word for word."

Tim wasn't buying it, but he grudgingly put the matter on hold. *It was the old man, and I don't really want to know what he said.* Shut the fuck up! he commanded the taunting voice. "Well, this caller was a woman, and she was trying to make Mags think there was something going on between me and Nicole."

Billy guffawed. "Damn, that could be anybody. This place has more grapevine than a winery. I'm guessing it was Tatiana. But she sure as hell doesn't drive an old crate like a Cutlass unless her sugar daddy cut her loose and she had to trade in the Bentley."

Tatiana was sounding more and more like the probable culprit. And if Tatiana had once been tight with Nicole, she could have easily secured their phone number.

Maybe the Cutlass, and the peculiarly hostile woman he believed drove it, was completely unrelated to the phone call.

"I'm sorry if Maggie was upset," Billy offered. "Give her my best, will you?"

"Yeah, whatever," he said, knowing he wouldn't. "Later."

He was too distracted to ride Warlock or even to give his full attention to Kat's lesson. He kept glancing over his shoulder to see if a white Oldsmobile had rolled into the dirt parking area. Damn this meth paranoia – what good was it to be this paranoid without the benefit of being high at the same time? He craved crystal so intensely it was all he could do not to double over. According to the Twelve-Step canon, he should call his de facto sponsor Father Bob ASAP, but he didn't want to. He wasn't up for a sermon, not even from the only priest he'd ever respected. Better to tough out the craving. After all, unlike Maggie he couldn't run over to the neighborhood supermarket for his fix. (*But maybe Ryan knows someone who can get it*) "Goddamn it, no!" he swore at the voice under his breath. Sandy and Kat didn't appear to have heard him, but a passing horsewoman shot him a perturbed glance.

Driving Kat home, he thought he saw the ominous Cutlass everywhere – in his rearview mirror, in the opposite left turn lane, rolling out of the fucking McDonalds drive-thru. He realized that he was startling at every white sedan on the road, regardless of make and model, and that his hypervigilance was making Kat nervous. He made himself keep his eyes strictly on the road until they reached their apartment complex.

"Look!" Kat pointed out excitedly. "There's Abuelito's car!"

Spotting Armando's silver Lexus in one of the guest parking spaces near their unit, Tim felt his blood chill. Oh God, what if something had happened to Maggie?

Kat dashed ahead of him along the narrow walkway that led to their front door,

but he was not far behind. "Mommy!" Kat exclaimed. "When did Abuelo and 'Lita get

– " And then she broke off. Maggie, wrapped in her robe and swollen with tears, was

flanked on either side of the sofa by her grim-faced parents. She leaped up unsteadily to

hug Kat, turning frightened, bloodshot eyes toward him. "Sweetie, Timmy – don't let

them make me go away," she begged.

"You know I won't, Mags." He clasped her waist.

"Mommy's leaving?" Kat said, fear welling in her voice.

"No," Tim said firmly.

Armando arose. "I think we should talk about this, just us grownups."

"My child is staying right here!" Maggie retorted. Kat was ashen.

Tim leaned down to Kat. "Your abuelo is right, babe. Why don't you take

Thumper for a walk around the complex? I promise you, no one's going anywhere."

"Sweetie, do as Daddy says," Maggie seconded, sniffling. She couldn't bear to

subject Kat to yet another highly-charged emotional scene. "Don't worry, mi niña. It's

going to be fine." She kissed Kat's cheek.

Kat unenthusiastically headed for the side patio where the dog was.

"All right," Tim said. "Who's going to tell me what's going on?" Maggie clung

to him like a terrified child.

"Tim, we know Magdalena has a very bad drinking problem," Eva said gently.

"You should have told us earlier. We want to help."

"Maldigalo, he's the last one to take charge," Armando erupted. "Can't even

support his family – look at this squalor!"

"Hey, this squalor costs us $1800 a month, plus utilities," Tim objected. Accustomed to Armando's not infrequent outbursts, he didn't take especial offense at the insult.

"It's no place to raise a family!" Armando insisted. "Why did you leave that beautiful house in Del Mar?"

Eva colored. "Armando, Papa, that house was too run down."

"Not to mention the fact it's haunted," Tim tossed in. "That's why your daughter's sick, Armando, Eva."

"Don't," Maggie whispered, feebly pressing a palm on his chest.

As for her parents, Eva's taut expression told him she already knew about the house, but not Armando, for he responded in overt scorn. "Ha – haunted. That's for foolish old women and *nacos*, simple-minded peasants."

"Well," Tim said heavily, "this is beside the point. What's this about wanting to take Mags away?"

"In our family, me hijo, we handle these things in private," Eva explained, stepping forward to touch Maggie's shoulder. Maggie pointedly recoiled. "We thought if Maggie could come home for a while, with us to take care of her and maybe some counseling from Father Contreras, who's so kind – "

"No, I won't go," Maggie said.

Tim sat down in their lone, shabbier-than-chic upholstered armchair, taking Maggie into his lap. He gestured for the Floreses to resume their seats on the sofa. "I can take care of Maggie."

"Si, you are doing a fantastic job," scoffed Armando.

Eva started to scold her volatile husband in Spanish, but Tim warned her off with a wave. "Look, I know I'm to blame for Maggie's problem in a lot of ways. She's had to be the strong one for so many years. It all seems to have caught up with her now that I can finally share some of the responsibility."

"Eloquent," Maggie seethed at him. "This is not *your* fault. It's the Shadow Man. And I'll never leave you and Kat."

"Only for a little while, mi niña," Armando tried to coax.

"I know," Eva brightened. "All of you – Maggie, Tim, and Katya – can come stay with us. We can even move her horse to a stable in Orange County."

Armando appeared to be on the verge of barking at his wife. Tim hastened to ward off a fresh eruption. "Eva, I know you guys just want to help – "

"*Stop!*" Maggie screamed, jumping up from his lap. "Stop it! Do any of you realize how humiliating this is? How much I hate myself as it is? Everyone just shut the fuck up and leave me alone!" She flew out the sliding glass door that Kat had left ajar.

Tim was heading after her, but Armando cautioned him back. "Let her be, son," he said, not unkindly. "She needs to be with her daughter. To remember what it is to be a mother."

A good thing Maggie had stormed out – she'd have gone ballistic over Armando's Old World sexism, however well-meaning.

Eva seemed less certain. "But she's so … intoxicated. What if she should take a fall and frighten the niña?"

"Yeah, I'd better go get them both," Tim concurred.

Kat burst back in with the leashed spaniel. "Daddy, Mommy just drove away in her robe." Though she looked stricken, her voice was eerily level.

The Floreses gasped, and Tim went into panic mode. "Oh Christ, I've got to go after her." She must have had her keys in the pocket of her robe.

"I want to come too, Daddy."

"No, Kat. Stay here with Abuelo and Abuelita." He had no time to argue with any of them. No time to think, to freak out, to absorb the unreality closing in on him from every corner like a fog.

He screeched out of the complex, eyes peeled for a 2000 blue Accord with an anti-Bush bumpersticker. His first stop was the nearby Longs Drugs, where he hoped she'd gone to buy liquor, but when he didn't find her car in the lot, he cursed himself for having squandered more time. Traffic was heavy as Sierra turned into Via de la Valle; it was the beginning of rush hour, and cars clogged the entrances for both directions of the 5. She couldn't have gotten far, he told himself. Even with the detour at Longs, how could he be more than a minute or so behind her? Unless she had inexplicably gone north on Sierra toward Cardiff, away from the business district, the freeway onramps.

Five minutes after bolting into his car after her, he realized he had lost her. Misjudged her direction, her route. Perhaps she herself was making it up as she drove along, drunk and frantic with shame. God-fucking-damn it, what had possessed Armando and Eva to improvise an "intervention," however lovingly intended? He could have told them first-hand how useless – no, worse, how dangerous – such choreographed confrontations were. Maybe these textbooks interventions were effective for people so genuinely in denial that they had no idea they had a problem. But for addicts with a modicum of self-awareness, while the humiliation was bad enough, the ensuing

alienation from those they loved and trusted was the real killer. It meant the death of any

hope, delusional though it was, of being loved without judgment. The acute self-

knowledge of having horribly, horribly fucked up worsened a thousand times by the

confirmation of others. He'd tried to support Mags by not judging her, not

condescending to harp on the obvious, trusting her to eventually find her own will to help

herself. As he'd said to Bob, he'd sought to be for her what Diana had been for him.

Maggie herself had struggled to deal with his meth addiction for years with patience and

tolerance, but they were both too hooked on the drama of arguments and ultimatums,

forgiveness and failures. A nonlinear narrative that had proven a maze, a perpetual

motion without destination.

Fuck. No time for thinking, he reminded himself. At least not for that kind of

thinking. Logic, practical reasoning, had to take precedence over abstract puzzling. He

swung into a convenience store lot to clear his head. Deduction: she had not taken her

purse, ergo she had no money, credit cards, or checks to buy more alcohol or even to

check into a motel to get away from them all and sleep off her inebriation. She'd fallen

out of touch with most of her local friends except for Ryan, and he was bound to be still

at work, at UCSD. And she didn't have her cellphone with her, because he remembered

seeing it on the coffee table.

Which left him with two clear, almost equally abhorrent possibilities: either she'd

gone to the barn to find Billy O'Donnell – or back to the house in Del Mar, ground zero

for psychic disintegration.

He had no choice but to check out both places. He got back on Via de la Valle

east, from which he could pick up El Camino Real south, toward the stables. Nearing the

ranch, he called home on his own cell. Eva answered, and her worried tone told him that

they had not heard from Maggie.

"I haven't found her yet, Eva, but I will. She can't have gotten far."

"Por Dios, what if she's been in an accident?"

"No, I'm sure I'd have come across it. I'm going to look in a couple of more

places. But call me if she turns up there or if you hear anything. Kat knows this

number."

No blue Honda – or white Cutlass, for that matter – in the barn's parking area.

However, Billy's Ford pickup was still there. Tim briefly debated with himself whether

to seek out O'Donnell and apprize him of the situation, if only to ask him to alert them if

she did show up. He decided he pretty much had to, but he'd tell Billy *after* he checked

at the evil house, the domain of the Shadow Man he'd insanely hoped they might have

sent back to a hell he didn't even believe in. Maybe that was the problem.

But as he put the car into reverse, Billy, with the great chestnut Oldenburg on a

lead, plainly spotted him across the clearing. Shit, Tim thought, might as well talk to the

jerk now. He shifted back into park and climbed out of the car.

"Forget something?" Billy said, not an unreasonable question given that Tim and

Kat had departed the ranch only an hour before.

"Have you seen Maggie by any chance?"

Billy's brows knit together. "No. Why?"

"Man, if you do see her, call me right away." Tim turned back toward his car.

"Hold on," Billy said, dropping the tone of faint sarcasm he usually deployed in their terse exchanges. "What's wrong?"

"Nothing – we had a fight, she was upset, and just drove off."

"No – I mean, what's really wrong?"

Restless to get back on the road toward the Del Mar house, Tim sighed. "It's the Shadow Man," he snapped.

"Fuck. Goddamn. Get over to that house."

"That's where I'm headed." Tim jumped back into his car, resolving to ponder the extent of Billy's awareness of the "weird shit" at the house later. Later, after he'd located Maggie.

He almost wept with relief upon turning onto La Amatista Road and sighting her Accord parked curbside across the street from the house. But where was Maggie? He didn't know anything about the people leasing the house, but Maggie must have marched up to their door, perhaps to demand a reckoning with the place's longer-term occupant.

Tim rapped the brass knocker urgently. But the moment the door was opened, by a tall, extremely thin woman in a sports bra and yoga pants, his nostrils burned at the familiar, intoxicating, terrible smell of a crank pipe. *No!* He froze because some deep part of him wanted to push past the woman, rush inside, and find not Maggie but his former, other great love and fill himself up with it.

"Are you here looking for the crazy drunk chick?" the skinny woman demanded in the rapid-fire, passionless delivery of a tweaker. "She's not here. A neighbor offered to take her to AA or somewhere like it. The chick was way too plastered to drive, and she was talking like a lunatic about haunted houses and bullshit."

The words registered with him mentally, but he still couldn't move or speak. Just one hit, one hit to get him through this nightmare.

Tires screeched up, startling both him and the tweaker woman. Billy O'Donnell leaped out of the dusty pickup truck. "Is she in there?" he asked, hurrying up the steps.

His meth-scented trance broken, Tim was too alarmed to be annoyed by the horse trainer's presumptuousness in following him. "This woman says some neighbor took her to AA."

"Or some other detox place. I'm not sure." Now the woman was plainly irritated by the intrusion, starting to ease shut the door.

"Which neighbor?" Billy grilled.

"I don't know – one of these soccer moms around here."

"Did she know Maggie?"

"Look, guys, I have a shitload of work to do and I've already wasted too much time on this ridiculous crap." Meth edge bleeding into meth paranoia. He recognized that too. "Like I said, I don't know which one or where she lives, only that she really came to my rescue because this woman was seriously out of control."

Tim saw this was going nowhere. "Fine. Enjoy your shitload of crank – oh, I mean, work." He urged Billy back down the front steps to the curb.

"What the fuck are you doing?" Billy challenged him. "We need to ask what the neighbor looked like, at least."

"Trust me, it would've been useless. That chick was tweaking, and that was all she was going to give us. She's probably ditching her shit right now, thinking this whole thing's a DEA setup." Fleetingly he wondered if the woman had started using meth

before – or after – moving into the house.

Billy seemed to grudgingly accept this explanation. "Maggie was friendly with

this couple who lived around here. Husband and wife Yuppies – "

Tim's phone rang. He grabbed it from his shirt pocket. "Yeah."

"Me hijo, she just called." Eva actually did sound as if she were crying in relief.

"She's on her way to a clinic."

Tim exhaled deeply. "Thank God. What clinic?"

"She wouldn't tell me – I don't think she was sure of the name. But she said

she'd call again tonight, after she was checked in and had gotten some rest."

Tim didn't like not knowing more specifics, but at least Mags was alive and safe.

"How's Kat?"

"She's being so brave like always, Tim, trying to calm down her abuelo and me."

His heart swelled. Destroy him, even destroy Mags, but please, please spare Kat.

He wasn't sure whether he was addressing the mental plea to the fates or to the Shadow

Man. "OK, Eva. I'll be home in a couple minutes."

Billy was watching him expectantly, but at last Tim garnered sufficient

composure to tell him – politely, for Maggie's sake – to mind his own business. "She

really is going to some clinic. She's had a little problem with alcohol lately. Thanks for

the backup, man, but I need to get home to my kid." He folded up the phone and

repocketed it.

Billy obviously got the message, but his eyes remained wary. "Watch your back. If I learned one thing from being around this house it's that just when you think you've got a bead on whatever's inside there it comes right back to bite your ass."

Tim suppressed the impulse to mimic Kat and reply with a scornful "Duh." Instead, he managed a more adult – and pointed – response. "Look, I know you're concerned about Maggie. But I don't suppose I need to tell you I'm uncomfortable with your allusions to all the time you spent with her before we got back together."

"Fair enough. But watch your back, dude."

At home the atmosphere was considerably less frantic than the one he had left, but still tense and morose. Kat sat on the floor cuddling Thumper and pretending to watch TV, while her grandparents conversed quietly – in Spanish, amazingly enough for Armando – in the kitchenette, nursing cups of coffee. Tim tried to persuade Armando and Eva to head back to Newport now that they'd heard from Maggie, but they refused to budge until she called again. "And what if you need to go to Maggie? Who will look after Kat?" Eva said.

"Yeah, I guess that's true." He thought of a pretext for getting them out of the apartment, if only temporarily, so he could talk to Kat in private. "You know, Maggie's car is still across the street from the Del Mar house. I'm afraid if we just leave it there it'll get towed."

Armando, who much preferred action to words, nodded. "You have another key for it? We'll go over there and Eva can drive Magdalena's car back."

"Thanks." Tim removed the extra key from his chain and handed it to Armando.

Kat endured their kisses goodbye but didn't move from the floor or avert her eyes from the television screen. Nor did she stir after they left. Tim got down on his knees beside her. "Mommy's going to be fine. I give you my word, Kat."

She tolerated his hug with little more enthusiasm than she had her grandparents' embraces. "Daddy, I did it. I called Abuelita and told her about Mommy and the wine."

Oh Jesus. Small wonder Kat was so keenly upset. "And now you think it's your fault Mommy drove off like that? Kit-Kat, that's so not true."

"Is so."

"No it isn't. You told Abuelita because you love Mommy and were worried about her. I should've done that myself."

"You didn't 'cause you knew she'd run away."

"No, Kat. I was just plain chickenshit."

Usually she giggled when he let her "catch" him swearing, but not even a flicker of a smile altered her grave expression. She said nothing, still refusing to meet his eyes.

"Katya, look at me." He gently pointed her chin toward him. "You did the right thing. It was wrong to let her go on like that. We were losing a little bit more of her every day. And one day we might have lost her entirely."

Tears sprang to her eyes. "I was so scared she'd die, Daddy. Just like with you."

Now she reciprocated his hug. "She's not going to die. And it's because you helped save her."

But even as he comforted her, *watch your back* echoed ominously in his mind.

For several hours they waited. Eva made everyone sandwiches but no one ate much. Conversation was so strained that Tim popped in a DVD, *Finding Nemo*, that they could all feign watching without having to struggle to come up with small talk. Just after nine the phone pealed. Tim caught it on the first ring. "Yeah?"

"Querido, it's me." She sounded groggy, but not drunk. He nodded to Kat and the Floreses.

"Babe, how are you feeling? OK?"

"Yeah, a little sleepy. They gave me something."

Common detox therapy, he knew, to administer moderate dosages of Librium or Valium to ease the miseries of withdrawal. Of course, the key was "moderate"; his own home remedy had landed him in the hospital and cost him his senior year of baseball. "Where are you, Mags?"

"I'm at … oh, what's it called. CWSC. Some sobriety center just for women."

He jotted down the initials. He'd never heard of such a place, but knew that there were almost as many specialized rehabs as there were phone-book attorneys and car dealers. To meet a need – or to create one? *Stop it*, he chastised himself. "Can I talk to your doctor or therapist, baby?"

"She said she'd call tomorrow. I love you, Timmy. I need to atone."

Fuck, had they already initiated the bombardment with Twelve Steps crap about making amends? Even so, "atone" was a peculiar word choice. "I love you too, Mags."

"Lemme talk to Kat before I fall asleep."

He turned the phone over to Kat and, not waiting to brief Armando and Eva, grabbed the yellow pages and flipped to the "A" section.

No "CWRC" – could it possibly be "Christian Women's Recovery Center,"
whose modest ad offered inpatient detox, rehab, counseling, residential services – in fact,
pretty much everything offered by all of the treatment centers listed – except for the
promise of "Christian 12-Step Recovery." The place sounded legit, and was even
"covered by most insurance plans." The location was in Lakeside, which he had some
vague notion was in east San Diego County. But the "Christian" appellation bothered
him, not simply because it suggested a rather more Biblical sense of "atonement," but
because it reminded him of the metal fish decal on that creepy woman's Oldsmobile.
Jesus-jumped-up Christ, what if she had somehow been the one to chauffeur Maggie to
this Christian rehab?

Kat, looking greatly encouraged, was handing the phone to Eva and Armando.
They tried almost comically to hold the receiver between his right and her left ear, talking
at once and looking no less heartened than Kat. Tim wanted to blame his apprehensions
on his admitted prejudice against "Christian" anything, whether the Coalition or the
Science Monitor. But he just couldn't shake his hunch that something about the
circumstances was wrong.

He wasn't about to rain on Kat's parade, not after all she'd been through, but after
he tucked her and the dog into bed, he decided to air his concerns to Maggie's parents. "I
know you guys are anxious to get back to Newport. But I'm not sure about this place."

Armando, helping Eva on with her coat, stopped mid-sleeve. "Why not? She
sounded so hopeful."

"And she said they gave her some medicine," Eva added, sliding her arm into the
coat sleeve herself.

"It's Christian. Not Catholic. Are you two OK with that?"

As he'd anticipated, they were visibly disconcerted by the information. He often thought they had cut him as much slack as they had over the years because he was at least nominally a Catholic. "Well, as soon as she's gotten the alcohol out of her system, she can go to another type of clinic," Armando reasoned, albeit somewhat unconvincingly.

"Or come stay with us," Eva said, reviving her earlier mantra.

"If Maggie had chosen this place, I'd say fine, that's what she needs for whatever reason. But she was taken there by someone who may or may not have had a religion agenda."

"She said it was a nice lady named Ruth," Eva said.

Ruth. If ever there was a name that agreed with the glowering woman at Starbucks, that was it. But he had to stay rational. "Yeah, and this Ruth's motives may have been entirely altruistic. But if you two don't mind, I'm going to talk to a friend of mine and see what he knows about this clinic. He's a Catholic priest – and a recovering alcoholic."

At this, Eva actually hugged him, and Armando nodded his vigorous approval. "Yes, get Father's opinion," he said. "Then we'll know better if this is the right place for Maggie."

"It's too late to call him now, but I will first thing in the morning. I'll let you know what he thinks." Tim's intention was to ring up Father Bob as soon as the Floreses departed, but he wanted complete privacy, since he also intended to disclose his own dangerous temptation at the house this afternoon.

Accepting his assurance, Armando and Eva left at last. What a long, upsetting day it had been for them, too, Tim mused as he escorted them to their car. Returning inside, he grabbed a bottle of beer and called Father Bob at the rectory.

He told Father Bob everything, from his discovery of Maggie's parents at the apartment attempting a ham-handed intervention, to finding her car at the Del Mar house, the meth woman, his daughter's guilt, and now this bizarre Christian rehab center. He almost choked up relating the traumatic effects on Kat. The only reason he wasn't sobbing outright was that with Kat sleeping, or so he hoped, one room away, he didn't dare indulge the luxury of breaking down.

"Tim, you're exhausted," Bob warned, though sympathetically.

"Please don't feed me that 'hungry-angry-lonely-tired' shit. What the hell kind of Jesus joint did this woman take Maggie to?"

A brief pause. "It's not a cult, Tim, or a racket. But you're right, it is strongly evangelical. Clearly that's the orientation of this woman good enough to take Maggie there. But it doesn't necessarily indicate a planned abduction for purposes of indoctrination."

"So you say. Maggie told me she had to atone, as if they've already gotten to her."

"Come on, Tim. Haven't most Catholics, practicing or lapsed, heard a good deal about atonement?"

He had to concede the point. "It's just that she's so vulnerable right now."

"And so are you, kiddo. Don't be afraid to ask for or accept help. From Maggie's parents, from me, from other people in recovery."

"I'll be fine. I'm telling you one thing, though – tomorrow I'm calling that goddamn property management office and telling 'em to evict that meth freak. It's not only the temptation, Bob. It's that people who smoke it are damn likely to blow the roof off the house in the process."

"Tim, if you're going to relapse, knowing where you can find it is immaterial."

More Twelve-Stepping. "Whatever. But Mags – I don't care if that center's not a cult. I want her out of there."

"Don't you think that Maggie, once she's detoxified her body, will come to the same conclusion?"

"Under ordinary circumstances, yes. But this is no cute little Meg Ryan chick-flick about alcoholism. It's *him*. Just when you think you're in the clear he fucks with your head until you're your own worst nightmare." He hated to paraphrase Billy O'Donnell, but the observation was undeniably on point.

Father sighed. "It isn't 'him.' It's not a ghost or the Devil. It's life, Tim."

He laughed humorlessly. "Man, now who's sounding like the atheist?"

Father Bob chuckled as well. "Tim, I'm going to pray for you especially tonight. I advise you to pray too. Before you object and launch into a discourse against the Higher Power aspect of the program, I want you to simply say yes. Humor me."

"I don't really know how to pray."

"Doesn't matter. Drag out your San Juan de la Cruz, read the 'Dark Night of the Soul' and some of the other poems. Read them closely but don't get distracted by intellection. Read them in Spanish, especially if yours is as rusty as mine."

"Probably rustier, which is pretty embarrassing given Mags and her family."

"All the better. Just read the poems, Tim. It'll help. I swear it."

"All right, Father Zossima. I'll do it."

"Call me tomorrow after you've discussed Maggie's care with her counselor or doctor. And try to get a decent night's sleep."

"I'm sure the poems will work better than Seconal." But in truth, he was beyond fatigued. "Thanks, Bob. Really."

"Be well, Tim. Talk to you tomorrow."

CHAPTER 4

Not long after Tim returned from taking Kat to school, the social worker from the Christian Women's Sobriety Center called. At first she sounded generically pleasant, totally secular. She referred to Maggie as "Mrs. Emerson," and Tim wasn't about to correct her lest the disclosure that they'd not yet gotten around to remarrying would preclude him from visits and decision-making.

Mrs. Emerson, the social worker explained, would undergo a two to four day detoxification period supervised, of course, by a physician. After that, she would "transition" into the customary 28-day rehab program, upon whose completion she would be referred either to a sober-living situation or discharged outright. As with all non-court-ordered rehabs, Mrs. Emerson's participation was 100% voluntary.

It was the standard spiel, he well knew. But he had a hunch that the devil, so to speak, was in the details. "When can I see her?"

"Family visits are for two hours each weekend day, on site. Because so many of our patients and clients are also recovering from abusive relationships, we usually don't incorporate spouses or partners into family therapy perhaps as much as other programs."

"That's not an issue with us."

"Mr. Emerson, according to your wife, you yourself are a recovering substance abuser." Now the voice was lecturesome.

"That doesn't make me a goddamn wife beater," he snapped.

Whether it was the mild sacrilege or the direct challenge, his retort prompted the woman to respond with open hostility. "One might consider numerous years of sporadic abandonment, failure to pay child support, use of illegal drugs in the family home – not to mention the emotional stress of coping with a criminal lifestyle – a form of spousal abuse." She was lawyeristic, ice-cold.

"She told you all this?"

"In our initial admissions interview, yes."

"She was drunk and terrified, for Christ's sake!"

"Mr. Emerson, as the representative of a Christian institution I'm going to ask you to refrain from profanity."

"Fuck that," he seethed. "I'm coming to get Maggie today before you fanatical Jeezoids plant any more bullshit in her head. Spousal abuse my ass!"

"She self-admitted, Mr. Emerson." He could all but picture the woman's smirk. "You would have to obtain legal conservatorship to check her out against her will. Otherwise, what would keep a *literal* batterer from doing the same to his very victim?"

The emphatic "literal" made him even angrier. So angry, in fact, that he actually calmed down enough to recognize that his outbursts were not serving either his or Maggie's cause. "OK. But I'm coming to see her."

"We generally don't recommend visits during detoxification, with patient-clients so heavily medicated and vulnerable to psychological distress. And of course, we'd have to get Mrs. Emerson's consent."

"Look, you can't have it both ways. Either she's too zoned out to handle visitors or she's rational enough to consent."

"This isn't a logic problem, Mr. Emerson. It's about empowering your wife's recovery."

Bullshit. It's about your "Christian" agenda, artlessly camouflaged in a quasi-feminist discourse of "empowerment." "Will you ask her to consent to see me, then?" he asked through clenched teeth.

"Certainly. Please understand, sir, we're not trying to interfere in your marital relations. We're simply committed to setting her on the path to sobriety and spiritual health."

He bit back another obscenity. "I want that too," he forced himself to reply.

He spent the rest of the morning on the phone: delivering a toned-down version of this conversation with the clinical social worker to Armando and Eva, reassuring them that Father Bob said the clinic was on the up and up; calling the property management office responsible for leasing the house to report he'd stopped by and found the current resident using drugs. The manager coughed nervously. "Are you absolutely sure? Liz

Yeager is a litigation partner at one of San Diego's top insurance defense firms. She's

paid rent in full through next January."

"I don't care. There's got to be something in the lease about illegal activities."

"Of course, that's standard. All I'm saying is that we had better be prepared to

prove it, because she's just the type to sue if she claims we've evicted her without just

cause."

His head ached, frustration mingling with an urge to get high that intensified the

more he had to focus on the tenant's meth use. "I can't prove it. I didn't take pictures."

"Your word against hers, Tim. You sure you want to take this fight on?"

"Ah, fuck it. But if that house explodes from a bong gone bad, I hope we're the

ones filing the lawsuit."

He hung up the phone feeling utterly thwarted.

He was keenly conscious as well of Maggie's absence; even when she was

smashed or sleeping, he was strengthened simply by knowing she was near. The

apartment felt vacant, too quiet. He supposed it was not a good idea for him to be

entirely alone today, but he didn't want to go to a meeting, where cellphones were

verboten, in case Mags or even that goddamn Jesussy social worker called. He was too

edgy to read or watch TV, and he chose not to ride lest Warlock, a sensitive if good-

natured horse, would intuit his tension and act up. Don't be afraid to accept or ask for

help, Father Bob had advised. But when he called Bob, the rectory housekeeper told him

the priest was occupied all afternoon overseeing a parish food drive.

He walked the dog, forced himself to prepare and eat a pathetic lunch of

Campbell's Chicken Noodle soup and a bagel. They were almost out of groceries; what in God's name would he do about Kat's dinner tonight? Even she, he feared, was tiring

of pizza. By early afternoon he couldn't stand waiting for the phone to ring any longer.

What if the social worker had just ignored his request to get Maggie's approval for a

visit? Just as he picked up his cell to call the clinic, their land-line trilled.

"Sweetie, it's me."

"Mags! How are you?"

"'K." She still sounded heavily sedated.

"I'm going to drive out there and bring you some of your stuff."

"Don't, Tim."

"Why not?"

"Because I need to suffer. We killed our baby."

He should have seen this one coming. If she'd blurted out to those holy rollers

that she'd had an abortion, what fodder she was handing them for manipulation.

"Maggie, listen to me carefully. I know you're doped up, but can you listen?"

"Uh-huh."

"That was no more a baby than an appleseed's an apple. You and I both know

that."

"I have to suffer, Timmy. Don't come. Please." The line went dead.

Tim slammed his fist into the wall, startling Thumper and creating a spiderweb of

cracks in the plaster. But the physical pain did nothing to dull the rage that seemed to

threaten to burst from his chest. Rage at the old man for having somehow found a perfect

vehicle for his destructive will in the Jesus clinic and whoever the hell had dragged her

there.

Then he simply broke down and cried. It didn't make him feel any better, but at least he didn't have to worry about alarming Kat. Kat. He needed to pull himself together for her sake. He staggered to the kitchen sink and splashed cold water on his face.

And now the fucking phone was ringing again, no doubt someone bearing still more foul tidings. "Yeah," he groaned into the receiver.

"Hey, Tim. You sound sick." It was Ryan.

"Man, you don't know the half of it."

"Uh-oh. I'm afraid to ask."

Ryan's phrase recalled to him again Father Bob's counsel about asking for help. "Look, you want to hang out tonight? Smoke a little weed and maybe watch some old *Mystery Science Theater* videos?"

"Actually, I have a date, for the first Friday night in months. How about tomorrow, though?"

"Cool. See you around seven or so."

In a way he was almost relieved to have an extra day to regroup, to muster up the energy to relate once more the events of the past 24 hours. The company would probably do Kat some good as well. She loved Ryan, and maybe between the three of them they could dream up an alternative for dinner other than the inevitable pizza. He wouldn't break out the weed until after she'd gone to bed.

He sometimes wondered how much Kat understood about his drug addiction. Schools started kids on those "D.A.R.E." programs practically at kindergarten these days. Clearly she'd recognized her mother's drinking problem almost from the get-go.

Damn shame they couldn't insert *X-Files*-like computer chips in kids at birth, programming in them an aversion to drugs. Could that have saved him, or Maggie, from the machinations of the Shadow Man? And even if, like Father Bob, you wanted to be empirical about it, Kat had to be considered at high risk for addiction given her family history.

No. If I can finally get him, get him for good, my daughter will be OK. If he had to sacrifice himself, or, God forbid, Maggie, on the altar of the old man's malignancy, it would be worth it to save Kat.

He picked Kat up from school and took her to the stables, but he maintained a low profile at the ranch. If Ryan had guessed from one word that something was wrong, it had to be scrawled all over his face, and he felt too emotionally spent to trust himself to come up with a good lie. Most of all, he wanted to avoid O'Donnell. Kat seemed able to lose herself in her beloved Sugar, eagerly accepting Rhonda's invitation to join her and her granddaughter Hayley on a trail ride. Tim went to Warlock's stall, slipped the fancy leather halter Nicole had bought over the horse's muzzle, and led him to the large, easternmost riding arena, which was seldom used because it faced Old El Camino Real and many of the school horses were spooked by the automobile traffic. In the center of the ring he removed Warlock's halter, gave the horse a slap on the rump. Warlock deigned to take a few trotting steps before stopping twenty feet away from Tim to roll luxuriantly in the dirt.

It was the damndest sight, one that usually made him smile, this massive horse scratching his back on the soil, all four heavy and feathered hooves kicking at the sky. But today Tim watched the stunt as dispassionately as though it were unfolding on a dimensionless snowy screen. The horse clambered to his feet, shook himself off, and proceeded to trot unbidden, farting loudly with each beat of the hooves. Tim had to chuckle, but it felt like a reflex and brought no warmth to his heart.

He let Warlock frolic for an hour, after which he put the horse back and went to the car to wait for Kat. He'd lied and told her he'd yet to hear from her mother today, and as always, she seemed not to believe him. Maybe that know-it-all cowboy was right about him; the whole fucking world evidently found him transparent. Had to be due to the drugs, because if he'd tipped his pitches the way he apparently telegraphed his most innocuous fibs, he'd never have made it out of Little League.

"I have an idea," he said to Kat once she rejoined him. "Why don't we find some really cool restaurant for dinner tonight? You know, the kind where we both have to act like grownups."

"Can't we go see Mommy instead?" she asked, but the note of resignation told him she already knew the answer.

"No, Mommy's still resting. Rest is what she needs to get better."

"Yeah, we can go to a restaurant," she replied quietly. Without the distraction of Sugar and the trail ride, Kat was as transparently worried as he.

He was determined to keep her from becoming overwhelmed by upset. Given their budget and Maggie's indisposition for much of the time since their reconciliation, he had little first-hand knowledge of area restaurants other than the Chinese place, Bully's, and Armando's La Jolla. There was a Thai place on Via de la Valle that Dennis was always raving about, but Tim was afraid the cuisine might be too eclectic for Kat's tastebuds. As he pored over the yellow page Restaurant Guide in a state of perplexity,

Eva called to check on Kat and ask if he'd heard anything more from Maggie. He fed

Eva the same vague "resting" line he'd tried with Kat, only his former mother-in-law

seemed to accept it. Maybe if Maggie was still acting bizarrely after the detox he'd enlist

her folks' assistance in wresting her away from Jeezopolis and its evangelical agenda.

The prospect of Armando venting his fatherly temper on that smarmy social worker was

certainly tempting. But in the interim, there was no sense in getting them worked up

again about a situation over which none of them had much control.

Eva applauded his notion about taking Kat out to dinner to get her mind off the

upsetting circumstances. "Yes, try to keep her busy with fun things. That's what Papa

and I did when Maggie was trying to find you in Los Angeles last fall." She suggested

the Chart House in Cardiff, where she had taken Maggie and Kat as a "moving day" treat.

"Wouldn't that just remind her of Maggie?"

"Me hijo, she's not going to *not* think about her mother. Why not go to a place

where her memories of Magdalena are nice ones?"

"All right. I guess it's better than just picking a restaurant out of the phone book."

Chart House was a chain and a rather pricey one to boot, but maybe Eva was on to

something.

"So sweet of you to want to take her out like a little lady. You are a good father,

Tim."

"Hm, better late than never."

"I always knew Maggie had not misplaced her faith in you. You've had your

troubles, but you're a nice boy."

No one had called him a "boy" since he actually was one, and he was both touched and slightly embarrassed. "I'll be in touch, Eva. Thanks for the restaurant tip."

Kat was, in fact, delighted to go to the Chart House, to have an occasion to wear one of the pretty dresses her 'Lita had given her for Christmas. And as Eva had predicted, she seemed to welcome the opportunity to talk about her mother in happier times. "Mommy kept making fun of our waiter," she told Tim once they were seated at a linen-dressed table with an ocean view. "He was a big geek and he was flirting with her."

The food itself was expensive and unmemorable, but if the outing had served to temporarily lift Kat's spirits, it'd be worth eating peanut butter and jelly sandwiches for dinner for the rest of the month.

Kat was able to speak briefly with Maggie the next morning, but whether the child sensed anything disturbing about her mother's state of mind Tim had no clue. To him, Maggie sounded no less zonked than she had the night of her first call, the main difference being that this time, she informed him at the outset that she'd phoned for the sole purpose of talking to Kat. "We can't talk until you open your mind," she murmured. He knew those words had been imposed upon her, but it was pointless to argue with her when she remained so groggy. What were they pumping into her, goddamn Demerol? Bob may have claimed that this Womens Christians Recovery Whatever was a legitimate treatment program, but to Tim, it was sounding more and more like a cult.

As soon as he dropped Kat off for her full day of riding and helping Rhonda out as a "working student," Tim drove straight to the rectory of Saint Thomas Aquinas in

Carlsbad. Father Bob was busy preparing tomorrow's Homily, and had a full afternoon of confessions ahead, but made time for the update on Maggie. "They're definitely brainwashing her," Tim declared. "How do I get her out of there?"

Father Bob volunteered to call the social worker, though he reluctantly concurred with her that the only way to forcibly remove Maggie from the program was to have her declared legally incompetent.

"Fuck, suddenly I'm helpless without a lawyer," Tim grumbled, thinking of the property manager's advice about Liz Yeager. "Screw it – I'm going to drive out there and talk to Maggie face to face."

"Do what you need to do, Tim. But I don't think it's wise to show up there looking for a fight. Maggie's not herself right now, that's obvious. But until she's no longer under sedation, you can't know how much of this 'brainwashing' is simply drug-induced confusion."

The priest proposed a compromise solution. "If by Monday she's still dazed and spouting extreme religious views clearly not her own, I'll go out to the Center and meet with her. They can't stonewall me, as a fellow clergy, the way they can you."

It was the best he could settle for. At least he trusted Bob to be as suspicious as he about evangelical proselytizing.

Kat surprised him, however, when he arrived to pick her up at the stables. She asked if she might spend the night at her riding friend Sabrina's house. "Are you sure you're up for it, baby?"

She nodded. "They have an inside swimming pool."

"Wow. Next time invite me." Barely April, it was still too cool to use their apartment complex's pool at night.

She regarded him pensively. "But I'll stay home with you and Thumper if you want."

"Don't worry about us, Kit-Kat. Ryan's coming over and we're just gonna hang out and watch movies."

She looked mightily relieved.

Tim shut the trunk on her tack box and horse treats, and was just opening the drivers side door when – *goddamn it!* – he spotted Billy O'Donnell, astride Westcott, approaching them. Apparently dodging him two days in a row was too much to hope for.

"Daddy, open the trunk. I want to give Westcott a carrot," Kat urged.

"Oh no you don't," Billy said in good humor, dismounting next to the car. "Not unless you want to clean carrot chaw off his bit."

"It's only carrot," Kat replied. "I'll clean it."

"We need to get home if you're going to Sabrina's tonight," Tim said carefully.

She was petting the Oldenburg's nose, affording Tim the opportunity to toss a pointed glance at Billy. O'Donnell was a cowboy but he wasn't stupid, and Tim was sure the message had been conveyed: things were not well with Maggie.

Billy shook his head ruefully.

"Come on, Kat," Tim coaxed.

"I'll see you guys later," Billy said, and to Tim's irritation, sounded like he meant it.

Ryan was visibly distressed to learn of Maggie's circumstances, of her disintegration. "I can't believe it. It's just so not like her."

Tim mindlessly rolled a joint. "It isn't her. It's that goddamn, fucking house."

"She used to say when she was living there that it was driving her to drink. She worried about it." Ryan stared at the TV screen, a basketball game, but he was plainly gathering his thoughts rather than attending to the score. "Did she tell you about the woman who first rented the house? She died of an OD."

Tim raised his lighter to the joint and drew in deeply, holding the smoke in his lungs for a few moments. He exhaled and passed it to Ryan. "No, she didn't tell me a whole lot about what happened there. The renter OD'd? That's awful." An earlier incarnation of the crank-smoking lawyer?

Ryan took a hit off the joint. "Maybe there's a rational explanation. Methane gas or radon, something underneath the house that affects the people living there. You ought to hire a geologist or an environmental surveyor."

Tim pondered it. "Huh. So maybe the ghosts and shit are hallucinations?"

Ryan chuckled dryly. "I don't know if I'm ready to go that far. I happen to believe the haunting was real. But the tendency toward alcoholism and drug addiction might be a separate thing."

"Fuck," Tim sighed. "All I know is that something inexplicably turned Mags first into a drunk and now into Sue Bridehead."

"'Done because we are too menny,'" Ryan quoted, with another dry laugh. "Either this is good pot or my memory of Victorian lit isn't as hazy as I thought."

"Give yourself a laurel and hardy handshake."

"Oh God," Ryan carped. "From Thomas Hardy to Mel Brooks."

"My bad." But not even the potent marijuana numbed his worries. "You know, if I thought it'd do any good I'd go over there and torch the place myself. Burn it to the ground. If they send me up for arson, well, been there, done that."

Ryan looked at him thoughtfully. "That must have been hell."

"At the time I thought it was. But this is worse." He fastened a roach clip to the dwindling cigarette. "Did Mags tell you how I hooked up with another guy when I was in there?"

Ryan shrugged. "I'd have done the same thing."

Tim burst into hoarse laughter. "Yeah, but you're gay!"

"Fuck, I'd have played boy-toy to the burliest bulldyke in a women's prison if that's what I needed to do to survive."

Tim was struck by how common-sensical a light Ryan's comment cast upon his own sordid experience. "I hate my complications."

"Really? I love mine."

The good-natured sarcasm dislodged his stoned self-absorption. He glanced at the basketball game. "Who's winning?"

"I couldn't even tell you who's playing."

"Hey, man, we went to UCLA. We're supposed to give a shit about basketball."

Ryan squinted at the screen. "Guess what – that *is* UCLA, and we're beating LSU."

"Oh yeah, the Big Baby. I completely spaced out that this is Final Four weekend."

"Hard to imagine you'd have anything else on your mind," Ryan quipped.

Tim began rolling another joint. "I can't tell you how much I need to be stoned."

"Let me ask you something that I hope won't offend you."

"How'll I know until after you've asked and I'm already either offended or not?"

"About the prison thing," Ryan ventured.

"What, you want to know about sleazy prison sex?" He was too stoned and too preoccupied with the present to be squeamish about the topic.

"Sort of. What did you think of man love?"

Tim couldn't judge whether Ryan was grinning because he was joking or because he was proud of himself for having the nerve to ask. "Um, I don't know. Have you ever fucked a woman?"

"Only in the pejorative sense."

Tim was utterly baffled. "Man, that's too weird … pejorative sense of fucked or of woman?"

"Forget it – not even I'm sure what I meant." Ryan swigged his beer.

But Tim was unwilling to have Ryan think him either hypocrite or homophobe for not answering. "Physically, fucking's fucking, isn't it? Except – OK, now I might offend you here. But the thing that really grossed me out was sucking dick. I'd rather do anything other than that."

Ryan only laughed. "Guess what – you're not gay."

"Well, how do you feel about giving a woman head?" Mags hated with a passion the phrase *eating pussy*; she thought so pleasurable a practice merited more dignified description.

"I never have, and you couldn't pay me."

"Must mean you're gay."

"How droll of you to notice."

Tim was aching with laughter. This truly was first-rate weed. What was especially hilarious was that they'd gotten it from Ryan a month before, who obviously had no recollection of the gesture. But on a night like tonight, who needed or wanted short-term memory?

They ended up ordering a pizza after all and watching the DVD of *Manos, Hands of Fate*. Father Bob called at some point, but Tim let the machine pick up. He was far too wasted to converse, much less with the priest. By midnight Ryan's head was sufficiently clear for him to drive. After he left Tim smoked another joint in front of what seemed like endless reels of sports highlights on TV.

He fell into bed fully clothed in his jeans and T-shirt, thoroughly stoned yet somehow cognizant that everyone would view his behavior this night as classic Tim Emerson Fuck-Up. Yep, he'd fucked up again. What if it had been Kat calling instead of Bob, or Maggie, come to her senses and needing him? What if the dog got sick from all the pizza scraps? What if Ryan really wasn't OK to drive and wound up killing himself or someone else on the freeway? A dead dreamless sleep could not claim him soon enough.

Now that the drugs were wearing off, she started to dream again. She found herself back in the small Westwood apartment she and Tim had shared their last year of college. All the night people were there – Dan, Ryan, Heather the dominatrix, Julie

Nash, raised a fundamentalist Christian and now the biggest stoner of the group. They were doing lines of meth on the coffee table, and that "Lies, Lies, Lies" song blasted on the radio. But where was Tim? She threw open the bedroom door and discovered him naked and face down on their bed, with the muscular, tattooed Ed on top and thrusting into him. Tim's eyes were glassy and he didn't see her, but Ed did. He withdrew his huge, engorged penis and greeted her. "It's little Maggie of the flowers," he said, as though he'd been expecting her.

Repulsed, she backed out of the bedroom. But the night people had disappeared, leaving only a sweet-faced, sixtyish woman with a sporty auburn bob and chic glasses. "I'll help you, honey," the nice lady said. "I know a place where they'll take real good care of you." Such a kind, sympathetic voice, devoid of judgment or disgust. For at once Maggie realized that she was terribly drunk and in her robe and pajamas, and she was horrified that everyone had seen her in such a state.

"Come along, dear." The nice lady locked an arm in hers and led her outside, only outside was no longer Westwood but Del Mar, and they were leaving the evil house, the shadow house.

"What about my car?" Maggie mumbled as the woman helped her into a generic white sedan.

"Don't worry about anything, honey. Now, strap in."

She fell back against the passenger seat head rest, shut her eyes for a moment. When she reopened them she saw that they were on the freeway, and the nice lady was wearing a crazy grin, weaving in and out of traffic, even passing other cars on the shoulder.

"Slow down! You're going to kill us!" Maggie cried.

The grin just widened, stretching across the woman's face until it literally cracked off like a plaster death mask, revealing *him*. *"Puta*. Greaser. Baby-killer," he taunted. "He never should have come back. You'd have lost him but saved yourself and your brat, you stupid *Mexicana*."

Baby-killer. Baby-killer. Baby-killer.

She woke up, shivering not only from fear but also from the chill of comprehension.

She had to get out of here, get home to Tim and Kat.

She threw on her robe, nicely laundered by the clinic staff, and ignoring the half-dozen other slumbering women in the dorm-like room, hurried out to the upstairs reception area where a night nurse sat sentry. "Can't you sleep, Mrs. Emerson? Maybe we cut back on your medication too soon."

"No – I need to use the phone. I have to call my husband."

"I'm sorry," the nurse replied, sounding as if she meant it. "Phone access for patients ends at eight p.m. I'm sure it will keep until the morning."

"I need to leave. I have to get to my family."

"That would be expressly against your treating physician's orders, Mrs. Emerson. You're still detoxifying."

Maggie tossed up her hands. "I know the rules. You can't hold me here. Give me the damn release form to sign."

"Can't I at least get Pastor Owens to come counsel you, dear?" wheedled the nurse. "Sometimes it's best to leave our decision-making to the Lord, especially when we least feel like surrendering to Him."

"The release form," Maggie repeated.

Looking heartsick, the nurse located the appropriate form in her desk drawer. There was nothing "Jesussy," as Tim would say, about this document; it was a standard release from liability testifying that she had checked out against express medical advice. Maggie scrawled her signature. "I don't suppose you'd lend me fifty cents for the pay phone, or will I have to hit up one of the other patients?"

The nurse clucked. "I can't allow you to use the phone because that could be construed as approval of your unauthorized discharge."

Damn, she'd have to hope the operator would allow her to charge the call to her Working Assets account, despite not having the card with its code. The very idea that she'd run off without her purse, without ID, was almost as frightening as the blackout itself, and the memory recovered tonight in her dream.

The pay phone was down the hall, near the residential wing of the clinic. Maggie punched in "O." Luck was with her, for the operator told her she could charge the call to her local AT & T number. Maggie dialed her home number. Four, five rings, then the machine and her own recorded voice: "Hi, you've reached the Flores-Emerson home. Please leave a message and we'll get back to you." The long beep that followed indicated at least one message already taped.

How strange. It was nearly two a.m., and Tim was the world's lightest sleeper, a residual effect of years of methamphetamine use. "Tim, it's me. Wake up. Querido, wake the hell up!" She was all but shouting, hoping at least to rouse Kat. "I need you to come pick me up right away. I don't belong here. It was all his – "

The machine cut her off.

She tried Tim's cellphone, which rang a dozen times before she gave up and simply called a cab.

She climbed into the taxi in the same robe and pajamas in which she'd arrived at the clinic, but the graveyard-shift cabbie was fortunately not the garrulous type, especially once assured he'd be paid with a credit card upon reaching their destination in Solana Beach. It was bound to be one hefty fare.

Something was gravely wrong, she worried over the miles of mostly empty freeway. Dear God, had Kat taken ill? Had Tim gone off on a meth binge? She'd just talked to him – hadn't she? – that morning. Or had she dreamed that too? Maybe she had, and Tim and Kat were in Newport with her parents.

Just let them be all right. The prayer seemed pitiably futile, for now she knew for certain that the Shadow Man was far from done with them.

The cabbie probably made record time in the long drive from Lakeside to Solana Beach, given the absence of traffic and his own leaden foot, but to Maggie the trek felt endless. At last they pulled into the apartment complex. Tim's car as well as her own was in its assigned outdoor space. "Wait right here while I get my credit card," she instructed the driver. At least they hadn't confiscated her keys at the clinic; no, they were tucked into the plastic zipper bag with the comb, toothbrush, and toothpaste furnished to her.

She pushed open the front door. "Tim? Kat?" she called, as Thumper bounded up to greet her. The living room light was on, the coffee table littered with empty Corona bottles and a large, empty pizza box from Oggi's. *Is there any more beer?* teased her brain.

The driver honked outside. "Shit." But the mess in the living room somewhat reassured her that no new crisis had struck. She located her purse on the kitchen counter, grabbed her American Express card, and hastened back outside to pay her fare, including a generous tip. She didn't wait for the receipt, simply snatched back her card and reentered the apartment. She checked Kat's room first, but its darkness told her that either her daughter had been indeed taken back to Newport by Pa and Mama, or else was at a friend's house. For surely Tim wouldn't have been ordering pizza if something bad had happened to Kat.

The light was on in the master bedroom, where she found him sound asleep in his clothes, his head sandwiched between two pillows.

He's drunk. Maybe you can sneak a drink before waking him. You know there's a new bottle of vodka stashed in the garment bag with your winter coat.

She bent over the bed and shook his shoulders with all the vigor she could muster. "Tim, damn it! Wake up!"

He grumbled something that sort of sounded like, "I'm so stoned," and pushed his face deeper into the pillows.

"Tim!" She shook him again.

Gingerly he lifted his head, opened his eyes, and realized he wasn't dreaming. "Mags!"

He reached for her, but she raised a cautious hand. "Where's Kat?"

"Hm, she's at somebody's house ... " Wake up, goddamn it, he ordered himself. "Sabrina's."

Only then did she permit him to embrace her. He held her so tightly he might have crushed her, and she might have let him, too. But first things first. "Sweetie, I need you to do me a favor. Get rid of all the alcohol in the house."

"Ryan and I drank all the beer."

Just like college days. "There's still wine in the refrigerator and a bottle of vodka inside my garment bag in the front closet."

He stumbled to his feet, located both bottles, and emptied their contents into the kitchen sink. He was profoundly ashamed that she'd found him in such a sorry condition, but resolved to postpone, for now, his inevitable guilt trip. "How did you get home? Forget it – I'm just so happy you're here."

"I'm cold. Let me make some tea and then I'll tell you what's been going on."

"No, I'll make the tea, babe. Get into bed."

Because she was still unsteady on her feet from two and a half days under heavy sedation, she acquiesced. She was still shaking, too – was it from the drugs, the withdrawal, or simply abject fear?

None of them was safe.

She heard the microwave's beep; a moment later he was setting a mug of green tea on the nightstand beside her. She took a small sip, savoring the heat, the pale nutty flavor. "This is perfect."

"Oh, Mags. When you said you didn't want to see me, I thought – "

"I didn't want you to see me that way. And I was so out of it that I believed them when they said I was bad and needed to suffer. Timmy, it still kills me that I'm a vile alcoholic and have put you and Kat through all this." She cried against his chest.

"Hey, remember who you're talking to." He pressed his lips against her temple.

It felt good to cry, to just lean into him and let him comfort her. "Oh, look," she apologized, when her tears were finally spent. "I've snotted all over your shirt."

"Ha. I'm surprised you didn't get a contact high. We smoked a lot of reefer tonight." He yanked the shirt over his head and tossed it aside.

"Stop right there," she said with a weak smile as he reached to undo the top button of his jeans. "I need to tell you things, and the sight of you naked is too distracting."

"Sorry."

And he looked so chastened she almost giggled. But the impulse died before the corners of her mouth could so much as twitch. "OK. I totally blacked out. The last thing I remembered was arguing with Mama and Pa, and then you and Kat walking in. The next thing I knew, I was in this place with all these nodding pious people, spilling out my life story and begging them to somehow get me a drink."

She told him of her dream, omitting the first part with the night people and, God help her, himself and Ed, beginning rather with the kindly woman who lured her away from the Del Mar house with a promise of help. He paled when she recounted how the woman had metamorphosed into the Shadow Man. "I'm absolutely certain, Tim, that some version of this dream is what really happened."

"You did go to the house," he confirmed, trying to mask how unnerved he was. "Our bitch tenant said a neighbor woman had driven you off. You told your parents it was someone named Ruth."

"Oh, I believe there was a woman. He's powerful, Tim, but I don't think he drives cars."

His brow furrowed. "You mean, he, like, possessed somebody, this Ruth person?"

"Yes, something like that. I wonder who she was."

He didn't. "Can you remember from your dream what she looked like?"

Maggie struggled to recapture the precise image. "She was around sixty ... short curly red hair, kind of hip glasses for an older woman."

"Fuck. Same lady." Maggie had exactly described the woman at Starbucks. "Was she driving a white Oldsmobile?"

"How in the world did you know that?"

"Because she was giving Kat and me the evil eye in front of Starbucks the other day. I think she was watching us at the barn, too. She may have even been the one who called you with the lie about me and Nicole."

Maggie's hand flew to her throat. "Oh my God – she was that close to Kat? Tim, we've got to do something, get away from here to some place where he can't get to us or Kat!" But she knew the thought was irrational even as she gave voice to it. They'd lived in the house, breathed it, him, into their lungs. There was no escape.

"Maybe we should raze the house," he said, with no great conviction.

"I don't think we could legally do that. It's Kat's, not ours, and the trustees wouldn't allow it."

"Hell, it probably wouldn't work anyway. Your idea's better – let's pack it in, find some isolated little town in Canada, and play each other's guard dog when it comes to drugs or booze. Either that or join a Doomsday cult."

"I'm sure you thought I had."

"I did. Or that he'd compelled you to. I pictured all the women in burqas or red hoods like in *The Handmaid's Tale*."

Again she managed a wan smile. "None that I saw, but then I was pretty dopey." She clasped her hands around the warm mug. "We can't go underground, like some '60s fugitives. If it were just you and me, it'd be an option. But how could we make Kat live like that?" She recalled a detail from her dream that she'd also deliberately left out, the old man's taunt, *He never should've come back. You'd have lost him but saved yourself and your brat.* No, she'd never tell Tim; it would shatter him.

The little lost boy. The old man had failed in his mission to keep Tim forever broken and fragmentary. And now he was exacting his revenge.

"I don't know," he said, lighting a cigarette. He coughed, lungs still burning from the weed. "But no matter what, Kat's got to come first. I'd kill myself, slit my own throat on those goddamn stairs, if I thought it would finally appease him."

"God, don't talk like that!"

"Don't worry. I'm afraid it'd be as useless as tearing down the house. Theoretically, Mags, what if you, Kat, and I are all killed in a car accident? *Theoretically*," he reiterated as she turned gray. "Does that mean people with no connection to us but who just happen to live in that house will suddenly stop turning into addicts?"

She hated even to humor his hypothetical, but needed to say her piece. "I think it's his presence that's toxic, that drives people to drink and drugs and to beat their children."

"Toxic, eh? Ryan suggested maybe it's like a cancer cluster there, with toxic shit in the ground that causes people to go nuts."

"I wish it were that easy," she sighed, rubbing his thigh.

"Whatever the case, we're not going to solve it tonight. You look so worn out."

"I am," she admitted. "But will you fuck me anyway?"

"OK, but I gotta tell you, it's not a lot of fun for me when you don't come." He hoped his candor wouldn't hurt her feelings.

And she feared he would be hurt if she told him that sometimes the closeness was as important as orgasm. Hurt, or else think her retro, antifeminist. The bizarre thing was that she did want him physically tonight. If they were damned, they were damned together, and hurtling themselves into the lost time of mad sex might be their lone gesture of defiance. After all, hadn't the Shadow Man been attempting to deny them even that small temporal pleasure by sending her into the repressive arms of the local Taliban?

"Well," she said coyly, taking his hand and pressing it between her legs, "I guess you're just going to have to make me come." Pleased by the sparkle in his eyes, she playfully twisted away to strip off her robe, her pajamas, and good God, some awful white cotton briefs clearly foisted onto her at the clinic. Who the hell wore panties with pajamas? Sober Christian women, she deduced.

"Leave the light on. I want to see you," she said, watching him cast off his jeans, boxer shorts. She hoped that somehow *he*, too, could see them, was forced to see them, and would be tortured by their transitory refusal of his dominion.

Tim sensed what she was thinking, and a heady wave of love as well as lust surged in his heart, his groin. "So you want me to work for it, huh?" He eased her back, deliberately draped her knees over his shoulders, and buried his mouth and tongue in her, sucking, teasing her clitoris, feeling the little bud stiffen and her vulva moisten with her own juices and his saliva. After her first climax he hastily slipped on a condom and pulled her forward on top of him. They fucked for hours, for as long as they had since college or their wedding night in Las Vegas, and just like in the John Donne poem, the sun was rising when they at last fell back sated.

And little more than two miles away, a mother awakened to find her child dangling limply from a rope tied to the upper frame of her expensive wrought-iron canopy bed.

CHAPTER 5

They took Sunday off from worry. After picking up Kat from Sabrina's home in Rancho Santa Fe, they went as a family to late-morning Mass, on to brunch at Jake's at the Beach. The day was unusually brisk but clear, the kind of weather some locals called "freezing," but tourists, refugees from the icy spring thaws of much of the rest of the country, strolled along the shoreline in shorts, their bare feet tickled by wave foam from the chilly ocean.

Though aware the uplift of her spirits was but temporary, Maggie felt fortified enough to call her parents while Tim helped Kat with her homework. She spoke with her father first, which was good, since he seemed most eager to take her at her word that she'd hit bottom, seen the error of her ways, and would be fine from hereon in. She loved her father all the more this evening because he was not of particularly analytical bent. Eva, on the other hand, was not so easily pacified. "Are you going to start attending meetings now?"

"Tim wants me to go with him tomorrow," Maggie replied, which was true, although she'd yet to commit to such a public gesture.

"Maggie, there's something else." Eva lowered her voice. "Tim said that the reason this has happened to you is the house. The ghost."

Maggie knew that a part of her mother was desperate to attribute the perfect child's fall from grace to external, malignant forces. In a way, so was she. And yet ... "Mama, it's hard to know for sure."

"You must take the priest over there. The one who's friends with Tim."

Maggie's lips twisted; Tim had conveyed to her Father Bob's skepticism. "I'll ask him, Mama."

"Don't take any chances, me hija. Papa thinks this is all foolishness. But there are dark things in this world, much as reasonable men want to believe it's not so."

More things in heaven and earth. Dark things. She longed to tell her mother precisely how dark. But Eva would only worry more, as well as continue to beat the drum for a priestly intercession.

And she'd sworn, vowed, to take the day off from trouble. Trouble that made her wonder whether there wasn't still a bottle stashed away somewhere.

She told her mother that she loved her, then joined Tim and Kat cutting and pasting together a pictorial book report on the life of Saint Teresa, the Little Flower.

He understood that she recoiled at the thought of putting her wounds on display, but reassured her this was an "open" meeting, and that he'd happily represent her as attending simply as his wife, his moral support. "These meetings aren't scary, Maggie.

If anything, they're kind of like theatre of the absurd." He was still trying to convince

her to accompany him as they dressed to take Kat to school Monday morning.

"But Father Bob knows about my drinking." She rifled through the bottom

drawer in search of a particular powder-blue sweater.

"What do you think he's going to do – stand up there and point and say

'J'accuse'?"

She bit back a grudging smile. "No, but – "

Ring!

"I hate the fucking telephone," Tim complained, snapping up the receiver.

"Yeah?"

"Hi, it's Mark over at Sunset Property Management."

"Yeah, we talked the other day," Tim said, recognizing the name and voice. He

hoped the company had found the balls – or the evidence – to evict their tweaking tenant.

"I'm afraid I have some unfortunate news about your lessee Liz Yeager. She, um,

passed away."

His pulse accelerated. "Oh God."

Maggie, noting his tone and sudden pallor, grabbed onto his arm. "What?" she

whispered, fearing the response.

"Just a sec, Mark." Tim smothered the receiver mouthpiece with his palm. "It's

the house. Tenant's dead." He was forced to be blunt lest she think a catastrophe had

befallen a family member or friend.

She clutched his arm even tighter; he felt her nails digging into his skin. He

uncovered the mouthpiece. "How did it happen?"

Silence.

"We're entitled to know," Tim pressed, even though he wasn't sure they were.

"Suicide. Her mother discovered her early yesterday morning."

Early yesterday morning. He closed his eyes, willing himself to concentrate only on her talon-like, desperate grip.

"Obviously," fumbled the property manager, "there'll be the matter of refunds and re-listing to see to."

"I'll be in touch." He hung up and seized Maggie by the shoulders. "Listen to me. We are not going to freak out or anatomize this right now. We're not gonna do it." She looked so stricken, so despondent. "We're dropping Kat off, then we're hitting the meeting. After that we can deal."

She could do no more than nod. She had to follow his lead here or she'd surely yank free of him and speed to the nearest liquor store. The desire for comforting poison stirred her every pulse point – at her wrists, her throat, even in her loins.

Somehow they managed to extemporize faux-ordinary chatter on the short drive to Kat's school. Kat kissed each of them goodbye and bounded from the car, catching up with a couple of friends in identical dull green plaid jumpers and snowy white cotton blouses. Maggie turned to Tim. "Oh my God. What are we going to do?"

"Maggie, I'm going to be selfish here. *I* can't deal with it right now."

"I'm sorry, baby." She leaned over to stroke his leg. How quickly she'd grown accustomed to letting him be the strong one, the one to keep them afloat while she flailed in the deep. A year hadn't yet passed since she had all but given him up for dead, less time still since she had welcomed him home, though with a keen sensitivity as to how fragile he was, how much he needed for her to be strong. There could be no more alternation between them, one waxing as the other waned, ebbing as the other crashed against the shore. That was the otherness – not complementarity – that had allowed the Shadow Man to seep into the space between them.

Nonetheless, she tensed as they walked toward the meeting hall, her hand turning clammy in his. Father Bob came up, his greeting friendly and discretely impersonal, but she was sure she blushed. As promised, Tim introduced her to a few people as his wife, "checking up on how I spend my mornings." Maggie was certain that all of them – the feisty little bird-woman named Norma, the hugely obese, soft-spoken man named Boyd, the pouting punk-rock chick whose name she somehow missed – saw through the subterfuge.

"You have a very nice husband," Norma said. "You're lucky. Most good-looking men don't have a brain in their heads, and the handful who end up here have usually lushed or doped away both their looks and their brains."

Maggie wasn't quite sure how to respond. "Tim's always kept his looks," she said inanely. God, what a ditzy thing to say, as if she'd stayed with Tim solely because he'd held up physically.

Norma cackled. "I'm not surprised. Something tells me that one was born beautiful."

For some vague reason Maggie found the phrase unsettling. "Yes, I believe he was," she said slowly, frowning because the notion struck her as inexplicably portentous.

Boyd, the very large man, led the meeting, with Norma performing in her customary role of secretary. Boyd talked about his ongoing difficulties in accepting his powerlessness over alcohol despite fifteen years of sobriety, and various people chimed in to share their experiences. Maggie paid close attention, although she didn't find the discussion especially encouraging. Mainly it served to remind her that never again could she enjoy a cerveza with Mexican food, a relaxing glass or two of wine at the end of a taxing day. Fifteen years sober and people were still obsessing over alcohol! Perhaps she ought to look into hypnosis.

Tim noted both her skepticism and attentiveness. He envied her the latter. Still in a state of shock over Liz Yeager's suicide and its timing, he couldn't yet process it, could not yet think past the thrum of *oh God, God, it killed her, he killed her* beating in his brain. And he dreaded moving past the shock, because a course of action was no longer an option but an imperative.

And he knew, too, he'd have to ask for, and accept help.

Admit you have a problem. *Hi, I'm Tim, and there's a ghost after my family.*

Admit your powerlessness. *I don't know what the fuck to do; people are dying, and sooner or later my daughter's life will be destroyed.*

Only a Higher Power (as you understand it) can restore sanity. *Um, OK, I'll try, I really will. Bob's right; how can I believe in a ghost but not some kind of metaphysical counterforce to it?*

Well, he started to argue with himself, and then everyone was standing for the concluding prayer circle.

The assembly dispersed. "Are you free for an hour?" he asked Bob, meeting Maggie's eyes. She gave him a slight nod.

"Sure," the priest said.

They rendezvoused at the St. Thomas Aquinas rectory. It was Maggie's first

venture into Father Bob's old-fashioned study, with its wood and leather, barristers

bookcases, portraits of Pope John Paul II and Pope Benedict. She listened mutely to

Tim's narrative: her dream that had restored what alcohol madness had blacked out; the

involvement of the woman Ruth in Maggie's short-lived institutionalization and the

apparent stalking of Tim and Kat; the news about Liz Yeager and his sense of personal

complicity. Maggie colored at his disclosure that Yeager must have killed herself right

around the time they were having crazy defiant sex, but throughout, Father Bob remained

inscrutable.

Tim was impatient for a reaction. "Any thoughts?" he goaded.

Father Bob folded his hands atop the desk behind which he must have counseled

scores of doubters, drunks, mourners, and prospective brides and grooms. "It *is*

uncanny," he began.

"But you still think it's all in our heads," Tim finished for him.

"Sweetie, let's hear what Bob has to say," Maggie chided gently. She thought

better of this priest for not immediately breaking out the garlic and holy water.

Father Bob smiled at her before looking back at Tim. "Some months ago, Tim, I

told you that what mattered was that you believed in your grandfather's presence in that

house."

"But Liz Yeager didn't," Tim pointed out. "And for all we know she was a

fucking clean-living Mormon before she moved in there."

"There was Judy Showalter, too," Maggie added. "The tenant who ended up

dying of a drug overdose."

"It's no longer for me to say I understand what's going on with the house." Bob unfolded his hands and looked directly at them.

Tim appreciated the concession. But now what? "Do you agree it would be morally wrong to let another tenant move in there?"

"Yes. Or at least, morally perilous."

"Tim, I think so too," Maggie said, "but the trust is going to fight us if we try to keep it empty. They're bound by law to protect Kat's financial interests."

"Fine," Tim said. "Then I'll move in. You and Kat can go stay with your folks."

Maggie and Father Bob objected simultaneously. He extended a palm toward her. "You first, Maggie."

"Thank you. Tim, that's insane. What would it accomplish?"

"Um, saving the life of another unsuspecting stranger?"

"Far be it for me to discourage altruism," Father Bob said. "But what happens to Maggie and Kat if they end up losing you to that – that madness?"

"Exactly, Tim! I couldn't bear to lose you at this point. Oh God, what more proof would I need that Kat and I are damned too?"

Frustrated, Tim lit a cigarette. "What do you suggest then?"

"I'll explore Church channels for exorcism," Bob said, though his discomfort with the idea was evident.

"It won't work," Tim rejoined. "Something tells me the Amityville Horror over there will be as oblivious to incense and Latin as it was to the witch doctor Maggie brought in."

"She was a Wiccan, not a witch doctor," Maggie corrected. "And why not at least try exorcism? After all, your grandfather was Catholic, wasn't he?"

"Yeah, but obviously he isn't practicing."

Father Bob removed an ashtray from a drawer and passed it to him. "The Monsignor keeps saying we need to make this a nonsmoking rectory but fortunately for you, I believe in strict separation of church and state."

"Tim, let's give the exorcism a shot," Maggie said. "If it doesn't work, the worst that happens is that we're back to square one."

"I have to warn you that the Church permits exorcism only in exceptional cases," Bob said. "Whether your situation will qualify is, frankly, beyond my area of expertise."

"Fuck, don't they teach you Jesuits anything useful in the seminary?"

Maggie wasn't convinced Tim had abandoned his foolhardy idea about moving into the house. What if that was precisely what the old man wanted? To victimize Tim all over again? His remark that he would slit his throat on the staircase to appease the Shadow Man nagged at her. "Father Bob, what would you do if you were in our situation?"

"Trust that God is infinitely more powerful than the destructive forces within that house. Lean on each other and put your daughter first. And move far away from here and try to start over," he replied somberly.

She looked at Tim. "Then why can't we do that?"

Her pleading eyes broke his heart, but he held his ground. "You know why. Kat's been exposed. Unless we find some way to resolve this permanently, she's as good as doomed, and we probably are too."

"Turn it over, Tim," Father Bob tried.

"I can't and I won't. I'll pray for faith and you can pray for it for me. But in the meantime I'm not going to just sit around waiting for the other shoe to drop. For Maggie or me to relapse or for something awful to happen to Kat or even the next person unlucky enough to move in there. I lost years of my life surrendering to the dark. This time I'm going down fighting."

Father Bob looked unhappy. "In that case, I'll start investigating the protocols for exorcism."

"If you insist on this dog-and-pony show, I have one request," Tim said. "I don't want you involved, Bob. I don't want your relapse on my conscience."

"Tim, that's irrational," the priest said.

"So's the thing we're dealing with."

"Let's not get ahead of ourselves until I've consulted with the Bishop," Bob cautioned.

Maggie sensed a standoff, and she decided to use it as an opportunity. "Tim, would it be all right with you if I spoke with Father Bob alone for a few minutes, about my drinking?"

Tim guessed that wasn't her true intent, but could scarcely refuse. "No problem. I'll wait in the car." He shot Father Bob another warning look. "I'm serious about your not being there, Bob."

He left the study, and Maggie pulled her chair a little closer to the desk. "I'm really afraid for him, Father. I'm afraid he's going to get obsessed with some literary idea of heroic self-sacrifice and do something crazy."

"I know, Maggie. He wants to go it alone and that's dangerous for all of you."

"Do you think … that maybe Tim's absence of religious faith is somehow feeding into the persistence of this destructive force, as you call it?" She kept thinking of Tim five months before trying to beat down the horrible apparition with a cross that meant no more to him than a couple of random sticks of wood joined together.

From Father Bob's creased forehead she inferred that the thought had occurred to him as well. "I think it's complicated, Maggie. Tim's unwavering belief in that ghost and its power might also account for its apparent persistence."

"But I believe in that, too. I lived in that house for months. I saw and heard things so far beyond explanation I questioned my own sanity, and this was long before I knew anything about how Tim's grandfather had abused him there."

He regarded her starkly. "Are you absolutely convinced your alcoholism is a direct result of having lived in that house?"

She hesitated. Was she? "I don't know. The house, the old man, are factors, of that I'm sure. But … I always liked a drink or two. I just never had a problem controlling it before."

His smile was reassuring if ironical. "Join the club."

"I guess I have. Though I suppose you think me a wimp for not standing up and declaring myself a fellow traveler at the meeting."

"Not in the least. It's about deeds, not words, Maggie. I hope you keep coming. It's not a magic formula for staying sober, but, to paraphrase you, it can be a significant factor."

"I was terrified I'd see someone I knew. Isn't that ridiculous?"

He chuckled. "When I first started attending meetings, I was certain I'd see half my parishioners. Odd that we're more concerned about people seeing us trying to get sober than we were about them seeing us drunk."

"Ah, but I thought I could hide it so well."

"Me too. I had blind faith in Listerine."

"And Lifesaver mints," she said, smiling back. Despite not having planned to discuss her drinking, talking about it with him did make her feel a little better, a little less ashamed. Maybe they really were giving the house and the old man too much power over them. But she knew Tim would never accept that.

Father Bob seemed to guess what she was thinking. "Has Tim always been an atheist?"

"Yes, for as long as I've known him. I imagine that a child repeatedly beaten with no one intervening to stop it loses faith at an early age."

"Either that, or becomes very devout."

"No wonder he believes in evil but not good. I think it's easier to believe in evil, anyway. Ghosts or not, there's so much evidence of it everywhere you look."

"Evil's usually another name for things we feel we can't control. Good, on the other hand, really is up to us."

"Now you're sounding very priestly," she teased. "My parents would approve."

"I wish I had more sage counsel to impart. Now, let's go find Tim and see if we can talk him out of whatever crazy ideas he may be entertaining."

He had wandered into the church, to think, to say a silent though hollow prayer for the poor woman who'd offed herself. He was as certain that prayer was futile as he was that Mags and Father Bob were fretting over him in the rectory. Tim's eyes drifted above the plain wooden pews to the altar, behind which loomed a good old-fashioned crucified Jesus, not one of your sanitized, Protestantized risen Christs with upraised arms and beatific gaze. No doubt about it, St. Thomas's was an older church, with homely plaster Stations of the Cross; waxy statues of Mary, John the Baptist (with head attached), the Holy Family; stained glass saints and niches with candles and a coin till. Nice and dark in here, though. An overlit church was too reminiscent of an AA meeting hall.

He attempted to reason himself out of disbelief. If the old man's vicious spirit had survived physical death, didn't it then follow that everyone's did, that humans really did have a soul, a *numen,* that exceeded the sum total of their material existence? No, he argued; evil at its core was merely energy, the will to power, to destroy. The creative force, the *élan vital*, was a property of nature, of the living, which was why no one ever seemed to be haunted by benign spirits like Casper or Geena Davis and Alec Baldwin in *Beetlejuice*. Or by the Marshmallow Ghosts, for that matter, from that book Maggie had discovered. He vaguely remembered it was a gift from … from whom? Hadn't it been given to him by his grandparents' maid? "Maid" was what they'd called the cleaning lady or domestic technician or whatever the proper euphemism was nowadays. He sort of recalled the cleaning lady; she was Mexican and she used to bring her son or nephew to the house. The kid was around his age and they used to throw around the baseball and terrorize the neighbors with games of "doorbell dodge." The cleaning lady didn't live in, and he wasn't sure how often she and the kid came to the house, or if they'd been there

every summer he and his family had. But Tim was pretty sure the woman had given him
The Marshmallow Ghosts, and that he and the little nephew or son had read it together
two or three times in anticipation of a Halloween that seemed, in the middle of summer,
impossibly distant.

He shuddered. A mild but unmistakable nausea was stirring in him, as it did
whenever he allowed himself to think back to those summers, even if the particular
memory had nothing to do with the old man. He'd actually had to throw up both after
writing about it and reading it aloud during his last stint in rehab. He even preferred
dealing with memories of himself at the lowest point of addiction, of prison and the rape
and Ed, and those recollections were sickening enough. But awful though they'd been,
those experiences had somehow served as outposts along his circuitous path back to
Maggie and Kat, to sobriety. His own secular, personalized Stations of the Cross.
Station One – he ODs and ends up booted off the baseball team. Station Four – he shoots
up for the first time. Six! Gang-rape in the prison showers. Seven! He sells his ass to
Ed. Ten! Oops, he "forgets" to lock or close the door in Echo Park. Twelve – he leaves
the syringe in Maggie's kitchen. He briefly visualized each scene as a gray plaster
tableau along the side walls of the church.

Then he looked up at the cross above the altar. "Gonna strike me dead?" he
dared.

The doors creaked behind him. Father Bob poked in. Tim waved, got up,
genuflecting as he left the pew, an old habit resuscitated by Kat's scolding whenever he
forgot. He joined Father Bob and Maggie outside the church. "Sorry, no epiphanies," he
said.

"Keep trying," Father Bob said.

"When's Kat's Easter break again?" It was the first thing he asked after bidding a curbside goodbye to the priest and pulling onto the street.

"Next week," she said warily. "Tim, please tell me you're not still thinking about moving back into the house."

"Correction – I won't be moving 'back.' You and Kat lived there for those months, not me."

"Correction – 'not I,'" she teased, desperate to defuse this new obsession.

"Yeah, but think how pompous 'I' would've sounded."

"Tim, come on. We went over this with Father Bob."

He kept his eyes on the road. "The thing has to be confronted, Mags, and no amount of religious mumbo-jumbo – Catholic or otherwise – is going to do the job. I need to find out what he wants."

"And what if he wants you dead? What if he wants us all dead?" She was trembling.

"Don't you think if he wanted to kill us – or if he could do it – he would have already? Look at Liz Yeager or Judy what's-her-name."

"That's just it. We're stronger than he is. We have to remember that."

"Or what? The terrorists will win?" he mocked. "Uh-uh. And if we really are stronger than he is, we have to stand him down, let him try to do his worst. Maybe when he finally realizes he's the one doomed to futility, he'll throw in the ghostly towel."

"Fine," she said, deciding to match his obstinacy. "Then the operative word is 'we.' And 'us.' I'm coming with you."

He flinched. "No fucking way."

"Yes fucking way. We know that his strategy with us has been to divide and conquer." Then she played her wild card. "If you don't let me do this with you, I'll simply tell the trustees that you're planning to live there alone. They won't OK it unless they believe Kat's included."

He swore under his breath. He wouldn't – couldn't – back down. "All right. I don't like it, but you've already been exposed to it anyway."

Not expecting him to call her bluff, she was forced to up the stakes. "I have another condition, and it's nonnegotiable. Ryan and Billy have to agree to stay there with us."

"Jesus fucking Christ, why?"

At least now his stubbornness had to vie with his displeasure. "Because you and I are especially vulnerable, for reasons I don't have to enumerate. And Ryan and Billy aren't affected. They spent more time at the house than anyone other than Kat and I when we were living there. They experienced things. And so far they both seem to be immune."

Tim's knuckles whitened around the steering wheel. "Immune so far as we know. I don't give a shit about O'Donnell, but I'd feel pretty goddamn bad if the old man got to Ryan."

"Tim, either it's already happened and it hasn't shown up yet, or they're somehow not susceptible."

"Kind of like an HIV test," he said bitterly.

Maggie's turn to wince. "Baby, I'm not trying to make you feel bad. But remember what you said the other night about playing each other's guard dog? We can't trust ourselves to do that, alone in that house. You know he'll try to turn us against each other."

"OK, but why not just have Ryan?"

"Because I can wheedle him," she admitted rather sheepishly.

He glanced in the rearview mirror (*no Oldsmobile*), signaled right, and pulled off the freeway even though they were several miles north of the Via de la Valle exit. He stopped in the lot of a minimart/gas station. Maggie presumed he needed cigarettes, but he made no move to get out of the car. "I need to know," he said, looking at her levelly. "Did you have an affair with O'Donnell?"

"We were good friends," she said, choosing her words with equal parts care and candor. "We slept together once. That's all."

The news came as no shock, but Tim still felt like he'd been kicked in the gut, and by a horse with the massive hooves of Warlock, no less. He was at a rare loss for words.

She saw the naked pain in his eyes. His skin tautened across his cheekbones, his jawline. "I never stopped loving you. And he knew it too."

Jealousy, hurt, anger, and disappointment contended with a struggle to understand. They'd been estranged, and he, of course, had thrown her over for Ed and his seductive supply of crystal. "Were you drunk?" he asked at length.

"A little."

He wanted that knowledge to soften the blow, but it didn't much. "What would've happened if I hadn't come back?"

"Nothing. He's married and I would still love you."

He inhaled jaggedly. He didn't doubt her sincerity. But it still hurt like hell. "Don't ask me to be around him, Maggie. Not at the house, not even at the barn."

She hated to paw at the fresh wound, but his resolve to move into the house left her with few options. "I understand why you feel that way. But these are my conditions. If you truly can't accept them, that's fine. That means the plan's scrapped and we come up with a different tactic for dealing with the house." Even if, God forbid, he abruptly reversed course and agreed to her terms, Billy's presence might provide a needed distraction against Tim's engulfment by the old man and his own obsession.

He folded his arms across atop the steering wheel and rested his forehead against them. Mentally he pitted what seemed like two worst-case scenarios against each other: temporarily sharing a dwelling with her ex-lover or letting the house be, allowing another ill-fated tenant to take up residence as well as granting still more foul substance to the shadow darkening his life, Maggie's, and most terrible of all, Kat's. He cursed himself for half-wishing she was still confined among the She-zoids.

"Do you need more time to think it over?" she prodded gently.

He raised his head. "No. If you want O'Donnell and Ryan there, that's how it will have to be. Assuming they're crazy enough to accept the invitation, which won't exactly convince me they're as stable as you seem to think."

She was none too sure herself that they would agree; she was still reeling from the fact that Tim had. "I'll ask them to come over tomorrow night, after Kat's gone to bed."

"Can't I be in bed too?"

"That's up to you," she replied, knowing full well that from hereon in, he was not going to let Billy and herself out of his sight.

Tim seldom looked at the local newspaper save for the Thursday entertainment tabloid; aside from the Arts section the *Union-Tribune*'s overall right-wing slant rankled him. Getting the daily Los Angeles *Times* felt familiar and normal. But he was determined to see Liz Yeager's obituary, although for reasons obscure even to him. Not surprisingly, Monday was too soon for the death notice. On Tuesday, however, it was the lead obit. "Elizabeth A. Yeager, 39, Partner with Sherman, Davenport Law Firm." A picture of a much fuller-faced woman than the tweaker he'd encountered only the Thursday before. Probably at the family's request, no cause of death was reported, simply that Yeager had died Sunday morning at her Del Mar home.

Nice going, old man.

The rest of the obituary was pro forma, detailing Yeager's educational background and professional accomplishments. She had been active in the Junior League (ugh!), the local Republican Party (double ugh!), and the county bar association. She'd left behind her no widower, no children. According to the paper, she was survived solely by a sister, Greta Beatty, of Sacramento, and her mother Ruth, also of Del Mar.

Ruth?

More ominous still, services were to be held at the Living Word of Christ Fellowship Assembly, which by its name sounded evangelical.

Maggie was in the shower, which offered him an opportunity to explore his inchoate theory. He called the property management office. "Hey, Mark, we're thinking seriously about moving back into the house. ASAP."

"My understanding is that Miss Yeager's mother wants to move out all of their belongings by the weekend. Bad memories and all. So it may work out for you."

Despite the rather crass sentiment, the agent had unwittingly provided him with an entry. "'Their'?" Tim probed. "The mother lived with her?"

"She's not on the lease but she'd been staying there. Obviously Miss Yeager was a lady with a lot of problems." A perfunctory "tsk."

"You ever meet the mother?"

"Twice, I think. Why?"

"I know this sounds bizarre, but what does she look like?"

"I'm bad with faces, but I do remember she had these Lisa Loeb-ish glasses. You know, the kind so geeky they're hip? My wife has the same frames."

Steeeeeeeeee-rike!

He had no doubt it was the same woman. But what did it mean? he pondered. "One last question, Mark. Did our phone number or e-mail address appear anywhere on the lease?"

"Quite possibly. Would you like me to check?"

"No, that's OK." Tim knew what the manager would find. Ruth Yeager was plainly the source of both the malicious phone call and the weird Instant Message warning about the Shadow Man.

He didn't find it especially mysterious that Liz Yeager had lied and said a neighbor had carted Maggie away; the unfortunate attorney no doubt wanted to be done with the entire incident. But Maggie's belief that her escort to the Christian rehab center had been somehow "possessed" by the old man was confirmed by this latest discovery. The old guy had sicced Ruth Yeager on them like a vicious dog, or what did occult-types call it, a "familiar." Would her stalking and harassment escalate into more direct forms of threat in the aftermath of her daughter's death?

Maggie emerged from the bedroom, toweling dry her hair. He informed her of this new, disconcerting development. "She probably dragged me off to the place she really wanted to take her daughter," Maggie inferred.

The hint of compassion in her tone irked him. "Yeah, that's one way of looking at it." In truth, he'd been mildly irritated with her ever since yesterday's admission that she had slept with Billy O'Donnell.

Maggie intuited as much. How typically male – he took for granted her forgiveness of his own extended, infinitely more appalling affair, but viewed her lone indiscretion as grounds for an open-ended sulk. "How ought I look at it?" she asked, fighting not to answer his sarcasm with her own.

"You may have stumbled right into her lair, but don't forget she was giving me and Kat the evil eye only the day before. Thanks to his influence, she's got a fucking vendetta against us." He lit a cigarette and began to pace.

"If you think that's a real possibility, we ought to reconsider moving into the house," she countered. "We'd be sitting ducks for her."

Flustered, he mashed out the cigarette. "Aren't you even listening? She was stalking Kat and me already, at the barn, and then outside of Starbucks. For all we know she's camped outside this place right now in her creepy Oldsmobile. What difference will it make if we're in the house or not?"

Maggie was as disturbed by the paranoid tinge to his thinking as she was by the possibility he was correct. "Tim, if we start seeing threats around every corner, we *will* go insane. Let's at least deal with one monster at a time."

He bristled at the probably unintentional echo of one of AA's central adages, with considerable effort let it pass. "All I'm saying is that we need to be on the lookout for this Ruth woman. I just wish we could stash Kat with your parents today instead of Friday."

Finally a point on which they agreed. She knew Kat would fight them over the enforced vacation in Newport away from them, away from Sugar and the stables. Nor did she expect their daughter to accept the "husband and wife sobriety retreat" premise she and Tim had concocted. But Kat's safety was paramount. Maybe Tim was right about the imperative of seeing this nightmare through to its conclusion. Either that or live in terror the rest of their lives.

She was nervous, too, about tonight's planned entreaty to Ryan and Billy. Why would they want to get involved in such a lunatic scheme? And how foolish of her not to have foreseen Tim's resentment of her past entanglement with Billy. So much for honesty between equal partners. It would be too easy to blame the old man's influence for her error in judgment. Her naiveté in admitting she'd slept with Billy and Tim's seething response were all too terrestrial.

Her fingers clenched as the longing for a chilled class of chardonnay or Pinot Grigio, something cold and dry, gripped her. Perhaps she could invent an errand for him to run, alone, giving herself a tiny window to make it to and from the store.

He sat down in front of the laptop to tend to the work she had delegated to him out of alcohol and neglect. Her craving intensified. "I'm claustrophobic," she said. "I'm going to get dressed and go for a little drive."

Large brown eyes fixed her in open concern. "Let's find a meeting instead. I think there's one in Encinitas at eleven."

Abashed by her own transparency, she was defensive. "It's not what you think – I just need some alone time. We've been living in each other's pockets since Saturday night."

He got up. "Guard dogs, Maggie."

She averted her eyes, defeated. "Oh God. I want a drink so bad."

"It's tough," he said, easing his arms around her waist. "I'm not going to lie and say it isn't."

She rubbed his arms briskly. "I hate it. I hate that I want it this bad, even after everything I've put us all through. I hate that you're still doing my work for me and that the thought of returning to it makes me panic. I hate that I can't trust myself to have just one drink anymore, that we don't dare serve liquor tonight."

"They'll live."

She touched his face. *Born beautiful.* The phrase still reasonlessly bothered her. "I have another confession. A part of me hopes that if we can finally destroy the Shadow Man, I'll be able to go back to having a margarita every once in a while."

"I'm not going to give you the Program spiel about that, Mags. Who knows? Maybe once he's gone we won't want to get high or drunk as much."

At least for the moment they seemed to have arrived at a kind of truce. She just hoped it lasted through the evening.

Ryan and Billy showed up at around nine, in time to bid a sleepy but undeniably suspicious Kat goodnight. Everyone looked tense, Maggie noted, urging them to take seats at the dining table. Tim poured the coffee mechanically. He appeared to be trying very hard not to display any particular hostility toward Billy, but she could see it in the slight furrow of his brow, hear it in his polite but terse comments.

"We have dessert too, as promised," Maggie said, nervously placing a plate of Pepperidge Farm soft-baked chocolate-chip cookies on the table. Nobody reached for one.

Tim proceeded to outline the situation and his strategy for resolving it with such dispassionate efficiency Maggie was half-surprised he hadn't worked a Power Point into the presentation. His was a streamlined version but it touched on every salient fact, including this morning's discovery about Liz Yeager's mother. The sole matter he glossed over was Father Bob's proposed exorcism, which he dismissed as mere "Jesussy shadow-boxing."

Ryan raised a mock-schoolroom hand. "First question. What if after a week nothing's happened to convince you that the problem's been taken care of?"

"We'll deal with that if it happens. But nothing suggests to me that this ghost is very self-disciplined."

Billy's gaze fell upon Maggie. "I'll do whatever's needed. But why do both of you have to be there? Isn't that, um, redundant?"

"I won't let Tim do it without me," Maggie replied, even as she saw Tim's eyes flash. "This involves me and Kat as much as Tim. I'm not going to sit on the sidelines."

Ryan frowned. "I know I mentioned this to Tim the other night, but – "

"You remember the other night?" Tim cracked.

"Vaguely. But have you ruled out every scientific explanation?"

"Toxic dump? Indian burial ground?" Tim challenged. "I'll send a geologist out there tomorrow if you want, man. But my gut tells me that's not the case."

"I agree, " Billy said. "Otherwise, why wouldn't everybody else in your family be affected?"

Tim shrugged stiffly.

Billy went on. "But since we're talking about exhausting every possibility, do you have all the information about this guy, your grandfather, that you're going to need in order to get rid of him?"

Sore subject, Maggie thought. It was all she could do not to cringe.

Tim looked patently uncomfortable. Ryan spoke up as well. "Yeah, what exactly do you remember about him? Did you ever ask your parents why he was such a mean bastard to you? That strikes me as key."

Tim darkened, and Maggie held her breath. "I can't talk to my parents about this because they're in total denial," he said, almost snapped. "I've discussed it with my sister. She agrees with me that he was just a vicious son of a bitch who probably had done the same thing to my dad. Toughen up the boy, you know."

"What was your grandfather's job?" Ryan asked.

"Doctor. GP."

"So much for the Hippocratic oath," Billy observed. "And your grandmother just stood by silently?"

"Yup. Asshole men and passive women run in my family."

"Hey," Maggie objected. "And Diana's far from passive either."

Tim's forehead was glistening. "I meant, until this generation. Jesus!" He got up from the table. "Gotta pee – be right back." The urge to vomit was intensifying, the innocuous dinner of roast chicken and salad battling its way toward his throat.

"Houston, we've got a problem," Billy remarked the moment Tim disappeared into the master bedroom.

Maggie's heart ached for Tim. "You guys have to understand. This subject is very painful for him."

"How's he gonna defeat this thing if he can't even talk about it?" Billy posed.

Ryan dropped his voice to a near-whisper. "Do you think maybe Tim was molested?"

Maggie grimaced. "I don't know, Ryan. But somehow I doubt it." Given the anguished candor of his journal, why would he have withheld a molestation? "Either he wasn't, or he's repressed the memory."

"From what I've heard, repressed memory is pretty much bullshit," Billy said.

Ryan nodded. "Same here. Too bad he can't talk to his parents about this, though. We all could learn something that might turn out to be important."

"You remember them, Ryan," Maggie said. "They're so – closed. And Tim's dad is always so hard on him."

"So we move forward without a possible major piece of the puzzle," Billy concluded. "You in, Ryan?"

"Oh yeah, I'm in. I'll bone up on *Hell House* and *The Haunting* and every other ghost story I can think of for prep."

"What about the daytime?" Billy asked Maggie. "I can't take the whole week off work on this short notice, and Ryan probably can't either."

Tim reemerged, ashen but composed. "I'll ask my sister to come down too. She's clearly not susceptible."

"Tim, she won't want to leave Wes and the baby," Maggie protested. "And she's back at work to boot."

"She'll come if I ask her." Why hadn't he thought of this earlier? "Maybe we can let Ryan and Billy off the hook."

Maggie ignored their guests' hopeful expressions. "No, I want them with us. Even if Diana agrees, you and I are too much responsibility for one person alone. And Billy and Ryan can spell her at night."

Tim heaved a sigh. "At this rate we're going to need HBO and catering."

Maggie looked at Billy and Ryan. "Please, you guys. I need you."

Tim bristled at the plea but held his tongue.

"OK," Ryan said. "When do you want us at the Overlook Hotel?"

"By Sunday night," Tim said. "Bring sleeping bags, because the place will be empty."

"No, we'll pick up some air mattresses," Maggie amended. "And I can't thank you two enough."

"Save your thanks until this is behind us," Billy said.

Despite his expressed assurance, Tim was surprised by how easy it was to convince Diana to join them once she learned of their predicament. But like Maggie, her agreement hinged on a stipulation, one he found perhaps even more distasteful. "We have to confront Mother and Dad about this," Diana said flatly. "For your good. For my good. And it could help us get to the bottom of what's been going on in that house."

He was glad he'd yet to have breakfast; that sick feeling from gut to gorge was stirring in him again. "*You* can confront them. I refuse to subject myself to their bullshit denial and Dad's inevitable attempt to blame it all on me."

"I'll be there and I won't let them get away with that. It'll be two against two, Tim. What's the worst that could happen?"

"Well, I could puke all over Mom's nice Berber carpet, for one."

"We'll do it at my house where between Brandon and the cat vomit's part of the feng shui. You and Maggie drive up here after you drop Kat off. I'll put Maggie and Wes to work in the kitchen while we corner Mother and Dad in the study."

"Forget it. Forget the whole thing. Mags and I will fend for ourselves by daylight, or else hang around the library until Ryan's done."

"No way," she said with an incredulous laugh. "I'm not letting you rescind the invitation. The situation at that house has bothered me ever since Maggie told me about it." Her voice softened. "Timmy, don't you want to see Mother and Dad squirm? All we do by never bringing it up is sustain their cozy little cocoon. They don't deserve that comfort zone. They haven't earned it."

He hadn't appreciated the depth of her resentment against their parents. "Maybe I could go through with it if you gave me a trank first," he said hesitantly.

"I shouldn't, but I will, if you really think you need it."

"Either that or some Alka Seltzer. Gotta go."

He nearly bowled Maggie over in his haste to get to the bathroom. Violent streams of coffee spewed from his gut into the toilet.

"Diana's on board, I hope?" Maggie asked twenty minutes later on the drive to the meeting.

"Yeah. She's bringing Wes and the kid, too. Don't panic – they're going to stay at the Four Seasons while she's with us at the house."

"That's great. I'm glad they could both get time off."

"She said they'd just hand over their appointments to their partners." He swallowed hard, still tasting bile. Christ, if he hurled at the AA meeting everyone would think he was drunk like that poor old lady.

Father Bob was awaiting them in the Lutheran church's parking lot. He motioned for them to stay in the car.

His reasons for ensuring their privacy quickly became obvious. "The bishop has turned down the petition for exorcism," he said quietly. "On grounds of insufficient documentation."

Maggie hadn't expected Bob to sound so discouraged, given his more humanistic interpretation of the disturbances at the house. She was disappointed as well, although Tim wore a stubborn, tell-me-something-I-don't-already-know expression. "Good God," she said, "what kind of documentation does he require?"

"The Church actually works with recognized experts in parapsychology."

"Ghostbusters!" Tim carped. "I told you, Bob, some churchy exorcism would be a waste of time. Now it seems we don't even qualify."

"I can still come and bless the house."

"Oh no you don't. Send us some generic priest if you want, but you're not going anywhere near there."

"We may follow up with the parapsychologists eventually," Maggie said. "In the meantime, I, for one, would welcome your blessing on both of us."

"Come by the church after the meeting and I'll make it a formal blessing," the priest said. Maggie feared he wouldn't approve of their revised plan to stage a morbid species of house party. But Tim's defiant atheism not withstanding, she resolved to hold Father Bob to his promised blessing.

He was so apprehensive about the pending confrontation with his parents that Diana actually insisted he take a Xanax shortly after he and Maggie arrived in Los Feliz. Two hours earlier they had deposited an unhappy but resigned Kat with her grandparents in Newport Beach, although she had brightened somewhat at the promises of Disneyland, the Long Beach Aquarium, and a day at the doggie salon for Thumper. Damn it, why couldn't his parents be more like Maggie's? What you saw was what you got. Armando could be excitable and Eva overprotective, but the Floreses seemed incapable of manipulation or hidden agendas. That they loved him and accepted him once again as part of their family he could not doubt.

Not like Jack and Beth Emerson, who regarded him with the same rueful resignation Kat did her compulsory vacation in Newport. His months of sobriety had evidently done very little to convince his parents that his life was salvageable. All they seemed to see in him was lost promise and bleak prospects. Clean or tweaking, he was still a Fuckup, an unemployed ne'er-do-well with no plans or future, unable to support his family without the charity of kin.

"Would you quit obsessing?" Diana scolded as they sipped Pellegrino water in the living room and awaited their parents' arrival. Brandon gurgled in his playpen; Maggie and Wes, per Diana's instructions, were busy in the kitchen assembling a seafood lasagna.

"I'm just hoping you stocked up on 'Oops.'"

"You're so funny."

"Yeah, well, we'll see how Mom and Dad enjoy my standup routine." He scrutinized his sister; she was the picture of tranquility save for a glint of steel in her eyes. "Why's this so important to you?"

"Because it's been bugging me for twenty-five years. And because lately ... "

"What?"

"I swear, I should have done my residency in psych. Because I see them displacing with Brandon, as if now he's assumed the mantle of their great white hope. They're reinvesting, you know?"

Horrified, Tim glanced over at the white-blond infant pawing around in his playpen. "That sucks. I don't care if they've given up on me, but they don't get another shot with him. Maybe you guys are the ones who should move far away."

Diana shook her head. "I hate estrangements, Tim. They serve only to reinforce all the things people are determined not to say to each other. Besides," she shrugged, "I have my own theory about the Del Mar house."

"Oh?"

"Maybe what's keeping Granddad's viciousness alive, so to speak, is the sheer force of our collective family repression. Remember *Forbidden Planet*, where the monster turns out to be Walter Pidgeon's Id?" Like Tim, she was a fan of vintage sci-fi movies, cheesy and classic ones alike.

"Morbius," he said, nodding. "Do you have it on DVD? I want to borrow it."

"What do you think of my theory?"

"I guess it's as good as any," he demurred, although he privately thought her hypothesis facile.

Outside, first one car door, then another, slammed. His parents in Dad's stubborn Buy American Cadillac Escalade. Tim's stomach lurched.

Maggie and Wes must have heard the sound too, for they came out of the kitchen, she with a bright red apron over her blouse and slacks, he with a light coating of flour on his shirt front. "The Béchamel was being temperamental," he explained, brushing at his shirt.

Diana welcomed her parents inside. Stiff and cursory embraces, handshakes. As always, Jack and Beth looked fit, lightly suntanned, neat but California casual in attire. Beth immediately scooped up Brandon. "Here's my big boy," she cooed.

Jack too smiled at the baby in apparently genuine affection. It creeped Tim out.

"What a shame Katya couldn't come," Beth said to Maggie. "She's doing well?"

"She's thriving," Maggie said. "My folks have planned a whole week of theme parks. I'm afraid they're the ones who are going to need a vacation." She tried to ignore Wes pouring red wine for his in-laws.

"Katya's still the budding equestrienne?" Jack asked.

"Oh yes. Tim rides with her all the time. There's this beautiful Friesian whose owner we know." Maggie felt as if she was prattling but couldn't stop herself.

"Why would you want to ride a big draft horse like that?" Tim's father asked him. "That's not exactly a trail animal."

Tim was grateful for the Xanax, which kept his annoyance on a purely cerebral plane. "Friesians aren't draft horses, strictly speaking."

"What do you mean? They're built to pull carts."

"Martha Stewart rides hers, doesn't she?" Diana tried.

Tim didn't see why it mattered one way or the other to his father whether he rode a draft horse or a camel, except as a pretext for impugning his judgment. "I like this horse. The owner wants to sell him to us."

This was news to Maggie. "Really, Tim? If only we could swing it."

Ugh! Wrong thing to say, for Tim looked pained and his father mildly satisfied. "Sounds like Armando and Eva may be ending up with their own Calumet Farms down there," Jack said dryly.

Tim's temper flared despite the tranquilizer. "I wouldn't let them, or anyone, buy that horse for me. Either we can afford him on our own or we can't."

Wes took his stab at defusing the tense exchange. "It all comes down to how you choose to spend your entertainment dollars. We probably spend twice as much on skiing in the winter than what it would cost you to maintain a horse for a year."

Knowing his father was about to point out the obvious – that Wes and Diana actually had "entertainment dollars" to spend – Tim decided to beat him to the draw. "The only way we could afford Warlock would be to move into the stall with him and go herbivore ourselves."

"That reminds me – something smells awfully yummy from the kitchen," Beth piped up, reluctantly passing Brandon to Wes.

"It's that seafood lasagna you two like so well," Diana said with a tight smile. "Wes, why don't you and Maggie go check on how dinner's coming along? Have you made the Greek salad yet?"

"Let me help, too," Beth said, starting to follow them.

"No, Mother," Diana said. "Tim and I need to talk to you and Dad in the study."

Tim's stomach lurched anew, even though it had been his idea that they have The Talk before dinner rather than after to lessen the chances he'd blow chow. But they hadn't at all rehearsed or even informally gone over how exactly the subject would be broached.

Both Jack and Beth looked wary. Diana ushered them into the study and shut the door behind them. "Please don't tell me you're back on drugs again," Jack said to Tim with a withering glance.

"You're the doctor – you tell me," Tim retorted.

"Please," Beth objected mildly, "can't we simply have a pleasant evening?"

"That's up to you and Dad," Diana replied. "Have a seat."

Tim noted that she had shrewdly arranged for their parents to sit together on the plump chintz sofa, leaving one leather armchair and a swiveling seat at the desk for herself and him either to occupy or ignore. He remained standing, and so did she.

"This is about the Del Mar house," Diana began, folding her arms.

"Diana, we've told you," Beth said, "we don't know why Mother Ginny left it to Katya and not to – "

"You really have no idea?" Tim interrupted. "Neither one of you?" His stomach was constricting but the Pellegrino was staying put, at least for the time being.

"Obviously," his father said impatiently, "Mother wasn't about to leave it to you. She might as well have bought you the methamphetamine herself. If you two want to challenge the will so that Tim can sell it to buy horses and avoid having to find a job, that's up to you."

Sighing, Diana unfolded her arms. "How can you two not get it? Grandma clearly left Kat the house because she felt bad about what Granddad did to Tim every summer we spent there."

Don't puke, don't puke. He tried to focus on his parents' obvious discomfort. "Why did that old bastard hate me so much?" he demanded.

His mother seemed on the verge of tears but his father didn't flinch. "Dad was a disciplinarian. I don't approve of his methods, but he was of another generation."

Diana rolled her eyes. "Oh, come on. There's 'spare the rod' and then there's outright child abuse."

"This is all water under the bridge," Beth clucked.

"I suppose you blame all of your drug problems on this?" Jack challenged Tim.

"Yeah, in part," Tim said. His parents' defensiveness had an oddly calming effect upon him. He was seized by a desire to drive the blade in deeper and twist it a few times. "When you beat the living shit out of a kid for no reason, the kid usually turns out warped in some way."

"Tim, didn't you hear Dad?" Beth implored. "We didn't approve."

"Then why the hell didn't you try to stop it?" Diana exclaimed. "Do you think Wes and I would stand by and let Dad or Wes's father beat Brandon within an inch of his life? Would Tim and Maggie stand by if it were Kat? Granddad was sadistic, but you two were equally responsible."

Tim was impressed by her soft-spoken fury. What good fortune that Kat had inherited Diana's temperament.

His mother looked crestfallen, but his father remained combative if superficially unruffled. "In the first place, your grandfather was not a sadist. Did he ever break any bones or seriously injure your brother in any way?"

"Both he and Ginny thought Tim was the most beautiful child they'd ever seen," Beth murmured, shaking her head.

Jack shot her an exasperated look. "That's hardly the point. What I'm saying is that Dad spanked you because that's how he believed unruly children were disciplined. A man's entitled to make the rules in his own house, which is why we didn't interfere. He never spanked you when they came to see us in Pasadena, or have you conveniently forgotten that?"

"So, theoretically," Tim mocked, "you'd have let him molest me or Di as long as it was in his own house."

Finally Jack erupted. "Of course not! Are you declaring that occurred too?"

His father looked so outraged that Tim was half-tempted to lie and answer in the affirmative. The only thing that kept him from doing so was his incredulity that his father regarded the beatings as mere "spanking." Fresh anger swept over him. "No, I didn't get raped until I went to prison for that 'much needed wakeup call,' as you put it. But whether you're beaten with a bare fist, a belt, or a bunch of strangers' dicks, you still feel the same helplessness and guilt, like you somehow deserved it simply for existing." How flat and distant his words sounded, and he was startled to see their effect on his parents and sister. Tears streamed down Diana's cheeks, while his mother looked shell-shocked, his father suddenly weary, old. Tim feared he had overplayed his hand.

"Have you had an HIV test?" his father asked woodenly.

"Yeah, two of 'em, six months apart. So far so good."

"Well." His father cleared his throat. "Thank God for that."

Even this constipated form of sympathy made him uncomfortable. Damn it, he'd definitely lost the upper hand. He brushed away Diana's arm around his shoulder. "I don't hold you responsible for what happened in the pen," he said rather awkwardly.

"What I – we – really need to know is whether or not there was something going on with Granddad other than the fact that he was a 'disciplinarian.'"

"Such as?" his father said, defensive again. But that was OK; at least the defensiveness was familiar.

"Did he hit the sauce? Did he have his own little cache of prescription drugs?"

"Oh, no," Beth said, as if shocked by the suggestion. "They were very clean-living." She looked to her husband. "I think the only time they even had wine was at Thanksgiving and Christmas."

"What about their lives before they moved to Del Mar? When was that, anyway? Mid-1960s?" Diana asked, at last taking the swivel chair and scooting closer to the couch.

"Yes, 1967. I can't imagine why this is of such interest to you all of a sudden," Jack said crossly.

"If Tim and I are going to understand – not forgive, mind you, but understand – why he was subjected to that kind of treatment, we need all the facts," Diana replied.

"If you want my opinion, we're all better off focusing on the present," Jack complained. "And I'm sure – "

"Jeez, Dad, who do you think you are, Mark McGwire?"

" – and I'm sure neither of you will make any mistakes as parents," Jack went on, ignoring Tim's interruption. Beth nodded.

"Humor us," Diana goaded.

"You know I grew up in Chicago. My parents moved to Del Mar for the climate, and to be closer to us." Jack's tone made clear his desire to wrap up the conversation.

"Do you have any old picture albums?" Tim asked abruptly, though he wasn't sure of what use any such mementos might be.

"Oh, Tim," Beth said with a short sigh, "probably stashed away in the basement somewhere. It will take weeks to find them."

If there was one thing he could count on, it was his parents' unapologetic lack of sentimentality. "What about the old man's personal effects?" he tried anyway.

"Or Grandma's," Diana added.

"Mother streamlined her life considerably when she moved into assisted living," Jack said. "Neither of them was a packrat."

"That's the right idea," Beth affirmed. "All this talk is reminding me to undertake a thorough spring cleaning."

Tim saw that no more water was to be squeezed from this pair of stones. He wasn't sure they'd learned anything they hadn't known already: Jack and Beth were determined not to delve into the past's fusty photographs and forgotten keepsakes lest they be forced to confront their own complicity. Words alone were insufficient against such heavily fortified, practiced denial.

Even Diana, it seemed, was ready to adjourn. "We'll talk about this again," she said, getting to her feet. "Wes and I are going to spend next week at the Four Seasons in Carlsbad, hanging out with Tim and Maggie. But when we get back, Mother, you and I are going to comb through the basement."

Typically his mother pretended to misunderstand. "That's sweet of you, honey. I'm sure I'll be able to use an extra pair of hands."

Tim took perverse satisfaction in how relieved his parents looked to be "dismissed," but as soon as they left the room he collapsed into the armchair, doubled up in nausea. "Let me get you some water and a few crackers," Diana said, briefly tousling his hair.

She left, and he cradled his head in his hands, elbows wobbling on his knees and eyes squeezed shut. He was certain that lifting his head would produce a paroxysm of dry heaves.

He heard light footsteps approaching. The perfume he smelled was Maggie's. The scent should have sickened him, but it didn't. It comforted him. Her hand was cool on the back of his neck.

After a couple of minutes, he was able to straighten up. He rested back, eyes still closed. "That was an exercise in futility," he breathed.

"Maybe," Maggie said noncommittally. Five minutes before, she had asked Diana how the "family meeting" had gone, and the answer had been a preoccupied "I'm not sure," not a declaration of defeat. But perhaps Tim had been seeking something entirely different and personal from the confrontation.

He looked spent, waxen. "I don't think I can eat."

"Fake it. Push the food around your plate the way Kat does with broccoli."

Her reference to Kat cheered him, but now the tranquilizer was making him drowsy. "I'd better have some coffee or I'm going to fall asleep in the broccoli." Yet instead of getting up, he drew her into his lap. "We're really going to do this, aren't we, Mags."

"Yes, querido." She coaxed a loose strand of hair behind his ear. "You know, we're not likely to have much privacy once we're at the house. Want to make a date for later tonight?" They hadn't had sex all week, a fact she attributed in part to stress but mostly to her revelation about Billy.

"Wish we didn't have to wait." He slipped his hand under her blouse.

She hopped out of his lap. "Be a good boy at the dinner table and I'll take care of dessert."

Somehow he survived dinner, the highlight of which came when Diana and Wes's cat, a rambunctious Siamese named Uncle Renie, snagged a begging claw in the lace tablecloth and damn near pulled six complete place settings, plus stemware and several serving dishes, onto the floor. Tim got to laughing at the cat's near-miss and couldn't stop, not even with Maggie kicking him under the table and his father glaring at him. Ultimately he had to retreat to the kitchen until the laughing fit exhausted itself.

Coffee and dessert, more forced chit-chat about topics no one presumably cared about – the Dodgers' prospects, gasoline prices, the last movie anyone had rented or actually gone to the trouble to see in a theater. Not so much as a veiled allusion to the face-off in the study. Diana was right; they humored their parents by allowing them to be so comfortable, reinforced their self-deluded conviction that theirs was the most normal of families except, of course, for his fucked-uppedness. Too bad they weren't coming to the little house party in Del Mar; let them try to be complacent when the old man manifested his ghastly will. Even then, they'd likely find a way to deny and rationalize.

They lacked the imagination to be haunted, and in a strange way he felt sorry for them.

Part Three: The House

This only is denied to God: the power to undo the past.

Agathon (448 BC - 400 BC), from Aristotle, Nicomachean Ethics

CHAPTER 1

The house felt empty, despite the property manager's helpful referral to a furniture rental outlet that supplied bare basics – beds, a cheap velveteen couch, a God-awful pressboard dinette set with four vinyl-upholstered chairs. From their apartment Maggie and Tim brought bedding, a coffee maker, boombox and CDs; Ryan was contributing his small TV and DVD player. Remarkably, no trace of the previous occupants was evident, and a perfunctory cleanup had been carried out. But the house felt derelict, bereft of human impress.

The house was icy cold, too, far colder than Maggie remembered, though she reminded herself she'd lived in it only from late August through early November, generally mild months in San Diego. But if outside the weather was bright and brisk, high 60s, inside the house it might have been the dead of a New England winter.

Now that they were actually in the house, they tacitly agreed not to discuss their purpose, not until Ryan and Billy joined them in a few hours. They tried to keep busy, building a fire, making up the beds, stocking the refrigerator and pantry with groceries. Upon realizing they'd forgotten the box of plates and cups they'd packed, they drove back together to Solana Beach to retrieve it. Neither wanted to leave the other alone in the house for even a few minutes.

"You know what?" Maggie said, scooping Peet's French Roast into the filter basket. "I don't want to sleep in the master bedroom." She suspected it was there that Liz Yeager had taken her own life.

"Me either. Let's take Kat's old room. Ryan and Billy can duke it out over the other two."

She guessed that Kat's former bedroom had not been the one in which he'd stayed as a child. His room must have been the smallest of the three bedrooms, the one she had used as an office. The site of her first optical illusion, or so she'd believed at the time: the old man's fedora in a shadowy corner.

Their coffee cups full, they sat down on the carpet in front of the fire, the rental couch being singularly, if predictably, lumpy and unwelcoming. "It feels so strange being here again," Maggie said. "It must for you too."

"Yeah. But not in the way I expected. I'm not having flashbacks or anything. But I feel like an interloper."

For a moment neither of them spoke. They didn't need to; that sensation of inhospitability surely emanated from the old man.

"Father Bob gave me a rosary and some holy water after Mass yesterday," she said at length. Ordinarily she wasn't the least compelled to attend Sunday Mass in Kat's absence, but she figured they needed all the spiritual fortification they could get on the eve of this "experiment."

"I saw him handing you something, and I figured it was Catholic contraband. I didn't ask you about it because I didn't want to know."

She studied his face, the motion of the flames flickering across his cheeks. "You're so good about going to Mass when you don't believe."

"I like going. I even like the Mass, except when the sermon's too full of fire and brimstone. But the theatricality of it – I thought it was cool even as a little kid."

She remembered the spectral child in the baseball costume. "You were such a beautiful little boy."

He grimaced. "So I've been told. What little boy wants to be thought of as 'beautiful'?"

"Too girly?"

"Too aesthetic."

"And yet you like the aesthetics of the Mass."

"Sure. If religion's going to be bullshit, it ought to at least be entertaining. That's why I can't fathom the appeal of Protestantism. Such boring, spartan self-deception."

The fire went out. Crackling and blazing but a moment before, it extinguished without a sputter, the log's entrails giving out a black, sour smoke that reeked of mildew and stale urine. The fetid stench drove them back, their coffee spilling on the carpet and on each other.

"Holy fuck!" Tim exclaimed.

Maggie frantically threw open the sliding glass door, urging him onto the deck with her. They gulped the fresh salty air. "Oh my God," she coughed.

"Don't tell me this ever happened before!"

She shook her head, waving away billows of the nasty smoke drifting outside. "It's as if somebody dumped a bucket of pee on that fire."

"'Somebody'?" Tim said, coughing as well. "Looks like the old guy doesn't like being ignored."

Maggie was especially disturbed by the flagrancy of the gesture. It was the sort of crass malice more typically associated, she recalled from her Internet research months back, with common poltergeists.

And then it hit her – the old man was mocking Tim's comment that he enjoyed theatricality.

"What are you thinking?" he asked nervously.

No holding back – not here, of all places. "He was listening to us," she said, trembling at the knowledge.

"Jesus Christ – 'fire and brimstone.'"

"And theatricality." Now it felt nearly as cold on the deck as it had inside, and she hugged her shoulders.

Tim was equally unnerved. It was one thing to speak of the Shadow Man in the abstract, and quite another to recognize him as a sentient being. The thought of him lying in wait, listening, fashioning a macabre response, was somehow more disconcerting, more *real*, than the pus-seeping grotesquery he'd attempted to beat down with Father Bob's cross last November. "Maybe we shouldn't hang out here until Ryan and Billy show up," he said, albeit reluctantly, for he hated to concede that the old man had won

the opening skirmish.

Maggie agreed. She didn't like the anger that glinted in his eye along with the

unease. "Let's go to the beach for a couple of hours. I'll leave the deck door open to air

out the living room."

They forced themselves to go back inside for the car keys and his cigarettes. "I'm

going to grab a bottle of water," Maggie told him, and went into the kitchen. She'd

forgotten to move some of the bottles from the case to the refrigerator anyway.

She opened the pantry door, stooped down to pull out the plastic-wrapped case of

Arrowhead on the lowest shelf. Glimpsing something behind the water, she peered closer

and saw a large, unopened bottle of Stolichnaya vodka.

Her heart jumped. She stared at the bottle, struggling against the impulse to reach

for it, stuff it into her overnight bag, ask him to run out to the car for something …

No. She shoved the case of water back onto the shelf, blocking the vodka from

her sight and grasp. She scratched open the plastic wrap and grabbed a water bottle, then

shut the pantry door on her temptation.

But she couldn't make herself tell Tim about it, even though – or because? – she

knew he'd remove the vodka bottle from the cupboard and pour it down the drain. She

cursed her own cowardice.

At the beach they walked along the shore and she did her best to respond to his

anxious comments about the house, the Shadow Man. All she could think about was that

1.75 milliliter bottle inside the pantry. If only she could find a way to transfer some of

the vodka into the one of the Arrowhead bottles, she could conceivably sip from it without anyone – Tim, Billy, Ryan, or Diana – the wiser. She even had a tin of Altoids in

her purse to disguise the smell. She wished she could think of an excuse for going back

to the apartment one time more, where she could surreptitiously grab a funnel from the

kitchen.

"Mags, what is it? You haven't heard a word of what I've been saying."

She glanced up at him. She couldn't make out his eyes behind his sunglasses, but

she knew they were searching hers. "I was thinking I ought to sprinkle some of Father

Bob's holy water over the fireplace," she started, but the lie sounded foul to her ears,

almost as obnoxious as the stench from the hearth. She steeled herself. "No, that's not

true. Sweetheart, I found a bottle of vodka in the kitchen cupboard. And you have to

throw it away because it's tormenting me." She was shaking as if she'd awakened from a

blurry binge to crave that gulp of vodka as imperatively as air.

He pulled her to him, and she shut her eyes against the warmth of his chest. She

felt his heart pounding under his shirt. "That's exactly how it was for me when I came to

the house looking for you and she was smoking meth. I could almost feel it in my veins."

"Just promise me you'll ditch that bottle."

"I will, baby."

She gently eased free of the embrace. Relief battled with regret over confiding in

him. "What if it were left there on purpose? By that poor woman's crazy mother or

somehow, even by him?"

"Whoever moved 'em out probably just missed it," he said a bit automatically.

He was visibly distressed.

"Tim, maybe we should abandon this. Cut our losses and do what Father Bob recommended, move far away from here and try to put it out of our minds."

"No way. I'm not going to let him win this time. The more we retreat, the stronger he gets." His tone became more tender. "That was really brave of you to tell me about the vodka."

"No, brave would've been calling out to you the moment I discovered it."

He squeezed her hand. "We need to go back, to show him we're not scared off by the stink of smoldering piss or a stupid bottle of booze. Besides, Ryan and Billy will be there in an hour."

She saw that he would resist any effort to persuade him otherwise. "All right, but the first thing you have to do is get rid of that bottle of vodka."

"I'll go you one better – I'll scour the rest of the house for any others to put your mind at ease."

He *was* resolute, possessed by the unwavering desire to search every cupboard, closet, and nook for the crystal meth he was sure awaited him as well. He had no doubt that Ruth, the evangelizing madwoman further crazed by her daughter's death, had planted the vodka for Maggie, and certainly she had also set aside some of Liz's residual meth for him. With any luck the woman had thought to provide a clean syringe, too, because he could already feel the wild rush of the injection.

There was no fighting it; he despised himself for lacking Maggie's strength even while he knew that the crystal would provide him with the jolt of courage he needed to do battle with the old man. He needed to be at the top of his game, more than if he were gearing up to start the seventh game of a World Series against the New York Yankees. Shattering over half a year's abstinence suddenly seemed inconsequential.

Despite their having left the deck door wide open, the stale urine smell remained pervasive and wisps of smoke lingered in the living room. As promised, Tim went to the pantry, found the giant bottle of Stolichnaya on the bottom shelf, and summarily emptied its contents down the kitchen drain. Sickened by the putrid odor, Maggie stayed on the redwood deck. He brought her a chair from the cheap dinette set. "I'm going to do a quick check of the rest of the house. Can I bring you anything else, babe?"

"No. Just be quick – and be careful."

He returned to the kitchen, rifled through the empty drawers, peered under the sink, on top of the refrigerator. Nothing, but he had a hunch his prize wouldn't be in the kitchen where Maggie might have come across it. He ran up the stairs, fast and reckless to spite the old man, and though his skin crawled, went into the master bedroom. Damp and empty save for the rent-a-bed, the room was at least free of the awful pee smell. Christ, how could they stand to remain in the house with that stench, and who would blame Ryan, Diana, or O'Donnell if they backed out of the plan? Was that what the old man wanted, to repel them? Was it possible he felt threatened by their presence?

He threw open the door to the walk-in closet. It smelled faintly of women's perfume and mothballs, but was bare, no items left on the floor or upper shelf.

On to the master bathroom. Nothing in the medicine chest or in the cabinet beneath the basin. There were three drawers in the bathroom console, each of which he swiftly opened and shut upon finding it also empty. But just as he was starting to feel frustrated, he noticed that the top drawer didn't appear flush with its brethren. He eased out the drawer, shut it again. It still would not close completely. He glimpsed his own slight smile in the bathroom mirror as he carefully pulled the drawer all the way out of the console. Taped to the back was a Zip-Lock bag containing a good two grams of the white powder as familiar to him as his own form in the mirror.

He ripped the bag free. No syringe, damn it. He fumbled in his jeans pocket for something to cut the powder into a line. He found a matchbook and a dollar bill.

He poured enough for a nice fat line onto the counter next to the sink, stuffed the resealed bag into his pocket. He used the side of the matchbook to form a good line and then rolled the bill, happily a fairly crisp one, into a straw and bent his head down, holding the dollar to his right nostril. He snorted the powder into his nose. It was icy and burning and he shut his eyes, moaning in anticipation of the rush. "Oh man," he gasped. "Oh God." What felt like pure, delirious electricity flooded his brain, his body. He raised his head, opening his eyes, and saw in the mirror behind him a cadaverously skinny woman in a faded flannel nightgown, sunken eyes bulging, a rope tight around her neck. It was Liz Yeager and she was dead, but her cracked white lips were moving. "Trapped with him," she croaked.

He spun around. She was gone.

The full thousand-watt rush hit him, exploded into a blinding sunburst as it collided with animal terror.

He flew out of the room, down the stairs and out onto the deck, too wired and panicked to worry that Maggie would recognize he was tweaking. He was hyperventilating and couldn't speak.

"Oh my God, Tim! What happened?"

He bent over the redwood railing, choking for breath, hair hanging over his face.

She stroked his back with an anxious hand. "Calm down, sweetie. I'm going to call Diana and see if they've arrived in Carlsbad – "

"No!" At that moment he realized that she did know. He began to cry jaggedly. "I'm so … scared." And wired. After months drug-free, he had no physical tolerance, and he'd snorted so damn much.

She was snapping open her cellphone, but he tore it out of her hand and hurled it far over the railing into the wooded grounds of the adjacent property down the hill. "No!"

She went white, and he saw fear in her eyes. "Tim, listen to me. What's happening to you isn't your fault. Please let me get you some help."

Now the words poured out from him. "Don't call Di – she'll be so goddamn disappointed to see me like this – Christ, Mags, I didn't mean to throw the phone, and now we don't have a phone and they're both here, she says she's trapped with him – "

"The stink's not so bad inside now, Timmy. Let's go inside – "

"No – you have to listen to me – there are two of them – "

"I'm listening."

"She came, Mags – so pathetic and defeated in her old nightgown – and said she was trapped with him. Oh God!" He tore at his hair.

She tugged his arm sharply. "Sweetie, let's get out of here. This was a bad idea. We've walked right into his trap."

He wanted to run, to run as fast and as far as he could, but then the old guy would win, once and for all, and they'd be doomed. "We can't. I can't. You go and I'll stay.

It'll be OK, Mags. It just freaked me out to see her like that." The panic was ebbing, and

he felt as ecstatically high as he had the first time he'd smoked meth, and suddenly

fearless. "I'll go get the phone but not a word to Di or anybody, OK? Why upset her?"

"No, I'll go get it," she insisted. "You stay put, baby."

"Just swear you won't call Diana."

"I won't. Holler if you need me."

"OK, but I won't be caught off-guard next time, now that I know they're both

here."

"Stay right here on the deck where I can see you, all right?"

He nodded impatiently. "I'm not letting him drive me out. That's what he

wants."

"Just stay put. I'll be right back."

He lit a cigarette with shaking hands. "Yeah, yeah." He wondered if he might

sneak another line in her absence.

Maggie hurried out the front door, sick at heart. Why, why had they not

anticipated this particular peril? It was so obvious, given their respective vulnerabilities.

She'd miscalculated in telling him about the vodka, blamed herself for not mustering the

fortitude to throw it away herself. What if Tim's entrapment led to a full-scale relapse?

No, she couldn't permit herself to consider that dreadful possibility. She needed

to stick to the immediate crisis – retrieving the phone and somehow calming Tim until

the drug's effects waned. And who was the "she" he was raving about? His

grandmother? Ruth? The apparition of her daughter? Or maybe there was no woman at

all, but simply a hallucination triggered by the meth.

To her consternation, the backyard of the house down the hill was enclosed by a high wooden fence, leaving her with no recourse but to ask the resident, if he or she was home, for permission to search for the phone. She glanced over her shoulder toward the redwood deck. He was still there, smoking, and he waved to her. She waved back, then rounded the corner to the front of the house.

The door was answered by a bored-looking teenage girl disinclined to challenge Maggie's impromptu explanation that her child had tossed the phone over the deck as a prank. But it took her nearly ten minutes to locate the cellphone nestled in a large potted plant, and after she did, she looked again to the deck and found it empty. She thanked the teen, and as soon as the door closed behind her she broke her promise to Tim and punched in Diana's mobile phone number.

Diana answered. "Hello?"

Maggie could tell right away that Diana was in transit. "Hi, it's Maggie. What's your ETA?"

"We're almost in Carlsbad. We thought we'd have an early dinner, then get to bed by nine so I can be in Del Mar first thing in the morning. Are your friends there yet?"

Maggie had all but forgotten about Ryan and Billy. "They'll be here shortly, but I need you to come over as soon as you've checked in at the hotel." She drew in a sharp breath. "Someone planted meth in the house and Tim's wired out of his skull."

"Oh no. I'll be over as soon as I can."

She decided to tell Diana about the vodka later; for the present, she was loath to characterize herself as somehow more virtuous than Tim in the face of temptation.

Thank God she'd been able to resist. Otherwise both of them were likely to have been completely intoxicated well before Ryan and Billy arrived. Wasted and vulnerable.

She found Tim perched tensely at the dinette, scribbling rapidly into a yellow legal pad. "We need to chronicle every fucking weird thing that happens," he explained, pen racing across paper. "The thing with the fire, and the smell – you're right, it's not so bad now – and the vodka and crystal and the woman's ghost … "

She winced, realizing he'd been at the crystal again. How much had he discovered, and how in the world would they manage to wrest it away from him? She had to trust that Diana would come armed with a potent sedative.

"Good thinking," she humored him. She kept her sweater on; the horrid odor was indeed almost dissipated, but the house remained bone-achingly cold. She went to the kitchen to reheat a cup of cold coffee in the microwave.

"You know what?" he called from the dining room. "It occurred to me that as far as we know, Liz Yeager's the only tenant of the house who actually died in it. Is that right?"

"Yes, I think so." So it was in fact Liz's spirit he'd encountered – or believed he had. Hurry up, Ryan and Billy, she beckoned silently.

"But then, why would he want her here? Unless he's using her, like he did when she was alive. And we know he's the one who inspired the crazy mother to drag you off to Jeezopolis."

"I don't know, sweetie." She took a seat across from him.

"I don't want you to worry, either, that because I'm high now we're totally back at square one. Once we're done at this fucking house I'm clean again. I'm not lying to you, Mags. I'll never go back to where I was."

But you are, she thought. "OK. But you must know he wants you high, just like he wants me drunk."

"Yeah, but I can outsmart him. I think better when I'm high. Clearer. And my intuition is all amped up."

Doorbell. Maggie leaped up.

She found Ryan on the doorsteps holding the TV. "Have I missed anything?" he joked.

She gave him a look. "Oh, yeah."

"Hey, man," Tim said, coming into the entry. "Let's hook that fucker up. Cable still works, don't you think?"

Ryan's expression didn't change, but Maggie sensed he realized Tim was tweaking. "Where's the co-axial cable? And Jesus, did your previous tenant have an incontinent cat?"

"Damn, you have a good 'smeller,'" Maggie said, feigning light-heartedness.

"I'll tell you everything that's happened once what's-his-face gets here," Tim said. "Better still, you can read it. I wrote it all down."

"'It all'? How long have you guys been here?"

"Couple hours. Let's hook up the TV first."

Tim knelt down to unwind the coiled cable protruding from the wall, and Ryan's eyes met hers. She wondered if Billy, less experienced with the signs of meth use, would be able to tell as well.

With the cable connected to the television, Ryan sat down on the lumpy couch with the legal pad, Tim hovering over him and providing a rapid-fire running commentary on the text. Billy arrived just as Ryan started reading. "Hey, Billy," Ryan greeted pleasantly.

Tim glowered. "Let the games begin," he mocked. "Maggie must be happy now – here's someone who'll judge me for sure."

Billy regarded him cautiously. "What's biting your ass?"

"Don't," Maggie warned Tim. "Excuse us." She dragged him by the arm into the kitchen. "I don't blame you for being high, but if you start acting like an asshole that's another story." Inwardly she wanted to weep – the situation was agonizingly familiar.

"OK, I'll back off."

"You'd better," she said curtly, "or I'm calling both Diana and Father Bob."

He yanked her close to him. "I'm really horny. Wouldn't it piss off the old man if we fucked right in his own bedroom?"

She jerked away. "Cool it. I mean it, Tim."

They returned to their guests in the living room. Ryan was perusing Tim's notes, with Billy reading over his shoulder. Both looked troubled. "Shit," Ryan said. "I wish we'd gotten here sooner."

Billy looked from Maggie to Tim, then back again to her. "You guys shouldn't be here at all. Let's scrub the deal."

"No fucking way," Tim shot back. "I'm not throwing in the towel that easily. It's what he wants."

"Bullshit. He wants you to stay – that's what the booze and drugs were for."

"You don't know what the fuck you're talking about," Tim spat. Maggie squeezed his arm hard.

"Look," Ryan interceded, "none of us knows exactly what he's after. Now that we're all here, we need to formulate a concrete plan of action."

"Let me go get my weed," Tim said, and rushed upstairs.

Billy regarded Maggie sternly. "Get out. I'm serious."

"I can't. He won't go and I won't leave him."

"He's out of his head. Who the hell knows what he saw up in that bathroom?"

Ryan also dropped his voice. "Tim's on the edge, Maggie. What if he pulls a Jack Nicholson in *The Shining*? Maybe that's what the old man really wants."

The suggestion unnerved her, but she knew that Tim couldn't be persuaded to leave the house. "His sister should be here within an hour. I'm hoping she'll give him something to knock him out for a while so we can find his meth and get rid of it." She gave Billy a sideways look. "And you *are* judging him. That's not fair. This is beyond his control."

"You fought it," he rejoined.

"I wasn't an addict for virtually all of my adult life," she said frostily.

"Ssh," Ryan cautioned.

Tim was back with a couple of joints. Maggie feared they were decoys, and that he'd done still more crystal upstairs. Dear God, what if he gave himself a heart attack or stroke?

"See anything weird up there?" Ryan asked.

"Uh-uh, but I only went into our room. I need to get way stoned before I can go into the master bedroom again."

Ryan alone accepted a hit from the joint, and then with no great enthusiasm. Maggie guessed that he too was mainly humoring Tim, doing his part to keep Tim from thoroughly spinning out from the speed. The pot made Tim less garrulous but more paranoid. "Why's that dead woman here? What if it's just him in a different shape?" he demanded of no one in particular.

Billy was rereading Tim's notes (or pretending to). Maggie had seldom seen him looking so tense. Ryan switched on the TV, found a rerun on the Sci-Fi Channel of *The X-Files*. "Maybe this will give us some ideas."

"Not unless the ghost is actually an alien," Maggie said, trying to play along.

"Shape-shifters," Tim said, enrapt by the screen. "I hope this is one with the alien bounty hunter."

Good, Maggie thought, get distracted by the show. Unfortunately, this episode was one of the more whimsical ones: Mulder trapped in the Bermuda Triangle circa World War II and Scully, aided by the Lone Gunmen, trying to reach him. Tim quickly lost interest. "We should have a séance," he announced.

"*No*," Maggie and Billy said simultaneously.

Tim's eyes narrowed. "Collusion?" he accused. "When did you two decide this?"

"Tim, we didn't." She sat down beside him on the floor, wrapped her arms over his shoulders.

"Yeah, right."

"Why not hold a séance?" Ryan said. "I mean, as soon as our heads are clear. When I'm stoned, I see dead people as if I were that kid in *The Sixth Sense*."

He wasn't stoned, but Maggie was grateful for his diplomacy. Tim's paranoia needed no further stoking. "I just remember Darlene Zarlengo saying that séances were for summoning spirits, not getting rid of them."

"Her word might carry more weight if she'd actually gotten rid of yours," Billy said, setting aside the notepad. "The main problem's that we're all too suggestible. Each one of us has a pretty firm idea what this ghost is about. How could we trust anything to come out of a séance?"

Tim scowled. "What do *you* think he's about, cowboy?"

"I think he hates your guts and by extension, your wife and kid's," Billy replied. "I thought we were all here to try and figure out why."

"Because he's a fucking psycho asshole!" Tim snapped.

"Oh, Christ," Ryan said. "Is it me, or is that smell getting worse?"

He was right. Whereas before the stench had receded to an almost ignorable level, now it was back in full potency, reeking not only of stale urine but also of rotting meat, overwhelming the pleasant pungency of smoldering marijuana. All four of them dashed for refuge on the deck. For a moment Maggie even forgot about Tim's condition. "What are we going to do about that? It's intolerable!"

"I told you he wants us gone," Tim rasped.

"Pisses me off to make it that easy for him," Ryan said, gulping air. "What would happen, I wonder, if we brought in one of those ionic breeze air purifying machines?"

"Those are expensive," Maggie fretted.

"I have to admit I don't like the idea of being stunk out of here either," Billy said, his jaw setting. "We could split the cost of the machine and if it's useless, return it."

"You all should go and let me deal with this alone," Tim said. "Let him do his worst – at least it'll be over, one way or another."

Billy regarded him in open annoyance. "Quit being such a goddamn drama queen. Besides, he's already KO'd you in the opening round."

The doorbell chimed, and Maggie yanked Tim back inside before he could react in anger to Billy's words. Bizarrely, not even the slightest whiff of the horrid odor marked the living room anymore, only the damp briny smell of the sea.

Tim froze at the sight of Diana, who was not expected until the next morning. "You lied!" he said to Maggie. "You told her everything!"

"Maggie told me nothing, Mr. Paranoid," Diana said. "I just thought I'd drop by and see how everyone's doing."

Ryan and Billy came inside, too, and Maggie noted them sniffing in surprise at the air. She introduced them to Diana, who greeted them cordially before turning back to her brother. "Come into the kitchen for a sec, Tim. I want to show you something I found that has to do with Granddad."

He was suspicious. "What? Show it here."

"No, it's kind of personal. C'mon."

He reluctantly followed her out of the room. Maggie allowed herself to exhale. "Thank God."

"This is lunacy, Maggie," Billy said.

"Even if we decided to call the whole thing off, Tim's got his heels dug in," she said. "Please, you guys. Hang in here with us."

Ryan wrapped an arm over her shoulder. "As long as we can hold the stink-bomb at bay."

She looked back at Billy. "I know you think we're crazy."

"No, not you or even Tim. This experiment is. Worse than crazy – it's a lot more dangerous than we'd counted on."

"I never dreamed there'd be the vodka and meth," she conceded.

"Or the smell," Ryan said. "That's a new trick, isn't it?"

"If Tim's right, maybe when you were here before, the ghost didn't want you to leave," Billy said.

"I don't think that was it. The little boy was protecting us." She cast a worried glance in the direction of the kitchen.

Ryan grimaced. "I feel like we need to draw Venn diagrams."

Diana appeared at the dining room entry. "Ryan, Billy, can you guys give me a hand with him?"

Tim slumped over the dinette table as if passed out, although when he mumbled something unintelligible Maggie realized he was semiconscious. He didn't resist Ryan

and Billy hoisting him to his feet, under Diana's instruction, and guiding him to the couch. "I want to keep an eye on his blood pressure," she told Maggie. "It's on the low side, believe it or not." She folded the cuff and meter into the tote bag serving as her medical valise.

"What did you give him?" Maggie asked, passing a palm over his clammy forehead.

"Haloperidol and diazepam. He was so wired he actually bought it when I told him it was morphine."

"That reminds me," Maggie said. "I need to find what's left of the meth." She felt the back pocket of his jeans. "Voila." She removed the plastic bag of powder, handed it to Billy. "Will you do the honors?"

He went to dispose of it into the downstairs toilet.

With Tim prone and now breathing deeply, the rest of them took seats on the carpet. The television, muted but still on, flashed a rerun of *Seinfeld*.

"I don't know what I would have done without you," Maggie said to Diana.

Diana was having her turn skimming Tim's notes. "Damn. You sure you still want to go through with this?"

"So long as Tim is, I'm resigned," Maggie said.

"It's freezing in here," Ryan said. "Mind if I try making another fire?"

"If you want to risk getting stunk out again." Maggie eyed Tim. "Will someone come with me upstairs? I want to get the blanket from our bed for him."

Billy volunteered, but they encountered no ghosts, noxious miasmas, or strange noises on the second floor. Maggie tore the thermal blanket off the bed in Kat's old room. "I'm afraid I'm going to have to ask you and Ryan to move the bed from the master suite down into the living room. Unless one of you is willing to sleep in that room."

"I don't know. I have a theory, and I bet Ryan's thought of the same thing."

They stopped on the landing, the staircase chilly but otherwise innocuous. "What?"

"Didn't you say that the grandfather was actually nice to Tim's sister?"

"Yes. She told me she still feels guilty about it."

"Well, I'm thinking, she shows up and that smell evaporates like it was never here. Betcha Ryan's fire does OK, too."

His stubborn calm was reassuring. "Maybe. But what happens when she leaves?"

"I suggest we use the next few hours to map out a real course of action. My guess is that she'll stay the night to make sure her brother's OK."

They descended the stairs. Just as Billy had predicted, the fire was crackling robustly, without even a trace of the noxious odor. Maggie covered Tim with the blanket; he appeared simply to be in a sound sleep. Either Ryan or Diana had put on a fresh pot of coffee, and its pleasant aroma scented the room only half an hour before virtually uninhabitable.

"How's his blood pressure?" Maggie asked, sinking to her knees beside the couch.

"He's still a little hypotensive. I'm glad I got here before he could do any more of that stuff."

Ryan chafed his hands in front of the fire. "So what does everybody think? Was the woman's ghost Tim saw a hallucination or are we dealing with a squatter?"

"Given the meth, I'm voting for hallucination," Diana said.

"Me too," Billy seconded. "Plus, he'd seen her before when she was alive. It'd be different if Maggie or Ryan had been the one."

Ryan nodded. "The suggestibility thing again."

Maggie wasn't so certain. Tim's point earlier, however meth-frenetic, about Liz Yeager's status as the only resident to have died in the house resonated. "Does it matter if she was a hallucination or a real spirit? She's not the one out to get us."

"I was saying to Maggie upstairs, we've got to have a blueprint if we're gonna stay in this house. We can't just sit around waiting to react."

"Let's have some coffee and sandwiches while we brainstorm," Maggie suggested. "I raided the deli at Ralphs today."

They fashioned sandwiches of Black Forest ham and Swiss cheese, added sides of dill potato salad and cornichons. Eschewing the dinette, they took their plates and mugs back into the living room and reclaimed places on the floor around the fireplace. "This is the most bizarre picnic I've ever been to," Ryan remarked.

"Tomorrow I'll dash over to Pier 1 and buy some oversized pillows so at least we'll have something to rest against," Maggie said.

Diana took up the yellow legal pad again. "I'll take minutes."

"I think we ought to start by stating what the goal of this whole deal is, and then work backwards as to how to reach it," Billy said.

"Isn't it obvious?" Maggie said. "We want to get rid of the old man. The Shadow Man."

"But what, specifically, do you mean by getting rid of him? Destroying him? Getting him out of this house? Or just out of your lives?" Billy pressed.

Tim muttered something in his sleep. Maggie leaned over to plant a brief kiss on his temple. Then she replied to Billy's question. "I want for him to have no power over us."

Ryan tossed another log into the fire. "Then it seems to me we've got to figure out why he has such a vendetta against you guys. It always comes back to the why of it."

"I believe he's punishing me for somehow reintegrating that little boy's spirit – Tim's spirit – with Tim," Maggie said slowly. "Before Kat and I moved in here, the old man must have been content to know he had Tim as a child trapped here with him, while Tim the adult was stuck in a kind of living death."

"'Trapped with him,'" Diana pronounced. "According to Tim's notes, that's what the woman's ghost said to him."

"Maybe that explains the crystal," Ryan mused. "It might be that the old man's trying to screw Tim up enough to reclaim the part of his personality that had been trapped here all these years."

"If that's the case, Tim's idea – that he doesn't want you two here – would have to be wrong," Billy cautioned.

Diana raised her pen from the notepad on which she'd been jotting down their speculations. "Bottom line, we can't be 100 percent sure what my grandfather's ghost does want. I wish my parents had given us some inkling why Granddad so had it in for

Tim in the first place."

"You'd think they'd have wondered themselves," Ryan said.

"Unless they already know why and aren't saying," Billy added.

Tim sat up abruptly, tossing aside the blanket, and started to laugh. "I watch him

while he sleeps. I can see him." He laughed again, childishly, crazily.

Maggie and Diana raced over to flank him. He kept laughing that weirdly

childish laugh even as they urged him to lie back down. "I can see him," he chortled.

Then he began to cough and choke. Diana pried open his mouth to check his airway.

"He's OK. Come on, Timmy. Calm down. Big deep breaths. Come on." Gradually his

breathing slowed and his pallor gave way to faint color. "Maggie, will you hand me my

tote? I'm going to give him a little more diazepam."

"Oh my God, what's wrong with him?" Maggie was so upset she almost

requested a sedative for herself. Ryan and Billy looked almost as shaken as she.

Diana fished in her bag for a bindle and fresh syringe. "His heart rate's almost

back to normal. He'll be fine."

"What the hell was he saying?" Ryan asked. "Who watches who sleeping?"

"That must refer to the old man," Billy said. "But why was he laughing about it?"

Diana administered the injection to Tim's bicep. "I hate to be a wet blanket, but

that was probably just a temporary brain glitch due to the meth." She gave them an

apologetic smile. "My husband's a neurologist. I'll get his opinion before making mine

the definitive one."

"How long until Tim's in his right mind and can tell us himself if it means anything?" Ryan asked.

Diana rearranged the blanket over him. "Barring any more episodes like that, he'll probably stay out until morning." A shadow passed over her. "He's going to feel so awful."

"I know it," Maggie said unhappily. "One of the reasons I never much liked crystal was the horrible depression when you come down."

Ryan nodded. "But that's exactly how it hooks you. You'll do anything to avoid crashing."

"Guess I'm the nerd here," Billy said ironically. "I've never done meth and from what I've seen and heard, I never plan to. Christ."

"Same here," Diana said. "I can count the times I've even smoked pot on the fingers of one hand. I didn't like it." She picked up the pen and notepad again. "But just in case that was some kind of trance, I'm going to make a note of it."

"Write down too that we were talking about why your grandfather hated Tim when that happened," Ryan advised. "What if he did watch Tim while he slept?"

"That sounds more like effect than cause of the old man's hatred," Billy said. "And why would Tim refer to himself in the third person?"

Maggie frowned. "There are only three bedrooms. Where did everybody sleep, Diana, when your family spent summers here?"

"There was a fold-out sofa down here, where my parents slept. When I was in my teens, I took it over, because I stayed up later than they did."

"Ever hear people walking around upstairs after they'd gone to bed?" Billy asked.

Diana shrugged. "I might have, but I wouldn't have thought anything of it. My mother's an inveterate putterer at bedtime."

"Tim was a sound sleeper?" Ryan posed.

"He was."

"He slept soundly when I first got to know him, too," Maggie said wistfully. "Now he wakes up if I so much as shift in bed." She drained her mug. "Anyone want more coffee?"

"Yeah, bring the whole pot out," Ryan said.

She fetched the carafe, refilled everyone's cup. "I guess none of us will be doing much sleeping tonight."

Ryan stared into the fire, which still blazed and cracked. "It creeps me out to imagine the grandfather going into a kid's room and watching him sleep."

"Or maybe Tim was the one watching the old man sleep," Billy posited. "Still doesn't make sense. Diana's probably right about not reading too much into it."

"And let's face it," Diana said, "we've all been pretty much watching Tim sleep for the last hour."

"True," Ryan granted.

"Excuse me, I'm going to call Wes and give him an update," Diana said. "Can I bring anybody something else from the kitchen?"

"Tell Wes we're sorry we stole you earlier than planned," Maggie replied.

"It's OK. It gives him and Brandon some extra male-bonding time. He's probably showing our son how to belch the alphabet. Be right back."

"Here's a thought," Billy said. "Unless you can think of a way to deal with the stench short of a $300 contraption that might not even work, why can't we confine our ghost hunting to the night? It's obvious Diana's some kind of safeguard against the old dude's tricks."

"That's a great idea," Ryan said. "She can spend the day with her family, and Maggie, you and Tim can just go back to your apartment."

She glanced at Tim dubiously. "I'm not opposed as a matter of principle, but I suspect Tim's going to say we'll never be able to accomplish anything if we simply drive the old man underground."

Billy looked impatient. "Forgive my saying so, but look where Tim's ideas for dealing with this have gotten him so far, and we haven't even spent an entire night here yet."

"I can't commit until he's thinking clearly and I can talk to him about it." Billy's skepticism about Tim's judgment made her all the more protective. It was easy for Billy to second-guess; after all, he had no investment in the outcome of this endeavor.

They stayed up past midnight, speculating and hypothesizing until arriving at the non-conclusion that they were little closer to guessing at the Shadow Man's motives than they had been at the start of the evening. As for the relevance of the cryptic words Tim had spoken, all they could do was wait for the Haldol and Valium to wear off. Maggie knew she was the only one convinced of the insufficiency of Diana's scientific interpretation, despite the fact that Wes supported the diagnosis as well.

They played poker for pennies until exhaustion at last got the better of caffeine. Maggie chose to sleep on the floor next to Tim, allowing Diana the bed in Kat's old room. Billy volunteered to take the master bedroom, a brave move as far as the rest of them were concerned. But he scoffed at their admiration. "I'm so tired a ghost could crawl right into bed next to me and I'd sleep right through it."

Maggie was dead-tired, too, but sleep didn't come easily. Her mind incessantly replayed the day's unsettling events, and she could only fear what her dreams might bring. And while Diana had assured her that Tim's blood pressure was stabilized, what if he experienced a new crisis in the night? "Why do you want to destroy us?" she whispered into the near-darkness, the last log's flames now reduced to a few sputtering embers. The silence that answered seemed volitional, not an absence but a deliberate withholding of some secret.

CHAPTER 2

She finally drifted off, but her sleep was fitful, her dreams vaguely ominous fragments broken up by moments of wakefulness in which she touched Tim or listened for his heartbeat. She was determined he not awaken before she did, awaken to the crushing post-meth depression exacerbated by guilt over his relapse. He would need her.

Dawn painted the dark living room a smoky gray. She staggered up to draw the drapes lest the fledgling light rouse Tim. As she was pulling the curtains together she was startled by his quiet, wretched voice behind her. "Leave them open."

She spun around. He was lying on his side but it was too dim to make out his expression. "How are you feeling?" She left the drapes open and knelt down next to him.

"I'm sure you can imagine."

His despairing tone distressed her. She lay a hand on his cheek. "Can I get you anything, baby?"

He said nothing.

"Tim, it wasn't your fault."

"Bullshit. No one forced it up my nose."

"Maybe not literally, but – "

"Don't console me, Maggie." He sighed. "Did you get rid of the rest of it?"

"Yes."

"Fuck."

"You don't really mean that."

Silence again.

"Maybe Diana could give you something to make you feel better," she tried.

"Did we smoke the second joint?"

She located it on a saucer he'd been using for an ashtray. Though uncertain about the clinical wisdom of his smoking it, she took a chance it might ease his withdrawal pangs and handed the joint to him along with his lighter.

He took two, three deep hits before slowly exhaling. "What a drug addict I am." The tone of despair had been replaced by one of resignation.

"Yes, but you're my drug addict."

"C'mere." He patted the couch.

She stretched out on top of him, holding out the saucer-ashtray as he continued smoking the joint. Thank God for the pot.

"I swear, Mags, I'll never do it again."

"I believe you, Timmy. That bastard just caught us off-guard."

"It's Crazy Ruth, too. We've got to watch out for her."

With the marijuana evidently allaying the intensity of his misery, her fatigue was overtaking her. She suppressed a yawn against his shoulder. Damn it, why couldn't everything be OK? Why couldn't she and Tim just lie here like cats, drowsy and safe? But the thought of cats brought to mind Kat and the imperative that had brought them back into this haunted house. She was wide awake again.

"Did anything happen after Di knocked me out?" he asked, passing his fingers through her hair.

"No," she lied. She wanted to consult with Diana about the stability of his condition before informing him of his brief "trance."

"That's weird."

"Not really. Ryan and Billy think that Diana's presence makes him retreat. We even had a decent fire in the fireplace."

"Hm. I wouldn't take that to the bank."

"But he was fond of her, wasn't he?"

"Yeah. I still think it's a ruse." The joint was now a smoldering roach, and he snuffed it out in the saucer. "Will you get my pot and papers, babe? They're in my shaving case."

Given the weed's effects on his equilibrium she could scarcely refuse. She crept up the stairs and into Kat's old room. Diana was sleeping, but stirred as Maggie foraged in the weak light for Tim's shaving kit. "Is Tim all right?"

"He seems to be. Go back to sleep."

"Come get me if you need me." Diana reburied her face in the pillow.

Maggie found the marijuana and rolling papers, and tiptoed out of the room into the upstairs hallway. She jumped at the creaking of the master bedroom door. Billy, looking alert and awake despite his boxer shorts and T-shirt, waved her over. She stuffed the bag with the weed and papers into her robe pocket – she knew he'd disapprove of this unorthodox use of "medical marijuana" – and stepped inside the master suite. "From the looks of you, you're regretting your bravado in taking this room," she teased in a low voice.

He didn't smile. "I saw the woman's ghost. In her flannel nightgown with a big rope-burn around her neck."

Reflexively Maggie's hand flew to the base of her own throat. "How horrible, Billy. Did she say anything?"

He looked troubled. "I was so blown away to wake up and have her standing by the bed, I'm not sure. I think she said, 'My mother' or maybe, 'the mother.' Then she was gone."

"Dear God. Tim was just saying we need to be really careful about the mother."

"Has he come to?"

"Yes. He's upset about the crystal. But I think he'll be all right. I want to get Diana's opinion before I say anything about his 'brain glitch,' though."

"That's smart."

"I'd better get back downstairs before he comes looking for me and, God forbid, runs into Liz again himself. When did it happen, Billy?"

"'Bout an hour ago. It was still dark. I woke up feeling like I was being stared at, and there she was."

"Come downstairs, then, and get some coffee. I can't believe you've stayed in here for a whole hour."

"I'm still waiting to see if she'd come back. When I heard someone in the hallway I thought it might be her. Besides, Tim probably needs you to himself right now."

She listened for irony but heard none. On impulse she kissed his cheek. "Thanks for being a damn macho fool and sticking with us."

"That's macho redneck fool," he corrected with a weary smile.

Tim didn't resist Diana's order that he use Valium instead of pot to treat the discomforts of crashing, although had she not been supervising, he'd have combined the two. The pathetic truth, one he could not in conscience attribute to his grandfather's malice, was that he loved being high, being in an altered state; he devoured it like a starving man, embraced its myriad physical sensations almost as he did those of sex. Twelve Step philosophy mandated avoidance of all intoxicants, not simply the one on which the addict or drunk was dependent, but it was a dictate he knew he could never adhere to. His only realistic hope was to restrict himself to the more benign substances, and he despised himself for falling short of even this modest objective – not the least because his lapse had played right into the old man's hands.

He did object, however, to the general proposal, presented by Ryan, that they forego the house by day and reconvene the next night after Tim had fully recuperated. "Hell, no! We might as well wave a goddamn white flag." He massaged his temples. "I knew it was a mistake to turn this into a house party. Why don't all of you go home and let me take care of this by myself like I wanted to all along?"

Diana attempted to appease him. "No one is waving a white flag. You need rest."

"And I need to get to work," Ryan said apologetically.

"Me too," Billy echoed.

Tim was all the more rankled by the usually opinionated O'Donnell's uncharacteristic reticence. "Fine – everybody leave. I mean it. But don't expect me to skulk off like a cat with a singed tail with the rest of you."

"Can't we compromise?" Maggie pleaded. "Why don't you and I go home for the day so that Diana can at least have some time with Wes and Brandon? We can all meet back here at six tonight."

He agreed only because he figured he'd caused her enough upset for twenty-four hours. Besides, he could smoke weed freely if Diana wasn't around, and he knew his sister was no more inclined to leave him alone in the house than Maggie was.

Despite the pot and Valium, his nerves were raw, growing more so once they were back in the Solana Beach apartment and Maggie insisted he go to bed. For one, it felt disorienting not to have Kat or even Thumper around, though Mags promised they'd call their daughter later in the day before heading back to Del Mar. Second, Maggie acted as if she had something else on her mind in addition to his relapse, something he couldn't quite coax from the tip of her tongue. Every time he brought up the Shadow Man or the house she hushed him. "Why don't we let it rest for a few hours? Tonight we can rehash everything that's happened so far."

Her eyes were circled, and he urged her to lie down with him for a nap. But she was as restless beside him as if she, not he, were the one coming down from a crystal binge. He fought back a twinge of residual paranoia that wondered whether her preoccupation had anything to do with O'Donnell. "Mags, maybe you should take one of my Valium." Diana had written him a prescription for thirty, which they'd stopped to fill at Longs Drugs.

"No, I'm just overtired. A Valium would probably put me out for a week." She shifted again on the bed. "How about a blowjob?"

Her stab at levity seemed strained. "Fine with me, but I don't exactly see how that'd relax you."

"It would. It'd make me feel like I was doing something to help you feel better. Between the pot and the Valium I'm feeling pretty useless." Her hand slipped beneath the blanket, caressed his scrotum.

He knew she was trying to distract him but his penis stiffened, oblivious of her ulterior motives. He groaned in pleasure as she lapped at him. Fucking had always been what they'd done when one or the other of them didn't want to talk. Fucking was *theirs* every bit as much as Kat was. Small wonder each had felt the other's sexual betrayal so keenly.

What began as an impulsive blowjob soon turned into fucking in earnest. He came so explosively that he had to assume the meth was still active in his system. Or maybe not – for her climax seemed as intense as his. "Oh God," she breathed against his shoulder. "Now I could take a lovely nap."

Plus it pisses him off, he thought with no minor satisfaction, although he was grateful they'd left no one back at the house to be subject to his wrath. "I'm glad we came back here if just for this. I don't really like the idea of him watching us, even if it does piss him off."

She colored. "What makes you say that?"

"What, that it makes him mad?"

"No – that he watches us."

He was slightly taken aback by her disquiet. "Wouldn't you assume he was watching us? We know he listens." He was determined to pluck out the heart of whatever mystery she was concealing from him. "Mags, we have to tell each other everything, remember?"

She looked away for a moment. "Last night – Diana says it was just some kind of neurological spasm from the crystal, but I think you went into a trance. You said stuff."

"What! What the fuck did I say? Please don't tell me he spoke through me." His heart was banging.

"No, no – it was you. But you said … " She wrapped the blanket around her shoulders as if chilled.

"Maggie, what?"

"You said, "He watches him while he sleeps. I can see him.'"

"Jesus Christ, who watches whom, and why the fuck would I say that?"

"I have no idea, baby."

"And you weren't going to tell me about this?" He didn't mean to snap at her but the disclosure was alarming.

"I knew it would upset you, and Diana said – "

"Yeah, she said it was a brain-fart. She doesn't know what she's talking about." He sat up and furiously lit a cigarette. "Anything else you all decided I was better off not knowing?"

"Billy saw Liz Yeager's ghost, too, early this morning. She said something like, 'my mother.'"

He heard in her tart tone that she was irked with him. But his mind was ajumble from these new, bewildering revelations. "What if Liz Yeager was trying to – ah, fuck it. We ought to track down the Jeezoid mother before she bursts in on us with a hatchet."

"These are precisely the things I wanted to put on hold until tonight. If we can't have even a temporary reprieve, I'm going to lose my mind."

"I know," he said guiltily. "It's just that *he* never takes a reprieve. But I'm sorry I bit your head off." He set his cigarette in the ashtray and wrapped his arms around her. "One day this will be over and I'll make it up to you. All of it."

"Can we have another baby?"

"Sure. Think of the money we'll save on condoms." He still had strong doubts about their emotional as well as financial ability to raise another child. But in the unlikely event that this hypothetical future came to pass, he supposed they would deal with a new baby if that was really what she wanted.

She seemed consoled by his promise, falling into a light sleep in his arms. Were it not for the Valium he would have obsessed over her account of his "trance," but thanks to the tranquilizer, he was able only to mull it over. *He watches him while he sleeps.* Who had been speaking through him? Or did the words have something to do with Maggie's notion that the old man's brutality had fragmented his developing psyche as a child? Hence the third-person pronoun. But who was the "I," then, who could "see" the ambiguous "him"? Tonight he'd grill them all for clues about his demeanor, his tone of voice, during the strange event.

Or was the trance somehow linked to the apparition of Liz Yeager? With O'Donnell having seen it, there could be no doubt the specter was real. Liz had to have been warning them about Ruth, the obvious source of the crystal and vodka. Or perhaps the spirit wanted them to summon her deranged mother in hopes of breaking free of the old man. "Trapped with him." Tim was angered as much as troubled by the old man's – the house's – spiteful defiance of their expectations. They'd foreseen none of it – not the drugs or booze, nor the ghost of Liz Yeager, nor his enigmatic trance.

He downed another Valium and eventually fell asleep himself. Not usually a vivid dreamer, he observed rather than participated in a drowsy scenario in which they had their second child, a little boy who spoke only Spanish, of which Tim could not understand even a word. The child kept laughing at their confusion, not a whimsical childish laugh but a mocking, contemptuous one. It was highly annoying, and he told Maggie he knew it had been a mistake to have another kid when they couldn't afford it.

He opened his eyes and realized who the child was and what he'd been saying. *Lo miro. Cuando esta durmiendo. Puedo verlo.* "Maggie!" he called, seeing her no longer beside him. Hearing the shower running, he swung his legs over the side of the bed and hurried naked into the adjacent bathroom. Through the frosted shower door her silhouette undulated beneath the spray. He slid the door open. "I have to tell you something!"

Startled, she switched off the steamy water. "Is something wrong?" She stepped

out of the tub, grabbing a thick towel from the rack to fashion a sarong around her

dripping body.

"Mags, I had this dream, and I know whose voice it was!" Not even all the

Valium he'd ingested could dull his agitation.

"Who?" She twisted her dripping hair into a knot.

"There was this kid I used to play with at the house. His name was – fuck, what

was his name? – Emilio? Enzo? He was the son or nephew of the Mexican cleaning

lady." He paused to catch his breath. "I saw him in my dream."

"That's amazing, sweetie," she said, although she looked puzzled. "Did this little

boy used to say things like that?"

"No, but he was saying it in my dream, in Spanish. *Lo miro. Cuando esta

durmiendo. Puedo verlo.* That's it exactly, isn't it?"

Her eyes widened. "Si."

"He – the kid – he spoke English with me back then but usually in Spanish with

his mom or aunt. He must have seen the old man watching me. Or maybe he means the

old man's watching me now." He clasped her wet shoulders. "This has to be

significant."

"I agree, baby. But now what?"

"I don't know – let me think. Does the trance mean that Alberto -- that was his

name – is dead? Or telepathic?"

"Or maybe you're the one who's telepathic."

He scoffed. "Nah." He switched the shower back on, hoping the rush of hot water would sharpen his thinking. He felt certain that the dream was an important breakthrough. Now the challenge lay in figuring out how best to exploit it.

He hated to admit it, but he was looking forward to input from the rest of them tonight. Maybe Diana would remember something pertinent about Alberto. And he still wasn't sure what to make of Liz's ghost and whether its purpose served or countered the old man's.

Despite his meth crisis, it was beginning to look as if their inaugural session at the house hadn't been a complete waste of time.

Diana, Ryan, and Billy were already gathered on the front steps when Tim and Maggie drove up. Tim intuited the trio had arranged to arrive early, probably thinking to head off another possible trap laid for Maggie or him. He was mildly vexed by the show of solicitousness but refrained from comment as he twisted the house-key in the lock. If he flew off the handle over the trivial, they'd all think he was still suffering from a meth hangover.

He and Maggie had stopped at Pier 1 to buy the oversized floor pillows and a cheap wicker coffee table, all of which made the living room somewhat more inviting. The sun was beginning its westward descent, casting a transient warmth over the deck, the living room. But underneath the warmth the house remained cold and clammy, and Ryan hastened to place a dry log inside the fireplace.

Tim was about to inform them of his dream when he caught eye of the yellow legal pad on the floor near the hearth. He picked it up to scan his own scrawls, then the additional albeit cryptic entries in Diana's hand: "Goal?" "Vendetta." "Screw Tim up

again – dis-integrate?" Then he read, to his great shock, Spanish words: *"Lo miro.*

Cuando esta durmiendo. Puedo verlo. " "Holy fuck, Di – why'd you write my trance

words in Spanish?"

"I did not, and that wasn't a trance," she protested, snatching the notepad from

him. Her expression swiftly turned incredulous. "Oh my God, I did write it down in

Spanish. How could that be?"

"I'll tell you how," Tim said.

He recounted his dream and how it had jogged memories of Alberto, his

childhood playmate. Neither Billy nor Diana, regardless of the Spanish words she'd

evidently scribbled into the notepad, seemed entirely persuaded of the dream's relevance,

but Ryan was receptive. "Does this mean Alberto's ghost is here too? This place is

getting more crowded than the island on *Lost*."

"Or those words could have been 'residual,'" Maggie said, invoking the term

she'd learned upon her initial foray last fall into paranormal inquiry. "Something from

the past that both Tim and Diana picked up on."

"That laughing was the kind you'd expect from a mean kid," Ryan remarked.

"Laughing?" Tim thought of the child's spiteful chortling in his dream.

"Yeah, you had this weird laughter," Ryan confirmed.

Diana looked flustered. "So we're going to dismiss any rational explanation out

of hand?"

"Hell, yeah," Tim said. "If you ask me, irrational is still grasping at the straws of a scientific interpretation despite everything that's been going on here since the old man died and – " He mimicked Jack Emerson. "—'Mother went into assisted living.'"

That at least coaxed a smile from Diana. "Keeping an open mind doesn't mean totally discounting more conventional possibilities, Timmy. Some of these things could be coincidence."

Tim glared at Billy, who remained poker-faced. "You're being unusually diffident."

"Just listening, dude."

Scowl deepening, Tim addressed Diana again. "One way to figure out whether that was Alberto's ghost last night or just a blip from the past is to determine if he's alive. Do you remember the cleaning lady's last name?"

"I don't even remember her first name. And I have no memory of the little boy."

He noticed doubt creep into Billy's eyes, and even Ryan's. "OK, now I've got a Spanish-speaking imaginary friend," he huffed.

"I wasn't implying that he didn't exist," Diana said. "During our summers here I spent most of my time at the beach scoping out guys."

Placated, Tim dropped his defensiveness. "You need to call Mom and ask her what the cleaning lady's name was."

"I take it your folks don't know what you're up to right now," Billy said at last.

"No," Diana replied. "Tim thinks I'm a rigid empiricist – my dad makes me look like spokeswoman for the Psychic Friends Network. Both my parents are in denial about Granddad's mistreatment of Tim."

It was a subject Tim loathed. "Will you call Mom?" he pressed.

"Right now?"

"Well, in the next hour or so, before they're tucked in bed in front of 'The O'Reilly Factor.'" He tapped the legal pad against his knee. "Next item. What do we make of Liz Yeager's ghost? Do we assume she has a separate agenda from the old man's?"

"For better or worse," Billy said, "she seems able to communicate. It's possible she'll tell us herself what she wants."

"Maybe. Her Jesussy mother's been infected too. But instead of getting wasted, she's taken on his hatred."

Maggie nodded in agreement. "I'm convinced of that, too. Liz's ghost was likely telling Billy that her mother is a threat."

"Or that she's the one who planted the vodka and crystal," Ryan said.

"But what if," Tim thought aloud, "her ghost and even my trance-thing and the Spanish words are red herrings, and he's trying to distract us from himself? We'd have to admit it's working."

"That's reaching," Billy said firmly. "And it's unknowable, anyway. We're better off dealing with each phenomenon as if it's free-standing."

Tim bristled at O'Donnell's dismissiveness. "What do you suggest? I don't see any of us doing much 'dealing,' period."

"It's true – all we're doing is bouncing ideas back and forth," Ryan said. "At the risk of being shouted down again, I propose we try holding a séance."

Tim was intrigued. "Like with a Ouija board?"

"Sure," Ryan replied. "Yes, we're suggestible, as Billy puts it. So what? We're all doing a pretty good job serving as each other's bullshit meter. The worst that could happen is that it'd be inconclusive."

"I'm for giving it a shot," Tim said. "Come on, you guys. Like Ryan says, what's the worst that could happen?"

"I'd feel better if it was just Ryan and Diana doing the table-tapping," Billy said. "You and I have seen the Liz ghost, and both of us and Maggie have seen the old man. One of us is bound to subconsciously influence whatever comes out of a séance."

"I saw the old guy's now-you-see-it, now-you-don't face in the photograph," Ryan reminded.

"Great," Diana said. "Now it's just me communing with the dead?"

"Of course not," Ryan assured her. "Anything we learn from the séance we'll take with a grain of salt. But why not try and see what happens?"

"Where do we buy a Ouija board?" Tim asked.

"Haven't you ever seen *The Uninvited*?" Ryan said. "We can make our own. Cut out letters, put them in a circle, and use an upside-down wine glass for a pointer."

"We don't have any wine glasses here, and there are only four chairs with the dinette set," Maggie rejoined.

Tim saw that she was the least enthusiastic of them all. "Someone can run over to Longs and get a cheap glass and a folding chair. Why don't you go get 'em, Di? I want to see if the stink comes back once you leave."

"Fine. I'll call Mother on the drive over."

"We'll walk you out to the car," Billy said. "There's something bizarre on the roof of the house next door that I want to show everybody."

Tim was skeptical. "What, a grilled cheese sandwich that looks like the Virgin Mary?"

"You'll see."

More suspicious than curious, Tim accompanied the others out the front door into the twilight and toward the neighboring house. He saw nothing the least peculiar on its roof, only Mediterranean tiles and a chimney.

"Listen," Billy addressed them. "It struck me that we might be telegraphing what we're planning or expecting to the ghost – *ghosts* – in the house. Maggie and Tim said they're sure he was listening when he launched the first stink bomb yesterday."

Tim wanted to scoff on general principle, but the point was a valid one. "Yeah, maybe we should be more selective about what we say in there."

"That's assuming he can't read our minds telepathically or eavesdrop on us out here," Ryan pointed out, zipping his leather bomber jacket. The fog was rolling in, and it was turning as chilly outside as it was within the house.

"For the sake of our collective sanity, let's assume he can't," Maggie said. "Why don't we go out to dinner where we can discuss this freely? We'll get the glass and chair on the way home."

Man, did she hate being back in the house, Tim reflected. He wished he could persuade her to sit out this experiment, though at the same time he was selfishly comforted by her refusal to leave his side.

They went to Tim and Maggie's regular Chinese restaurant in a strip-mall off Del Mar Heights Road. Because it was a Monday night they were seated immediately in a booth. Billy and Ryan ordered beers, and Tim longed for one too, but refrained in deference to Maggie, and echoed her and Diana's requests for Perrier. Maggie smiled awkwardly. "You know, you guys," she said to Ryan and Billy, "you can have beer at the house. I'm not going to wrest the bottles away from you and start chug-a-lugging."

"Frankly, I'd rather have my wits about me when I'm in that house," Ryan said, opening his menu. "I hope this place has hot mustard. Unless it's painful, it might as well be French's."

"It's quite hot," Maggie said. "Let's get some egg rolls and then decide on the entrees after."

Tim wasn't especially hungry, so he let the others debate the merits of Kung Pao this and Szechuan that. He had to point out, however, an item on the menu called "shong," and he dared Ryan to ask the waiter how the "schlong" was.

Ryan broke up. "I will, if you go over to the bartender and ask him if those chairs are his only stool samples."

"Quit," Diana begged amid their wild laughter.

"You guys are brutal," Billy concurred with a chuckle.

"At UCLA we'd stay up all night trying to outdo each other with bad puns and word games," Ryan explained to Diana and Billy.

"Ha – remember 'Regina Dentata'?" Tim said, smiling.

"'Queen with teeth'?" Diana squealed.

"Our friend Julie, but why?" Maggie said, dipping her egg roll into sweet and sour sauce.

"She was taking that feminist theory class where the professor was fixated on the vagina dentata," Ryan replied. "But if anyone should have been the Queen with teeth, it was Dan's catty boyfriend Louis."

"Good to know the taxpayers of California got their money's worth by you guys," Billy commented.

"Maggie's the one who thought of the Seven Deadly Personality Disorders," Ryan said.

"What were they?" Diana asked.

Maggie laughed. "I can't remember them all. One was the Orange County Personality Disorder. Tim and Ryan have Pisces Personality Disorder. Oh, and sorry, Diana, but there was a USC Personality Disorder."

"That's all right – we thought anyone who went to UCLA was a bozo, a geek, or Tragically Hip."

"I hope I fell into the Tragically Hip category," Maggie said.

"Is this zero-sum?" Ryan pretended to balk. "I'll take 'geek,' then, which leaves 'bozo' to you, Tim."

Tim didn't want to spoil the relative light-heartedness by reminding them of their purported reason for dining out. However, it seemed to him that they'd be better off saving their merriment for the house, to spite the old man, and using this time away from it for more somber discourse. "Don't forget to call Mom before we head back," he said to his sister.

"I will. You should eat something."

Obligingly he chopsticked a garlic shrimp. "I have a feeling the old man's going to try to scare the fuck out of us at the séance."

"All I know is if anybody starts spewing green vomit, I'm out of there," Ryan said.

"Please, we're eating," Maggie objected.

"The Liz ghost is pretty scary in its own right," Billy said matter-of-factly, helping himself to more tangerine beef.

"I'm telling you, man, I still think she could be one of his tricks," Tim said.

Billy appeared unswayed. "If it's your theory that he wants to scare or stink us out of the house, why would the Liz ghost have warned about her mother?"

Tim saw that Maggie had stopped eating. He wished he could ease her apprehension. "Did you ever sprinkle Father Bob's holy water around, babe?"

"No, I completely forgot."

"Tonight would seem a good time for it."

She gave him a wry smile that told him she was aware he was humoring her. "I know you don't believe but it certainly couldn't hurt."

"Amen to that." Diana raised her water glass.

"I keep thinking about the old man paying attention to all our ideas and plans," Ryan said. "Maybe we could use the séance to throw a red herring his way."

"Such as?" Tim posed.

"We could float an alternate theory about why we think he's after you guys and see if he reacts."

"Yeah, that might get him to drop his guard," Tim agreed. "But an alternate theory assumes we have a dominant one. Or did I miss that too?"

"We could pretend to believe he wants something in particular and offer to leave the house if he lets us know what it is," Diana suggested.

"But what if Tim's right and all he really wants is for us to leave?" Ryan countered.

"Why are we assuming he'll cooperate at all?" Tim asked. "Just because he's sentient doesn't mean he's rational."

"Sort of like you," Ryan quipped.

"Ha ha. You and your stool samples."

"Not that again," Diana groaned.

"You hung out with these losers in college?" Billy teased Maggie.

Tim didn't like her grateful smile. "We're getting off-topic."

Maggie refolded her napkin in her lap. "We probably can agree that the old man – the Shadow Man – is untrustworthy no matter what he might or might not do during this séance. The Liz ghost, on the other hand, seems to want to communicate. I think we should concentrate on her. Maybe she can tell us something."

"We also need to find out about Alberto, the cleaning lady's kid," Tim said. "I'm positive he plays some part too."

"I can take a hint," Diana said, getting up. "I'm going to the ladies room. I'll call Mother while I'm in there." She headed for the restrooms.

Ryan drained his beer. "Tim, do you remember your grandfather having any dealings with that kid?"

"Uh-uh. I just remember throwing around a baseball with him, reading the books his mom gave me, or running around the neighborhood. They didn't live in. I never remember them being there at night, which is why I'm sort of confused about the 'He watches him sleeping' thing."

Maggie arched an eyebrow. "The mother gave you books?"

"Mother or aunt, yeah. Those books you found and gave to Kat. I thought I told you."

"Nice cleaning lady," Billy observed.

"I just hope my mom remembers her name."

Diana returned as the waiter was setting the bill and a plate of plastic-wrapped fortune cookies on the table. "Mother said the cleaning lady's first name was Inez," she announced. "She doesn't think she ever knew her last name, though."

Tim leaned forward. "Did she remember the kid?"

"Yep. She offered it without my needing to ask. 'Inez used to bring her little boy with her to play with Timmy.'"

"Hm. Well, at least this proves he's not a figment of my imagination."

"Did your mother wonder why you were asking about the cleaning lady?" Maggie inquired.

"I told her that Tim and I had a bet on it."

Ryan grabbed a fortune cookie. "Who won the bet?"

Diana smiled. "I did, of course."

"What, did you tell her I swore the woman's name was Hazel?" Tim said.

Ryan cracked open his cookie and pulled out the coiled white slip. "This is an odd fortune. 'You long to see the great pyramids of Egypt.'"

"Do you?" Maggie asked.

"Not especially."

Nor did the rest of them find messages ominous or insightful. They split the bill five ways and left the restaurant.

They stopped at Rite-Aid for the wine glass, poster paper for the letters, and a folding chair. Tim remained outside the store to smoke a cigarette. He thought about the fateful day, not even two weeks before, that he had taken Kat for ice cream and spotted Ruth Yeager in front of Starbucks glowering at him. He couldn't help but sense that everything was at last coming to a head.

Maggie joined him outside. "They're in line. Did I ever tell you I hate Rite-Aid? They could stock the same as Bloomingdales and still feel cheesy."

"It's those blue carts." He squeezed her cold hand. "I know you're not thrilled by the séance. It'll probably come to nothing anyway."

"I just feel like we're flying blind, Tim. I'm starting to rethink the idea of simply burning the place to the ground."

"I'm not ruling that out either, depending on where we stand by the end of the week."

"I envy your faith."

"You're joking." He tossed away his expired cigarette.

"I mean, your faith that this awful situation can be resolved."

"When I was a kid, Mags, I had it in my head that so long as I didn't cry, he didn't win." He willed the garlic shrimp to stay put in his stomach. "But he won anyway. I'm not going to let him do it again."

"I love you."

"I'll never understand why, but I'm glad. It'd be pretty pathetic for me to have loved you since I was twenty years old and now realize you'd just been tolerating me all this time."

They shared a quiet kiss in the dark, and it struck him that the only faith that really counted was the heroic faith she'd always had in him.

She wanted to believe that Tim, through sheer doggedness, could not only stand down the old man but somehow extinguish him as well. She was heartened that he seemed to have rebounded from the meth landmine. But the moment they stepped back inside the cold house she was overwhelmed anew by feelings of anxiety and hopelessness. The fire in the hearth had gone out completely, although the log was barely charred. At least no residual foul odor tainted the interior. Yet there was something else in the house, intangible and unutterable but perceptible nonetheless – something that bespoke of late trespass. The back of her neck tingled. "You guys, I think that woman has been in here."

"What woman? The mother?" Billy asked.

She nodded.

Billy stooped to unzip his duffelbag, from which he removed a handgun. "Told you I was a redneck," he said tensely to his stunned companions. Maggie couldn't bring herself to scold him, nor, apparently, could the others.

They searched the house, including the closets, the garage, the side yard that had been Thumper's run, but discovered no signs of intrusion. Maggie was convinced, however, that Ruth Yeager had been there. Perhaps she'd come to plant more landmines. Though Maggie felt a little sheepish that they'd come across no evidence of an interloper, she was amazed that no one expressed the least doubt about her declaration. "Did you make sure the locks were changed?" Ryan asked as they reconvened in the living room. Tim relit the fire in the hearth.

"I just assumed," Maggie fumbled. "But then, maybe we didn't give the property manager enough time to see to the locks."

"That does it," Billy said. "No one sleeps here until the locks are changed."

Maggie threw Tim an imploring look before he could protest. "All right, all right," he grumbled, closing the fireplace screen. "In that case, let's stop wasting time and get started on the séance."

Diana folded her arms. "Before we do, I have to tell you, Billy, I have seriously mixed feelings about that gun. I'm glad you had it on the chance the crazy woman was still here. But in this atmosphere, I think having a gun around is like chainsmoking next to a powderkeg."

Tim looked rather satisfied, and Maggie expected Billy to take umbrage. But his expression was thoughtful. "I understand your concern. But what happens if even after the locks are changed that woman breaks in with a carving knife? She's obviously

unhinged."

"There's no proof she's violent," Diana reasoned. "And the atmosphere here – "

"Oh, just say it, Di," Tim interrupted. "The ghosts."

She rolled her eyes at him. "OK, what happens if the ghosts decide to play tricks

with our eyes, you shoot at what appears to be an intruder, and end up blowing a big hole

in one of us?"

"Can't we table the debate over gun control until after the séance?" Tim proposed.

"I'd rather we postpone the séance until we know the locksmith's been here,"

Maggie said, avoiding Tim's eyes. Let him think her a wimp childishly spooked by

Ouija boards. Misapprehension was still preferable to disclosing the actual cause of her

trepidation – her worry that he would be overtaken by another trance episode whether due

to a spiritual presence or the power of his own subconscious.

"Come on, Mags. She's not coming back tonight, not with all of us here and Billy

the Kid locked and loaded."

She relented. "OK, but this time I'm going to take the minutes. The last thing I

want to do is handle a wine glass." Especially given the possibility that Ruth had stashed

more temptations around the house.

Ryan cut the poster paper into small white squares, passed them along to Diana,

who marked them with block alphabet letters, plus "YES," "NO," and numbers 0-9.

They arranged the squares in a circle atop the pressboard dinette table. The overhead,

faux-chandelier lamp had a dimmer, which Ryan adjusted first to near-darkness, then,

reluctantly, to muted light to quell objections that no one could read the letters. Maggie took the precaution of sprinkling Father Bob's holy water around the table before claiming the newly purchased folding chair. She uncapped her pen and flipped the notepad over to a blank page.

Tim, Diana, Billy, and Ryan took the dinette chairs and leaned forward to touch their fingertips to the base of the upturned wine glass. "No jokes," Diana warned. Then she asked somberly, "Is there anyone here who would like to speak with us?"

No movement of the glass, no sound other than that of their own breathing. Maggie doodled absently but kept her eyes fixed on the glass, on Tim.

A minute, then another, of silence and no response. Diana spoke again. "Liz, you've shown yourself to Tim and Billy. Are you here?"

Still nothing.

"I guess we have to be patient," Diana said.

"We know you're listening, old man," Tim baited in a low voice. "Or are you afraid to show your real self to Di?"

"Timmy, we agreed to let me do the talking," Diana reproached quietly.

"But what if he really is too chickenshit to do anything in front of you?"

Maggie glanced at Ryan, who stared at the glass but was obviously suppressing laughter. Billy simply looked alert.

"I thought we were also trying to contact Liz," Diana rejoined.

"We're not gonna contact anybody if you two keep bickering like ten-year olds over the last Ding Dong," Billy said acidly.

"Let's not talk at all for a few minutes and just concentrate on the glass," Diana said.

Maggie supposed that the glass's motionlessness indicated that no one's subconscious mind was exerting undue influence. Or was it her own mind inadvertently willing the glass to remain still? She assumed she alone felt neither impatient nor disappointed with the lack of ghostly response so far.

Ten minutes must have elapsed before Billy finally spoke. "Why don't we give it a rest for a while?"

"No shit – my arm's starting to cramp," Ryan agreed, withdrawing his hand from the glass.

"I'm sure it's a trick," Tim said, leaning back in his chair. "Damn. What were you managing to write all this time, Mags? The great American novel?"

"Write?" she repeated, confused. "I was just doodling – " She broke off as she saw that not aimless scribbles but line after line of the page was filled with a cursive hand utterly unlike her own.

She flung away the legal pad as if it were toxic and leaped up. "I didn't write any of that!" Oh God, which of the dead souls had commandeered her hand to inscribe what she feared was some horrible, portentous message?

Tim dashed to her side. "It's OK, baby. It must be Alberto again. What does it say?"

"I'm afraid to look – no, Tim, don't pick it up! Please, let somebody else read it. Diana?"

Diana got up from the table, brightened the overhead light, and picked up the notepad. She frowned as she scanned the page, flipped it over to the next. Maggie was appalled. She'd had no awareness at all that she'd been writing, much less two pages' worth of scrawl.

"What's it say?" Ryan asked. "Is it in Spanish?"

"No, it's in English." Diana handed the legal pad to Billy. "You read it aloud. I'm feeling a little headachy."

"OK. It says, uh, 'The poison is the shame and secrecy. If he dies here he'll be trapped too. Leave, leave, leave. It's too late. Check the books. No, make her leave now.'" He cleared his throat. "I can't make out the rest – it's in some weird code or language … " He peered more closely. "I see. It's the same thing, only backwards. Then it's repeated again left to right."

"Maybe the ghost speaks Hebrew," Ryan cracked.

"Let me see," Tim said.

As Billy extended the pad a low moan sounded from the living room. A woman's moan. Maggie knew right away whose it was, knew even before they all hastened into the living room and froze, collectively aghast. Ruth Yeager slumped on the couch, eyes unseeing behind her tortoiseshell glasses, a horrible white viscous substance roping out of her gaping mouth and snaking into the air beside her, self-propelled, as if struggling to coalesce into a shape. Although the fire in the hearth still blazed, the room – or was it the substance itself? – reeked of sour body odor.

None of them could speak or move. The undulations of the mucus-like matter were almost hypnotic; the thick single strand apparently emanating from the woman's mouth was now sprouting multiple, wispy tentacles, one of which seemed to be crudely forming a hand with long stringy fingers.

The hand was reaching in their direction when Diana cried out, "I've got to help that poor woman!" Her words jolted the rest of them out of near-stupor. As Diana hurried to the couch, the white substance abruptly lost its animation and crumpled into an inert tangle of spiderweb-like filaments across the woman's body and onto the floor. The odor of perspiration receded.

"I knew she was here," Maggie whispered, holding fast to Tim's arm.

"That's Liz's mother?" Billy whispered back.

Maggie nodded, watching Diana feel for the woman's pulse, brush aside the grotesque threads to check inside her mouth and throat. "She's alive but unconscious," Diana said, gently shifting Ruth into a prone position, placing sofa cushions under her feet. "Somebody call 911."

The woman's eyes snapped open. She sat up ramrod-straight. "Where is my daughter?" she demanded.

"Ma'am, you need to lie back down," Diana urged.

Ruth glared past her at the others, her burning eyes fixing on Maggie and Tim. "My daughter is barely cold and you two are back to reconsecrate this house to Satan," she accused. "It's because of you that Elizabeth died. Don't try to deny it."

Despite the venom in her words and eyes, she spoke as calmly as if reciting a bus schedule.

Tim stared her down. "I'm calling 911 all right. This lunatic broke into our house. Is the phone in your purse, Maggie?"

Maggie barely heard him. She couldn't look away from the crazy woman, remembering all the more clearly the feigned kindness with which Ruth offered to assist her, along with the revelation that the old man was acting through this woman, animating

her no less surely than he had the hideous white substance.

Ruth stood, amazingly steady on her feet for a woman who had regained

consciousness mere moments before. "I'm leaving," she gloated. "You can't make me

stay. I'm the one who should report you to the police for bringing me here." She

straightened her blouse, then marched out the front door.

Astonished, they exchanged glances but no one seemed eager to speak. Maggie

was finding it difficult to shake the dream-like sensation that had befallen her from the

instant she saw Ruth on the sofa with that horrible living gunk streaming out of her

mouth.

"Am I the only one who thinks we should call the cops?" Tim challenged.

"I'd make sure our visitor didn't stash any more drugs before I invited the police

in," Ryan said. "And how the hell will we explain to them that godawful ectoplasm?"

"Ectoplasm," Diana echoed. "Yes, that must've been what it was."

Maggie observed that Diana appeared most shaken of them all. Tonight's

manifestation defied any desperate hope that the disturbances might be understood

scientifically.

"Why would we even have to mention that snot-like shit?" Tim asked.

"So you just want to tell 'em we found the woman plopped unconscious on the

couch?" Billy said.

"Why not? Take it from someone who knows, it's still a B and E. I'm sure glad

you brought that gun. She scares me a hell of a lot more than the ghosts."

Maggie sensed that Tim was becoming agitated. "Sweetie, your pacing's making me nervous. Come sit down by the fire with me."

Billy took a seat beside Diana. "Are you OK?"

She forced a tight smile. "Fine. Just a little freaked out."

"Join the crowd," Ryan said, sitting down on her other side. "I'm not spending the night here with Ectoplasm Woman running around with a house key."

"I thought that was already decided," Tim retorted. "So do we call the cops or not?"

"Yes," Maggie said. "They probably won't do anything, but I think we want to have it on record."

"In case she comes back and murders us," Tim elaborated.

Diana gave him a distasteful look. "We get the picture, Tim. But yes, let's call the police."

Billy and Ryan weren't as convinced. "You know they're going to see her as a pathetic grief-stricken mother," Ryan said.

"Who left of her own accord," Billy added. "Like Ryan says, we'd better triple-check that she didn't deposit more dope here. Talk about a set-up."

Maggie was anxious to leave. "I don't know. Maybe we should just call it a night and deal with Ruth in the morning. *After* I've called the locksmith."

"Not yet," Tim protested. "Aren't we at least going to discuss what happened and what it could mean?"

Once again everyone fell silent.

"Come on," Tim said. "Didn't I predict he would pull out all the stops tonight?"

"What do you want, dude, a blue ribbon?" Billy returned irritably.

"No, just for you guys to admit I was right."

"So what happened bolstered your argument that he wants to scare us out of here. What about the writing?" Billy said.

"I think Liz was doing the writing," Maggie ventured, trying not to shudder. "Didn't it say 'make her leave now'? That probably referred to Ruth."

Ryan retrieved the notepad. "'The poison is the shame and secrecy,'" he read. "I guess that could be an allusion to her drug problem."

"To the effects of this house," Maggie said.

"'If he dies he'll be trapped too,'" Ryan went on. "That's either a threat or a warning. Probably directed at Tim."

"When I saw her yesterday she said she was trapped with him," Tim allowed. "OK, I'm starting to buy that the message came from Liz, not the old man."

"But what does 'Check the books' mean?" Ryan wondered.

"Maybe the books you mentioned over dinner?" Billy suggested.

Tim's eyes lit up. "Wow, maybe. Mags, where are those books?"

"In Kat's room, I presume." She supported any interpretation likely to encourage him to return to Solana Beach.

Diana craned her neck to reread the notepad still in Ryan's hands. "I don't think the thing with Ruth was meant to scare us, per se. 'Make her leave now,' and then the writing gets confused, reversed. I think he staged that scene with Ruth as a warning to Liz."

"I disagree," Billy said, but his subtly pointed tone told Maggie and, she trusted, the others that he meant the opposite. He was cautioning them again against revealing their thoughts in the presence of the Shadow Man.

That was, of course, assuming the vicious entity didn't glean Billy's meaning as well.

The fog hugging the coast seemed not only denser but closer; over her shoulder the house disappeared before they had even swung right from La Amatista Road onto Camino del Mar north. If only it would disappear into the haze forever.

She asked him if he accepted Diana's notion that the macabre tableau in the living room had been enacted for the benefit of Liz's spirit. "Could be," he said. "Or he might've been killing two birds with one stone – warning her and freaking us out."

"Didn't it seem like he was deliberately not responding at the séance? That's why it makes sense the writing was Liz's. I wonder if she spoke Spanish. She might have guided Diana's hand last night."

"That was Alberto," he said stubbornly. "I feel it in my gut." He pulled into a liquor store lot. "I'm low on smokes. Need anything?"

A drink, desperately, which was the reason she opted to wait in the car rather than subjecting herself to walls and walls of bottles while he was buying cigarettes. She promised to honk the horn if Ruth emerged from the damp gray to accost her, but the five minutes it took for him to return were happily uneventful.

Back on the road he switched on the fog-lamps. "Talk about a night we all should've stayed put," he remarked, nearing Sierra. At the screaming siren of a fire truck behind them he jerked the wheel right to allow the engine to screech past and roar through the intersection at Via de la Valle. But they caught sight of it again less than a mile farther – in the parking lot of their own apartment complex. "Oh Christ," Tim swore, slamming on the brakes just short of the driveway.

"Tim, it can't be!"

"Want to bet?"

Another shrieking engine tore into the lot from Sierra. Even in the thick fog billowing black smoke was visible from the door and windows of their unit. For one irrational moment Maggie thought Kat and Thumper were within and started to run toward the apartment, but Tim restrained her. Other residents, some in pajamas and robes, huddled anxiously on the asphalt. "Those are the tenants!" One neighbor pointed them out to a firefighter in his yellow heavy gear and hat bearing a captain's insignia.

He jogged up to them. "Anybody else inside?" Behind him other firefighters aimed a large hose into the smoke.

"No, thank God," Maggie replied, shivering convulsively. "Is it only our apartment? How did it start?" As if she didn't already know.

"It's confined to your unit. Too soon to tell what may have caused it. You'd better look for another place to sleep tonight."

"I'm sure you'll find it was arson," Tim said, his voice level but tinged with anger. "There's this crazy woman who's been stalking us." He shot Maggie a glance that said *See? I told them all we should've called the cops.*

More smoke but no sign of flames. The captain took their cellphone number and assured them investigators would be in contact. From the amount of smoke Maggie knew that the fire, though short-lived, had been intense. She felt a sharp pang. How many of their keepsakes had been damaged or destroyed? Photographs, Kat's drawings and school papers, items of sentimental if not monetary value. Beloved books, home videos of Kat's birthday parties, their college graduation, wedding reception. Smoke and tears stung her eyes.

Another neighbor, a gay gentleman in his sixties they knew mainly from witnessing his regular harangues directed at skateboard-banging teens in the common areas, approached them. "Perhaps the damage won't be as extensive as you fear," he tried to console.

Maggie swiped at her eyes. "Thanks. We're just grateful our daughter and dog are with my parents this week."

"Yes, that's what's most important," the neighbor sympathized.

Tim looked even more shellshocked than he had upon discovering Ruth bathed in ectoplasm on the rent-a-couch. "This is unreal," he said woodenly. "What are we going to tell Kat?"

The neighbor, who introduced himself as Ben, invited them in for coffee, but they politely declined, preferring to wait for a last consultation with the fire captain. The fire crew appeared to be withdrawing the hose, and the smoke was now indistinguishable from the still dense fog. The fog had probably impeded the fire's spread, Maggie pondered, for the night air was so damp that her skin and clothing felt wet.

At last the captain returned to them. "We found some apparent traces of an accelerant in the smaller of the two bedrooms."

Maggie gasped. "Oh my God, our daughter's room."

"We can't say for sure until the arson investigators have a look in the morning. Right now we're treating the site as a crime scene, so unfortunately, you folks won't be able to get in to see what you can salvage until the tape comes down."

"I'm telling you, we know who's responsible," Tim said. He was pale, almost spectral.

"The arson team will be eager to hear about it," the captain said. "You can also refer your insurance representative to them."

"Jesus Christ, do we even have insurance?" Tim asked Maggie, despair darkening his eyes against the chalky white of his face.

"Yes, renters insurance, sweetie," she confirmed. She'd taken a policy out years before, around the time she'd made her first major upgrade to her computer system.

The captain chuckled. "My wife takes care of all our bills too. I hate paperwork." He started to move away. "Good luck to both of you. We'll be in touch."

They retreated to the car, where it was at least dry and relatively warm. Tim slammed a fist against the dashboard. "God-fucking-damnit!"

"I know, baby." Her own shock was giving way to a locust's swarm of worries and fears. How would they tell Kat? Where would they live? And what if Ruth, acting as instrument of the old man's malice, was not satisfied to destroy merely their property, their peace of mind, next time?

They were too numb, too disconsolate, to share the misfortune with anyone else tonight. Tim suggested they check into a modest beach motel for the night. "No, let's go to the Marriott. It'll be expensive but Allstate will probably reimburse us." Or so she hoped. Her primary concern was the additional security of a big bright chain-hotel compared to the uncomfortable accessibility of a humbler local inn.

Either he agreed with her rationale or was too weary to object. They drove in silence to the Del Mar Marriott just east of the 5, removed their overnight suitcases from the trunk, and checked in charging the room on Maggie's Visa card. Riding the elevator to the fourth floor, Tim remarked dully, "I can't even remember the last time I had a credit card. How useless am I?"

On a different occasion she would have tried to tease him out of his self-pity, but any capacity she had for levity, much less gallows humor, had run dry. What about in-progress work assignments lost on the computer in the fire? What about their tax documents stuffed into a night table? She was certain that Tim couldn't hate Ruth Yeager more than she did. Bad enough that the literally misguided woman had sneaked into the Del Mar house; the violation of their actual home, their child's home, felt as savage as a rape.

"I want to get drunk," she said to Tim, dropping her overnight bag onto the floor of this impersonally attractive hotel room they couldn't afford. She wasn't telling him so he might stop her; she was merely making known her intention.

He regarded her blankly, said nothing.

"I wonder if it would be cheaper to order wine from room service than to raid the mini-bar," she said, and then burst into sobs.

He began to cry as well, and for a long time they simply wept together, holding on to each other on the strange bed. She no longer craved a drink, only the oblivion it might have brought.

Her tears subsided an eternity later. "How do we begin to deal with this?"

His expression was empty. "We let the police handle Ruth – and we get the fuck out of town." His voice was weighted with defeat.

Alarmed by his tone, she sat up. "You don't mean that!"

"Like hell I don't. What if Kat had been home?"

Why wasn't she relieved? Hadn't she been begging him to reconsider the mad plan to force a confrontation with the Shadow Man, to accept instead Father Bob's recommendation that they move far away and try to start over?

He was surrendering, and she knew instinctively it would destroy him. "Kat's staying with Mama and Pa, whether she likes it or not, until we know it's safe. And even if Ruth is arrested, Tim, who's to say he won't find another proxy? You've been right all along – we need to defeat him once and for all."

"I'm not sure I know how anymore – if I ever did."

"But think about it. Despite the fire – "

"That's one big 'despite.'"

"Yes, I know. But hear me out. In the last twenty-four hours we've gotten two potentially valuable pieces of the puzzle – the little boy Alberto's possible role and this business about 'checking the books.'"

"The books are probably burned to a crisp. That's the obvious reason he sent loony Ruth over there to play with matches. Fuck, why did I stop for cigarettes? We might have gotten home in time to stop her."

Temporarily at a loss, she struggled to offer something of comfort. "Well, we don't even know for certain those are the books Liz was talking about."

At last a glimmer of interest from him. "What other books could she have meant?"

"Automatic writing – that's the phrase I've been trying to think of all night." It had been nagging at the fringes of her consciousness from the time she'd discovered the writing until – well, until the first fire engine tore into their apartment complex.

"Yeah. Didn't Yeats fool around with that?"

"Uh-huh. Claimed he based some of his later symbolism on it."

"Ah. So Liz might have been trying to write a poem," he joked grimly. "Fuck, we're all frustrated poets:

'If but some vengeful god would call to me

From up the sky, and laugh: "Thou suffering thing,

Know that thy sorrow is my ecstasy,

That thy love's loss is my hate's profiting!"

Then would I bear, and clench myself, and die,

Steeled by the sense of ire unmerited;

Half-eased, too, that a Powerfuller than I

Had willed and meted me the tears I shed.'

But not so,'" he quoted. The manic recitation appeared to have exhausted him.

"Very good," she praised wryly. "Or are you simply channeling the ghost of Thomas Hardy now?"

"'Check the books,'" he said slowly, as if he hadn't heard her. "To me, that sounds almost like accountant-speak. You know, as in 'doctoring the books.'"

"Could be. If he was listening in, he might have thought Liz was referring to those old books of yours. That doesn't mean she was."

"Where exactly did you find those books?"

So many details she hadn't told him, not because she'd meant to deliberately withhold them but rather because she'd inanely believed the Shadow Man was finished troubling them and thus the finer points of her account of the haunting were irrelevant. "I found them in the crawlspace above the downstairs closet. Where you used to hide from him as a kid."

He flinched. "Was anything else up there?"

"Your baseball mitt, which I also gave to Kat, and a box of table linens."

His pallor had turned faintly green. "That was a pretty big storage space, as I recall. We should look check it again – " He bolted up from the bed and dashed into the bathroom. She heard him retching through the closed door.

Was it finally becoming too much for them? She recognized that she herself was veering dangerously near her breaking point; what about Tim, whose life had seemed to career from trauma to trauma probably from the first time his grandfather raised a hand to him.

Several minutes passed after the sound of the toilet flushing, and he still hadn't emerged. Maggie got up from the bed and rapped lightly on the bathroom door. "Is everything OK, sweetie?" When there was no response she opened the door.

He was slumped on the floor between the toilet and the bathtub, his eyes open but heavy-lidded and sightless. He didn't react to her repeated cries of his name, her efforts to shake him out of stupor.

Tim, it appeared, had reached his breaking point.

CHAPTER 3

As Tim's treating physician, Diana insisted he be accorded priority triage status at the Scripps Hospital ER in La Jolla, and he was wheeled, still unresponsive, into an examination room. Maggie clasped his hand, scarcely hearing Diana's calm, clinical voice explain to the ER doctor Tim's drug history, his ingestion of a large amount of methamphetamine the day before, her treatment with medication of his extreme agitation. Maggie knew that Diana shared her own fear that Tim had suffered a stroke. Nor did Diana neglect to mention his "brief neurological episode" the night before; it was clear that she now regarded the "trance" as symptomatic, not supernatural.

Tim was taken off for tests, while Maggie and Diana waited in the examining room. It was more cubicle than room, actually, overlit and bounded by curtains. Diana explained various procedures – CT scan, ultrasound, EEG, MRI – but to Maggie they all sounded arcane and frightening.

"Wes thinks it's a stroke, doesn't he?" Maggie asked, dreading the reply.

"Unlike Senator Frist, Wes can't diagnose from afar," Diana said, trying without much success to forge a reassuring smile. "He wanted to come, too, but somebody had to stay with Brandon."

"The fire – it was just too much." Thank God she had resisted the mini-bar. What if she'd been drunk?

"Unreal. It's a miracle you both haven't broken down."

"Tim was ready to call it quits with the house. Why did I talk him out of it?" Anguished, she wondered if his uncharacteristic resignation derived from an instinct for self-preservation, if he'd sensed that the stress was becoming too much for him.

"Don't blame yourself. The meth was obviously the precipitating cause for – for whatever this is."

Meth, the shadow over them from the first night they'd met. Perhaps meth, and not the enduring malice of Tim's dead grandfather, had been the true Shadow Man all along.

The automatic writing, the ectoplasm, even the terrible coup de gras of the fire, seemed like the remotest of memories as she waited with Diana for news about Tim. Moaning from an adjacent cubicle: someone had broken a leg. The voice of a confused elderly woman asking whether she was at Scripps or Sharp. The impersonal cheerfulness of nurses and aides. And of course, the stinging antiseptic odor of hospital. *Please don't let him have had a stroke.*

She was too tense even to glance at her watch. At least an hour, maybe longer, dragged by before the stocky, babyfaced ER doctor returned. Preliminary test results did

not indicate stroke or another neurological abnormality, he said, although they couldn't

yet be conclusively ruled out. Tim remained mute and nonresponsive.

Maggie was both relieved and bewildered. "What could it be, then?"

"We'd like to admit him to psych for observation," the doctor stated.

She felt as if she'd been punched. "Are you saying my husband has lost his

mind?" Suddenly this possibility frightened her almost as much as the idea of a stroke.

Diana too looked stricken.

"Again, we have more tests to run," the ER doctor continued. "But he's

presenting catatonic features with no evidence of organic injury or anomaly. This isn't to

say his condition isn't substance related."

"And stress-induced," Diana pointed out. "Maggie, it's probably just temporary.

What is it called? – a 'brief reactive psychosis.'"

"That's so DSM-III, Doctor," the ER physician jested. "It's called 'brief

psychotic disorder' now, and yes, it's entirely possible that it's the proper diagnosis.

We'll know more over the next twenty-four hours."

As his "wife," Maggie completed the paperwork for his admission. One of these

days they had to get officially remarried, she thought in passing; what if the hospital had

required proof of his marital status? She and Diana were allowed to see him before he

was transferred to the psychiatric ward. He lay motionless on a gurney; his eyes looked

at them but didn't see them, and his face seemed chiseled in wax. He looked like a

beautiful cadaver.

She combed his hair with her fingers. "It's going to be fine, sweetie. You're going to be fine." She kissed his forehead.

And she wished she could curl up inside his injured psyche like a cat and soothe him to peace.

An hour later she was back in the hotel room at the Marriott, exhausted, disconsolate, and alone. The mini-bar no longer held the slightest allure. She stripped to her underwear and surrendered to the far stronger temptation of leaden and dreamless sleep.

She awakened at sunrise, overcome by anxiety, feeling inadequate to deal with the tangle of immediate concerns. Tim first. She called Scripps for an update. No change, but he was being treated with medication and a positive response might take some time. More neurological tests were scheduled for the morning, so she was advised not to visit before noon.

She ordered room service coffee, hoping a jolt of caffeine would compensate for the emotional energy whose reserves felt utterly drained. She gulped down a cup, then called the police to find out when she could survey the damage at the Solana Beach apartment. She was referred to the fire department's arson unit, and she arranged to meet an investigator at the apartment around eight.

There was no sense in calling her parents and Kat until she knew exactly how much of their home had been destroyed. She at once welcomed and dreaded Armando and Eva's inevitable sympathy, their promises of financial assistance. She was torn over whether to tell them of Tim's collapse. Trying to embrace the hope that his breakdown was a direct consequence of the meth and the trauma of the fire, she hesitated to frighten

Kat and her parents while there remained a chance he'd make a swift recovery. If only

the laptop, which she believed she'd last seen him using in the bedroom, had been spared,

she resolved to research "brief psychotic disorder" on her own. Diana was likely to soft-

peddle his condition to her, and the Scripps doctor had couched everything in vague

clinical terms, as wary of committing to a diagnosis as a ladies man was to one woman.

However, that the master bedroom turned out to have only minor smoke damage

was of marginal comfort against the shock of seeing how ravaged the rest of the

apartment was. She cried at the sight of Kat's bedroom in charred ruins, at the blackened

skeleton of the girlish wicker furniture, the clumps of ash that had been stuffed toys, the

closet full of incinerated clothes. The living room had not fared much better. Her

beautiful shabby-chic sofa from Maison Luxe was a blackened hulk, their entertainment

system, dining room set, shelves and shelves of books recognizable but both flame- and

water-damaged beyond recovery. Everything reeked of acrid smoke.

The arson investigator, a sharply dressed African American man in his forties,

explained that traces of lighter fluid had been detected in Kat's bedroom; in fact, an

empty can had already been discovered in a nearby dumpster. Plans were to canvass

neighbors, ask if any had seen or heard a possible intruder who had jimmied the sliding

glass door that opened on the patio. Omitting the detail of the ectoplasm, Maggie told

him about Ruth Yeager and her bizarre intrusion the night before at the Del Mar house.

"Tim and I think she may irrationally blame us for her daughter's suicide." She

confessed she had no idea where the woman was living, but was fairly sure the property

managers knew how to contact Ruth. Officer Gilbert assured her he'd look into it, gave her his card so she and her insurance agent – oh God, she needed to call Allstate too – could contact him. No Joe Friday automaton, he seemed sympathetic, even helping her throw some belongings from the master bedroom – clothes, framed photos, and yes, the laptop, which she'd located under the bed – into her car. Vandals weren't likely in this neighborhood, he offered, but why take a chance?

While she was driving back to the Marriott Diana called. "Wes talked himself in as a consult on Timmy's case. He's been at Scripps since seven, and he just confirmed to me that there's no way Tim had a stroke."

Maggie allowed herself to feel relief. By the light of day she could deal with crazy, but brain damaged was another story. "Now I guess we have to hope he responds to the drugs. Is it OK for me to go see him?"

"Wes said they're still running tests, but more to rule out than rule in. Why don't you go around lunchtime? I'll go when Wes gets back mid-afternoon."

She agreed; that gave her a couple of hours to call the insurance agent, her parents, and to find out anything she could about "brief psychotic disorder" on the Internet.

The Allstate rep promised to start the paperwork on their claim, but warned it would not be paid until a final report was issued by the arson investigators. Although she realized it was standard procedure, she resented the impersonal suggestion that they had staged the fire in order to collect on the insurance.

As for her parents, she found herself forced into the role of cool-headed consoler; Eva was this side of hysterical to hear of the fire, out-"what-iffing" even Maggie herself the night before, while Armando ranted about the shoddiness of the apartment complex and was insisting upon buying them a "more suitable" condo right away, threatening to do so by phone if need be. Maggie didn't disclose the arson aspect – better for her father to blame faulty wiring or construction – and told them that Tim had suffered only a panic attack they'd both mistaken as a coronary, and had been hospitalized as a mere precautionary measure.

Then Kat came on the line. "Our apartment burned down, Mommy?" she asked soberly.

Maggie wished she could embrace her daughter, so calm, so brave, as always. "It's going to be all right, baby. We can buy everything again brand new. That'll be fun, huh?"

"Is Daddy sick?"

"Just a little shaken up and tired. I'll give him a big hug from you."

"Mommy, why can't we move back to our old house?"

Maggie winced. She'd told her parents that she and Tim had been notified of the fire while at the "sobriety retreat"; Kat's question was a patent reminder of the big lie that had landed them in this unhappy situation. On the other hand, what if Ruth had tried to incinerate their apartment with all of them in it? *Stop, you're sounding like Mama.* "We'll decide all that later, sweetie," she said, wondering why Kat, who was so intuitive, remained so attached to the Del Mar house. Perhaps she associated it with her father's return.

Kat made her promise to visit Sugar now that they were "back," and Maggie asked her to try extra-hard to reassure her frantic Abuelita. After ending the call, Maggie opened the laptop and hooked up to the high-speed connection provided for the room.

Good God, 89 e-mail messages. She eschewed the mailbox to Google "brief psychotic disorder," but was soon frustrated by the sheer volume of information as well as by the impossibility, at least from her perspective, of establishing whether Tim's condition had been brought on by stress, drugs, or a combination of the two. Reluctantly she decided to leave his diagnosis to the doctors.

It was close to eleven; she might as well depart for the fifteen-minute drive to Scripps. Maybe the tests were over and Tim had been returned to his room.

He had not been, according to the staffer at the hospital's lobby-level general information desk, but Dr. Hewitt would be right down to meet her. Maggie needed a few seconds before she recalled that Hewitt was Wes's last name.

In a couple of minutes Wes stepped out of an elevator. She gave him a hug. "Some vacation, huh? How is he?"

"About the same," he said gently. "But Diana said she told you that there's no sign of organic abnormality. That's good news, Maggie."

"It is. But I just want him to snap out of this."

"I'm no psychiatrist, but I'm confident he will. I don't buy the notion he's an undiagnosed schizophrenic or schizo-affective."

"What?" She was incredulous.

Wes took her elbow. "Let's get some coffee in the cafeteria. And that's not the diagnosis, only a possibility the psych folks have been floating. I've told them that as the only one present who's known Tim for years, I disagree emphatically."

They purchased coffees and took a table in the busy, fluorescent-lit cafeteria. "What would even make them think he was schizophrenic?" she asked. "Schizophrenics are delusional, nonfunctional. I mean, aren't they? Dear God, you or Diana didn't tell

them about the haunting, did you?"

He chuckled dryly. "No. Jeez, that ectoplasm. Since we also believe that the

house is haunted, we'd be obliged to commit ourselves."

"I tell you, Wes, shrinks and their ilk are the crazy ones." She thought of the

psychological interventions foisted upon her at the place Tim had dubbed "Jeezopolis."

"Some of them, sure. I think in this case, it's a more of matter of prejudice about

patients with extensive drug histories."

She cocked an eyebrow. "Really?"

"Apparently it's become quite the rage in the addiction medicine community to

assign what they call a 'dual diagnosis' to almost every substance abuser they treat.

Again, I'm not a psychiatrist, and maybe in many instances it's valid. But when certain

diagnostic practices suddenly become ubiquitous, it makes me a little leery."

"Is this like every bratty kid being labeled ADD and put on Ritalin?" She was

comforted by his good-natured skepticism.

"You didn't hear that from me," he said with a wink. "But I was reading an

article in *The Nation* a while back called 'A Disease for Every Pill.'"

She couldn't have been more grateful for Wes's involvement in Tim's case. She

feared to think how she would have reacted to an unfamiliar doctor grimly telling her that

Tim was hopelessly, chronically psychotic.

But Wes's reassurance was no preparation for the psych ward and the fresh shock

of realizing this was where Tim had been placed. Not exactly a snake pit – no

straitjacketed lunatics shambling about the halls moaning and screaming at invisible tormenters. Everything was clean and bright. But the floor was locked, with the words

"ELOPEMENT RISK" printed prominently above the exit, and the few patients being led

to or from rooms by nurses wore the same dull, sightless expressions as Tim.

At the nurses station Wes introduced Dr. Crowe, a lanky man with a close-

trimmed graying beard and a full head of curly brown hair, as the psychiatrist assigned to

Tim. Dr. Crowe was as dry and dispassionate as – well, as Jack Emerson. "According to

Dr. Hewitt and Dr. Emerson-Hewitt, your husband has no history of catatonic episodes.

Is this also your experience?"

Catatonic. The word, finally uttered, chilled her. "Yes, and we've been together

for the better part of twelve, thirteen years." She made an effort not to sound hostile or

defensive.

"What about paranoia unrelated to meth use?"

She shook her head. "Tim's never been erratic when he's clean." He thinks

we're all in denial, she observed irritably.

"Has he ever been diagnosed with a personality disorder – borderline, antisocial,

et cetera?"

"I have no idea," she admitted, ridiculously remembering another of the facetious

Seven Deadly Personality Disorders: the Pluperfect Disorder.

"For the time being, our working diagnosis is brief psychotic disorder, substance-

related. Subject to revision depending on how long he remains symptomatic. Assuming

he recuperates within the protocol for BPD, I strongly recommend a course of inpatient

treatment for the drug problem. Our own McDonalds Center is tops in the county. You

might want to stop by there on your way out and pick up some literature."

"I will," she lied. "Can I see him now?"

"I'll take Maggie to his room," Wes offered. They moved away from Dr. Crowe and the nurses station sufficiently for Wes to add sotto voce, "Great bedside manner, eh?"

"Jesus. A shrink ought to have better people skills."

"Don't need people skills when you're mainly a pill dispenser."

"That reminds me – what kinds of drugs are they treating him with?"

"Risperidone. It's a nice little antipsychotic with minimal potential for side effects. And a sedative. He's going to be pretty groggy."

And so he was; his eyes were closed and he lay still as a corpse in the hospital bed, hooked up to IVs for medication, fluids, and nourishment. She touched his cool face, but he gave no indication he knew she was there. "How do we know he's not just sleeping?" she asked Wes.

Tim's eyes snapped open, but the brown orbs were hard and blank. "Backwards backwards backwards backwards backwards," he intoned under his breath.

"Timmy, it's me, Maggie."

But he seemed to be looking past her. "Backwards backwards backwards," he repeated.

Bewildered, she glanced up at Wes. "Is he getting worse?"

"No. He may need his meds adjusted." He leaned over to press the bedside pager.

"Come on, Wes, be straight with me."

"I am, honey. Catatonic patients don't always present with complete muteness or immobility."

Tim had fallen silent again, but his lips seemed still to be forming the same word. A psych nurse appeared, and Wes told her about the "vocalization." She didn't look especially alarmed, concurring that Dr. Crowe would likely want to increase the sedative component of the med cocktail.

Maggie kept searching his eyes for some spark of recognition. And what was the significance of "backwards"? Was it a reference to the backward writing they believed dictated by the spirit of Liz Yeager last night?

She stayed at his bedside, stroking his hair, until the nurse returned from her consult with Crowe and administered the additional dosage through the IV. Sleep overtook him quickly. Maggie kissed him. "I'll be back tonight, sweetie."

Tonight. No facing down ghosts this evening, nor, perhaps, ever again. She needed to tell Ryan and Billy the "house party" was over. Her heart sank at the prospect of more phone calls relaying more bad news. She supposed she could inform Billy in person, given her vow to Kat that she would visit Sugar. At once she longed to be at the barn, watching the horses and riders, breathing the hay-scented air. Petting Warlock, feeding him treats over which he'd slobber his gratitude. Literally homeless, she yearned for the stable's rustic welcome.

On the drive north she reflected on the bizarre course her life had taken from the time she and Kat first moved to San Diego County last summer. They had embarked upon a new life with such a sense of promise: a real house, not an apartment or condo, to live in, and one with an ocean view; the little community of horses, friendly faces, and essentially harmless busybodies just across the freeway at Camino Equestrian; a benign but enjoyable flirtation with Billy. But the interlude was spoiled by the Shadow Man crashing the party, insisting his toxic presence be acknowledged, poisoning her as insidiously as he had Tim. Was the Shadow Man gloating now, with their apartment destroyed and Tim hospitalized in a psychotic state? Or did he plan to humble them further, stopping only when they were all ruined? The desire for a drink still gnawed at her, even though that was what he wanted, too, to complement Tom's meth relapse and breakdown. Damn it. She resolved to call Father Bob if the craving grew any stronger.

The arena closest to Rhonda's school was a whirl of young helmeted riders on Easter break. The usual convocation of "moms" watched from the picnic table, and Rhonda stood near her tack room talking on the phone. Maggie's nostalgia made her feel guilty – after all, the innocent early weeks at the barn were ones during which she'd been determined Tim was no longer part of her life. She parked near the Tack 'n' Snack. She wanted to pick up some treats for Sugar and Warlock.

Kim waved from behind the counter. "Hey, stranger. Is Kat home from vacation yet?"

"Not yet," Maggie replied, hoping her pleasant tone didn't sound as forced to Kim's ears as it did to her own. She set a bag of Mrs. Pasture's horse cookies on the counter.

Kim rang her up. "Three twenty-one. Is Tim with you? I think Warlock misses him."

"No, he's busy. I'm afraid Warlock and Sugar will find me a poor substitute for Tim and Kat."

Kim grinned. "Not with those cookies they won't."

Stepping out of the store, Maggie scanned the back arenas for Billy. His truck was in the dirt lot, but all three of the back rings – the dressage, jumping, and all-purpose arenas – were in use by riders. She supposed he'd turn up somewhere.

She went to visit Sugar first, whose stall was in a breezeway. The sweet-natured palomino chewed her treat daintily while Maggie stroked her bose. "Kat loves you and misses you, Sugar," she cooed. "She'll be back before you know it." As soon as she said it she began to worry anew; notwithstanding her father's grandiose plans to purchase them a new home long-distance, Kat was due back in school this Monday, and they had no place to live other than a hotel room. And Kat would need a new uniform, school supplies …

"Hey, I thought I saw your car."

She looked up at Billy, ordered herself not to cry. "That crazy woman set fire to our apartment, Billy, and Tim's in the hospital."

"Jesus Christ, that's terrible! Is he gonna be OK?"

She realized she'd inadvertently implied that Tim had been injured in the fire. "We weren't home. Tim just kind of … " Her voice wavered. "He kind of lost it. He's been so strong for me the last few months, and the fire was simply too much."

Billy's expression was thoughtful. "That's still terrible. I'm really sorry, Maggie. I hope he's better soon."

"That's what I'm praying for. I want to kick myself for making most of the time since he's been home all about me and my drinking. And he gets this stubborn head of steam that makes me forget how fragile he is."

Billy gave Sugar a pat, then touched her arm. "Come on, let's go see Warlock."

Maggie presumed he felt uncomfortable talking about Tim; thus she was a bit surprised when he stayed on the subject as they strolled out of the breezeway. "Tim's not strong," he said, "but he's a fighter. Sometimes that's better than strong."

"You mean, as in better to be lucky than smart?" They neared the dry riverbed; Warlock's stall was in sight, and the keen-eyed Friesian spotted them. He whinnied in anticipation, dancing in front of the gate to his corral.

"Oh, Tim's smart – too smart for his own good." The familiar irony had crept into his voice. "But that's not the point. Taking care of someone who's fragile – but fights it anyway – is both a good thing and a bad thing."

The irony was gone. Indeed, he looked deeply sad, as she'd never seen him before. She stopped walking, despite Warlock's impatience ten feet away. "Does she fight it?" she asked quietly.

He shook his head. "No. She feels safe. Tim's probably never felt safe in his life."

Her eyes misted, not just for her own predicament or even solely for Tim's, but for Billy and his wife's. "What sad sacks we all are," she said with a pained smile.

"Eh, we're better off than a lot," he replied with a shrug. "My mother was a huge admirer of Rose Kennedy. Whenever anyone bitched and moaned about a run of bad luck, Mom always said, 'Think of everything Rose Kennedy has had to bear!' It was her Irish version of the starving children in India."

"You must miss her."

"Yep, that I do." He cocked his head toward Warlock, now kicking a large hoof against the lowermost pipe of his corral. "Let's stop torturing the big guy and give him a cookie."

Maggie knew he wasn't typically one to indulge a spoiled horse's demands, so she guessed he felt awkward discussing his late mother. Strange that he had mentioned only a hard-drinking stepfather. Something told her that his biological father had never played a significant part in his life.

Whatever the case, Warlock was undeniably thrilled for the company and horse cookies. He ate with more enthusiasm than any animal she'd ever seen, begging for a fresh treat before he'd even finished chewing the prior one, spraying streams of cookie-flecked saliva on the corral pipes, her arm, his own broad chest. She would recount his gusto tonight to Tim, whether he was aware of her presence or not.

And then she was seized by a bold impulse. "Billy, I want to ride Warlock."

He gave her a look. "To prove ... ?"

"To prove nothing. I want to ride him in one of the rings, maybe for fifteen or twenty minutes."

"OK. You want to use Tim's saddle or Nicole's?"

Maggie was surprised by his assent, having fully expected him to argue with her that Warlock was too big and headstrong and unpredictable, and she too inexperienced and stressed out. But her impulse didn't dissipate for his lack of resistance. "Tim's, I guess. Nicole rides English and I want something more to hold on to." She laughed darkly. "And no, this horse is not a phallic symbol."

"'Cept when he's dressed up like Tinkerbelle. Who said he was a phallic symbol?" He grabbed Warlock's halter looped over the gate, slid it over the horse's broad nose.

"I just don't want you to think this is some kind of symbolic gesture," she said. Watching him lead Warlock out of the stall, she was excited rather than nervous, wishing that Kat were present to witness her finally getting astride any horse.

"Sometimes a horse is just a horse," he quipped.

He guided Warlock into the crossties and secured the chains to each side of the halter. Maggie curried Warlock's coat but gladly allowed Billy to pick those gigantic hooves and put on the blanket, saddle, and bridle. Unlike Tim, she had no choice but to use the mounting block to get on the horse. Billy held him steady as she stepped into the left stirrup and swung her right leg over to reach the other. How broad Warlock was – her inner thighs stretched to their limit across his massive back. Billy shortened the stirrups for her, adjusted the reins in her hands. "Hold 'em just like two ice cream cones," he advised.

"I think I remember that." Her heartbeat quickened, but she felt no fear, and she tapped her heels against Warlock's sides.

He moved ahead of the mounting block at a lazy pace, Billy strolling alongside. She needed a few moments to orient herself to being so high up, several more to relax into the motion of his walk. On Billy's insistence she'd borrowed a helmet from Kim. She urged Warlock into the now empty dressage arena with its iceplant rather than fenced perimeter. Warlock lowered his head to munch on the iceplant, stretching the reins against his bowed neck. "Don't let him do that," Billy called, just outside the ring. "The world isn't his salad bar, and you're in the saddle to ride, not to let him stuff himself."

She gave Warlock another gentle kick, and he reluctantly lifted his head to resume his leisurely if heavy-hoofed amble. She circled the arena twice, focusing on the movement, the light wind against her face and rippling his long mane, the occasional flicker of his ears. "How do I get him to trot?" she asked Billy, who supervised, arms folded at the top of the arena.

"Give him a sharp kick with both heels and make a clicking sound. And prepare yourself – he's got a big bouncy trot."

No exaggeration there; the bumpy verticality of his gait almost startled her right out of the saddle, and she instinctively yanked on the reins, halting him. "Damn it. He just caught me off-guard."

"You probably want to try posting."

She looked at him sheepishly. "What's posting, again?"

"Push yourself up in the saddle with each beat of the trot, moving with his outside shoulder."

She'd seen Kat and other riders "post" a thousand times. Warlock's trot was still bouncy and lumbering, but by posting she no longer felt in danger of losing her balance.

Unwilling to press her luck, she limited her ride to just over twenty minutes. It was a good thing, too, for when she dismounted her legs were rubber and Billy had to prop her up. "Don't you want to canter him too?" he teased.

She felt exhilarated, proud of herself regardless of her wobbly legs. Yet the enchantment dissipated only moments after her feet touched the ground, and worry reclaimed her with a vengeance. How could she have been gallivanting around on Warlock with her family's residence in literal ruins, her child bereft of all her worldly belongings save for a spaniel and a horse, Tim catatonic in a psych ward? She had to –

"Stop, Maggie," Billy said gently. "Take a few minutes to rest on your laurels." He touched her face, and for an awful instant she feared he would kiss her and she would let him. But he turned away to refasten the crosstie chains to Warlock's halter.

Blushing, she was relieved his attention had shifted to Warlock. "I have to go. I'll talk to you later."

And because she was craving a drink more keenly than ever, she drove directly from the stables to the St. Thomas Aquinas rectory in search of Father Bob.

Even though he was a priest, she anticipated some hint of "I told you so" in his reaction to their ill-fated sojourn at the house. But his primary response was concern – for Tim, obviously, but also for her. "Promise me you won't go back to that house," he said. "Let me appeal again to the bishop about an exorcism."

"I'm fine with that." She sipped the coffee the housekeeper had brought her. "Tim and I talked facetiously about burning the house down. It's as if the old man knew it, too, and sent that madwoman to set fire to our apartment."

"I hope the police have her in custody, for her safety as well as yours. Will they call you?"

She massaged her forehead. "Yeah. Or maybe I'm supposed to call them." She was becoming punchy from worry and fatigue.

"I'd like to visit Tim tonight, if that's all right with you."

"Of course. We could sure use a miracle."

"He fought his way back from addiction, Maggie. I'm confident he'll fight his way out of this."

"I worry so much about him. What if one of these days he has no fight left?"

"God's not like Tim's grandfather, even though I sometimes fear he conflates the two. I do believe in God's mercy. I hope you can believe in it, too."

"'The quality of mercy is not strained,'" she quoted automatically. "Ought we to show mercy, then, toward Ruth, or even toward the soul of that wicked old man?"

"For that poor deranged woman, certainly. And I'll say a Mass for the late Dr. Emerson's soul. As for you and Tim, the best way to show the grandfather mercy is to remove yourselves from the reach of his influence."

She started to rise from the comfortable leather chair, but a sense of unfinished business urged her to remain seated. "One more thing, Father. I can't believe this happened in light of the fire and Tim's breakdown. It's almost as bad as drinking, but … today, when I was at the stables, I found myself physically attracted to someone else. It was just for a moment, but I feel like for that moment I was betraying Tim."

He regarded her kindly. "We're not Protestants, Maggie. Unlike our friend Jimmy Carter, we don't have to flog ourselves over having 'lust in the heart.'"

"I love Tim, and more, I'm *in* love with him. He's always been the one. How could I have even momentarily wanted anyone else?"

"Saint Francis referred to the body as 'Brother Ass,' as you probably remember from catechism. It's the nature of mules to be contrary." He was smiling, but his eyes were serious. "As a fellow alcoholic, though, I'm glad you let this off your chest.

Especially at a time like this, excessive self-recrimination can put you on a path toward drinking."

"Damn that Brother Ass," she said wryly. "I'm glad I told you too. I may be making a real pest of myself for the next few weeks, Father."

He rose with her to press her hand warmly. "You could never be a pest, Maggie. And I'm not saying that because I'm a priest, or an alcoholic. I know pests when I see them, and see them I do, I have to admit."

"I'll let them know to expect you at the hospital," she said. "Maybe Tim can absorb a little of your faith through osmosis."

"Try to have faith, too, Maggie. Be careful, but don't forget to have a little faith."

Ryan met her at the hospital, insisting she let him take her to dinner after she saw Tim. She'd called him to deliver the latest bleak news on the drive to La Jolla, and with UCSD just across the freeway, he left work early to catch up with her at Scripps. "Why don't you crash with me until you find a place to live? The Marriott must be a fortune."

"I can't plan for anything until Tim's better."

Ryan offered as well to visit Tim with her, but Maggie asked him to wait in the lobby instead. She knew Tim, were he able to choose, would rather none of them see him in his current shape. She rode the elevator up to the psych ward alone. Dr. Crowe was not on the floor; a nurse introduced her to another psychiatrist, a pretty Indian woman named Dr. Thekdi. Although Dr. Thekdi's manner was less clinical than Crowe's, she regretfully told Maggie that Tim's condition was the same.

Maggie fought despair. "You don't think this proves he's schizophrenic or something like that?" she had to ask.

"From everything you and his brother-in-law and sister have said, he seems too high-functioning for that particular diagnosis. The main complication is his history of long-term methamphetamine dependency."

"Until Monday night, he'd been clean for over seven months," Maggie said.

"Until Tim becomes responsive we're fumbling a bit in the dark," Dr. Thekdi admitted. "But I'm wondering if the heavy meth use might have masked an affective illness."

"You mean, like manic-depression?"

"Maybe."

Maggie chewed her lower lip, thinking. While this possibility struck her as less alarming than that of schizophrenia, she still found it hard to believe that he'd been suffering all along from a serious emotional disorder. His bursts of energy, incapability of deep sleep, and flashes of impulsiveness seemed to her habits engrained by crystal, ones that would probably require years rather than months to unlearn. Nonetheless, she granted that Dr. Thekdi was right insofar as the nature of his problem was impossible to determine so long as he remained unresponsive.

Diana sat at Tim's bedside, reading aloud to him from the LA *Times* sports page. Baseball stories. "I'm taking the chance that any sensory stimulation is helpful," she explained. "It's completely unscientific."

Maggie perused his stony, mask-like face, half-open staring eyes. "Come home, sweetie," she said, caressing his face. The gesture recalled to her Billy's fleeting touch, and she felt herself color.

But if Diana noticed she didn't mention it. "My mother called today. I didn't tell her about Tim. Wes thinks I should have."

"Oh no, I agree with you. He wouldn't want them to know."

"Wes's thinking is that since they helped do this to him, they ought to see the consequences." Diana looked distressed. "And here I am, enabling their denial as always."

"Even if you are, Diana, I still think you're doing the right thing. He'd hate for Jack and Beth to see him this helpless."

"There's something else," Diana said. "Mother said she found a big box of our grandmother's picture albums in the basement. I'm having her Fed-Ex it to me at the hotel."

Maggie was intrigued, despite her promise to Father Bob about putting the house and its influence behind them. "Wow, I wonder what you'll find."

"After last night I'm as determined as you guys to get to the bottom of what's going on. Any news on that Ruth woman?"

"Not yet. I'm almost relieved Tim's in a locked ward if she's still running around."

"I hear that. What would you think if Wes and I checked out of the Four Seasons and took a room at the Marriott where you are? It's a lot closer to Scripps and we can all hunker down in case Ruth's still at large."

"That'd be great," Maggie said, meaning it. "But what about the Fed-Ex package?"

"It should arrive tomorrow morning. We'll wait to check out until we get it."

"I suppose it's too much to hope that the box will give us a few clues about why your grandfather was so vicious."

"Who knows? Mother didn't even bother to look. She's made her life's work nurturing a lack of curiosity."

Maggie felt sorry for Tim and Diana. How lonely it must be for them to hold their parents in such contempt. Perhaps that was why the siblings each had chosen a partner whose disposition was nothing like that of Jack or Beth. Wes was warm, fun-loving, compassionate, while she herself was anything but uncurious. Just because she'd promised Father Bob she'd steer clear of the house didn't mean she couldn't help Diana root through the Fed-Ex box in good conscience.

Soon as I get out of here I'm going to take a long hot shower in a clean private bathroom. No, better still, I'm going to rip off all my clothes and jump naked into the ocean and I'll drown myself if someone calls the cops or maybe even if someone doesn't. I don't care if it's cold. I don't care if I die because it's better to burn out than to fade away

Why is this train moving backwards? Backwards backwards backwards. I'm getting motion-sick. Backwards and too fast. Don't hurl or he'll call you a pussy. Maggie's a blur at the station. The station's just a dark space in the smoke

OK, I can deal with this. As long as I've got crystal I can deal with all of it. It's not a bad bargain when fucking God knows I don't exactly have many options. And I've always known how to hide pain. He taught me that much. Don't think about it, don't puke or else Ed might cut off the crystal. With crystal I can get through anything

Dead now. Peaceful. Calm kaleidoscope glitter. Little candle flickering. Quiet. Quiet. Ssh. Pure quiet. Safe quiet. Poor raped murdered Tim. I'm not Tim. Warm cool quiet

Holy shit, no! No! This isn't real – don't let them, don't pin back my bad arm it's full of screws and pins Jesus Christ no one to help no one ever helps. He's back from the dead and it's him, they're all him, his smell his grunts and he's fucking won again, waiting and waiting all these years he's one again

Backwards backwards

Don't show fear. I'm so fucking scared. Goddamn Andy Chase and his paranoia. Goddamn the fucking cops. Mags swears she'll wait, she'll visit every week God I hope I can get some drugs in there. Don't tell Kat I'm a con, Maggie – tell her I did something noble, joined the Peace Corps or Shining Path. Ha, I've never done anything noble in my life. Even Kat probably knows that. Damn Andy and his fucking paranoia

Divorced. She says she still loves me but she doesn't. We're divorced now. She'll find someone else – what fucking slob wouldn't be a step up from a tweaker? Where is that son of a bitch with the crystal? It's only been twenty goddamn minutes? Can't be, my watch must be wrong. Wish I could blow my brains out. Oh God I gotta slam. Hurry the fuck up! I hear a car – no, it's some goddamn UPS truck. Ha ha, what can Brown do for you? Bring me some fucking meth, that's what, ha ha ha. Maggie, Maggie – mi pequena flor. Help me to die

Jesus Christ I've been shot! Oh my fucking God my arm my arm and why didn't I throw a curve outside my arm my arm my arm

Will this backwards train ever slow down I can't see a damn thing just the blurred crystals of the kaleidoscope Di gave me for my sixth birthday but it's broken all I see is blur racing by

Don't stop here! For Christ's sake, don't stop here – don't slow down now. Don't make me go back there. Please God don't stop here –

'Cept for baseball I hate summer. Sometimes I think I should try to flunk a subject so I'd have to go to summer school. But then Dad would get mad and wouldn't be proud of me. And mom would complain how hot it gets in Pasadena and Di would sulk about not getting to see her Del Mar friends. So no matter what it'd be my fault.

Just like Father Avila said in confession when I told him I hated my granddad and wished he would die. Father said that's a sin and told me if I tried harder to be good Granddad wouldn't hit me. How much does that suck? Grownups sure aren't good at listening. Unless it's like a school thing where you have to memorize a poem or something dumb like that.

Granddad thinks I'm the one who doesn't listen. "That'll teach you to listen," he says after he hits me. Dad and Mom also say just listen to your grandfather and then he won't hit you. But I hear him all right, even though he never yells. It's just that I like to run up and down the stairs. I do it at home all the time and no one gets mad. I like to run. Dad says it's 'cause I'm a born athlete. But he never takes my part when we're in Del Mar.

And sometimes I make Granddad mad on purpose, because I hate him and maybe if I can just make him mad enough he'll drop dead. Like the time I told him fuck you. None of them even thought I knew that word. Granddad hit me that day with the dog chain so many times on my butt and back and legs and when I tried to get away he punched me in the stomach so hard I couldn't breathe. Grandma finally said That's enough, Charles, real calm as if asking him to turn down the sound on the TV. Dad and Mom told me to never use that word again and if I hadn't hurt so bad all over and could breathe better I would have said fuck you to them too. They sent me upstairs without dinner but I hurt too much to be hungry, even when Di snuck me a tuna sandwich a couple hours later.

Today was an OK day, I guess. Granddad only hit me once, for feeding crackers to the seagulls on the deck. All these birds – hundreds, I bet – came swooping over and covered everything with birdshit. I thought it was funny but Dad and Mom didn't and Granddad hit me with his belt. But at least I still got to go to the Del Mar Fair with Alberto and his mom. Get that brat out of my sight, Granddad said, so it worked out for me. At the fair we played some rigged games – I won a cheesy windup toy for popping a balloon with a dart – but mostly we ate all kinds of good junk like cotton candy and corndogs, and rode pretty much every ride. I'm really tired but it was an OK day.

Oh yeah, Alberto told me something kind of weird when we were on the Ferris wheel. He said he could read minds. I tested him and thought of the number five, and he guessed it. Then I thought how much I hated Granddad and he guessed that too. It was really cool. I promised not to tell anyone because he said his mom told him people would think it was the Devil. I swore not to say anything but I told him there was no such thing as the Devil – the priests and nuns just make that stuff up to scare kids into being good. Besides, if there was a Devil, he didn't have horns and a pitchfork. He was Granddad. Alberto got this funny grin and said he knew what Granddad thought, too, and it was really bad, but his mom said he could never tell because she'd lose her job and they'd have to go back to Mexico. What's wrong with Mexico? I said. Fernando Valenzuela's from Mexico so it has to be a neat place. But I didn't really want to know what Granddad was thinking anyway. Maybe it's that he's the one who wants to kill me. I don't think he would 'cause then he'd have to go to jail and everyone in the family would be embarrassed.

I'm so sleepy I can't think anymore. Sometimes I hate it when I think so much, but Dad says that's what will make me a great major league pitcher. For the Dodgers, I hope. So sleepy. No more thinking. Who is this man I see with my eyes closed, this tall man with messy hair and big worried eyes? Why's he telling me to open my eyes? Go

away, mister, I'm sleepy. I'm sorry you look so scared but I want to sleep. Sleep sleep.

He's hard to see in the fog and his voice – open your eyes! *– is fading. Sleep.*

CHAPTER 4

Safe in her hotel room for the night, Maggie found a voice-mail message from the arson investigator Officer Gilbert, informing her that the arson team had yet to track down Ruth Yeager. He was, however, confident they would be able to locate her. Too worn out to contemplate Ruth's whereabouts, Maggie decided to trust Gilbert's reassuring tone along with the double lock on her room door.

She slept, really slept, for the first time in two days. In her dreams she wasn't safe at all. She and Kat were driving down the freeway toward Scripps Hospital, pursued by Ruth in a speeding white sedan that loomed more and more massive in the rearview mirror. Maggie wanted to go faster but Kat kept begging her to slow down. "You'll get a ticket, Mommy!" Maggie tried to explain why a speeding ticket was the least of their worries but the words wouldn't come out right.

Then her car spun out of control, hitting the center median. It kept spinning and spinning like a wildly malfunctioning carnival ride. Kat was squealing, but in delight, not fear. "He can read minds, Mommy! But we can't tell anybody."

At last the car stopped spinning, and a police cruiser drove up. Ruth and her white sedan were nowhere to be seen; the freeway was virtually empty save for the police car and her own. Tim climbed out of the cop's passenger seat, unperturbed and eating cotton candy. He was sporting a bad haircut. "He won't kill me," he said matter-of-factly. "He doesn't want to go to jail." He handed the cotton candy to Kat. But Maggie was afraid to leave the car, afraid of the police, for at once she realized she was drunk. There was even an empty wine bottle in the backseat.

Panicked, she tried to restart the car, but the engine was dead. A grim-faced cop was moving toward her, hand on his gun. Tim and Kat had disappeared, and the policeman was barking at her to come out with her hands up. Then he metamorphosed into the old man, Tim's grandfather, and he was smiling insincerely. "This has all been one big misunderstanding, senorita. Timmy's a crazy little liar."

"You're the liar," she spat.

A fire truck tore up. "You call for the jaws of life?" the chief asked Tim's grandfather.

"It's kinder to let him die," the old man gloated.

"Tim!" Maggie screamed, noticing him sprawled unconscious on the right embankment. "Open your eyes, sweetie! Open your eyes!"

His eyelids didn't so much as flutter.

She woke herself up.

Why's this pretty lady bugging me now to open my eyes? Grownups sure suck.

When she called the hospital at dawn, the shift nurse told her that Tim had become agitated in the middle of the night and that once again his medications had been adjusted. Agonized, Maggie prayed her dream was no premonition. He was alive but he was suffering, and it was all because of the Shadow Man.

How strange it was, she mused pensively; she'd known him since they were both twenty, lived with him for years, married and divorced him, borne his child, but were it not for the Del Mar house, he might well have told her nothing of his traumatic childhood. Indeed, that was clearly what he'd preferred. To her endless *why?*s about his drug obsession he'd offer only the explanation that he was a fuckup. Was it the family legacy of denial, about which Diana was so bitter, that accounted for his reticence? Or was it guilt, shame, some core certainty that he'd deserved the abuse, probably aggravated by Jack Emerson's excessively high demands and expectations? Oh, if only Tim had confided in her, how much more patient and understanding she'd have been about his drug problem. Or would she? What if she'd turned it back on him, accused him of making excuses for his misbehavior? Regardless of their countless discussions about how the buzz-phrase "personal responsibility" was right-wing code for blaming the poor and people of color for systemic injustices, living with a drug addict tried the patience of Penelope, and God knew her forbearance had been tested. The trope of "personal responsibility" might well have been a useful weapon against her own frustration.

She recognized that she couldn't keep her word to Father Bob. She couldn't leave the house alone – the old mad had to be forced to answer for what he'd done to Tim. Tim had to be revenged.

At once she felt stronger than she had in months.

She was preparing to leave for Scripps when Diana appeared at her door carrying a large cardboard box. "Can you believe Fed-Ex came at seven thirty? Wes is downstairs with Brandon checking in."

Maggie regarded the box dubiously. "Tim had a bad night. Maybe we should do this later."

"I know. But at least he's comfortable now. We can go through the box after we see him. It's up to you." Diana set the carton on the dresser.

Maggie quickly decided that it might be more helpful to Tim if she discovered something pertinent in the box rather than spending the morning staring at him in his drug-induced semiconsciousness. "No, let's look now. Maybe there'll be an old family exorcism recipe in here."

"Wouldn't it be a hoot if my meek little grandmother was a practicing witch?"

"Or if she secretly poisoned him to death with her elderberry wine."

They say down on the bed and opened the box. The top item was a photo album. Maggie felt a twinge, thinking of her own photographs lost in the fire. But her sadness turned to revulsion at the first picture inside the album. A wedding photo. Of course, he wasn't old in it, just a tall, clean-cut ordinary man in a tuxedo, next to a sweetly smiling bride. "Yuck," Diana said, turning the page. Fortunately, the late Virginia Emerson had arranged the album chronologically, allowing them to skip through a variety of vacation shots, more wedding pictures, this time of Jack and Beth. They came across baby pictures of Diana and Tim, First Holy Communions, family Christmases in Pasadena.

"No summer photos in here," Diana remarked. "I hate to say it, but the only one I remember taking pictures in Del Mar is my dad."

"Well, let's see what else is in here. I wonder how the box I found in the crawlspace got separated from these things."

"Who knows?" Diana lifted another worn-looking album, marked "My Scrapbook," from the box.

At first glance this album too appeared to contain inconsequential items. Charles and Virginia's wedding notice, marriage license. Jack's – more properly "John Charles Emerson's" – Catholic school report cards. Copies of father and son's medical diplomas from Northwestern and USC, respectively. A souvenir menu from Antoine's in New Orleans, a homemade birthday card from Diana to Grandma. "All of this is rather sad," Diana said. "She saved these things and nobody even bothered to look. And I don't really want any of – " She broke off as she flipped open one of the last, blank pages.

"What?"

"Oh my God." Diana scanned a folded, yellowed newspaper section. "Here's – oh my God – the skeleton in the closet." With a trembling hand she extended the paper to Maggie.

It was the local section of the Chicago *Tribune*, dated January 24, 1967, and the headline just under the fold read "*Child Recants: Evanston MD Cleared of Molestation Charges.*"

According to the story, Dr. Charles Emerson, family practitioner, had been accused of sexual abuse by a seven-year-old boy patient. His license had been suspended while the police conducted a three-month investigation that culminated with the child's admission to his mother that he'd made the story up. "Jesus Christ, Diana! Your parents had to have known. How could they have subjected you and Tim to this monster?"

"He retired to California the same year. I'm sure Mother and Dad believed he was innocent."

"Do you?"

Diana shook her head. "Someone capable of such cruelty to a child – why wouldn't he be a molester too? Oh God, what if Tim's repressed the memory and it's finally caught up with him?"

"I don't think so, Diana. Repressed memory's been more or less discredited, right?"

"Yes, it has," Diana conceded.

"Besides," Maggie went on, "I think that what happened to him in prison would have brought it back to him if he'd somehow forced himself to forget." She shivered. "I believe ... I believe he beat Tim because it was some kind of perverse outlet for his pedophilia. The old man was the one doing the repressing, if you ask me."

The blood had drained from Diana's face. "Yeah. That's it, isn't it. All that twisted, frustrated desire. But why in God's name can't he let it go? Why didn't it die with him?"

"Check the books," Maggie recalled. "These must be the books that Liz was talking about – writing about, I mean." The old man's influence obviously didn't extend to his daughter-in-law in Pasadena. "Maybe this is what he never wanted us to know." But it didn't quite add up. In death Charles Emerson didn't seem driven by a warped undying lust so much as by an undying hatred.

Diana clearly agreed. "I have a feeling there's still more to this. Shall I call my parents and confront them with what we now know about Granddad?"

"Only if you're reasonably sure they won't just insist that the case was dropped and he was cleared."

"Ha. I'm reasonably sure that's exactly what they'll do."

"I just thought of something else." Maggie swallowed hard. "What if he molested that little boy Alberto? The cleaning lady's son."

Diana looked ill. "Oh Jesus. It's starting to fit together. Tim's right – we need to track down Alberto or his mother."

Maggie's horror was shifting to a strange exhilaration. "It *does* all fit together, Diana! Alberto ... 'check the books' ... and remember, Billy said that when he saw Liz's ghost her words were either 'my mother' or 'the mother.' I think Liz is trying to help us. I think the only way she can be free is for us to figure him out and destroy him."

"Poor Liz. Then we have to help her, too."

"It's all so horrible, so tragic."

"Thank God he died before I had Brandon. I'd have killed him if he so much as looked askance at my son." Diana was crying. "Why didn't I try harder to stop him from hurting Tim? I was a teenager, I knew it was wrong. I should've called Child Protective Services."

Maggie hugged her. "Need I remind you that you saved his life when you got him back into rehab?" Yet she understood how Diana felt: that irrational desire to intervene in the past, to wrest control retroactively of the events that had bodied forth so much anguish.

An hour later they drove to the hospital together, sufficiently composed to put on benign faces on the chance that Tim could sense their presence or, better still, had regained lucidity. "I wonder if we should hire a detective to find Inez and Alberto," Diana mused.

"That's not a bad idea. But it would be expensive."

Diana shrugged. "They charge by the day, and I bet this job wouldn't take very long. And don't worry about the money, Maggie. We know you guys are strapped."

Once upon a time, it seemed, she'd been able to support Kat and herself with no assistance from anyone. Finances had been tight, certainly, but she'd somehow managed. For the thousandth time she wondered if the late Virginia Emerson's bequest had been more curse than boon.

I can't figure this out how I can be sleeping, with my eyes closed, and still seeing him. That tall guy with the big worried eyes. The pretty lady's gone but he's still here, bugging me about the same old thing – "Open your eyes." He's almost as big a nag as Granddad is about the stairs, only this man doesn't seem angry or ready to hit me if I don't do what he says.

"I need to catch him watching me sleep," the guy pesters.

It's funny but I can argue with him without having to talk. What does that have to do with me? I ask. And besides, if you're asleep what do you care if someone's watching or not?

He kind of laughs. "The old epistemological conundrum, eh? The tree in the forest."

I'm not even sure he's speaking English anymore, so I don't answer.

"If I don't look then I'm no better than Dad or Mom refusing to see what's right under their noses," he keeps up.

If he's talking about his dad and mom, they sure sound a lot like mine. I'm starting to feel bad for him. It sucks to have parents like that, almost as much as it sucks to have a grandfather like Granddad. If I open my eyes, I say, will you leave me alone?

He nods. "I promise."

Oh, OK then, I say. I open my eyes.

Oh my fucking God! It's him!

Dr. Crowe met Maggie and Diana just inside the "elopement" door. His expression was grave. "An hour ago he became extremely agitated. He's heavily sedated now, but don't be alarmed by the restraints."

"Restraints?" Maggie repeated, frantic. "You mean he was moving around? Was he saying anything?"

"He was screaming 'no' and 'oh my God.' Typical psychotic verbalizations, I'm afraid."

Maggie broke away and hurried to Tim's room, Diana at her heels.

Tim no longer looked semiconscious; he was unconscious, heavy brown bands securing his arms to the bed. "They've knocked him out like a light," Maggie despaired. "How can we tell anything about his condition when he's like this?"

"I'm professionally obliged to trust my colleague's judgment," Diana said, though with a pointed lack of conviction. "I guess all we can do is wait out the sedation."

"What if he'd been coming to his senses and simply panicked to find himself in a psych ward?" Her frustration mingled with hope.

"I don't know, Maggie. I hope that's the case. Speaking off the record, I'd love to see Crowe proven wrong."

What a shame that the more sympathetic Dr. Thekdi had not been on duty during the episode of supposedly "psychotic" agitation, Maggie rued. But Diana was right; at this point they could do little more than wait.

By tacit agreement they didn't discuss the revelation discovered in Virginia Emerson's old scrapbook. In fact, they didn't talk much at all, their eyes fixed upon Tim. *Watching him sleep.* The notion now made her skin crawl. She was more convinced than ever that locating the adult Alberto and/or his mother would produce the final piece of the puzzle.

She found herself praying in earnest. Let him be all right, let us all be all right. Whether there was a god to hear her she had no more idea now than she had before the Shadow Man seeped into her life, and she didn't want to dwell on what the house's terrible phenomena bode for the nature of an afterlife. Nonetheless she prayed out of habit to the God and Jesus and Virgin Mary of her childhood, for regardless of their reality, they were enduring symbols of an unseen force for good. That, most of all, was what she hoped really existed.

Finally came a deep, drowsy sigh; he was stirring. Maggie bent over his bed. "Fuck," he mumbled under his breath, his lashes fluttering. She saw his wrists strain against the binds.

He seemed struggling to focus his heavy-lidded eyes on her, on Diana. "Take it slow, sweetie," Maggie said tenderly.

"I wanna leave," was his hoarse reply. He flexed his fingers, and that message was even clearer.

Diana checked his pulse. "You're doing OK. Pretty doped, huh?"

Another sigh, this one impatient. "Drugged. Not crazy." His voice was weak but the note of stubbornness was reassuringly familiar.

"I'm going to get Dr. Crowe," Diana said. "Be right back."

"Di."

She turned back. "Yeah, Timmy? Can I bring you something?"

"I need to talk to Dad."

Maggie and Diana both froze. His eyes darted from one to the other. "You guys know something."

"Tim, slow down," Maggie urged. "You've been really sick for the last couple of days – "

He scowled down at the arm restraints. "So I gather."

"Honey, I'll have those things removed right away," Diana said, and strode from the room.

Maggie fought back tears of relief. "I've been so worried – "

"I'm fine. Or I will be once I shake off this goddamn horse tranquilizer."

"I'm so sorry I had to bring you to the hospital. But I was scared – you just weren't there, Tim."

"You check that crawlspace?"

Before she could answer, Diana returned with Dr. Crowe. "Welcome back," he said gruffly. "I'm Douglas Crowe, your treating physician."

"Sorry I can't shake your hand," Tim mocked, pointedly waggling his fingers.

Crowe efficiently unfastened the restraints, cocked his head as Tim gingerly rubbed his left elbow.

"He has a bad arm," Maggie explained.

"Um-hm. Mrs. Emerson and Dr. Emerson-Hewitt, can I have a few moments in private?"

Reluctantly they retreated to the hallway. "I can't stand that guy," Diana said. "I should've let Wes come instead since he's a consult."

"They can't make him stay if he's coherent, can they?"

"No, but he's still fragile, Maggie. He ought to stay at least another night for observation."

Maggie hated to, but she concurred. "I know. He's already champing at the bit to plunge right back into the awful business with the house. And why in the world would he ask to see your father?"

"I haven't a clue. If he feels like telling off Dad now, can you imagine how he'll be after he finds out Mother and Dad knew about that investigation in Chicago?"

Maggie shook her head. "How do we put him off until he's strong enough to deal with it? You know Tim; he's not going to let it rest."

"Well, Dr. Charm is certainly going to advise him to stay another twelve hours, at the minimum. We have to back him up. Let him sulk and act impatient. They've got him so pumped up with meds he's not even going to be able to walk a straight line for hours."

Maggie couldn't resist a gallows jest. "Maybe we should have kept those damn restraints on after all."

Never, not in twenty years of embracing every form of chemical sensation, had he fought so furiously to clear his head. Instead of experiencing a welling panic at the first sign the drugs were wearing off and the desperate urge to keep feeding the fire, now he was frustrated that he couldn't simply will the alien substance out of his bloodstream. His mind was alert but his voice still feeble as he crossly answered the doctor's various questions obviously designed to test his cognitive functioning and perception of reality. Afraid of telling this condescending shrink about the backward train and the kaleidoscope, Tim said that all he remembered of the last two days were vague feelings of depression and discouragement over the fire.

The shrink wore his skepticism on his clinical white sleeve. "There aren't any wrong answers to these questions, Mr. Emerson," he chided.

"Whatever. I just want out of this place."

"What are we going to do about your drug problem?"

"I've been going to NA and AA. I'll start going again," he lied.

"I strongly recommend an inpatient treatment program in light of your drug history and your concomitant need for psychiatric care."

No fucking way! he longed to retort, but he sensed that continuing to be defensive would not further his objective, which was to get the hell out of this loony bin. Christ.

He bet that Ruth Yeager was still at large free as a bird, while he'd lain strapped to a hospital bed like a frothing Bedlamite. "Hmm. I'll give it some thought," he lied again, trying to sound reasonable.

"Give it some serious thought. Only two in ten meth addicts manage to stay clean on even a semi-permanent basis – "

"Thanks for the encouraging stats."

The doctor ignored his interruption. "We can discuss your treatment options a little later, after you've rested a bit more."

"No. I want to check out as soon as possible."

"That's highly inadvisable for another twenty-four hours. I'm sure your family will back me up."

His *family*? For a moment Tim thought that Crowe referred to his parents, but caught his own misapprehension before he could rage. "Maggie and my sister."

"And your brother-in-law Dr. Hewitt, who's been consulting on your case."

Good old Wes. He'd probably at least been able to dissuade these headshrinkers from prescribing a course of brain surgery. But Tim was sure he could make all of them agree that a prompt release was in order. Mags would want him with her, and Diana and Wes would agree that their oversight of his "condition" was more than sufficient in lieu of continued hospitalization.

Thus he was stunned – and highly suspicious – when Maggie and Diana endorsed Crowe's recommendation that his discharge be postponed until the following day. "You both think I'm crazy too," he accused. Again that hot anger welled in his throat, fighting against the effects of sedation.

"Tim, we don't even have a home to go to," Maggie pleaded.

She reached for his hand but he yanked it away. "By that reasoning I should hunker down here until we've put down first, last, and a deposit on a new place," he seethed.

"You're being melodramatic," Diana advised. "How bad can one more day be? We'll be around, and at least Ruth can't get at anybody in here."

"Fuck, she's probably being straitjacketed in the padded room next door as we speak." He wanted to scream. "And I need to talk to Dad."

"Why?" Diana challenged quietly.

"Because I just do." At this point he suspected any details would end up confirming to them that he was psychotic. "And I sure as hell ain't doing it from here."

Di remained unmoved but he saw in Maggie's eyes that she was beginning to waver. "Come on, Mags," he wheedled. "If I zone out again you can cart me right back here."

She briefly glanced at Diana. "Sweetie, please, just one more day."

"Did I tell you to stay 'just one more day' in Jeezopolis?"

Bad move, for she bristled. "Your hostility isn't exactly helping your case," she snapped.

"Sorry. But I want out."

Diana folded her arms. "Suppose I promise to get Dad down to San Diego by tomorrow so you can talk to him face to face, and Maggie promises to go look in the crawlspace under the stairs."

"Faulty premises," he pointed out.

"Why?"

"Because I can walk out of here and take care of both things myself."

"I'll tell you one thing you can't do on your own," Maggie said, plainly still irked with him. "You can't make either of us tell you what we found out about your grandfather."

"Jesus Christ, what?" Even his doped-down pulse quickened.

"No way," Diana said. "We'll tell you tomorrow when you've had twenty-four hours to get stronger."

He glowered at her euphemism. "You mean, not wig out again. How do I know you're not bluffing?"

"You noticed yourself that we looked like we'd found out something," Maggie replied.

"Yeah, but I'm crazy, remember?" he said, forcing an ironic smile. He hated to capitulate, loathed it in fact, but he had no doubt that they had learned something about the old man. Something major. It might even provide added ammunition for his interrogation of his father. Daunted, he rested back against the unyielding pillow, closed his eyes for a moment before he snapped them open again with a start. *Open your eyes.* "OK," he gave in, making a face. "But you guys better uphold your end of the deal."

"We'll tell you everything after you've checked out tomorrow," Diana said, the reproach gone from her voice.

"And get Dad down here and look in the crawlspace?" he reminded.

"Yes, that too," Diana said.

"Fine." He remained irritated by their intransigence, but he supposed that if he could endure nine months in state prison, he could get through the next twenty-four hours in a nut house. "Now, can I have a few minutes alone with Maggie so she doesn't start slipping Happy Pills into my coffee?"

Diana obliged, but Maggie's expression had softened considerably upon his concession to delay his emancipation. She let him grasp her hand and pull her closer. "Thanks for humoring us, sweetie. I know you'll be fine."

He guessed that she was the one doing the humoring, but let it go; he needed to make amends. "I don't want to be put on crazy medication, Mags. How ironic is that?"

"Querido, I can't tell you much more, but I think we really are on the brink of putting all this horror to rest forever. That's why we can't take any chances with your health."

He felt a mixture of annoyance and encouragement at her words. But then, he wasn't about to tell anyone about why he was determined to grill his father. Not until the time was right. "Delayed gratification sucks," he complained. "At least tell me about the apartment. Was the whole thing torched?"

"Pretty much everything but our bedroom. But that's something."

"Goddamn it. All Kat's stuff. How much have you told her?"

"About the fire, but not that it was deliberately set. And I told her and my folks that you just had an anxiety attack and were in the hospital to play it safe."

He planted a brief kiss on her knuckles. "Kat's smart – she must know it's bullshit."

"We'll call her later and you can tell her yourself that you're all right."

He was unsurprised that lunatics weren't provided a bedside telephone. "What about the arson investigation? How come they haven't hauled Ruth in yet?"

She looked uneasy. "They're having a problem finding her."

"Great. I'll betcha money some other Jeezoid's hiding her out."

"Could be. The police think we should get a restraining order."

"And how'll it get served if nobody knows where she is?"

A wan smile. "You're much easier to deal with when you're incommunicado."

"Ha ha. Docile and useful bodies."

"Well, docile at any rate."

Her half-hearted teasing assured him she wasn't treating him like a ticking bomb. "Make sure you don't go back to the house alone, Mags. Fuck, get Billy and his gun for backup."

She nodded. "I won't take any chances with myself, either."

"I still can't believe any of this." He swallowed with difficulty; his throat was drier than dirt.

She noticed, slipped off the side of the bed to pour water from a plastic pitcher into a plastic tumbler. "Here, sweetie."

Even the water tasted of hospital antiseptic. "Ugh. Nasty shit."

"We'll smuggle you up some goodies from Jack in the Box."

For some reason that idea made him laugh; the entire situation was so goddamn ludicrous.

"Are you hungry? I'll go get some now?" she asked.

"Nah. I'm going to try sleeping off the rest of this Thorazine or whatever crap they've pumped into me." At least for the moment he hoped never to feel the effects of drugs – any drugs – again, and now this was the feeling he wanted to prolong.

She patted his shoulder. "I'll be back in a couple of hours."

How he resented this drowsiness, but there was little point in fighting it. "'K. Be careful."

"I will. See you in a bit, sweetie."

He managed a half-wave.

Goddamn drugs.

CHAPTER 5

What a morning. First the shocking discovery that the old man had been investigated for child sexual abuse, then Tim's recuperation of his senses, and now, a brimming apprehension – or was it anticipation? – that the end was at last on the horizon. Diana said she felt it, too. "I'll get Dad to drive down come hell or high water. If facing off with him one more time is what Tim needs to heal, then I'm going to make it happen."

Maggie inferred that Diana still feared the possibility that her grandfather had molested Tim. "Do we tell Tim about the scrapbook before or after he meets up with your father?"

"Gosh. Maybe we should play that one by ear and see how Tim is tomorrow."

Back at the Marriott Maggie called her parents to deliver a species of update. She told Eva that the various tests showed Tim was fine, ready to be released the next day. She promised Kat she would talk to her daddy later in the afternoon. Kat accepted this – or pretended to – and moved on to describe all the cool toys and clothes her grandparents had been buying for her. "I'm glad I still have Daddy's books and glove," she added.

Maggie was taken aback. "You do, sweetie?"

"Yeah, I brought them with me."

Maggie wanted to sigh at the futility of the arson. It, too, had to indicate that the

Shadow Man was growing more desperate, less potent. "I'm glad you brought them

along too."

"Is Daddy really OK, Mommy?"

"When you talk to him this afternoon he'll tell you himself."

Kat turned the phone over to Armando, who was eager to tell her of a promising

condo for sale near 14th Street and Camino del Mar. "You all can walk to the beach!

And the owner's put in $50,000 worth of renovations."

She wasn't up to arguing with him. "Pa, it sounds great. Maybe we'll go look at

it this weekend."

"Not this weekend, muchacha," he scolded. "It's Easter."

Of course; that's why Kat had even been free to be shipped off to her

grandparents. "I forgot," she admitted meekly.

As usual, he softened. "And who could blame you, Magdalena, with that fire and

Tim's heart attack?"

"It wasn't a heart attack, Pa – just anxiety." This lie felt comfortable, since it was

closer, give or take the catatonic spell, to the truth.

But she lied anyway when she reassured him she'd make time tomorrow to attend

the Stations of the Cross and Sunday Mass on Easter. She figured that Jesus himself

would have understood.

After a quick stop at Starbucks for reinforcements, she drove to the stables. This time Billy wasn't hard to find. He was working with Westcott on a lunge line. Around and around the giant chestnut Oldenburg cantered, his lope graceful rather than lumbering like Warlock's. Billy signaled for her to wait. Clutching her steaming paper coffee cup in its brown sleeve, she leaned her elbows against the top rail of the arena.

Billy removed the lunge rope and Westcott's halter to leave the horse sniffing the earth in the arena. He joined her on the other side of the fence. "What goes? How's Tim?"

"He's better, and dead-set on picking up where we left off."

"Jesus, he doesn't want us all to move back into that house, I hope."

"No – not yet, thank God." Especially when he might make a reasonable case for them not having anywhere else to stay. "He wants me to give that crawlspace beneath the stairs one more look, and he thinks you should come with me, armed, as a matter of fact."

He let out a brief dry chuckle. "You yuppie liberals hate guns except when someone's out after your asses."

"Be that as it may. When are you free?"

"Contrary to what you may believe, I don't pack heat 24/7. I'd have to go home at lunch to get it, and it's forty minutes each way between here and Fallbrook."

"Will you do it?"

He brushed dust from his palms. "Sure. I'll meet you back here at two."

In a way she was glad for the delay. This way she could report to Tim that the plan was in motion without having to explain whatever she did or didn't find. She needed to balance her commitment to honesty against a determination not to upset him, the same conundrum she and Diana would face tomorrow.

At noon she was back at Scripps, a bag of Jack in the Box fare secreted in her leather satchel. But such subterfuge was probably unnecessary, for Tim had been moved to another room down a different corridor of the psychiatric floor, an area clearly reserved for less acutely disturbed patients. These digs had a telephone, a TV, and an unseen roommate behind the drawn curtain that bisected the room.

Tim was dozing lightly, but when he awakened he was dramatically more alert than he'd been earlier. His eyes, no longer heavy-lidded, brightened upon seeing her. "Mags! Did you go look in that crawlspace?"

"Not yet. Billy can't go until two." She decided it was wiser not to mention guns within earshot of the other patient.

He sat up in bed, glared as she adjusted the mattress, the pillow. "I'm not decrepit, you know."

"You're cranky enough to be an old fart, though. How do a Jumbo Jack, onion rings, and a chocolate shake sound?" She pulled the food bag from her purse.

He commandeered the milkshake, and they shared the burger and onion rings. They were finishing up when Wes appeared. "Eggbeaters and Jello don't ring your chimes, eh?" he smiled. "Glad to see you're off the IVs." He took up the clipboard from the end of the bed. "Good, you're only on Valium."

"I don't even want that. Will you tell that quack Crowe I don't need antidepressants or any of the other crap he wants me to take?"

"If you don't want to take them, don't." Wes replaced the clipboard. "Accept the prescription to get him off your back and then just don't fill it."

Maggie laughed. "You *are* a subversive, Wes."

"No," he scoffed good-naturedly. "But if a patient says he won't take a medication, it's his decision. You can't chase him around with a hypodermic needle."

Tim's brows knit together. "Do you think I need them, Wes?"

"Tim, I'm not a psychiatrist. Speaking as your brother-in-law, I've seen you do admirably well since you got out of rehab. As a doctor, I have to defer somewhat to Crowe's assessment. That doesn't mean I endorse it or not."

"What if it was thirty years from now and Brandon was in my situation?" Tim posed.

"I'd tell him the same thing I just told you."

Maggie bit her lower lip. Tim's hypothetical struck her as telling.

As for Tim, he now looked thoughtful. "Then Brandon's a lucky kid. Lucky enough, I hope, never to be in this position."

"You're also assuming he'll give a rat's ass about what his doddering father thinks," Wes replied.

Having anticipated his restlessness, Maggie had also stopped at Barnes and Noble for a book of New York *Times* crossword puzzles. They worked a few together, complaining about excessively arcane clues – "Who the hell knows 'river in southeastern Laos'?" – as if they were lazing away a Saturday afternoon in bed. They called Kat and he reassured her he was in the pink of health. But at twenty to two, he reminded Maggie of her appointment. "Let me know right away if you find anything," he added.

He sounded so certain that she would find something, though she was almost as sure she'd found only that one box in the storage space.

Regardless, her skin crawled as she and Billy pulled into the driveway. The house's outward innocuousness, even prettiness, seemed to mock them.

While she fumbled in her purse for the keys, Billy remarked, "I take it you haven't gotten around to changing the locks."

The matter had indeed slipped her mind entirely. "Damn! For all we know Ruth's been hiding out here."

"Let me go in first," he said, taking the gun out of the pocket of his jacket.

She turned the key in the lock but crept in behind him, staying close as they performed a wary walk-through. Everything appeared exactly as they had left it. "I forgot to check the fridge to see if anything's missing," Maggie said, gesturing back toward the kitchen. She tried to remember what should be within the refrigerator other than bottled water, a quart of half-and-half for coffee. Hadn't there been leftovers from the first night's dinner of deli sandwiches, some cold cuts and Swiss cheese?

"Coast is clear in there," Billy said, reaching for the knob on the downstairs closet door. "Crawlspace is in here?"

"Yes, there's a panel on the closet ceiling. You may need a chair to stand on."

He dragged one of the cheesy dinette chairs to the closet. Positive he'd find nothing of consequence, Maggie returned to the kitchen and opened the refrigerator door.

She stared at the alien jar and its contents.

Then she screamed, horror bursting savagely from her throat.

It was a fetus, perhaps nine or ten weeks developed, preserved in a jar of cloudy liquid.

She staggered to the sink barely in time to vomit her half of the fast-food lunch into the basin. She sobbed and retched at the same time, only distantly aware of Billy's voice on his cellphone calling the police. She couldn't think, couldn't think whether it was a good or bad idea to bring in the cops, or wonder when Ruth had managed to stow the gruesome jar in the refrigerator. It might have been an hour ago, it might have been just before they'd found her all but smothered in ectoplasm. And it didn't matter. All she could think about was the pickled fetus. Dear God, had her own – Tim and hers? – looked like that when she'd had the abortion seven weeks into an unplanned pregnancy?

Billy's arm clasped her shoulders. He led her through the dining room and into the living room, where he eased her onto the uncomfortable rent-a-sofa. She cried into her hands, angry tears over the malice of the gesture mingling with guilt, shame, irrational fear that a vengeful God was reminding her that she'd never have that second child, the beautiful little boy who would look just like Tim.

Billy kept his arm around her but didn't speak. What if he'd guessed the significance of the fetus and was judging her?

"The cops should be here soon," he said at last.

Though she'd ceased crying she was loath to raise her face, to look at him. And how could she ever tell Tim of the grisly discovery? "When do you suppose she put it there?" she said weakly.

"With the locks still the same, she could've done it anytime between the other night and half an hour ago."

"Why can't they find her? She's a demented Jesus freak, not the Unabomber!" Father Bob had urged her to extend mercy to Ruth, but that would have to be deferred until after the madwoman had been safely removed from society.

Two policemen arrived. Billy took them to the kitchen to show them the revolting object left by the trespasser. Upon the group's return to the front of the house, Maggie observed that one cop's face now bore a greenish hue. As she had with the arson investigator, she enumerated her reasons for believing that Ruth Yeager was stalking her family.

"You really need to file that TRO," the non-green cop advised.

"I know, but my husband's in the hospital and I haven't had the chance."

They told her to keep away from the house until the locks were changed or Ruth was in custody, then went to retrieve the evidence. "Why don't you go wait in the truck?" Billy suggested.

None too eager to lay eyes upon the jarred fetus again, she hurried out the front door and climbed into the Ford's cab. She closed her eyes but still saw the homunculus with its swollen space-alien head and webby inchoate limbs. She feared she might be sick again, and hoped she'd be able to bolt from the truck in time to spare the upholstery.

She took a few deep breaths and the nausea subsided. She watched the policemen traipse out the front door, one holding a dark plastic bag – oh God. Billy followed, clasping what looked to be a brown lidless carton. Had he forgotten something in the house two nights ago?

He climbed in beside her and set the carton between them. Up close, she recognized the tangle of old-style Christmas lights, but the red felt beneath it had been partially lifted, revealing neat stacks of Bank of America check boxes. She gasped. "Oh my God – I remember that box now, but I never thought to look underneath the Christmas stuff." *Check the books*.

"Given the dust, it's a safe bet that no one's looked inside for some time."

"They must belong to Tim's grandparents! He was so sure something would be up there. Did you peek?"

"No, so long as that nut-job lady has a key, I'm not real big on lingering in that house. Should I go back and lock the door, or would it be pointless?"

"Let's just get out of here." That image suspended in murky fluid was floating back into her mind.

He backed out of the driveway. "You know, I think she left that thing today. Maybe only a couple of hours ago."

Maggie's stomach churned. "Why?"

"'Cause I bet the old man had her do it to distract us from looking again in that storage space."

She glanced at the box in trepidation. "I hope to God there's something inside that will drive him straight back to hell." Fleetingly she considered telling him of the morning's scrapbook find, then thought better of it. She trusted him, but Tim would be hurt, not to mention jealous, if Billy knew about the alleged molestation before he did.

Diana, it turned out, had no such compunctions. Entering the hotel lobby with Billy, Maggie spotted Diana stepping out of the hotel gift shop, a plastic bag in her hand and Brandon in his baby cuddler pouch against her chest. "Wes forgot the shampoo at the Four Seasons," she explained. "What do you guys have there? Was it in the crawlspace?"

"It sure was," Maggie said, adding grimly. "And you won't believe what Ruth left for us in the refrigerator."

"Everything really is coming to a head," Diana marveled. "Did you tell Billy about the old newspaper?"

They stepped into an open elevator, joined by a natty businessman whose presence forestalled further elaboration.

They went to the Emerson-Hewitt suite where Diana put Brandon down for a nap. "Tell me about Ruth first," Diana said.

"I can't bear to yet," Maggie demurred. "Let's just say she's still at large and still doing his dirty work."

"What's this about an old newspaper?" Billy pressed.

"Back in Chicago, where my grandparents lived for most of the '60s, my grandfather was investigated for child molestation. A little boy patient."

"Holy shit. Nothing came of it?"

"The kid evidently recanted," Diana said. "But I'm sure you're drawing the same inference we did."

"We haven't told Tim yet," Maggie said nervously. "Come on, let's look at the checks. Maybe there'll be more clues."

Billy removed the lights and felt cloth. Along with the boxes of checks was a thick bundle of what appeared to be old bank statements bound by a fraying rubberband.

"Where do we begin?" Diana said, reaching for one of the boxes. "They probably saved this stuff for tax purposes." Her disappointment was audible.

"'Check the books,'" Maggie reminded her. "Tim said he thought that sounded like an accounting phrase. You guys, this is exactly what Liz wanted us to find!" She opened a box, discovering half a dozen dated check registers. "These are from the early 1980s. I guess we look for ones written in the summer time – " She broke off. "*No*! We look for ones made out to Inez!"

Diana lit up. "Of course!" She opened the box she'd dropped in her lap.

"I hate to rain on the parade, but what if they paid her in cash?" Billy said. "If she was undocumented, or simply didn't want to declare all her earnings, they might have."

"I've got to believe there's something in here," Maggie replied firmly. "Everybody start looking."

She scanned the first check register. None recorded to any Inez; virtually all seemed for typical household expenses, entered in a tidy feminine hand.

Nor did Diana or Billy have better luck with their boxes. "Damn, Billy's right," Diana said, "they must have paid her in cash."

By the time they reached the mid-1980s they were all a bit deflated. "Liz had to have led us to this box for a reason," Maggie insisted, flipping through the first register of 1985. More household expenses, it appeared, until an entry for 3/21 caught her eye. The payee was blandly listed as "Charity," but the word was followed by "Inez" in parentheses – and the amount was a staggering $50,000. "Here it is," she breathed, passing the register to Diana.

Diana's jaw dropped. "Sweet Jesus, was she blackmailing him?" She in turn handed the register to Billy.

"Or was he paying her off?" Billy said. "Either that or she was one hell of a housekeeper." He grabbed the bundle of bank statements. "Maybe there's a cancelled check. What's the date again?"

"March 21, 1985," Maggie said. Tim would have been twelve; presumably Alberto was around that age too. She chilled.

Billy rustled through the bank statement envelopes, separating out two and shuffling through cancelled checks. After several moments he stopped shuffling. "Here it is. Made out to cash, but endorsed by Inez Camacho. Fifty grand." He held up the check.

"That's it," Maggie said, heart racing. "It has to be hush money. But for what?"

Diana looked queasy. "I'm afraid to know."

Maggie too felt vaguely ill, certain that the little boy Alberto was somehow the key to Dr. Emerson's unlikely largesse. "We have to find Inez and hope she'll tell us now that the old man's dead."

"Would she have left San Diego?" Diana wondered.

"Let me get my laptop," Maggie said. "It'll make it easier to look in all the county area codes."

Returning to Diana's suite with the computer, she sat down at the writing table and logged online. "Let's start with the San Diego White Pages." Diana and Billy leaned over her shoulder as she typed in the name.

No "I. Camacho" in the 858 or 760 area codes. But miraculously, under 619 am address, on Centraloma Drive, and phone number popped up, not simply for "I. Camacho" but for "Camacho, Inez R."

Diana jotted down the number on a Marriott notepad. "That has to be her. It's an unusual name."

The room phone rang, startling them. "Hello?" Diana answered. "Yes, OK. That sounds fine. See you then." She returned the receiver to its cradle. "That was Dad. He said he'll be here tomorrow late morning."

Maggie cringed. Tim's cryptic demand for a meeting with his father had almost slipped her mind. Everything was happening so fast. "Why does he think Tim wants to see him?"

Diana groaned. "He thinks Tim's going to hit him up for money because of the fire."

Even Billy looked pained, and Maggie bit back anger. "He doesn't know Tim's been in the hospital?"

"Maggie, you know I decided not to tell him."

"What I wonder," Billy said, "is whether your father knew about this fifty-grand payout to the cleaning lady."

"I doubt it," Diana replied, lips twisting. "It's precisely the kind of thing he'd have made a point not to know."

Maggie had to agree. Jack Emerson may have been a rigid and unemotional man, but even Tim conceded his father was ethical to a fault. A real law-and-order type, to the extent that he alone in the family had supported the judge's prison sentence for his son.

Unbidden, the picture of the formaldehyde-preserved fetus flashed in her mind, and she winced reflexively.

Diana and Billy regarded her in patent concern. "Maggie, why don't we put Inez on hold for a while so you can lie down?"

Maggie appreciated the solicitude, but she needed to remain focused, to press onward if only to ward off the frightful image seared into her brain. "No, I'm OK. Let's call Inez now." She switched off the computer. "I should talk to her, don't you think? In case she's more comfortable speaking in Spanish."

"I'm ashamed I barely remember her at all," Diana said dully. "What an insensitive little ditz I was."

At that moment Maggie understood, understood that the Emersons' legacy to Diana was guilt, just as surely as for Tim it was self-destructiveness. The existence of an actual ghost was redundant.

She dialed the number. A woman's voice, with a light Spanish accent, answered. "I'm trying to reach Senora Inez Camacho," Maggie began tentatively. "Is this she?"

"No, this is her niece Elena. Tia Inez is at church for Holy Thursday. May I ask who's calling?"

"My name is Maggie Flores. Flores-Emerson." She held her breath, observed Diana and Billy doing the same.

"Emerson?" The woman sounded very suspicious. Clearly she recognized the name. "What does this concern, senora?"

"I'm married to Tim Emerson. Your tia worked for his grandfather years ago and Tim was friends with Alberto when they were little."

"My family has no interest in the Emersons. Please don't bother us again."

"Please," Maggie implored. "Por favor. This is a matter of life and death. Tim Emerson is in danger, and so may be our daughter, because of that terrible old man. Please tell Inez I must speak to her."

"The old man is dead – what danger can he be anymore?"

Anymore? Maggie noted the word. "I promise you, Elena, I wouldn't trouble your tia were this not extremely important. Will you at least take my number and tell Senora Camacho I called?"

"She doesn't like to speak on the phone. Her English isn't so good."

"Hablo espanol," Maggie tried.

"I will tell her," came the grudging reply.

Maggie gave Elena her cell number but couldn't be sure the niece would even pass along her message.

She said as much to Diana and Billy. "From the second I said the name Emerson the niece freaked out. They're still scared of him."

"Maybe for the same good reasons we are," Diana said pensively.

"What if he molested that little boy Alberto?" Maggie blurted.

"Oh my God," Diana said, but it was obvious the thought had already occurred to her as well.

"Fifty thousand's a lot of money," Billy mulled. "Twenty years ago it was even more so."

Diana was visibly shaken. "It's just too horrible to contemplate. And what kind of mother could be bought off for the rape of her child?"

"Um, ever heard of Michael Jackson?" Billy said.

Diana managed a humorless smile, but it vanished at the ring of Maggie's phone. To Maggie's great surprise the caller was Inez's niece Elena. "Tia Inez says you can come by and speak with her tomorrow morning at ten, before she goes to the Stations of the Cross." Elena sounded none too happy about it, either.

"Please tell her how grateful I am," Maggie said. "I swear to you, Elena, I mean her no harm."

Elena's sole response was to provide directions to the Camacho home in Point Loma some fifteen miles south.

Hanging up, Maggie realized she had a new problem. "Tim's being discharged tomorrow morning and he may need me if he's planning some confrontation with Jack," she fretted.

"I'll stick around to referee," Diana said. "Are you OK about going to see Inez alone?"

"I'll go with you," Billy offered.

"No, I'll go by myself. We don't want her to feel outnumbered, especially if she's hiding something."

Her mind moved on to the next quandary: how much to tell Tim about this afternoon's events and discoveries. His breakdown, though short-lived, had thrown a major wrench into her prior vow to keep nothing from him. She decided she'd tell him about the planned meeting with Inez but withhold the matters of the $50,000 check and the fetus in the jar. She'd allow that they'd unearthed the box of cancelled checks, hence learning Inez's full name, but not that his grandfather had paid the woman a disconcertingly large sum.

She found him playing chess with Ryan, a magnetic portable board resting on the side of his hospital bed. She felt his scrutiny on her face. He sensed something. "We've located Inez. I'm meeting with her tomorrow at ten," she said.

"Fuck, I want to go too."

"What about your dad?" she prodded. "He's due in San Diego between ten and eleven."

"Damn. His timing has always sucked. Did you look in that crawlspace?"

Her eyes briefly met Ryan's; did he guess as well that she was holding back? "Yes, and we found a box of cancelled checks, one of which was made out to Inez."

"Ha – 'check the books.' I knew it."

Ryan lifted up the chess board. "I should be going. I'll call you later, Maggie."

As Ryan kissed her cheek, Tim admonished, "No secrets."

Maggie took the chair Ryan had occupied. "Of course not, sweetie."

"You look sort of rattled."

Damn his intuition, damn him for knowing her so well. "I'm having a delayed reaction, I think, to everything that's happened." No lie, that; Tim's meth relapse, the séance, the fire, the dead fetus – all blurred into a disjointed, endless waking nightmare.

He reached for her hand. "Have you wanted to drink?" he asked softly.

"Oh God. It's a truism, isn't it? The times in your life that you most need a drink you can't have one."

"It'll be over soon, Mags. Once I talk to my dad and you talk to Inez, we'll know everything. I'm sure of it."

She couldn't speak the question that immediately came to mind: would the knowledge end up freeing or destroying them?

There's more to the picture than meets the eye. That line from an old Neil Young song kept playing in his mind. She was so pale and drawn, so determined to convince him that nothing more unsettling had occurred than the discovery of Inez's whereabouts. He didn't challenge her; he knew she was self-censoring to protect him. Until he was released from the hospital he was in no position to make any *mens sana in corpore sano* claims for himself.

Was the old man or his creature Ruth the one to have flexed a malignant tentacle at Maggie this day? Or was it the corrupt miasma of the house itself? Answers could wait, he supposed, wait until he'd escorted his father back to the scene of the crime and forced an answer to the paramount question.

Out of the blue and into the black repeated another line from the same Neil Young song. The black of clarity, not of cover, the black seen with open eyes in the dark.

The anger that had accumulated over a lifetime – well, his lifetime – now vied with an aching hunger to understand. The why was as important as the what. He clung to his anger for its familiarity and because he feared that to lose it would mean losing his purpose. All the years of tweaking had merely deferred and detoured his anger. Just as he'd been incapable of imagining life without crystal meth, now he couldn't envision his life without the impetus of anger. He was starting to sense that he had feared its resolution all along, and that the same held for Diana and his parents.

Mags remained with him through his bland dinner of what purportedly was a chicken cutlet and macaroni and cheese. "I bet the box spells 'macaroni' with a K," he joked. Just as she prepared to leave Dr. Crowe put in an appearance, mostly to lecture him over his expressed intention not to take the Depakote he'd been prescribed or to check directly into rehab. The shrink was somewhat placated by a promise to do the "ninety meetings/ninety days" dance as soon as he was released. Not a total lie; once he had his answers, his dreaded resolution, he'd resume regular attendance of meetings. For himself, and for Maggie.

More as a gesture toward her than for Dr. Crowe's benefit, as well as to escape the claustrophobic psych ward, he actually consented to attend the evening AA/NA meeting in one of the hospital's auditoria. Maggie looked pleased. He got dressed, promising not to use the excursion as a means to cut out from Scripps early. She offered to accompany him, but she looked so fatigued that he declined. He kissed her goodnight. "Rest up for the big day, Mags."

An aide escorted him out of the locked ward and down to a ground-level conference room. Thirty or so people, many in robes over hospital gowns, were taking seats; at the front of the room was the familiar podium and microphone, behind which a hippie-ish man with a walrus mustache and pot belly shifted his considerable heft from foot to foot. Soon he introduced himself as Ken, a counselor at the McDonalds Center and himself a recovering alcoholic. Tim guessed that Ken had replaced one addiction with another to Big Macs and French fries.

No surprises; the usual discussions of the Twelve Steps and struggles to achieve or maintain sobriety. He recalled telling Maggie a few weeks before that the chief benefit of meetings lay not in their content but in the discipline of attending. But since his first taste of Foucault at UCLA, he'd thought of discipline as subjugation internalized, self-policing, self-punishment. Tonight this philosophy seemed a perilous lens through which to regard an aspect of his own struggle, and he tried to lose himself in the patchwork accounts of others' battles, to mute the running editorial commentary in his mind that fortified his aloneness. Or was it his denial?

He wished he were elsewhere, somewhere safe with Maggie and Kat. Yet he recognized the imperative to be here, an imperative almost on a par with the one that compelled the planned confrontation tomorrow with his father, his grandfather, all of them walled up in that prison a thousand times more fetid and oppressive than the state penitentiary at Lancaster. No drugs to mitigate the horrors.

He took a deep breath, forced himself out of his head, and tried to concentrate on the current speaker, a gravel-voiced fortyish woman with the splotchy skin of an alcoholic and the haggardness of a tweaker. Her name was Toni, and she was on her fifth inpatient rehab in three years. "I just can't seem to stay clean more than a month or two. I've tried sober living homes, Antabuse, you name it." She swiped at tears. "Every time I think I've hit bottom, I sink a little deeper."

Sympathetic strangers comforted and advised. Tim wished Father Bob were present for the sake of the tortured woman. Bob was so good at pointing out common sense strategies minus the rote pieties of the Twelve Steps credo. Tim was ashamed he had no encouraging words to offer, not now, fresh off a relapse cannily engineered by the

Shadow Man but compliantly executed by he himself. And how to convey his present

certainty that it would never happen again, that the breakdown had extinguished that

visceral desire to be chemically *other,* which had simmered within him from early

adolescence? These suffering, well-meaning people would gently chide him about

hubris, only they'd call it "denial," remind him that recovery was a lifetime process

waged one day at a time for the rest of his life. That he needed to call his sponsor, work

and rework the totemic Steps, and never, ever drop his guard against considering himself

a *former* addict.

Christ, no fucking wonder this weepy Toni woman was disheartened. Reluctantly

he rose to speak. "My name's Tim and I just blew over seven months of being clean," he

said matter-of-factly. "But – call me crazy – " (he tried not to gulp) "—but I don't see

myself as back at square one. Linear thinking can become a prison – "

Stop the goddamn private puns!

" – I'd rather see it in terms of seven clean months with only one day high. I don't think

you forfeit your sober time when you relapse."

Most people, including Toni, regarded him with benign confusion. He hadn't

made himself very clear, he supposed in resignation. The moderator with the David

Crosby mustache looked a little irritated. "Thanks for sharing, Tim. But it's risky to

view even a one-day relapse as a meaningless blip on the screen. It's important for all of

us who relapse to return to our Steps and try to learn what made us forget or ignore our

disease, even for a day. Sounds like you need to watch out for that self-will run riot."

The man's rather patronizing tone didn't bother Tim other than to make him

choose to be pleasantly argumentative for its own sake. "But then it becomes like

Sisyphus and his fucking rock. Camus was right – in the face of that absurdity, why not commit suicide?"

A pasty man with frizzy red hair challenged him. "But Camus said that by owning his rock, Sisyphus made his life meaningful." He looked very self-satisfied. "Our addictions are our rocks. We need to own them anew every day. Maybe that's part of why you relapsed, Tim."

Now Tim was growing annoyed. He should've kept his big mouth shut. "Maybe. Whatever."

Ken smiled indulgently at the red-haired guy. "Now, James, don't take Tim's inventory."

"Sorry to Fourth-Step you, man," James said to Tim, though he didn't sound particularly apologetic.

Discipline, discipline. Christ, maybe what he really needed was electroconvulsive shock to purge his brain of all the intellectual flotsam. Forget Foucault; forget Baudrillard's book of the same name; forget the evasive dance of cerebration through which he eluded the scared but stubborn little kid resolved never to cry, the child whose secret tears he had smothered in a windstorm of drugs, resentment, obsessive yet strangely ineffectual love. He yearned to be purged, purified down to his essence, his truth – pure hate, pure love, pure comprehension.

And tomorrow would be the day.

He let go of the transitory annoyance, James's smirk, Ken's condescension, the cant and platitudes of those who likely themselves questioned on occasion the same axioms while clinging to them in place of a longed-for leap of faith as yet deferred.

The Garden of Gethsemane was crowded tonight.

CHAPTER 6

Fearing the images that sleep might bring and dangerously over-conscious of the mini-bar contents, Maggie had tried to fill the long night with mindless tasks: working on the itemization form from Allstate, watching reruns of *Roseanne* on Nickelodeon, leafing through the glossy fashion magazines she'd purchased earlier in the gift shop. At dawn an almost crushing fatigue caught up with her. But mere moments after she buried her face in pillow and sleep, her cellphone jangled.

"Damn, I woke you. Sorry."

Clutching the phone, she propped herself up on the bed with her free arm. "It's OK, Timmy. Want me to come get you?"

"No, go back to bed. I'll check myself out and take a cab."

"Don't be silly. I'll be there in half an hour."

A hot shower scalded her into a second wind. Knowing how impatient Tim was, she dashed into the AM/PM for a coffee instead of braving the line at Starbucks, also picking up the pack of Marlboros he'd requested. More than fully awake she was wired, and a nervousness akin to dread thrummed in her veins, an amorphous but insistent sense that after this day everything would be different.

It rained steadily on the drive to the hospital. She came upon him fully dressed and completing paperwork for a chipper little Asian nurse in his room. He pocketed slips for prescriptions she knew he had no intention of filling, and a minute later they were buzzed through the locked door.

The elevator door slid shut on them. Maggie feared that his first words would be a demand she make good on her promise to tell him all she'd learned during his hospitalization. Instead, he hugged an arm around her and said, "Did you get the cigs? I'm crawling the walls."

"They're right here in my purse."

"Good. Christ, I never want to be in a place like this again."

Even the outside grounds of the medical complex were nonsmoking, but he lit up anyway. "Ah, nirvana," he said, exhaling smoke and shielding the cigarette from the rain.

All the same, they hurried to the car. "It's barely eight," she said, twisting the key in the ignition. "Why don't we stop somewhere for breakfast?"

"Sure."

She intuited then that he shared her shapeless dread about the day, just as she saw her own fatigue and anxiety in his circled eyes.

They headed back up the 5. He switched the radio from Air America to music. 94.9 was playing "Californication," and the song struck her as a fitting dirge.

She took the Del Mar Heights exit west, suppressing a chill because the house on La Amatista Road was less than a mile away. That horrible house, Kat's windfall inheritance, a house not of death but of undying malice and pain. Even if they succeeded in permanently driving out the Shadow Man, the house would remain forever residually haunted, anguish and humiliation and terror seared into its invisible architecture. What if the same proved true for Tim and herself?

"I thought we'd go to Elijah's," she said, attempting to sound casual. She turned the car into the Del Mar Heights Village strip mall anchored by a Vons at one end and a Jack in the Box at the other.

"That's cool."

Elijah's was a restaurant and deli with umbrella'd outdoor tables and a classic New York style menu, located near the Vons end of the mall. "Good day for bagels and lox," Tim remarked.

She assumed he was being ironic. "I'm thinking about an omelet."

"Make it a veggie omelet or you'll rot in hell. It's Good Friday."

He was joking, of course, but she thought it an odd joke for him, of all people, to make. "Well, I need all the help I can get, so a veggie omelet it will be," she agreed.

The late spring storm precluded a table outside, so they claimed a place within. She wasn't especially hungry, but the coffee was a tonic. She glanced out the window at a good number of intrepid shoppers marching under umbrellas into Vons. "Can you believe people grocery-shop at this ungodly hour?"

He saw one woman in a jogging suit wrestle with a shopping cart stuck end-in to another. "Maybe at the end of the school year we should move from this area. It's so fucking lily-white. That can't be good for Kat."

She remembered how Tatiana had mistaken her for Kat's au pair during their first visit to the stables. But life after – after whatever happened today – seemed too remote to contemplate. "It's awfully homogenous here, I agree. More like Newport than Manhattan Beach."

"Why do only Jesussy right-wing nut jobs home-school their kids?"

"For obvious reasons. They don't want their kids exposed to Darwin and the 'homosexual agenda.'" She smiled. "Kat would mutiny if we tried to home-school her."

"Yeah, it's a bad idea. And she likes it where she is." A shadow of unhappiness passed over his face.

"Tim, let's not worry about the future right now, OK?"

She was positive that her entreaty would prompt him to raise the more proximate matter of yesterday's discovery. But when he said nothing she recognized that he was deliberately not asking. Perhaps he still felt too emotionally brittle to cope with any shocking revelations. More likely he wanted to keep his mind and sense of purpose clear for the looming encounter with his father.

Years ago, this was how he had been in college, in the minors, on the day he was slated to pitch. Getting in "the zone." He didn't exactly will himself into a Zen-like silence, but rather, he cultivated a steely single-mindedness that discouraged both the playful banter and the philosophical ruminations in which he otherwise delighted. How far they had come since his baseball days.

Yet as she looked across the table at him so somber and preoccupied, she marveled that she still saw in him the beautiful boy with the face of a Renaissance pagan deity and the recklessness of a fire-breather who'd turned up at one of Dan Ullman's impromptu parties looking to score some drugs. Did he look at her and see any remnant of the buoyant, flirtatious girl who'd stayed up with him until four a.m., long after even Dan had crashed, talking about the Camus-Sartre break over communism, the Kantian sublime, and where to find the best late-night burrito on the Westside?

In fact, he *was* looking at her. "Let's go back to the room," he said simply, and she knew what he was suggesting.

"Yes," she said.

Early in their relationship they'd agreed never to refer to sex as "making love," though not because they hadn't fallen fiercely in love the night they met. The phrase seemed somehow squeamish, more appropriate to the Lifetime Network ("Television for women!") and Christian discourses against premarital sex than to the intoxicating corporeality of their coupling. Before him she'd had four lovers, two in high school and two at UCLA, with whom she'd enjoyed sex, but none had been the profoundly sexual creature that Tim was, and none had discovered to her that aspect of her own being. She used to think it was because he was an exceptional athlete, by definition keenly in touch with his own physicality. But over time she came to believe that both his sexuality and athleticism stemmed from the same wild drive as his appetite for drugs, that desire to surrender consciousness to the present, the realm of the immediate beyond the tentacled reach of the past and black summons of the future.

Yet once in their hotel room they didn't rip off their clothes and fall together in a paroxysm of lust. They undressed casually, as though preparing merely to change into other garments or take a shared, leisurely nap. Atop sheets still rumpled from her abortive attempt at sleep they kissed, their legs entwining, his hand squeezing her breast, hers his penis. His mouth moved from hers to first one then the other nipple, his fingers to her vulva. She arched her back and urged his tousled head down lower until she felt his tongue exploring her clitoris, entering her. She loved the music of her own gasps and moans. She loved when he abruptly stopped, swung her around, and slid into her from behind. He thrust deeply, panting into her hair. Nearing orgasm, she stroked herself in rhythm with his movements inside her.

And when he spilled warm semen into her for the first time in forever, she laughed with all the reasonless joy of a madwoman.

He was smiling, too, though in his more characteristic ironical fashion. "It's Good Friday. We're going to hell for sure."

"You sure you know how to get to this place?" Eager though he was to hear what Inez Camacho might reveal about the old man and Alberto, he was reluctant to part company with her, even for a few hours. He walked her down to the car. Damn his father for being an inveterate morning person.

"I MapQuested it last night," she replied. "Good luck with your dad, sweetie. Don't let him get to you."

A lingering kiss goodbye, then she was off and he was heading back into the hotel. He went up to Diana and Wes's suite, where he presumed his father would appear first. "Hey, you're looking worlds better," Wes greeted.

"Amazing what leaving a loony bin does for you."

Diana, holding Brandon, emerged from the adjacent room with a quizzical expression. "Hi, honey. Did Maggie tell you – "

He cut her off. "Whatever you and Mags may have found out over the last couple of days, I want it to keep until after I've talked with Dad," he said firmly. "Right now I can only deal with one issue at a time."

"All right," Diana said, though her confusion was obvious.

"I don't want you guys hovering around trying to run interference, either." He lit a cigarette. "As soon as he gets here, I'll take him to the coffee shop. Nice public place, Di, no angry scenes. I swear."

"Dad's likely to be delayed by the rain. And why can't you order room service coffee? Wes and I'll hang out in the bedroom in case you need us."

"Your dad does have the bedside manner of a heart surgeon accustomed to losing patients on the table," Wes added.

"True enough. But I need to do this on my own."

They were clearly not happy with his decision, but he refused to yield. Couldn't yield, not if he had a prayer of getting at the truth. He felt a little guilty; Diana and Wes had been his mainstays during some of the worst times of his life. To this day they paid the premiums on his health insurance, their generosity guaranteeing that Scripps Hospital would not be stiffed for his short stay in the booby hatch. But their supervision of his

meeting with Jack Emerson was wholly incompatible with necessity.

Apprehensively Maggie swung off busy Nimitz Boulevard onto the rather pretty

side street that was Centraloma Drive. The houses were small but well-tended, most

fronted by patches of neat lawn, suggesting a slightly older neighborhood on the fringe of

a generally affluent area. Twenty years ago $50,000 had probably been a more than

sufficient down payment for a house on this street.

The source of her nerves lay in her awareness that she was intruding into a past

not her own, sniffing around secrets that had likely been long guarded if not put to rest.

She regretted that Diana hadn't been free to accompany her, for at least she wasn't a total

stranger to Inez Camacho. But Maggie felt it was more important for Diana to stay at the

hotel and mediate the unpleasantness between Tim and Jack Emerson. Tim, born

beautiful but grievously damaged in upbringing, Tim who was as much flesh of her flesh

as Kat, as vital to her consciousness as her own chi.

Born beautiful. At once she realized why that innocent phrase, uttered casually

by Norma before the AA meeting, had felt so portentous. How long had she intuited,

without knowing, that the old man had been a pedophile, warped to the point of rage by

frustrated desire for the strikingly beautiful child who was his grandson? If the perverted

desire had outlived the old man in his natural state, how could it ever be slaked?

She had no choice but to table the question, no choice but to get out of the car and

walk up to the front door of a small stucco house with Mediterranean trim. She rapped

twice with the tarnished brass knocker.

A woman around her own age, olive-skinned and ponytailed, answered. From the grim set of her jaw Maggie guessed this was the niece, Elena. "Tia Inez is in the kitchen having some tea," she said brusquely. "Follow me."

Maggie half-expected to find at the kitchen table a sad and wizened old abuela draped in a black mantilla and clutching a rosary in her gnarled hands. Instead, the woman sitting there, while careworn of face and with abundant silver in her short curly hair, looked like a reasonably fit and vital sixty-year-old, dressed in a simple sweater and skirt, and sipping tea from a nice china cup and saucer.

Maggie offered her hand. "Senora Camacho, gracias por su tiempo."

The woman's guarded eyes brightened slightly. "You are the wife of little Tim? How much time has passed," she replied in Spanish, shaking her head ruefully. "Elena, some tea for Senora Emerson. Then go."

Stoically Elena did as she was asked. With her niece out of the room, Inez turned back to Maggie. "Elena says you fear for your family. Because of *him*."

Usted está asustado debido a él. Maggie heard not the anticipated contempt or anger, but rather a weariness as deep and hollow as a benediction bell. She heard, too, that Inez didn't doubt the old man's power to terrify beyond the grave. Did Elena, of a different generation, scoff at her aunt for believing in ghosts and hauntings just as Armando chided Eva?

Maggie leaned forward to touch Inez's hand across the table. "Yes, Senora. That house in Del Mar now belongs to my family – Tim and me and our little girl – and his spirit seems bent on destroying us, whether we live in the house or not."

Inez tilted her head curiously. "But how can I help, Senora? He has done his damage to me and mine. May God protect you and yours."

"What damage?" Maggie asked gently.

The woman's thin lips pursed.

"Senora Camacho," Maggie tried again, "I beg you. Tim and I hope that if we can learn the old man's secret, we can cast out his evil spirit. We can all be free from him."

Inez clucked almost absently. "The old doctor was so cruel to little Tim. Such a pretty, high-spirited child. I should have called the social workers, senora. So much pain could have been spared us." A lone tear trickled from the corner of one eye.

Maggie clasped Inez's hand. "He was a doctor, Inez. He'd have lied his way out of it."

"Alberto – my son – he saw through the lies." No more tears, just a profound heaviness in Inez's voice and eyes. "My boy had a gift, Senora."

"He could tell when people were lying?"

"He knew what was in their hearts," she said, staring dully at Maggie's hand over her own. She looked stricken.

Maggie paused a moment before speaking again. "What did Alberto see in the old man's heart?"

"Lies. And the wickedest, most impure of thoughts about his own grandson." Inez squeezed shut her eyes as if against the horrifying image she'd evoked. "Senora, he *desired* his own grandchild. The parents let him beat the little boy because they thought it was better than him doing the other."

Maggie felt as if she'd received a boot in the stomach. For several seconds she couldn't catch her breath. Inez kept her eyes closed, rocking almost imperceptibly in her chair.

Or was it she herself swaying? Maggie managed to inhale, exhale. "And your son, Senora, he saw this in their hearts?"

"Yes." The eyes at last reopened, and they were impossibly old. "Senora, I must believe God sent you to me on this day for a reason. Lord Jesus died that our sins might be forgiven."

"Yes. I was raised to believe it."

"My Alberto was like Tim. High-spirited. The two of them liked to get into trouble." A faint smile curved her lips. "They ran around the street ringing doorbells and hiding. They left a jar of live snails for the lady next door because she was French."

Maggie wanted to hug her for conjuring a picture of innocence to counter the previous sordid one. "You know, we found the books you gave Tim."

"Oh yes, he loved books. It was the only time he'd sit still. I thought if perhaps he spent more time sitting still he would stay out of trouble with the old doctor. This was before Alberto told me why the old man was always beating him."

Maggie hated to ask, but had to. "Did the old man ever ... hit Alberto?"

Sighing, the woman rested her chin on her hand. "No, not that I ever knew, Senora. Alberto hated him too. Because he knew, of course. He teased the old man, even though I begged him not to."

"How would he tease him?"

"Ah, Senora, he would imitate Tim by running up and down the stairs or bouncing a ball indoors. Little things sure to anger the old man and remind him of your husband."

Maggie tensed, fearing the denouement.

"He never raised his voice, but he would scold Alberto," Inez continued. "Then one day I overheard Alberto answer him back. My little boy told him – " Inez covered her face with her hands, but when she lowered them those tired eyes remained dry. "He told the old doctor that he saw what was in his heart, this disgusting desire … The next thing I heard was a tumbling on the stairs. I ran out of the kitchen and found my little son broken on the bottom step. His neck was broken like a twig. The old doctor was coming down the stairs, and his face was – terrible." Finally the sobs broke through, quiet, weary sobs devoid of shock, hysteria.

Maggie got up from the table to embrace the woman's trembling shoulders. "I am so, so sorry," she whispered.

Straightening in her chair, Inez brushed away the comfort. "He insisted it was an accident. We were illegal – I didn't know what to do … "

"He gave you money, Senora?"

"Yes, he gave me money. I drove Alberto back to Mexico for a burial. No one ever knew."

The woman looked spent, her features carved in cracked stone. Maggie felt a blend of sadness and nausea. It appeared that the old man had sexually assaulted neither Tim nor Alberto, but he'd brutalized them, one lethally, and that was somehow better? She thought of Jack and Beth rationalizing *at least he's not molesting Tim*; she thought of the old man's fury at Alberto inextricably tangled up with his lust and hatred for Tim; all of it seemed at this moment beyond unraveling. Her search for answers had led her only to questions beyond human resolution.

"Are you going to tell the authorities?" Inez asked wretchedly.

"I don't know. Do you want me to? Do you think it's for the best, Senora?"

"I don't know either, Senora Emerson. This was so long ago."

"You never saw the old man again?"

Inez shook her head. "No. But I knew the lady who cleaned for one of the neighbors, and she said he took to drink. Almost never left the house."

This news too stunned Maggie too. How did this information jibe with Tim's remembrance in his rehab narrative of benign Christmas visits between the time they all quit summering in Del Mar and the old man's death? And a week ago he'd told her that his parents insisted that the *paterfamilias* barely touched liquor.

And then she felt foolish for even puzzling over the matter. Denial – the comforting lies people forced themselves to accept when the truth was not merely too awful but too messy and complicated to grasp.

Her suspicion that Elena had been listening from the adjacent room was confirmed when the niece appeared in the kitchen doorway, her expression icy. "No mas, Senora Emerson," she said sternly, adding in English, "I think you should leave now."

After the extended conversation in Spanish, the English words were jarring. But having clawed her way through the miserable secrets of two families, Maggie couldn't protest. "I am sorry for your family's suffering," she said, reverting to English as well. She patted Inez's stiffened shoulder. "Muchas gracias, Senora. You may have saved my family."

Inez didn't look up at her. "May God save us all."

At eleven, virtually on the dot, the phone in Diana's suite rang. Their father was in the lobby. "He's on his way up. He says the traffic's a nightmare in both directions," Diana relayed.

Tim had been playing with Brandon and a stuffed tortoise on the floor. He clambered to his feet, scooped up Brandon and handed him to Wes. He was amazed by the steady beat of his heart.

Diana greeted her father with a short hug and Wes shook his hand. Jack Emerson, in typical casual garb of polo-style shirt and twill slacks, said hello to his grandson before turning to Tim. "I'm sorry about the fire, Tim. Has it been officially ruled an arson?"

Tim caught the implication – *or did you stupidly start it yourself with one of those damn cigarettes?* -- but resisted the bait. "Yeah. Seems we're being stalked by this nut-case Jesus woman whose daughter was renting the house."

His father barely masked his skepticism – and his overall lack of interest. "I hope Maggie had the good sense to have renters insurance."

"They do – isn't that fortunate?" Diana broke in nervously.

Tim was growing restless with the futile attempts at small talk. "Look, Dad, I need to discuss something important with you. Why don't we do it over coffee downstairs?"

"Why don't I take out my checkbook and spare us the trip?" his father replied crossly.

"This isn't about money. Come on." Was it his imagination, or was his father testier than usual? Almost *defensive*. Might he possibly intuit what was coming?

For once Tim felt that he, not his father, was the one in control. They rode the elevator in silence. Tim waited until they stepped into the lobby to announce a change of plans. "You know what? Why don't we go for a drive instead? I bet you haven't been to your folks' house in ages."

His father tossed him a suspicious glance. "I remember it well enough. Besides, it's pouring rain. And why you all haven't been living there in the first place continues to escape me."

"I'll tell you on the drive over," Tim said, removing his sunglasses from his shirt pocket and putting them on. In doing so he realized that he'd left his cellphone in his and Maggie's room, but was disinclined to risk a potentially mind-changing delay by going back to retrieve it. His father probably had a phone in his car.

"What about the tenant?"

Tim was enjoying his father's efforts not to appear irrationally disinclined to revisit the house. "She broke the lease," he said tersely. "Let's go."

His father looked annoyed. "This is ridiculous," he muttered, but fumbled for his car keys.

Tim climbed into the passenger side of his father's silver Escalade. So typical of Jack Emerson to proudly drive the most environmentally-incorrect, arrogantly gas-guzzling automobile this side of a Hummer. But that argument would have to keep for another occasion. "You can just take the 5 one exit up – " Tim started to direct as his father steered onto Carmel Valley Road.

"The freeway's at a standstill," his father cut him off. "I'll take the back way."

Tim, unaware there *was* a back way, was momentarily taken aback but recovered quickly. "Our tenant – the one with the crazy mother – killed herself in the house a couple weeks ago," he said as they crossed under the freeway, heading west toward the ocean.

"And what, now you have the heebie-jeebies about living there?" Jack Emerson countered calmly.

"I've got the heebie-jeebies about living there, all right, but the dead woman's just the tip of the iceberg."

Irritation flickered in his father's expression. "Is this going to be the sequel to what we hashed over last weekend at your sister's house? I've nothing more to say on that subject, Tim. If I'd known you were still banging this drum I'd have saved myself an exasperating three-hours-plus drive."

"Well, *I* have something more to say on the subject, but it'll keep until we're at the house."

A block or so north on the old coast highway, a right turn at Del Mar Heights, and from there, mere moments to reach the house on La Amatista. Through the rain the gray ocean down the hill looked dull and opaque. His father parked across the street from the house, facing the Pacific.

Tim hopped out of the SUV, hoping that Maggie, distracted by the last few days' upheaval, had neglected to have the locks changed. No matter – if his key didn't work he'd find a way to break in. Might as well put his felony conviction to good use. And he could hardly be arrested for a forced entry into a house that was for all intents and purposes his.

What would the old man do in front of his own son, his partner in crime? His pulse sped up as he twisted the key in the lock. The front door clicked open.

Stepping inside, Tim cocked his head for his father to follow. "Come on in. Mi casa su casa."

He didn't miss the hint of distaste – and unease – that darted across his father's countenance as he entered. Tim felt a thrill of satisfaction. "It's clammy in here, don't you think?" he said.

"Mildew," his father said, making a face. "Place needs a thorough scouring, and not by those Merry Maid crews the property managers hire on the cheap."

"For once I agree. What this house has got is way beyond the Merry Maids' skill-set."

At this Jack Emerson clearly realized he was being toyed with. "Why did you drag me here, Tim?" he snapped.

"I could ask you the same question – except I have another one I need you to answer first."

"For Christ's sake, get to the point, then, and stop wasting our time."

Tim dropped his gamesmanship and met his father's eyes coldly. "Why, when we'd come here, did you sit by my bed watching me sleep?"

As soon as she spied the freeway Maggie despaired at the motionless lanes of cars. At least on the drive south the traffic had been stop-and-go. What she saw ahead looked to be all stop, LA-like congestion caused by the unexpected rain and onset of the holiday weekend. Deeply shaken by Inez's horrible account, Maggie was all the more upset to find this mundane yet insurmountable obstacle to her path back to Del Mar. The idea of going to a bar, even at this time of the morning, and waiting out the traffic jam with a few Bloody Marys, teased her like a sensuous perfume. But only for a moment; the Shadow Man had amassed more than enough casualties already.

Instead, she called Ryan at his apartment. "How do I get from Point Loma to Del Mar without taking the freeway?"

"Where are you?"

"On Sea World Drive, I think."

"Piece of cake. Go through Pacific Beach and La Jolla, and pick up the coast highway from North Torrey Pines. It'll take a while, but from what I hear the freeways are a mess."

She longed to blurt out *Ryan, the old man murdered little Alberto! He was a killer in life too!* But her urgency to forge a way home to Tim trumped further conversation.

"I don't know what you're talking about," Jack Emerson replied irritably, glancing over his shoulder toward the redwood deck, the ocean.

"I think you do. You watched me while I slept. Why?"

"And why are you so hell-bent on dredging up nonsense from the past? You seem to have a laundry list of grievances against your mother and me that you want to blame for your own mistakes. I won't play this game with you, Tim."

Out of the corner of his eye he noticed a light fog swirling in through the rain, indolent yet implacable, over the redwood railing. It was clammier than ever in the living room. "You watched me because you knew the old man was dangerous. Why can't you admit it?"

His father was starting to flush. A vein in his forehead pulsed and faint color deepened his tan. "I never slept well in this house. Too damn damp," he said impatiently. "Sometimes I'd look in on you kids."

"Why can't you admit you were trying to protect me? And why the hell didn't you try to protect me while he was beating me?"

That swirling fog was seeping through the glass of the closed sliding door, snaking inside through the misted pane in tendrils.

He realized it wasn't fog at all.

The same disgusting odor of stale sweat that had accompanied the ectoplasm draping Ruth Yeager the other night was creeping back as well. Reflexively Tim scanned the room, the doorway, for the crazy woman, but didn't see her.

"What is that God-awful smell?" his father demanded, nose wrinkling in revulsion. "This place needs to be fumigated. Let's get out of here."

Tim froze. Standing just inside the sliding glass door was the old man.

As if in a maddening dream, his father refused to follow the direction of Tim's horrified gaze. It was the old man, all right, in his fedora and overcoat, and he seemed no more composed of shadows than Tim and his father were.

And he was smiling.

Incredibly, his father still wouldn't look. "What the hell are you staring at, Tim? You look like Hamlet seeing the ghost."

He wanted to laugh at his father's unlikely literary allusion. *I am not Prince Hamlet, nor was meant to be.* He'd always been wildly decisive, so many impulsive bad decisions. "Dad, *look*," he implored, gesturing toward the Shadow Man who merely stood and sneered.

It really was like a bad dream, for Jack Emerson wouldn't even turn his head. "I think this noxious atmosphere is getting to you. I don't know what point you're trying to make, but – "

And then his father's entire being simply *quit*, as though he were an animatronic figure whose power source had abruptly switched off. His eyes went blank and his face rigid. He remained on his feet but seemed almost to be suspended by invisible wires from the ceiling.

Though he realized what was happening, Tim instinctively moved forward to ease his father – or the man who up until a moment ago had been his father – onto the sofa. He had to push; his father's body felt extraordinarily heavy, as if filled with wet, sour-smelling sand.

Fight him! Do what you never did when the old man was alive, and fight the son of a bitch!

"So Jack thought he was protecting you. How touching," taunted a voice, gruffer and crueler than his father's, a voice Tim recognized with a chill. Nearly as unsettling, his father's eyes stayed sightless and glassy, not registering the mocking words spoken through him.

Tim's fists clenched against the mounting urge to close his hands around the old man's throat and choke him into silence. "What the fuck do you want?" he cried. "Do you want me dead? Do you want us all dead? Goddamn it, tell me!"

The face no longer resembled his father's. "You grant me far too much power," was the snarling response. "I didn't turn you into a loser. Junkie. Queer. That's all your fine handiwork, Timmy."

Hot rage all but blinded him. He drew back a fist. "You fucking – asshole!" The insult seemed pathetically impotent.

"Speaking of assholes, doesn't yours miss getting reamed by your old pal Ed? Crouched in your little jail cell like a bitch in heat, a wet cock shoved up your ass so far you felt it all the way to your throat? You know you miss it," the old man baited, panting like a dog himself.

Wildly Tim lunged for the firetools, an andiron, anything sharp and lethal to ram into the old man's heart. He was pulling the weapon free from the stand when an icy translucent hand closed over his. "No! It's what he wants!" whispered a woman's bodiless voice.

He released the andiron and twisted around, expecting to see Liz in her dowdy flannel nightgown. No Liz ghost, only the old man contorting his father's body into a spasm of spiteful laughter, rocking back and forth mechanically on the ghastly rent-a-sofa. "Always knew you were a little coward, Timmy! I used to say to Jack and Beth, that brat's too pretty to grow up to be a man. Mark my words, he'll be a sissy and a faggot."

I'll kill him! It's the only way to end this. And to put an end to that odious stench that was now overpowering, the smell of ancient piss and body odor and decaying meat stinging his eyes and throat, his lungs. The old man continued to chortle, rollicking cruel laughter.

Tim fumbled again for the fire poker, but quickly withdrew his hand when this time the tool was as fiery to the touch as a piston.

"Jack, I said, you better keep an eye on that little pussy of a boy," the Shadow Man kept on. "He's girlier than Diana." His face suddenly twisted unpleasantly. "Damn that woman!"

The non sequitur startled Tim. "Shut the fuck up!" he screamed at the old man.

His outcry seemed to buoy the demon. "Or what? Little pussy boy is going to make me?"

Tim could no longer endure his jeers. He charged at his tormenter, knocking him off the sofa onto the floor, his hands circling the old man's neck even as the horrible odor enveloped him, seeped into his skin.

"Tim, no!"

Maggie's scream pierced the madness. He rolled off the old man, but his eyes were blind and his rubbery legs refused to support him when he attempted to stand. He keeled backwards, his head sharply striking one corner of the brick hearth. Welcome pain, welcome blackness.

Struggling not to choke on the fetid odor, Maggie took a step toward him, but at once Jack Emerson sprang to his feet to block her path. Only it wasn't Jack animating this body or the cruel, crazy grin stretching across the face. The Shadow Man was no longer a creature of shadows.

"Get out of my way," she ordered. "I'm not afraid of you." Not exactly the truth, and she suspected he knew as much. But let him call her bluff.

Semiconscious, Tim moaned. She tried to sidestep the wildly grinning old man. "Puta. Baby-killer," he hissed.

His breath reeked of putrefaction, forcing her to recoil. But his maledictions now struck her as gutless. "*You're* the baby-killer," she spat back. "A child molester and child murderer. Everyone's going to know about it – your family, the police – they're all going to know, and they'll all hate your memory."

The face convulsed and twisted as if made of putty. Then it seemed the spirit hurled away the human form it had temporarily usurped, violently shoving Jack Emerson to the floor. Filthy smoke billowed out of the fireplace that had a moment before been cold and still, blinding her. But she had to get to Tim. She staggered forward, stumbling once over Jack Emerson's legs. As she regained her balance a woman whispered in her ear, "Turn around!"

She spun around. Through the smoke she made out Ruth Yeager but two feet away, one upraised arm clutching a shiny carving knife.

Maggie jerked away but the blade caught the flesh of her right shoulder, and she gasped in pain. She heard rather than saw Ruth back away and stumble – over Jack, Tim, or a piece of furniture she couldn't say – and then the squish, then *ping*, of the knife driving into flesh, striking bone, followed by a horrible gurgling.

"Go to sleep," she heard that strange female murmur.

At first Maggie thought it was her imagination, unhinged by terror and the acute pain in her shoulder, tricking her into thinking that the foul and heavy smoke was dissipating. But within moments she could clearly discern not only her hands in front of her, one bloodied from clasping her shoulder, but also Tim and his father's crumpled shapes – and in the middle of the room that of Ruth Yeager, the knife that she still gripped protruding from her bleeding chest like a wooden stake pounded into a vampire. Maggie had left her purse and cellphone in the car; from the moment she realized where Tim and his father must have gone, her sole focus was getting to the house before the old man subjected them to a final, devastating salvo.

She crawled toward Tim. When she saw him lift a hand gingerly to his head and heard him mutter, "Shit," she turned to Jack Emerson. He was alive but unconscious. They needed an ambulance. Ruth appeared to be dead. While Maggie couldn't bring herself to go near her, she felt a twinge of pity and even forgiveness. She owed that much to the ghost of Liz, who had saved their lives.

"I'm so sorry you were caught up in this," she said softly into the quiet. "May both of you rest in peace."

EPILOGUE

One year later

Both Tim and Kat scolded her for deciding to skip Easter Mass. "You'd better go tonight, Mommy," Kat warned, while Tim shot her one of those *You're going to hell* looks that she never knew how seriously to take. She walked them to the car, marveling at how tall Kat was getting, how pretty she looked in her floral dress and pink straw hat. Despite the day's religious symbolism, Tim dressed in the same Johnny Cash black he'd worn for a year now. She didn't nag him about it. Grief kept its own calendar.

He had taken his father's death hard, blaming himself for the stroke Jack had clearly suffered upon the old man's violent dispossession of his body. Tim was inconsolable, convinced that his abortive attempt to strangle his grandfather had caused the aneurism that claimed Jack Emerson's life twelve hours later. Beth's ensuing disclosure about her husband's high blood pressure and his obstinate denial of the condition proved of no more comfort to Tim than the medical opinions of Diana and Wes had. He sought spiritual guidance from Father Bob, attended Mass at least twice a week,

but after a few months even he reached the unhappy conclusion that he needed

professional help in coping with his guilt. In therapy – and on antidepressants – since

August, he'd yet to cast off his nighted colors but was gradually rediscovering life, small

moments of joy with his wife and daughter, the energy to ride Warlock as well as to

coach Kat in softball and teach her how to surf. To lose himself in Maggie's arms and in

their physical desire once again.

He was genuinely pleased when she announced on New Year's Eve that she was

pregnant. For the first time since they'd moved into the ocean-view townhouse in Cardiff

by the Sea, he began to take interest in their new home, in readying the small third

bedroom for a nursery. It was another promising sign; for although everyone – his

mother, Diana, Armando and Eva, even Father Bob – had advised him to invest his not-

insubstantial inheritance in real estate, he repeatedly told Maggie that he felt like a ghoul,

a graverobber, for reaping the financial benefits of a death for which he felt so

responsible. But with a new baby coming, his obvious discomfort with the lovely

townhouse seemed to ebb.

It had taken her a while, too, to realize that his grief stemmed not simply from

misplaced guilt but also from the fact that he'd loved his father, indeed had always loved

him, despite the complications and estrangements, the misunderstandings and all the

words left tragically unsaid.

That the old man had intended for Tim to kill Jack she had no doubt. It was a

perfect revenge: Jack dead, Tim guilty of his murder. Liz's intervention had plainly

caught even the Shadow Man off-guard, distracting him from his purpose long enough for Maggie to confront him with the secrets he'd sought to keep well beyond his natural life. She supposed she should have been surprised by how little fight he put up once she forced his own truth upon him. Yet she wasn't surprised. Killing little Alberto Camacho and then purchasing his mother's silence were acts of cowardice, of desperation born of fear at the prospect of acknowledging his own perversity. Cowards trafficked in shadows; faced with truth, they disintegrated under the onus of their own masquerade.

Not that they were about to move back into the house. Half in jest, Wes and Diana proposed that they lease it to a mobster, just in case traces lingered of the old man's venomous presence. The current tenant was almost better than a mobster, a former Republican state congressman forced into retirement by scandal. As far as they knew, he and his wife were very happy in the house.

Despite her threat to the Shadow Man, Maggie hadn't gone to the police, out of consideration for Inez, who had surely suffered enough. She let Diana recount the lurid story of her grandfather's pedophilia and murder of Alberto to Beth Emerson, who seemed sincerely appalled. Tim had reacted with a mixture of disgust and resignation. "Poor Alberto," he said bitterly. "By comparison I got off easy."

Maggie still wondered if Alberto had been among the house's restive eidolons, or if, as she prayed, his spirit had roused itself from peace solely to jog Tim's memory. For without the crucial knowledge of Inez and her son's roles in the house's narrative, they might never have exhumed the origins of the haunting. Even had she discovered the checks and bank statements under what she'd dismissed as cast-off holiday ornaments, Inez's name would have meant nothing to her. She remained certain that Tim's dislocated spirit had deliberately sought her attention that day it drew her to the crawlspace, and the box with the mitt and books. It was so like Tim.

Ryan arrived to help her prepare for the informal Easter brunch she'd been planning for a week. "As one fallen Catholic to another," he said, carrying a tray of unfilled champagne flutes to the dining table, "I'm not going to another Mass until the Pope stops calling gays the problem of evil."

"Tim hates the Pope too," she replied good-naturedly from the spacious, modern kitchen where she mixed crabmeat, artichoke hearts, and cream cheese for a dip. "He's sworn off logical consistency, I guess, because it's *my* soul he's concerned about."

"I wouldn't worry. As soon as the fall quarter starts he'll lose his religion all over again." Tim had been accepted into UCSD's doctoral program in philosophy, and though he didn't admit as much, Maggie suspected his decision to pursue an advanced degree was informed by a sense of duty to his father's aspirations for him. Regardless, it was a decision she endorsed. Not only would he earn a fairly decent wage as a graduate teaching assistant, but the regular schedule and intellectual stimulation would do him good as well, especially since she'd reclaimed the bulk of her freelance assignments.

"I'm counting on you, Ryan, to keep an eye on him just in case some nubile undergrad puts the moves on him," Maggie joked, transferring the dip to a festive bowl. "Want to help me grate pepper-jack for the frittatas?"

"Not especially, but since you've got that bun in the oven, how can I refuse? Swear to me you and Tim aren't running around saying '*we're* pregnant.'"

"Hell, no," she laughed. "When he can share in the morning sickness, backaches, and hemorrhoids, he can be pregnant too. But not until then." She grabbed the bowl of oranges from the counter. "Or perhaps you'd prefer to ream the oranges?"

"You are so bad." He peeled the plastic wrapping from a block of cheese. "Are Diana and Wes coming?"

"No, unfortunately. They're off skiing in Tahoe this weekend. My folks are driving down, though. And a few people from the barn – Kat's teacher Sandy, Nicole and Greg – "

"No sellers' remorse from them after you guys bought Warlock?"

"Nicole now rides this gorgeous white Arabian mare that runs like a racehorse. Warlock, bless him, is built for style, not speed. Even Sugar's faster."

"Did you invite Billy? I haven't seen him since the ectoplasm night last year."

She began halving the oranges on a cutting board. "We really don't socialize much anymore." She fought a pang of melancholy. It wasn't something they'd deliberately agreed upon, nor anything so facile as "growing apart." Tim even seemed to have moved past his jealousy. Maybe it simply came down to the fact that in a way, the Shadow Man had brought her and Billy together. Now that he was at last destroyed, they had little else in common.

Or maybe it was simply that now, sober, pregnant, and with an emotionally frail husband and a daughter sufficiently mature to sense, if not understand, all that had brought them to this point, Maggie knew she couldn't afford even the fantasy risk of closeness with Billy.

"It's funny," Ryan remarked, "but I always expected somehow that his wife would show herself to all of us. Kind of like Boo Radley at the end of *To Kill a Mockingbird*."

"If only neuroses were as easy to get rid of as ghosts," she said ironically.

"That was your idea of 'easy'?"

She wiped her sticky hands on the bright red apron against which her belly bulged. "Maybe my memory's playing tricks on me, but in retrospect, I wonder if we didn't make it harder than it had to be. When I think about it, all we really needed was information."

Ryan fed a piece of cheese to Thumper, who was underfoot as usual. "Or maybe the old man finally drained his reserves of poison."

"Yeah, I've wondered that too. All that hatred has to be ultimately self-consuming, doesn't it?"

"I suppose, or else there'd probably be a hell of a lot more haunted houses."

"Do you think people as a rule are really so full of hate?"

"Yes. But you know me, an incurable Pollyanna."

Because she feared he was right she chose not to pursue the point. "Well, we're only the second owners of this place, and from what I could tell, the sellers were boringly well-adjusted."

"Ah, but this is a two-on-one. What if whoever's on the other side of the wall has a few overactive skeletons in the closet?"

She had to chuckle; his reflexive worst-case-scenario speculation reminded her of the doom-and-gloom Tarot readings he used to provide at Dan's house. "The owner's an airline pilot. If he's got a ghost, it's a nice quiet one."

Now he smiled as well. "There's a cool idea. Maybe all houses are haunted, and that's not necessarily a bad thing."

"Benign ghosts I can deal with." *Do* deal with, she added silently.

Beyond the balcony and the railroad track beneath it, gleams of light danced on the rippling ocean.

THE END

NOTE ON THE AUTHOR

Karin Coddon is a former English professor currently residing in Del Mar, California with her three cats and five minutes away from her two horses Donovan and Warlock. Her passions include animals, baseball, left-wing politics, and the poetry of Charles Baudelaire. She firmly believes she spent much of her childhood living in a haunted house.

www.ingramcontent.com/pod-product-compliance
Lightning Source LLC
Chambersburg PA
CBHW032252020726
47495CB00001B/74